Joy Dettman was born in Echuca in Victoria and now lives in Melbourne.

Joy, a mother of four, is a full-time writer and a published author of several award-winning stories and the highly acclaimed novels *Mallawindy*, *Jacaranda Blue* and *Goose Girl*.

Also by Joy Dettman

MALLAWINDY
JACARANDA BLUE
GOOSE GIRL

Joy Dettman

yesterday's
DUST

PAN
Pan Macmillan Australia

First published 2001 in Macmillan by Pan Macmillan Australia Pty Limited
This edition published 2002 in Pan by Pan Macmillan Australia Pty Limited
St Martins Tower, 31 Market Street, Sydney

National Library of Australia
cataloguing-in-publication data:

Dettman, Joy.
Yesterday's dust.

ISBN 0 330 36339 5.

1. Family – Australia – Fiction. I. Title.

A823.3

This is a work of fiction and all characters in this book are a creation
of the author's imagination.

Typeset by Midland Typesetters
Printed in Australia by McPherson's Printing Group

For Aaron, Dallas, Lachlan, Tristan and BD, who paint their more innocent pictures of life on the blank sides of my early drafts.

farewell, mallawindy

~

The corrugated iron roofs were as mirrors turned towards the late afternoon sun. A war of white light, a solar war, it blistered the thin skins of painted weatherboard, and the blisters burst and the pink and the green and the grey and the blue skin flaked and fell to the earth. It turned to dust. Red dust.

And the dogs rolled in the red dust and they scratched at their fleas, they sprawled on footpaths, slept in doorways, mated in the main street – smirking passive beasts, content with their lot.

Not so Amy O'Rouke, who stepped around a mustard mixed breed mastiff, her pale yellow dress swinging as she wiped sweat from her eyes, shooed at the flies, looking neither left to the bar, nor right to the group of faded women in their faded T-shirts – wrung out, strung out to dry in front of the shire hall.

Flies. They swarmed like bees in this place. In her hair. In her ears. In her eyes. Fresh meat, Amy O'Rouke, she was a blow-in and every fly in town knew it. Grim facts of life were the flies of Mallawindy, like the 'roo plagues and the rabbit plagues, like the wasted dreams and the suicides were facts of life in this cursed town. But life endured. Children were born – necessary fodder for two neighbouring cities that fed on Mallawindy's sons and daughters, who grew fast, ran early. Got away.

1

Some of them got away. Some of them found the Grand Central Hotel.

Amy couldn't walk through that door, drink and forget. In Sydney she could have walked into a bar, tossed down a vodka and tonic and no one would give her a sidewards glance. Or Melbourne. Cool place. Moist air. Dear Melbourne, too far away.

Up here?

'No can do, Amy,' she said.

The new teacher's wife, her place had been marked; a restricting little box prepared for her to crawl into, its label fixed, stuck on with immovable glue. But she didn't fit the ready-made box. Too old. Or too young. Fair of feature, fine of frame, and childless. Mutton dressed as lamb, the women in faded T-shirts whispered behind hands while their men stared at Amy O'Rouke with their hard, raping eyes.

She wasn't one of these people. Couldn't be one of them. Didn't want their box or their label, their social set, or their town. She dressed as she had in the city. She wore yellow sandals with heels, wore her city frocks, wore her yellow-rinsed hair hanging long. She had pretty hair. She'd always had pretty hair. It curled, just a little, just enough.

Her frock sticking to sweating knees, one foot was placed before the other, then one more. Her sandals had not been made for walking the rough surface of potholed country roads. Their high heels had been made for a city, as she had been made for a city, made for concrete paths and green parks and air-conditioned shopping centres.

Red dust scuffed up, puffed up with each step, it stuck between her sweating toes. Irritated. She shook her right foot, then her left, shaking dust and grit free, shaking some of it free. Most of it stuck.

Sun on her left, slowly falling to the west. But still hot. Reckless, abusive heat. Didn't it know that summer was over? She shook her head, smiled and walked forward. This town ignored the flyspecked calendars that hung on kitchen walls. April only days away.

2

April Fools' Day come Tuesday; a good day to go, but she couldn't wait until Tuesday. Shouldn't have waited this long.

One year, she'd promised Norman. She'd crossed seventy-five days off the calendar. Too many left to cross.

A truck roared by, spraying her with grit but creating a momentary breeze. She stilled her sandals until the truck and breeze had gone then, one yellow-shod foot placed before the other, she walked again. One step forward, then one step more.

Her shoulder bag, grown heavy too soon, she moved from left shoulder to right. All she was was in it. Packed in. Squeezed tight. Zipped up. Closed. A plastic card, twenty-five dollars, night cream, make-up and her gold earrings. Not a lot to show for fifty years of life.

The shoulder strap slipped. Her sunglasses, greased by sweat, slid. Her frock, sweat-soaked beneath her arms, rubbed. Sydney five hundred-odd kilometres east, Melbourne eight hundred south, Warran to the west, and the river, dirty water, grey trees, but cool, and close.

'The fast fix,' she said. 'Or – '

Fast was good. Fast was –

'Fast,' she said, stilling her feet. Her eyes closed, she turned around, once, twice. Tight circles, spinning circles, her shoulder bag joining the game; around and around she spun.

'Eenie meenie miney mo.' Around and around, her arms spread wide, handbag slapping. 'Eenie meenie miney mo. Which way will poor Amy go?' Then she stopped her whirling, a direction chosen by fate.

At the far end of town, near hidden behind tall creepers, Ben Burton's funny little house leaned. Amy glanced at its walls, then up to the chimney, and she smiled, tilting her head to the side, levelling the chimney, but not the small windows that had looked out on this town for over a hundred years. Wisdom came with the years and this house had grown wise. It hid from the cursed town, hid behind bougainvillea and tecoma, ornamental grapevines and the climbing rose. Cerise. Orange. Red. The wildfire blooming of wild things.

Only the wild could survive here, the wild and the strong. Amy wasn't wild, and she wasn't strong any more. She had tried. She'd given it one last try.

No creeper to hold me upright, she thought. No shade for my eyes to hide behind. If those creepers should die and fall, the mud bricks would crumble, return to the red dust and blow away in the next windstorm. She knew it, as she knew that another month, another week, another day, one more hour in this town would see her blowing away with the dust.

'*Pooof*. All gone, Amy.'

A glance at her watch. Near five. She turned her head, looking behind her, then to her left. Ellie Burton lived with her sons in this old house with its leaning chimney and creepers. She was standing at her front fence, one elbow on the time-eroded wood, her eyes turned south, to Daree, and to Melbourne, and to the South Pole.

Still mourning the man who got away, Amy thought.

Got away. Ran. One way or another.

A breath of cool air lifted from the old garden. Scent of red roses, scent of mint, of lavender. Scent of some place better. It drew Amy from the road, forcing her sandals to step high through the brittle dry grass, forcing her eyes to seek for snakes; then, stepping onto a bare red clay-patch beneath a gum tree, she leaned against the trunk, soaking up the cool of smooth cream bark, soaking up the scattered shade of sparse grey leaves while listening to the older woman's words.

Soft words, but no breeze to blow them away, they hung on the heavy air. Sad sound.

'Hail Mary full of grace, the Lord be with me. Blessed art thou – '

The rattle of a transport on the long straight road killed the words, and the whiff of stinking pigs in transit washed away the perfume of the garden. For a moment.

' – and blessed is the fruit of thy womb, Jesus. Hail Mary, full of grace, the Lord be with me. Blessed art – '

Movement from the right. Amy lifted her head in time to see

three small children scuttle across the road, dusty town urchins left to their own devices while their parents filled an hour or two at the Grand Central – not so grand.

A fly bit her shoulder. She brushed at it as she watched the urchins. Full up with cheek and questions, they climbed the wooden fence, watching the rosary beads slip through the fingers of the woman who prayed.

'Why do you come out here to say your bead prayers for?' Words from the mouth of a stunted redhead – one of the Dooleys. Amy could pick a Dooley. Everyone could pick a Dooley. They all looked like old Bill, their grandfather. And the Wests. Dusty little garden gnomes, big ears, big feet, pin heads – small clones of old Robbie.

They straddled the weather-beaten rail, edging closer to the woman, intrigued by the rhythm of the beads falling through a hand that fitted well into its box. It had no need for a label; it had its beads to hold on to, its prayer book to grasp each Sunday, it had Father Fogarty and two sons to lean on, and two daughters who had got away.

Amy had carried three sons and a daughter, for a time – a short time. Eleven weeks and sixteen weeks, twelve weeks, then twenty-one. Poor mite, the last one had tried to live for her. He'd lived for a day. She'd named him, touched him, kissed his unfinished face, then buried him and told Norman she wanted a divorce.

Twelve years ago.

Poor Norman. He wouldn't let her leave him. Another chance, he'd pleaded, a new start. A new town. They'd had too many new starts. Too many new towns. She was too old. Too tired. Too sad. And too hot.

'Mallawindy, the straw that broke the camel's back,' she said and she listened again to the urchins.

'My mother said you're still waiting for him to come home.'

Ellie Burton's only reply was the swish of her rosary beads as she slapped at a fly.

Mother of Ben, hairdresser cum newsagent; mother of the other one too, the tall dark one, rarely seen about town, John, the ex-priest – defrocked or disenchanted, or both – a silent man, existing in his uneasy discontent, as lost in this town as Amy.

He'd had a box ready made for him to return to, but its old label had worn away. The hermit, they labelled him these days. Couldn't understand a man who didn't drink, didn't smoke, didn't have a woman – though plenty in town would have had him, Amy thought as she brushed an ant from her sandal. She'd eyed him a couple of times. Tried to speak to him once.

'My mother said old Jack got drownded when I was little, so you might as well stop looking for him, because when you get drowned, you're dead, aren't you, and you can't never come back, can you?'

Jack Burton, the legend. Gone but not forgotten.

'Struck by lightning,' they said in town. 'Standing on Ben's bridge, he was,' they said. 'And he's still down there somewhere, feeding the fish. I haven't eaten a yabby since Christmas 1990,' they said.

Jack Burton had been big news when the removalist van delivered the new schoolteacher's furniture north in early January. Ellie's photograph had been in the Daree *Gazette* with a half-page write-up on Jack's quarter of a million dollar life insurance policy with AMP.

He'd remained big news all February while the insurance investigators nosed around town and Amy had tried to fit into her box, tried to turn the old schoolhouse into a home. Then March had come, and the investigators returned to Sydney, but Jack Burton, though missing, was not allowed to be dead until the courts declared him dead. He'd disappeared on Christmas Eve of 1990, and come Christmas of 1997, he'd be declared dead. That was the law, even though his eldest daughter had sighted him near the footbridge, just as a bolt of lightning had hit the earth.

'Fried, then flung into the river,' they said in town. 'But not a mark on the bridge.'

'I say, remember old Coll Martin, that got struck by lightning out at the racecourse? Burned him to a crisp, it did, and never a blade of grass that has grown on that spot o' dirt for eighty years,' Granny Bourke, the town historian, said.

The teacher's wife glanced at Ellie. Her sons were in their forties; she had to be sixty-odd, though she didn't look it. No stress lines, no bitter mouth – not a lot of anything, really, except her wide innocent green eyes, and her hair. She had a lot of hair. Only nine more months and she'd collect her quarter of a million.

Nine months – time enough for a conception and a birth.

A transport passed by, its breeze flipping up the hem of Amy's yellow frock, creating a breath of cool on sweating legs. She closed her eyes until the dust and grit settled, then she looked back at the town, her eyes half closed, the better to see, the better not to see the roofs, straining now to gather in the last swords of sun.

A slap at a gorged mosquito smeared blood onto the paler skin of the inner side of her elbow. She stared at it, and as she stared a fly landed on it. Licked blood.

Flies all day, mosquitoes all night, and no breathing space in between. They shared their hosts at sundown, supping together.

Ellie's hand also slapped at an insect, flicked at the hair she wore like a lopsided turban of fading straw. A slow smile touched Amy's lips. The older woman flicked again, and the turban tumbled as a long plaited rope fell free to her knees. But fast hands caught it and deft fingers found the escaping pins; they removed them, recoiled the rope and again settled the turban into place.

'My mother says long hair is hot and stupid and you get nits in it,' the small Dooley said. Was it a girl or boy? Hard to tell these days, faded shirts and shorts, basin-cut carrot hair. 'My mother said you probably come out here and say your prayers so he won't come back. She said she would, if she was you. She said you'll get a big Christmas present if he doesn't come back.'

'You're Marlene's boy, aren't you?'

'Yes, and she says that God is like Santa Claus and the tooth

7

fairy. That he's just pretend and there isn't even an Easter Bunny, so there.'

'Well, my goodness me! What a thing to tell a child! No wonder our old world is in such a mess.' Ellie crossed herself, her beads swishing. 'God is up there listening to you right now, love. He hears every word we say, and if we are good, he answers our prayers too.'

The teacher's wife sighed. She had been good. She had been very good. She'd tried hard to believe there was a God. Now she had as little faith in prayer as the urchins who turned on Ellie with their sharp little viper tongues.

Old Ellie Burton with her stupid long hair.
Drowned old Jack and said I don't care.
He's sunk in the river, and we boil all the water
'Cause our mother said that we ought ta.

The yellow frock eased away from the bark of the gum tree, the teacher's wife returned to the side of the road to continue on her way. One step at a time would do it. One yellow sandal placed before the other, each footfall carrying her on.

To the crossroad, and the signpost. 'Mallawindy: Population – ' Population all gone. Just a series of rusting bullet holes.

Barely did she glance at the signpost. With a wave of her hand she passed it by.

'Deduct one bullet hole,' she said. And her yellow sandals scuffed on through the pink powder dust.

technology

~

While Amy O'Rouke walked the narrow highway, Malcolm Fletcher sat before his bay window, glowering at his neighbour while listening to the thunk, thunk, thunk of a crowbar driving into hard clay. Like a heartbeat, it laboured on. Thunk. Thunk. Thunk.

Then it rested, and Malcolm breathed easier – until it began again.

Mad as a hatter, the fat man thought as he watched the crowbar placed to the side and a long-nosed shovel taken up. A neat, methodical worker was John Burton; he dug neat post holes, one after the other, day after day after thunking day. Sun and wind, mosquitoes and flies could not stop him. Only the lack of light forced the ex-priest away from his thunking.

Malcolm's two and a half hectares had been fenced by a local contractor, who had come with his boisterous tool, which in minutes corkscrewed out fine deep post holes. Noisy, but perhaps preferable to this infernal, eternal thunk.

His house plan had been chosen from many, chosen for the two bay windows in lounge and main bedroom; then Malcolm had asked the builder to turn the internal plan around, so the lounge room became the study, and the bedroom his kitchen. They charged a small fortune to do it, but the retired headmaster was now in possession of a not so small fortune. His neat little cottage had been worth every cent he'd paid for it; he lived in those two front rooms.

Life for Malcolm revolved around the preparation and the eating of good food, and his secret vice – writing; thus during daylight hours, the twin bay windows gave him the optimum view of the gravelled river road, and across the road to the old Burton farmhouse where Jack Burton had once ruled. Malcolm had sat at those windows for hours watching Jack's every move – and documenting them in detail.

But Jack was gone and the Burton house unoccupied – only his thunking son out there to stare at these days, and at night, no neighbourly light to burn. John crossed over the river to his rest, at odds with the sun – at odds with the world.

Malcolm sighed weightily and, with effort, moved his massive bulk from the window to his typewriter where he poked with distain at a key. Inspiration was a fossil in his brain, as it had been now for months, his stimuli rotting, caught on a snag at the bottom of the river, or blown to hell by his own gun. Whatever his fate, Jack was long gone.

On pleasant afternoons Malcolm still roamed the riverbank, forcing a passage between tall reeds and around the giant river gums. He climbed carefully over rotting timber, shone his flashlight into hollow logs, determined to find Jack's corpse, but like the insurance investigators, he'd found nothing. An accidental dip one cold evening, while fishing for a shoe with his walking stick, had brought on a pneumonic influenza, which had done his aging lungs no good at all – and the recovered shoe had been three sizes too small, and brown into the bargain. Jack Burton had only ever worn black shoes.

Admittedly, Malcolm thought, there would not be a lot of corpse left to find these days. Bones, yes; perhaps some of the heavier refuse would not yet have washed downstream. In Malcolm's novels, bodies, without fail, conveniently floated to the surface three to seven days after death, depending on the water temperature. He'd looked that one up in a book. If for some reason the bodies did not float, then the bones were assuredly found on a riverbank, bleached white. Jack had not floated, and his bones had not surfaced.

On many an afternoon Malcolm stood on the Mallawindy bridge, scanning the banks with his binoculars, while vehicles on the aged timber construction blasted him with their horns, the drivers cursing.

The bridge had been built a hundred years ago in the horse and buggy era. Traffic being infrequent then, one-way had been enough, but time had caught up with the Mallawindy bridge. There was now a give-way sign on the forest side, which applied to all vehicles. But not to pedestrians. Malcolm Fletcher should have been reclassified twenty-odd years ago; at seventy-six, he was a bulldozer of a man, a waddling traffic jam.

He'd never achieved his boyhood aim of six feet – missed out by an inch or three. Back in the seventies a doctor had weighed him in at twenty-six stone; he'd added a few kilograms since then. His mammoth thighs, by necessity, spread his knees, and his small feet resented their burden. Shoelaces had become an impossibility. Fighting his socks over spreading toes was a daily contest between will and belly, and changing his underpants, the battle of the bulge.

Life had become a burden to Malcolm. One morning he'd wake and decide that the day didn't justify the effort expended in putting on his shoes.

He glanced at his new typewriter. The electronic bastard of a thing taunted him. He looked guiltily at the phone, left off the hook these last weeks. His publisher was haunting him for Number 10. Coll M Chef-Marlet, Malcolm's alter-ego, had been churning out his novels since the mid eighties, but no new manuscript had been tabled in eighteen months and his publisher's gentle hints had lately become demands. They wanted to see a rough draft. They'd settle for a brief synopsis. He couldn't give them one; since mislaying his early work on Number 10. Coll M Chef-Marlet's word-well had been empty – as was Malcolm's current brandy bottle.

He'd escaped his publishers in December, flown first class to old England, convinced by the airlines that the first class seat would contain his bulk comfortably. It had contained it, held it captive too, while he'd eaten his way across the brown continent and over the sapphire waters, beyond green islands. He'd sipped on complimentary brandy, night and day, day and night, and he'd landed beneath the sad grey skies of home, his bowels seized, his legs bloated stumps, his balloon feet laughing at the new slip-on shoes bought for this long-promised trip home.

Two weightlifters had assisted him from the plane to an ambulance. His heart was not all that it should have been, and for three days his kidneys had threatened a shutdown. Nine days passed before he'd sighted the land of his birth; still, his flight insurance had paid for a private hospital ward, and the food served, though flavourless, had brought back memories of childhood.

Two months in all he had spent in England, trapped there because the plane that might have delivered him out of purgatory appeared worse than existence within it. Like a raging bull Malcolm had sought the world he'd left behind almost forty years earlier. He hadn't found it, but until he boarded another plane he couldn't get out of the bastard of a place that he had found.

Time and the wet grey skies eventually dulled memory of the flight in. On doctors' advice, he'd broken the return journey in Bangkok – and barely lived to rue that day. Had he been able, he would have prostrated himself on the good earth of Sydney's airport but, scarcely capable of hobbling, he'd hired a car instead and driven home.

Home?

Where did an immigrant call home? He'd spent ten thousand hours mourning what he'd left behind; he'd spent years visualising his homeland as it had been on the day he'd left, but slapped in the face by old England, Malcolm discovered he had no home.

Only this house. Only his hedged sixth of a hectare with its neat little garden, his neat little English trees, his hollyhocks at the door. For days after his return to Mallawindy, he had walked his garden, renewing acquaintance with tree and shrub, a rare smile irritating his belligerent features.

Today his face was set in more normal lines. He scowled at his bottle, accusing it for its empty state; then again he turned to the window, striving to force his mind out there to play.

Not a word. Not the hint of a plot presented itself. Nothing to see, thus nothing to write about.

'Such grand plans. Such grand plans.'

One's life, when one looks back on it, is filled with grand plans, he thought. He'd had grand plans for Ann, that dark-eyed mute who had spoken her first words in seven years to him. She was to have been his magnum opus. What a mind she had possessed. Wasted.

He sighed and again prodded at his typewriter. Not the whisper of an idea; not a thing to see from his window, even with his new binoculars. Only the grey grotesque trees lining the roadway, only the wind-flattened weeds at their feet, only a gust of red dust swept up from a fallowed paddock and flung in the face of the crowbar man. Only the cows queuing for their turn in the milking sheds. Only a white chicken feather flying by. And the sky darkening into lonely night, and that slow heartbeat of crowbar.

Thunk. Thunk. Thunk.

Late March, and the land gasping for rain that refused to come. Somewhere in Australia they were always needing rain – except when they got it. A mad land. Red and grey and flat, an ugly featureless land. But what a strange panorama from a plane's porthole. The narrow stretch of green border, the scant rivers crawling out of the green, like Dreamtime snakes heading off towards the dead centre. Wide, incredible land of extremes, its inhabitants screaming drought for five years, then flood for the next two, freezing in Tasmania and broiling in Darwin.

And Mallawindy. The river formed four-fifths of a circle around it, enclosing, protecting the town that had grown from water's union with red dust. A misbegotten thing, Mallawindy, as harsh as the land that had spawned it.

Ellie Burton's grandfather had bought, squatted on, or stolen more than his fair share of river frontage. The Burtons' river paddocks were green. Groups of young willow trees grew tall there, offering the cows a shady meal and shelter from the wind. Jim Watson's land, a few kilometres out of town, was burned a uniform brown, his dams were dry and his cows eating hay.

Malcolm had spent an hour on the bridge this morning, willing a motorboat to flush Jack's skull from the mud, bowl it up to the bank. The river too low, familiar snags were rearing their heads. They'd find the bastard's bones soon. Maybe then Malcolm would write Number 10, in which he planned to kill off his anti-hero.

Ten novels had always been his aim. Ten beautifully bound books on a library shelf would look better than nine. As a lad he'd visualised that long row of books, but he'd put childhood dreams behind him and for forty-odd years had attempted to pound his love of words into juvenile heads. To a large degree he had failed. He'd returned late to writing, and gained no success at all until he'd decided to immortalise Jack Burton in print.

His fingers poised over the keyboard, he urged them on. 'Make a start, Coll. Only make a start. Kill him off and be done with it.'

But how was he going to kill that conscienceless bastard? A lightning strike would give the game away. Suicide then? The fat man shook his head. Mack Curtin, or Jack Burton, was not the type to blow his own brains out. One of his women friends might be tempted to off him – with a knife. Or one of their husbands.

'So make it the husband.'

His middle finger hit the T. His electric typewriter made an entire row of Ts. He abhorred the abominable fool thing that defeated his heavy-handed, two finger, hunt-and-peck keyboard style. A bad buy. His second bad buy.

'Write it off as a tax loss. That and the trip home,' he said. 'Thieving swines,' he said.

He had been introduced to the wonders of the computer two years ago when his publisher began nagging about deadlines on Number 9. Still weakened after his bout of influenza, Ann had come to his aid. She still came when he called, but these days he did not call often. She had her own . . . small problems.

His rough manuscript she had somehow electronically scanned into David's laptop computer, and each night for a week she'd come with the machine. Malcolm, at her side, had watched ten fingers work as a single unit, while, at his command, she'd added, deleted, moved paragraphs from one page to the next. And when it was done, she'd printed the entire manuscript out in a night, then copied the data directly from the brains of the beast onto two small disks, one of which was packed off to the publisher with the manuscript. The second she'd put in his hand. Was it possible that the entire novel was contained on a small piece of plastic? The computer appeared to be a tool too good to be true.

A salesman had convinced him that a child could use the things, so he'd bought a large desk model; the instructions might as well have been written in Chinese; proving indubitably that the thing was indeed too good to be true.

Ten, twenty times he'd called Ann. There were those in town who, no doubt, could have tutored him, but only Ann knew of his secret vice. Ten, twenty times she had talked him into or out of a file, or sat patiently at his side, watching him bumble.

'Just treat it like an obstreperous child,' she had advised. 'Never fight it, or force it. It has a will of its own, and as long as you allow it to go its own way, it will do anything for you.'

That may have been the modern method of child raising, but it was contrary to what Malcolm had found in his years of pounding information into thick heads. An elbow jab to the ribs had achieved swifter and more satisfying results with the obstreperous.

Unable to contact her one evening after his screen had gone blue, he'd panicked, read the instruction manual, which mentioned nothing at all about not forcing it. However, when he'd given the machine an elbow jab and tossed the keyboard to the floor, it hit back. The bewildering bastard of a thing had gulped down three chapters of Number 10 and refused to regurgitate them.

The computer now sat idle in its corner, a sheet covering the blank, gloating face, replete with his last words. He loathed the dogmatic abomination, considered tossing it, with Jack, in the river.

'Aggressive bastard,' he snarled at it now, hating it, but wanting those chapters back. They hadn't been his best, but they had been a start. He wanted the large computer screen too, with its large text, or he wanted his antique Royal typewriter back. It had rolled over and died, like his dream of England had died. Maybe the world was trying to tell him something.

He slid the top drawer of his desk open, and his hand touched a red, cloth-wrapped parcel. The knowledge of what it contained calmed him, but with a deep, chin-trembling sigh he closed the drawer, and his hands returned to hover over flat grey plastic keys.

'Reasons for the murder. Come on, Coll, think. Think. Reason number one.'

Husband comes home, finds Jack . . . Mack in bed with his wife.

'Or perhaps allow him to blow his brains out. Finding his murdered daughter, finding Liza's bones, buried on the family property at Narrawee, may have pushed him over the edge. That was a possible.

'But not good enough. She'd been missing for twenty-odd years, and you cannot use it anyway. The son's return; did the son kill the father then bury him? He certainly has skill enough with a crowbar to have buried him deep.'

Fact and fiction now becoming confused, Malcolm stood, walked to his window, staring at John Burton, still out there, still thunking.

John had arrived home that Christmas Eve, only minutes before his father had disappeared. Had he perhaps dispensed with him? An interesting theory, but as Malcolm had been at the Burton property at the time of the disappearance, he knew it was illogical.

'Forget the logic. Put logic aside.'

So, John had done it later. Or killed him that night and buried him later.

'A possibility. A definite possibility.' The crowbar man had not only retreated from his church, but from life.

Why?

'Guilt? Obviously. So . . . so assuming he committed a mild case of patricide, where does that leave you?'

For minutes he gazed at the crowbar man, an unworthy replacement for Jack. No spark in his eye, no fire in his belly, and no women, thus no obligatory sex scene.

Ann had stated back in '91 that she'd last sighted her father beside the insane structure they now called Ben's Bridge. He'd had his gun with him. There had been several lightning strikes that evening. One may have homed in on him, fried him. It was also possible that he had fallen accidentally. Once only had Malcolm attempted the crossing of that footbridge. Three metres into it, he'd turned back. The thing had springs in it, and as the trees dried, the planks twisted and six-inch nails protruded. He, like Jack, had never learned to swim.

He sat again and hit the B with his middle finger then looked at his row of Bs while considering the bridge as a first line.

He hit the T. Quickly. Only three Ts this time. He selected a new line, and carefully typed in: *Ttthey haad nevvver fffouuund ttthe guuun.*

Excess letters deleted, he read his words aloud. And found the sentence lacking.

'Lighting struck the old shotgun – or, he aimed his shotgun at the thunderclouds, threatened by the bastard, lightning struck back. Mack was flung screaming to the river.'

'Better. Certainly visual.'

Malcolm sat forward. There was movement across the road. The grass widow Burton had come to milk her cows. She angered him. For years he'd wanted to pick Ellie Burton up by her ears and shake some sense into her. Laboriously he rose from his chair and waddled to his window, this time reaching for his binoculars as John stopped his thunking and left his crowbar upright in the post hole. Malcolm had him in his sights, clear and close up.

In the fading light the fallen priest was his father's image, the build, the colouring, the fine classic features. But not the mannerisms, stance or personality. John was a loner, nursing some deep guilt. Malcolm had on occasions made the effort to be neighbourly, to walk across the narrow road, but the ex-priest had little to say, and not once had he knocked on Malcolm's door.

'Too much of the mother in him. A victim born,' Malcolm admitted, aware that he was wasting his time attempting to create characters from the characterless. The binoculars placed down, he glanced at his bottle. Still empty. He'd have to get out, fill it before dark. His vision was not good for night driving. He lifted the large bottle, loving its form.

'Our game has ended, Coll. Perhaps we must face it together. It was a killer on the bones, and the hands are not as supple as of old. Perhaps we should retire. Travel the world. Enjoy our fame.'

His study walls were covered with framed book covers and other memorabilia. Few came to his house, and none, other than Ann, entered his study. It was a chaos of papers and pages, of stockpiled used brown envelopes he could not bring himself to toss away. Wall to ceiling bookshelves were packed with copies of his novels, supplied free by his publishers. He couldn't give them away, and thus give up his secret; he couldn't throw them away because he loved every one of them. And he wanted Number 10 to sit beside them.

He glanced up at the stacks of rubber-banded pages piled on the top shelf – early drafts of each of his novels. Six drafts of his first. He couldn't throw them away either.

'But out of chaos comes creation,' he said, picking up a page of text, his day's work, scanning it before tossing it high. The bottle upended, he squeezed it. A few drops dripped into his glass. Primed then, he sagged down to his writing chair, his finger prodding at a D for the damned. It led to an E.

Deeetermined to knooow the truth, Edward asked quuues-tions others shrank from asking, but on thiiiis particular evening as he watched the guilty pair he wishhhhed he was close enough to hear, or that his ssssight was goood enoughhh to lip rrrread . . .

the facts of the matter

~

Tuesday 1 April

'Let the rain pour down, and wash my face, let the sky grow grey and dre-aa-ry,' Jeff Rowan, the local lawman, sang as he showered. Every landowner within a fifty-kilometre radius was singing the same old song; clouds had gathered late last night, and this morning the scent of rain was on the wind.

'Oh, tell the sun, I don't want it to shine, for you've gone away, and left me tea-aa-ry.'

Jeff had the perfect nasal tones for country and western; what he lacked was an ear for music.

The water turned off, he stepped out. 'But not necessarily until tonight,' he said. 'Rain today will make the job that much bloody harder.' He towelled his hair, eyed his shoulders and waist in the small bathroom mirror. Not bad. No beer belly yet. He bent his knees and checked out his face. False teeth but plenty of hair. Not too tall, but tall enough. Still young enough.

'So what's wrong with her?' he said.

Jeff yearned for Kerrie Fogarty, the lanky infant mistress. He dreamt of her, but his dreams were better than his reality. She wasn't interested. Still, that wasn't the business of today. He dressed, donned his hat and boots, which gained him extra inches, then he headed for the river.

Amy O'Rouke had last been sighted on Thursday 27 March, wandering up the highway in her high-heeled sandals. Those eager to get away usually took the morning bus. Jeff had been considering his options for days now, but when Amy O'Rouke hadn't checked in with her mother by the following Monday, he decided he probably ought to drag the river. A dragging crew had been organised to do it this morning which was, incidentally, April Fools' Day.

He'd concentrate the search in the area below the bridge where one of his colleagues had pulled out another teacher's wife, old Malcolm Fletcher's wife, Jillian; she'd gone for the long dive thirty-odd years ago.

Teachers' wives didn't do well in Mallawindy, and that was a fact. One had taken off with a landowner and left her kids behind, another had just taken off, and now Amy O'Rouke, only in town a few months, had gone missing – probably topped herself, and who'd blame her?

Jeff had spoken to little Norman, the husband, and he'd had a word to the Indian doctor who visited the town one day a week. 'Menopausal,' the doctor had said. 'She is suffering from the deep depression. I am prescribing the HRT, Valium and antidepressant.' Norman had been less help; since his wife's disappearance he'd been swallowing her pills and not following the directions on the packets. Today he looked as if the hormones were starting to kick in.

'You can't do much good down here, Norm. Go home,' Jeff Rowan yelled, sighting the husband, knee deep in reeds.

Norman nodded, wiped at his eyes with a floral handkerchief and wandered deeper into the reeds, half in, half out of the water. Probably end up dragging him out tonight. Bloody Education Department had been scraping the bottom of the barrel when they dug up Norman and Amy O'Rouke, Jeff thought.

Kerrie Fogarty was trying to hold the fort, and Jeff was giving her what support he could. He would have loved to give her a bit more too – like he'd dreamt last night. She wasn't having any. Not getting any from anyone else in town either. She was no kid fresh out of teachers' college – had to be thirty-odd – probably been around the block a few times. The question in town was, had she been around it with a bloke or a lezzo.

'They're a bloody weird mob, teachers,' he said.

By nine-thirty he had two motorboat crews armed with grappling hooks, two rowboat crews prodding with oars and poles, and half a dozen walkers poking around tree roots and snags.

One of the boat crews thought they'd found the missing Amy at ten, but it turned out to be a dead pig, minus its legs. Somebody was eating free pork this week – Ellie Burton's pork; it still had her label on its ear.

With no sign of a yellow dress or yellow sandals found in the vicinity of the bridge, by late afternoon the boat crews had worked their way downstream, down past the Burton property where they scoured the reed banks, prodding mud and catching their grappling hooks on snags and willow roots.

Then they found it!

If not for an errant teacher's wife, Jack Burton's double-barrelled shotgun may have rested a hundred years in the mud.

It was old Bill Dooley who reeled it in. He hooked the trigger and, open-mouthed, watched his catch surface.

'Hey. I've got his bloody gun,' he yelled. 'Hey! I've fished out Jack's bloody old gun.'

'Hey, Dooley has found Jack's shotgun!' The call went out across the water, and weary searchers gathered on the bank for a smoko and to talk again of Jack and his insurance policy, while an old cow, trimming the fringe of the trailing willow tree in the tradition of her ancestors, stopped her labour a while. She stepped two paces into the water and turned an ear, the better to hear.

'Hey, Bessy. I pulled out his bloody old gun!' Dooley bellowed across the river to Bessy Bishop, sister of Ellie. 'He's blown his brains out, the poor bastard.'

And the cow lifted her head and she lowed out her message to the herd.

'Gone. Gone. Jack is gone.'

And Ellie's hens, scratching in the old fowl yard, heard her; they cluck-clucked and gossiped amongst themselves, and the rooster crowed.

'Jack-has-gone-to-hell. Jack-has-gone-to-hell.'

Across the river Bessy Bishop's dogs heard the call, and they howled to the ghost of the sun. 'Jack, Jack, Jack's gone. Jack, Jack, Jack's gone.'

All night the dogs of Mallawindy barked, and the cats wailed, and the rabbits courted and cavorted on the sand dunes out at Dead Man's Lane, but it was business as usual in the Central Hotel.

'It was finding his kid's bones that done it, pushed him over the edge. Didn't I always say it? Didn't I? Finding young Liza murdered, like they did. I mean, on his own bloody brother's property too. How are you gunna feel about that? How are you gunna live with that? He couldn't, the poor bastard. Blew himself to buggery. I bet you a dime to a dollar.'

'That's what must of done it, all right,' Mick Bourke, the publican agreed.

'When?' Henry Cooper, a recent blow-in, needed more details. Few in the bar had much time for blow-ins, except for a wizened-up old dame seated in her corner.

'Back in late 1990, it was, boy. His daughter – missing for twenty-odd years, she was – then they dug her up on his twin brother's property in Narrawee. Raped and murdered by the gardener, then buried under a rose bush while her little sister looked on.'

'Yeah!' Henry turned to Granny Bourke, busy lubricating her ninety-nine-year-old vocal cords with the stout she'd been drinking for seventy years, on doctor's advice.

'He had a tribe of kids, but he loved the one that got murdered. Took her everywhere with him, he did. Used to dress her up like a little princess. She won Miss Tiny Tot, you know, back in . . . back in '63. I remember when it happened.'

'Go down to the back, Gran,' Mick Bourke yelled.

'I'll go when I get my second stout, boy, and you remember who owns this hotel, and shut up. I'm talking here.'

'We can all bloody hear you talking. Go down the back and I'll give you your other stout.' Young Mick had inherited the management of the hotel from old Mick, but unlike his father he had never learned to manage Granny.

'I'll get it myself when I'm ready. That way I'm sure of getting it. You're too mean to spit, you are. You're getting too much like your bleedin' father.'

'You tell him, Gran,' many voices chorused.

Loud in the bar tonight. Like a flock of gaggling geese the drinkers competed for their time, and when they left the hotel, the news spilled out to the street corner.

'Did you hear they found Jack's gun?'

'Never would o' believed it of him. Never thought he'd be the type to blow his brains out.'

'Something snapped, they say, when they dug up his kid. That's what they reckon at the pub. We all got our snapping point.'

'I seen him in the pub the night it happened. He didn't look much different to me.'

'Snapped when he got home. Went off his rocker, they say.'

'Him and Charlie Owen were going at it hammer and tongs that night.'

'Jack and Charlie's missus had been going at it for five bloody years.'

Laughter on street corners as they watched a stranger's car drive into town, park.

'Looks like that insurance bloke's car again.'

'Or those bloody news hounds back. Doesn't take them long to sniff out a story, does it?'

The following day the men in boats forgot about Amy O'Rouke and began searching for Jack, or for what might be left of him, which wouldn't be too much after the shotgun had done its worst and the European carp and yabbies had had his bones to nibble on for six years.

For days fish played around the grappling hooks, darting, diving, knowing more than the men in the boats. They blew chuckle bubbles while the river flowed on through this red and grey land, and the clouds, refusing to mourn Jack's demise, moved away to drop their payload on a more deserving town.

The frogmen came then, came all the way from Sydney, and for another week they suited up and scoured the muddy water while the unemployed lined the riverbanks watching, waiting. And the newsmen came, their cameras aimed and ready.

No Jack Burton. No Amy O'Rouke either. By April's end, the little schoolmaster had returned to his classroom, where he stared into space while the students stared at him.

the party

~

So time moved on in Mallawindy, and the pages of the 'Burton & Dooley' calendars were turned, offering a photograph of twin calves for the flies to defile. May came in hot and left without a drink, then June arrived, a T-shirt June by day, but each night she spun her carpet of glistening ice over the bone-dry paddocks and the farmers cursed the blue sky and their dry dams; they bought hay for their stock and they waited.

By late July, all hope of rain was dead, but old Granny Bourke, born on 19 July 1897, had no intention of dying and wasn't too worried about the drought either. She was planning her hundredth birthday party.

'Only fifty guests, Gran,' her aging daughter-in-law stressed.

'I've got more than fifty bleedin' relatives.'

'Fifty, Gran. No more.'

Gran could, by tracing a line back far enough, claim relationship to most Mallawindy residents. Supplied with only fifty invitations, she found a way around the problem. *Milly and Joe Crocker and family. Bessy Bishop and family. Ellie Burton and family. Jim Watson and family.* She received few refusals.

Ellie coerced Bronwyn. Bronwyn coerced Ann. Ben said he'd pop in for a while, but Johnny said no.

The party was held in the residence at the rear of the hotel but the hundred and fifty guests spilled out to beer garden and bar, to ladies lounge and pool room. The marble clock on the mantelpiece had ticked its way to three-thirty. The cake long cut and demolished, the Daree *Gazette* photographer been and gone, still the old dame wasn't ready to give up her spot of limelight, though her legs were. Expecting the party now to come to her, she settled into her favourite chair, from where she could keep an eye on that clock.

'I say. I say, take Jillian Fletcher as an example,' she yelled. Didn't get any takers but she got a cigarette out, and lit it, singeing her sparse hair in the doing.

Few in town made it to eighty with their faculties intact. Old Gran may have had the body of a smoked goanna, but she possessed the memory of a rogue elephant and the logic of a city bean-counter. She had been living behind the hotel since her wedding night in 1914, ingesting nicotine, stout and the town's secrets on a daily basis.

'I say, take Jillian Fletcher.' A dogged old bird, she persisted, determined to capture a listener.

Bronwyn Burton heard her, but kept her distance. She wasn't feeling sociable today so she leaned against the wall, watching people, watching Ann, who stood by the window with Jeff Rowan, Kerrie and Ben. Ben was five-seven. Kerrie and Jeff stood eye to eye with him, but Ann, her hair pinned high, was half a head taller. Easy to find Ann in a crowd. Still thin as a rake handle; she could wear loose jeans and bulky sweaters and still look slim. Bronwyn looked at her own jutting breasts; she had inherited Ellie's buxom build and never, never, never wore bulky sweaters.

Two women joined the group. Bronwyn smiled, watching Ben evade Judy Watson's greeting kiss. Ann copped the kiss and she flashed her smile. Bronwyn envied her sister the strong teeth she'd inherited from their father. She had his determined jaw too, but not his eyes; still wide, still more black than brown in the cold afternoon light, still wanting to run, to get away – if only Bronwyn knew it.

Ann wasn't into fake kisses, though these days few would guess; she put on her party face with her make-up, carried her party manners in her shoulder bag. She'd strip them off, toss them onto the back seat as soon as she slid behind the steering wheel for the drive home.

Both Burton girls had their father's long hands. Bronwyn looked at her own now. No rings. Didn't want any either. Ann wore three; David had bought her an eternity ring for their fifth anniversary, wanting to lock the engagement and wedding ring more firmly onto her finger. They'd had a few bad years after Mandy's death, but he'd hung in there. He was a nice guy, more brother than in-law, an accepting guy and easy to be with, to talk to. But he wasn't here today and Bronwyn didn't feel like talking anyway.

Then Ann turned her head, her eyes scanning until she found her sister. Her hands high, she signed, 'Had enough.' For seven years she'd communicated with hand signs, and they were still put to good use in crowded rooms. 'Want go?' the hands asked.

'What you think?' Bronwyn's hands replied. Fast. Emphatic. God only knew why she'd agreed to put in an appearance. God alone knew why she did anything these days.

Her bag over her shoulder, she walked to the door, waiting there for Ann to make her break for freedom, and she was halfway across the room, too, when Bessy bailed her up. Bronwyn moaned, took a cigarette from her bag and lit up.

The ash grew long, longer. Outside in the biting wind wasn't an option. She was forced to walk to old Gran's side, or to her standard ashtray.

Granny squinted at her guest, measuring her up before offering a running commentary on their old connections.

'. . . anyway, when the bleeding war got my Jimmy, Katie, your great aunt on your grandma's side went into mourning and never came out of it. We buried her two years after the war ended. Blow-ins, the Granvilles – they had no staying power. Look at your grandmother. She was dead at forty.'

Bronwyn nodded, wondered how much blow-in Granville blood she carried. The way she was feeling today, she probably wouldn't make it to her thirty-first birthday. Sick and sore and sorry for herself, her world had been picked up and used as a bowling ball and she was one of the tenpins. Down.

She'd broken a front tooth in February. It had abscessed in March. Penicillin injected into her backside, penicillin by mouth before meals and some super bug killer to pop after meals, and not enough hours in a day to swallow what she had to swallow plus painkillers. She'd blown her cool when Jeff Rowan had pulled her up for speeding. Instead of flirting with him, as she had on previous occasions, she'd told him where to go, and where to put his ticket too. She'd blown her licence. That was in April. She'd told Nick where to go in May, told him to drop dead in June, and now it was July and things were looking worse.

The old dame drew hard on her cigarette, priming her brain for the next instalment of yesterday.

'She took to her bed, you know, after she lost her last one, and she never got out of it again. Bessy raised your mother.'

Didn't make much of a job of it, Bronwyn thought, but offered no comment. Get Granny going and you couldn't shut her up.

Bessy was talking, Ann was nodding, nodding, but looking at her watch, looking at Bronwyn.

'Save me,' the younger girl signed.

Ann smiled, backed away from Bessy, backed into fat old Fletch.

'No!' Bronwyn moaned aloud, aware that her sister would not be so eager to get away from him. What was he doing here anyway? He wasn't a relative. She considered asking the old dame, but Gran's mouth was moving again – or still.

'Now you take your mother, she's got staying power. She'll make old bones. You need staying power in this life, girlie. You need to find a reason to go on when there's no bleeding reason to go on.'

'Tell me about it, why don't you, Gran.'

'Humph,' Gran said, eyeing her guest up and down, but a bird in the hand was worth two in the bush. 'Never could see how anyone with half a mind could do hisself in. Better the devil you know than the devil you don't, I always say.'

'You may be right.'

'Now you take old Fletcher's wife. She done herself in, but she was as mad as a hatter, that one.'

'Married to that bloated old toad, who'd blame her?'

Granny chuckled awhile, eyeing the toad in question, but from the corner of her eye she saw Bronwyn sidling away. 'He wasn't such a bad-looking coot when he first come to town. Sort of baby-faced he was, and only a shadow of the man he is today.'

Bronwyn shrugged, lit another cigarette as Bessy joined her at Gran's ashtray.

'What are you on about now, you old reprobate?' Bessy was doubly related; not only had her maternal aunt forged a direct connection to Granny Bourke, but Mickey, her only son, had married one of her great-granddaughters.

The old dame basked a moment in the glow of attention as Ellie Burton followed on the heels of Bessy, Jim Watson one step behind.

Bronwyn caught Ann's eye, pointed her thumb towards the door, signed, 'Five minutes and I'm walking.' Ann nodded, and Bronwyn turned her eyes to Jim Watson, who looked like his mangy old blue heeler cattle dog.

'Having a good day, Gran?' he said, his red-rimmed, stubby lashed eyes not leaving Ellie.

'Humph,' the old dame replied before returning to her previous conversation. 'And Lou Evans. You'd remember her, Bessy. She drowned herself and her three kids, she did. Remember that day? Mad as a hatter, that woman was. Always was. Got herself born with a clubfoot, she did. No one ever thought she'd find a man and have a family, you know. Mad as a hatter.'

'Lou-lou with her built-up shoe?' Bessy said.

'To her dying day, Lou's old mother blamed the priest for her misfortune. Reckoned he put a jinx on her because of her marrying out of the church. He had a clubfoot, you see. O' course, Lou's father, him not being of the faith, he blamed the priest too. But not for the same reason, if you get me drift, girlie.' Granny jabbed Bronwyn with a witch's finger and she cackled.

Granny knew this town, knew every skeleton in every closet, every man who had ever strayed, every woman who had produced a child who did not bear his true father's name. Superstitions, adages slid readily from the old dame's tongue while her voice rose and fell, keeping time with the minute hand of an old marble clock that tick-ticked, tick-ticked, tick-ticked, much slower than its city counterpart.

Her eye wasn't straying far from that clock today, that old killer, Time. Someone had given it to her for a wedding present. Like a malevolent god, it had sat on this mantelpiece since the war of 1914, counting her girlhood away, counting her life's seconds down to nil.

'What's the time say, girlie?'

'Quarter to four.' Bronwyn yawned, her eyes straying back to Ellie and Jim Watson. He'd married Granny's youngest, and only recently buried her. Always keen on the Burtons' river frontage, he'd tried often enough to buy some of it, but Ellie wasn't selling. For his stock's sake, it looked as if Jim had decided to wed some of it.

Granny's eyes were also on Jim. 'He won't be a widower long, that one. Ugly as a bag full of whippets, but he'd be a good catch for your mother,' she hissed at Bronwyn from behind a hand.

'Over my dead body.'

'Haven't found no sign of your father's yet.'

Bronwyn ignored that one.

'He's no more drowned than I am, girlie. He wasn't mad, just bad. My word but he was a handsome devil when he first stepped into that bar. I never seen a nicer looking boy. They were a good-looking couple there for a few years – your mother and him.'

Bronwyn blew a perfect smoke ring at the ceiling. Jack wasn't mad, just bad. She'd go along with that. She glanced at Ellie. Her face was pink and Jim Watson was walking away, heading for the bar. He wouldn't get Ellie's river frontage, or any other frontage. Each year that passed, Jack Burton came closer to achieving sainthood status in Ellie's eyes.

'What's that sister of yours doing these days?'

'Bloody good question, Gran, and I wish she'd stop doing it.'

Granny Bourke looked at her guest, head to the side. 'Humph,' she said. 'Your mother was telling me that she was having another one?'

'Mum? Christ! Not Jim's, is it?'

'Your sister! Annie! Don't you go getting smart with me, girlie.'

Bronwyn smiled and looked at Ann's long sweater. It hid the six-month bulge, but there was so much length in her that her babies probably had room to sprawl out flat on their backs instead of rolling up in a heap. She never looked pregnant until the last weeks.

'Terrible about her first, wasn't it?' Granny's tongue worked around her teeth, it licked thin lips eager to rehash some old drama. Bronwyn wasn't playing ball. She lit another cigarette, and lit one for the old dame. 'Thanks, girlie. Your blood is still worth its bottling, even if you're not much of a talker today. What's wrong with you?'

'Nothing, Gran.' She sucked smoke, looked at the old dame; she liked her guts, and she sighed, tried. 'I see the newspaper photographer was here. You'll make headlines tomorrow.'

'Cruel buggers. I'm not worth photographing these days, but there was a time when I was the belle of this town.'

'Not a lot of competition in Mallawindy, Gran.'

'You've got your father's tongue, girlie, and it's laced with acid. He'll never be dead while you're alive.' She puffed smoke, closing her grey lizard eyelids against it, and Bronwyn moved back a pace, preparing again to edge away. Granny's eyes opened, caught her on the move.

'To tell you the truth, I miss your father. He livened this old town up.' She aimed her ash at the ashtray as a camera clicked, trapping the action. 'Everyone treating me like a two-headed freak show just because I turned a hundred,' she said. 'Nowhere else to go after ninety-nine, is there? Except the bleedin' cemetery, and I got no intention of going out there for a while yet. They're all dead out there, eh? No one to talk to.' She cackled again, but swallowed it as a camera flashed. 'Might as well hang a sign around my bleedin' neck,' she yelled. 'Get your last chance photographs here.

'Time waits for no man, girlie. From the day we're born we get dragged along towards the grave, like it or not,' she said, glowering at the two females standing in front of her clock. Hiding time.

Then a baby wailed and Bronwyn flinched. She loathed that plaintive wail. A woman moved to silence it, just as the hand of the mantle clock jerked forward, deducting another minute from Granny's life.

'You haven't started your family yet?'

'Not married, am I?' Ann had disappeared. Hopefully to the toilet.

'They don't let that stop them these days. Anyway, what's a pretty little thing like you doing not getting married? I thought you had a good bloke.' Gran's finger prodded and an ember fell onto her dress, bought new for this day.

Bronwyn swiped at it, knocked it to the floor, ground it into the carpet while the old girl glanced around, gnashing her jaws.

'Don't you dob on me. They'll nick my smokes.'

The screaming infant was only metres away, and its mother undoing the buttons on her blouse. Bronwyn swallowed hard, watched a pink balloon breast emerge, watched the small cannibalistic mouth bite in, suck. And the old lady watched her watch, her wicked eye roving from her guest's expression to her waist, then back again.

'You're not drinking much today, are you, girlie?'

'I'm on a diet.'

'Pull the other one. It's made out of rubber.'

Bronwyn glanced at the leg in question – more like a plucked sparrow's ankle than rubber. Hands like gnarled mallee roots. One was flung out, old fingers snaring a box of chocolates. She helped herself to one then offered the box. Bronwyn shook her head, but watched the old dame's hands work hard at removing the purple foil, watched her tongue urge the fingers on until thin lips closed around the chocolate and her tongue caressed it, pressed it, savouring the sweet.

'You got that look about you, you know.'

'What look is that, Gran?'

'That breeding look.' Granny sniggered, drooled chocolate. 'It's in the eyes.'

'Not for long,' Bronwyn muttered.

'What's that you say?'

'Nothing, Gran.'

'I'm not deaf yet, and I haven't lived for a hundred bleedin' years and not learned nothing either.'

Gran's tongue flicking in and out, reclaiming lost chocolate, she squinted at the young face. Large brown–green eyes, deep set today. A pretty face, but pale against the long nut-brown hair. High breasts beneath a dusty pink sweater, black slacks.

'Well you just put this in your modern little pipe and smoke it, girlie. It's an ill wind that sheds no good along its pathway, and new life was never "nothing" and that's a fact.'

Granny Bourke's words were like some virulent virus. They hit hard, hit Bronwyn below the belt. She ran for the toilet, lost her glass of wine, three corn crackers, and the dry biscuits she'd managed to keep down at breakfast time, but she found Ann.

It's an ill wind that sheds no good along its pathway.

'Are you okay, Bron?'

'I will be. I'm going up to Sydney tomorrow.'

'It's too late for that.'

'Shiiiiit. What am I going to do, Annie?'

'Sneak out through the bar. They won't miss us.'

a full set of teeth

~

Friday 8 August

Mallawindy had been battered by ill winds for weeks. Mini torna-does swept through, determined to flatten the town, to wipe it from the face of the land. They failed, but they shifted Bill Dooley's house a foot to the south, exposing his termite-riddled stumps. They lifted the roof from the new garage and dumped it on the Central. The hotel remained open for business.

The winds ripped a tree from the earth and it fell across the old river road and onto a panel van, just as young Bob West and old Vera Owen were getting down to business. Vera swore that Bob was a hero, that he'd thrown himself on top to protect her, but they were both naked from the waist down when cut from the wreckage. Only big Charlie, Vera's much cuckolded, truckie husband believed the story. Vera had always preferred the dominant position.

Ill winds were still wailing when Bessy Bishop came to the mud brick house on that Friday in August. She'd been born and raised in this house, knew every brick, every creaking board. Ben had bought it back in the eighties and lived alone there until his father went missing, when Ellie and John had moved in with him.

'Ellie!' Bessy bawled at the front door. The wind picked up her words, tossed them away.

She let herself in. 'Ellie. Where the hell are you?'

The kitchen was a small black hole, the dining room as dark and not a lot larger; twin doors and two deep steps down separated it from the lounge room, which was cluttered with furniture. The bedrooms might have made good walk-in wardrobes these days, but this morning Ellie wasn't in any of the rooms.

'Ellie! Are you up there? I'm not climbing those bloody stairs,' Bessy yelled up to the bedroom in the roof. Low beamed, larger than the downstairs rooms, it was Ellie's room. Always had been.

'Ellie!'

Born a gosling, old age had not turned Bessy into a swan. Some argument between her Granville/Vevers genes had set her pugnacious features at conception. Sun-dried, windblown, she wasn't a pretty sight today.

'Ellie!' On the back verandah, her face near lost beneath a thatch of steel-grey hair, she turned from east to west, her darting eyes scanning the back yard. 'For Christ's sake, will you answer me! I got something to tell you.'

'I'm in here. For goodness sake, stop your yelling, Bessy.' The reply came from the outdoor lavatory, a long path away.

'They've found him.'

'What?'

'They've found Jack.'

The chug-chug-a-lug, the rumble of water, the hiss of old pipes refilling the outdated overhead cistern, then Ellie emerged, her skirt blowing in the wind, her smile triumphant, her belief in prayer justified.

'Oh, shit.' Bessy turned her back to the wind and to Ellie; she took the makings from her pocket and rolled a cigarette.

'I was just going over to do the chooks, Bessy. Where has he been?'

Not bloody far from home, Bessy thought, but said: 'Don't you go over that bridge today. You'll get blown off the bloody thing.'

Ellie rinsed her hands at the garden tap and Bessy watched her, watched the water stream bend in the wind. She'd just heard some good news, but how to tell it was the problem. Trying hard to compose her features into a mask of concern, she lit the cigarette, pursing her lips around it, which hindered her satisfied smile but did not totally conceal it.

'Is he all right?'

'Come in out of the wind. We'll have a cup of tea and a talk about it.'

Her hands wiped on her khaki apron, Ellie walked up to the house, her smile becoming a quizzical frown. 'What's the matter?'

'Jeff Rowan just rung me up. He said it might be better coming from me than from him.' Ellie was staring at her now, so Bessy let it rip. 'They found his body out the Daree road a couple of days ago but held off saying anything until the experts had looked him over. But it's him.' She sucked smoke hard, controlling her lips, but not her eyes.

'No. Not Jack. No. It can't be Jack?'

'It's him, all right.' Bessy watched her sister sit down hard on the edge of the verandah and she sat beside her, placing an arm around her. 'I done it all wrong, love. I know that. I opened my mouth and put my big foot right in it, didn't I? But I've been looking for you for ten minutes. I've been right though your house. I could have pinched your handbag off the table.'

'There's not much in it.' Ellie was staring at her wedding ring, twisting it. 'It can't be Jack, Bessy. It's not Jack.'

'He's the right age, he's big, he's been dead around the right time, and he must have thought a bit of himself because they dug out the skull intact and it's still got a full set of teeth. I mean, who else of sixty-odd, with his own teeth, is missing from around here?'

A full set of natural teeth was as rare a find in Mallawindy as hen's molars. Dentists cost money, and meant a trip to Warran or Daree. Bessy sucked tobacco from her own set of dentures while with one hand she patted her sister's shoulder. 'Isn't it better to find his bo . . . I mean, you knew this could happen. You knew this was bound to happen sooner or later.'

Her hand in her apron pocket, Ellie's fingers played the rosary beads. Prayer beads, worry beads, they were always with her. 'It's not him, Bessy. It's not.'

'As they say, love, it's an ill wind that blows no good. You'll feel better about it if you can give him a proper funeral. You'll be able to forget about the bas – ' She sucked the word back with smoke, swallowed it. 'And you'll get his insurance money and no more bloody messing around. You can build yourself some new milking sheds.'

Eyes wide, her mouth open, Ellie lifted her head and stared at her sister. 'I don't want their money. I don't need a new milking shed either. I wouldn't take their money in exchange for . . . for Jack's life.'

'I know, love, but it's yours. You've paid the premiums for years.'

'I'll . . . I'll give it to the church.'

'My backside, you will! You gave your son to the church and look what it's done to him.'

Johnny rarely left the property. When he wasn't digging post holes and setting in new posts, he was stretching wires between them, or cutting hay, painting the old Burton house, milking cows. At it from daylight to dark, from Sunday to Sunday, he worked on, slowly, methodically, like a battery-driven robot. He'd keep on moving until his batteries finally ran down, then he'd start charging them up at the Central, start hitting the bottle and end up worse than his father, Bessy thought, though she never said it – not to Ellie.

Bessy worried about her silent nephew, but could not get close to him. No one could. The whole family hadn't been the same since Christmas 1990. Held together by some collective rubber band when Jack Burton had been around, his leaving had snapped it, sent them shooting off like scattered pebbles fired from a slingshot.

Look at Annie, playing mother earth, for Christ's sake. Never would have thought it of her. And look at Bronwyn; she was a loose cannon with a bloody short fuse, that one – and after the way she'd treated young Nick, it was a bloody wonder he was going to do the right thing by her too, and God help him. And Ellie – Ellie might have been her sister but she had the memory of a blind worm with its head cut off.

Ben had done okay. He'd never changed. Even as a kid he'd just continued on doing what had to be done, and doing it well. He'd shed ten years and grown an inch the day he'd built his bridge, or maybe he'd just stood taller.

He and Johnny were working wonders over the river, and the old house, given a long overdue coat of paint, had come up well – on the outside. They could have been renting it out, should have been, as Bessy frequently told them. Someone living at the house might stop people helping themselves to the chooks and pigs. But Johnny didn't want strangers wandering around the property, and what Johnny didn't want, Ellie didn't do. He slept at the old place when his moods were dark, or wandered there and kept Bessy's dogs barking all night long.

She turned again to her sister, who was now staring unseeing at a geranium barely surviving in an old milk urn. Like Ellie, it had made the transition over the bridge six years ago and it wasn't doing so well either. All stalks and no sap. Bessy stood, filled a watering can and poured water into the pot. 'Buck up, love. You knew they were looking for his body. Christ, they dragged that river for weeks.'

'Where did they find – ?'

'This side of Daree. In that bit of bush that comes down to the road, about three miles east of Charlie and Vera Owen's place. Only metres from the road, Jeff said.'

'Just laying there, out in all the weather?' Ellie was weeping now.

'No. No, love. He'd been buried. A couple of – '

'Buried? Buried!'

'Wouldn't have been much left of him if he hadn't of been buried! A couple of campers found him – or their dog did, when they were out walking. Around midday the day before yesterday. So Jeff was saying.'

'Then it's not him, Bessy. Who'd bury him?'

'Charlie bloody Owen, for one. He knew about Jack and Vera. He swore to everyone in town that he'd bury him one day. And he done it, didn't he?'

Ellie stared at the geranium, picked at a broken fingernail while Bessy leaned on a verandah post and blew smoke.

'They've got to do the official ID, which Jeff says is only a formality. They've took photos or X-rays of his teeth, so they need to know the name of his dentist. Then it's done and you get the money.'

'His dentist?'

'Dentists keep stuff for years. X-rays and the like, details of fillings and stuff. The cops always use dental records. You know that.'

Ellie nodded, nodded, her green eyes dripping.

'Nothing much found on the body. A few bits of clothes.' Bessy tossed her smoke into the garden but the wind blew it back to the verandah. Ellie flicked it away, watched sparks fly in the wind. 'They think you might recognise his clothes, love.'

'Are Benjie and Mickey back yet?' It was Ben's day off from the shop. He and Bessy's son had taken a load of pigs up to the Warran sale.

'The pig sale goes late. That's why Jeff rung me, I suppose. Though I don't know why he didn't drive over and tell Johnny. It might have been better coming from him than me.' Might not have either, she thought. He'd probably do a victory dance. 'I came straight down here as soon as I heard.'

Almost straight down. She didn't tell her sister about the book they'd been running at the pub since they'd found the gun. The odds on Jack being dead had fluctuated since. When the frogmen hadn't found his body in the river, they went up, when the insurance investigator packed up and left town they went down. Then Mrs Carter swore she'd seen Jack at the Sydney racetrack, and the odds had gone up again.

The population of Mallawindy, like AMP, was now not wholly convinced that Jack hadn't faked his disappearance, that he wasn't hiding out in Sydney, biding his time until Ellie got the money. Bessy had given the Central a quick call before coming to find her sister, using her inside information to place a bet – and getting a lousy two to one on Jack being dead.

'I told Jeff that I'd drive you down to Daree to talk to the Sydney blokes this afternoon, so we'd better get a move on.'

'I can't go to Daree. I've got *that* wedding tomorrow.'

'They need the name of his dentist.'

'Well I don't know it, Bessy.'

'Jeff said they're homicide bigwigs, love,' she said, watching her sister for reaction. There was none. 'You don't want them up here, do you, sniffing around, asking everybody bloody questions about him again? We only just got rid of the nosy bastards.'

'I'm not going down to Daree today. I've got to wash my hair and you know it takes hours to dry. Ring them up, Bessy. Tell them Jack used to go to a dentist somewhere in Melbourne. I never knew where. If he had a toothache, he'd just take off and go. You know that.'

'You paid his bills. You'll find the dentist's name on something. What about your old cheque butts?'

'I never paid for his dentist. He must have paid, or May and Sam might have. He kept his private things in his briefcase, and I told you a dozen times that Annie took it with her that night. I haven't got anything. Ben and Johnny burned most of the papers when they moved me over from the old place.' Ellie looked towards the house across the river, looked at the trees, their branches tossed by the wind. 'Ring Jeff and tell him that Annie might have something with the dentist's name on it. There might have been some old bills in the briefcase – that's if she's still got it.'

'She's told you she hasn't got it. I heard her tell you.'

'She has so got it. I saw her take it. She took it that night before Jack came home. I saw her put it in her car boot.'

'Yeah. Well, I'd keep her out of it if I were you. They annoyed Christ out of the poor kid when they found his gun. She's got enough on her plate these days, I wouldn't go mentioning his bloody briefcase to the cops or they'll be into her again.' She pulled a weed from the geranium pot, her fingers delving deep into the earth. She'd been looking forward to a trip to Daree, to getting the lowdown straight from the horse's mouth.

'Come on, love. Fix your hair and put a nice dress on and we'll get it over and done with. It will only take us a couple of hours and I'll dry your hair tonight with my hair dryer.'

'You tangled it the last time you tried to do that. Anyway, I've got to get the eggs before the chooks start pecking at them, and I'm worried about the little brindle heifer. I wish you'd keep your bull locked in, Bessy. She was too young when he got to her,' Ellie said as she walked off towards the river.

'That bridge is dangerous in this wind. I'll drive you around. And why don't you wear the tracksuit I bought for your birthday?'

'The pants are too tight when I bend over, and Benjie built that bridge for me. It's safe if you're careful.'

'If you crawl on your belly! The bloody thing will be alive today.'

'It's solid as a rock.'

'Rock being the operative word.' Bessy walked behind her sister through the side gate. 'I'm warning you. Those Sydney cops will be coming up here if you don't go down and talk to them. It'll be better for everyone if you keep it out of town.'

'I can't tell them anything that they don't know already.'

'You'd recognise his clothes, for Christ's sake.'

'So would you.'

'Not his underdaks.'

'Tell them . . . tell them he always wore Bonds briefs, size eighteen. And he never wore singlets. He wore black socks and black shoes, size nine. And he only ever bought Pelaco shirts because they have different sleeve lengths and he had long arms.

And he was wearing sports trousers that night. Grey.' Ellie walked ahead. Bessy attempted to keep up with her sister, who had extra inches and weight, who had longer legs and shorter years.

'For Christ's sake, wait up, will you?'

'Don't you come over the bridge, Bessy. You'll get blown off. Go and ring up Jeff. Remind him that we've got Bronwyn's wedding tomorrow, and tell him that the Sydney men will have to wait until . . . '

The rest of her words were lost to the wailing wind.

run, rabbit, run

~

Saturday 9 August

Panic came out of sleep, came for him out of the dark. It bit at his throat, constricting muscles that banded together until each one became that old familiar enemy. His throat cramped, drawing his mouth into a rictus smile. Scalp muscles gathered, squeezing his brain, chest muscles crushed his lungs. Each breath, hard fought for, was drawn in, pushed out. Fast panting breaths.

Coward. Weak little bastard.

Had to slow his breathing. He knew it. But rationality was dead. Couldn't think his way outside of panic. Only those words left in the cerebral mass to haunt him, to chase him to hell and haunt him there. Words he could trace back to near birth. Repetition had pounded them deep.

Thunk. Thunk. Thunk. Thunk.

Weak little bastard.

When all else was dust Johnny Burton would still hear his father's words. And run from them.

He ran now, that old inner running, that dream running, that leaden limb running. Couldn't get away.

Run, Johnny. Get the little ones and run for the river.
Run, Johnny, run, Johnny, run, run, run.
Here comes Daddy with his old shotgun.
He'll get by without his Johnny pie,
So run, Johnny, run, Johnny, run, run, run.

His limbs were swimming, shudder swimming in his bed, in his sweat. Hands dripping. Face, feet dripping while the damp sheet dragged, bunching, binding him, holding him down.

Fight me, you weak bastard.

Couldn't fight any more. Just wanted it to end now, wanted his brain to lie down and die. Die and let him get some sleep.

Failure. That's what he was and always had been. Failure. Weak little bastard. Running bastard.

He sucked on air, panting it in, and too fast out. His mouth was dry, his lips sandpaper, his tongue a lump of dry wood in his mouth, his eyes staring at a patch of not so dark, clinging to the patch of not so dark as the tremors shook his heavy frame.

Hold on to the lighter dark. Hold on to it and concentrate. Think white. Think light.

Look at the curtain, blowing, billowing with the breeze, like a white ghost in the dark. A white sail to carry you into the dawn. Ride it, and breathe over panic. Watch the curtain and breathe as it breathes. In and out. Slow now. Recognise it for what it is. A curtain, not the white sail of the old ferryman's boat come to carry you across the river to Hell. A curtain. Ellie's cheap nylon lace.

And outside that curtain the light was growing. Morning would come.

I shouldn't have slept, he thought. He knew not to fall asleep with the light off, but his head had been aching. He hadn't been able to force his eyes to read last night. That's what he did each night, read anything, read until his eyes rebelled and the book fell from his hand while the light glowed on.

Light had always stilled panic when he awoke in the night.

These last years he'd closed his door and left his light burning all night, sealing the light in with an old blanket placed against his door.

Ellie had bought him a torch when he was four or five years old and afraid of the dark. He'd slept with that torch beneath his pillow for weeks.

Don't let Daddy see it or he'll take it away, Johnny.

But Daddy saw it and he took it away, didn't he?

Weak, cowardly little bastard.

He'd taken a box of matches from the kitchen then and he'd slept with them in his pyjama pocket until the matchbox fell apart, but he'd found another box. Slept with his matches for years – until Liza had come to fill the cot and Ben had come to share his room. Ben hadn't been afraid of the dark. Ben had been there when he'd dreamed the bad dreams in the night. Ben with his funny little sighing snore. Soothing snore.

Ben in the room across the passage now. Ellie in her little room upstairs. Sleeping soundly.

And Jack Burton.

Dead.

He was dead.

Johnny Burton raised saliva enough to swallow. He was going to be okay. Morning was coming. Shadows were playing outside the curtain now. He could see the old oak tree, see its naked branches like grasping fingers.

Old eternal oak, the seed brought from Germany in a coat pocket. Always there, that tree, always outside that window.

A good climbing tree.

The shuddering had stilled, now wipe-out weariness came for him, wanting to drag him down again into sleep.

Insane agony, this weariness. Every bone, every muscle was begging for the release of sleep. Tired crept up from his feet to his legs, his back, his arms and higher. It crouched on his shoulders like a cat waiting, smiling, knowing its time would come to pounce, waiting to get him again in the dark, to curl over his face, suffocate him.

His eyes were stinging. He closed them, moistened them, and they wanted to remain closed. But he forced them to stare again at the curtain.

Intolerable, this weariness. When in his life had he been so intolerably tired?

He'd never been a good sleeper. Never game to sleep when he was a kid. Slept with one eye and both ears open.

Nothing to hear in this house. A silent old place. A safe old place. Close your eyes now and picture that old oak behind your eyes. It's bigger now than it was back then. How long does an oak tree continue to grow? How long is forever?

Shadow fingers swaying, playing, his mind began to wander into the outland of sleep.

A good old climbing tree, that one. The best. He'd known good times in this little old house with Grandpa. Gentle old man with his wide bed an eight-year-old could crawl into when the bad dreams came. Grandpa's house. Safe.

Good times with Grandpa and Mummy.

Be careful up that tree, Johnny. You'll fall.

I'm careful, Mummy.

He's a big boy, Ellie. Don't breed fear into him. Boys were born to climb trees.

Big boy. Big enough to have a pocketknife. Grandpa said so. Cut Daddy's head off with the pocketknife if he comes home and hurts Mummy again. Wait till he goes to sleep and just creep in and cut him and let all the blood out.

Cowardly, weak little bastard.

Our father, the destroyer, creator of crippling scars, hated be thy name. Thy time will come.

How many times had he planned his father's death? The fingers on his left hand held high, he stared at them, grey fingers in the grey light. Slowly he added the fingers of his right hand. Not enough fingers. How many times had he planned to kill his father? How many leaves fall from an oak tree?

The scars of childhood had split open. Old memories and pain were swamping John Burton. Wide scars, they had never healed, only a fine membrane had grown over them, sealing in the putrescent pus that exploded at will, bursting forth to poison him with that old childhood infection.

He'd hated his father at four, despised him at eight. Just a little boy, not much bigger than Ann's oldest boy now.

Man is only a frightened little boy, forced to grow tall, he thought.

Take the little ones away, Johnny. Do as I tell you. Get them away from me.

Mummy. She's come alive.

Fight me, you weak little bastard. I could take you with one hand tied behind my back. Come on. Have a go. I'll put my hand in my pocket. Have a go, you cowardly little mummy's boy.

Light was creeping out of the east like grey water. He needed the dawn. He needed light in which to work. Light to dig holes. Light to fill holes. To hammer. Fix. Fill his mind with doing and leave no room for memories.

He'd make a start on the old bedrooms over the river. Strip the wallpaper in Ann's old room and he'd get Ben to bring home some paint from the shop. White. Or something light. Pale blue, maybe. She'd loved blue.

Is the ocean water all blue if you put it in a cup, my Johnny? Is the stars still up on the sky when it is day time, my Johnny?

Questions. She'd never run out of questions. Talk? That one could have talked the leg off an iron pot.

Then nothing. She'd come home from Narrawee just a terrified little ghost of the one he'd waved away, her wide questioning eyes hidden behind a veil of fear.

John shook his head on the pillow, forcing his mind to return to the old house and to the fading wallpaper, and to the rotting window that refused to open. It was too small anyway. That room had always been dark. Maybe he'd talk to Ben about putting new windows in the two back bedrooms. And the old kitchen – a couple of long windows in there would improve it. Easy enough to do, too; it had never been lined. Maybe he'd make a start on the kitchen. New windows. New cupboards. It was a good-sized room. You could get a modern kitchen in there and have a separate eating area.

Sleep tried to grab him while his mind had turned its back; the old kitchen became a dream and he didn't know that it was a dream until it almost had its claws in. But he fought his way free of sleep and flung his legs from the tumbled bed, sitting a moment on its edge until his pulse rate steadied, then on bare feet he walked out the back to the bathroom, showering long, washing the dreams away.

He shaved, hating his face in the mirror, because it was his father's face, hating the straight nose and the heavy hair, darker in the morning light. Hating the well-shaped brows, and the eyes, the high cheekbones and the determined jaw, loathing the mouth that could have been his father's and the teeth. Straight. Strong.

Self-loathing.

He was taller than his father, a generous six foot three. Heavier bones, heavier wrists and shoulders, but hard work kept him slim. His hands and his feet were not his father's. He looked at his hand holding the razor, then, turning his face from the mirror, blindly scraped the dreams and dark overnight growth away. His thick hair, tamed by a splash of cold water, looked black beneath the light. He parted it, combed it to the side. Jack Burton had never parted his hair. Slowly then he dressed in khaki drill trousers, a T-shirt and an old windcheater, clothing his father's clone, disguising him, slowly rebuilding the working man his father had never been.

In the kitchen he boiled the jug, made coffee, strong, and he drank it while staring at the maddening clock, ticking too slow, the big hand jammed, like him, not wanting to move on.

He couldn't move on because he had nowhere to go. No place left for him. Out of touch with God, he'd told them when he'd left the church. But had he ever been in touch with God? I'm going home to find my faith, he'd said, but he'd lied, he'd looked them in the eye and he'd lied. Easier to lie. Easier than the truth.

His faith had been a crutch. He'd preached devotion, hiding a faithless boy in the ritual, the ecclesiastical claptrap of the Catholic church. He'd stood in the pulpit offering up words and baseless promises of miracles and deliverance – offering his own splintered crutch for the weak to lean on. But let them lean too heavily and the crutch snapped and they tumbled, fell flat on their faces.

He'd fallen on his face and he couldn't get up. Fallen in the mire and he didn't want to get up any more.

Tired. Tired eyes. Images moved before them – or behind them, shadow and dream, memory and moment swaying. He shook his head, turning to face the small window as he thought of another window, and the old man, dead these past fifteen years – the only priest he had trusted with his truth, or his half-truth. He'd even lied in the confessional.

Bless me, Father, for I have sinned.

What is your sin?

My life here is a lie, Father.

I am listening, my son.

At fifteen I promised to kill my father.

At fifteen you were a boy. Now you are a man. You did not kill him.

The boy in me wants to keep his promise. The boy in me dreams of it each night. I have cut all ties with my family because I'm afraid of my dreams.

Take some time. Go to your father and make your peace.

That I cannot, will not do.

If you still carry a desire for some childhood revenge within your heart, then you have no place here.

I am here to find forgiveness, to find the miracle that will allow me to forgive.

Here, miracles come only from labour. We plant a seed and

harvest a miracle of nature. Go to your father and plant your seed of forgiveness in his heart.

Plant a knife of steel in his heart. Plant an iron axe in his head. Plant a lead bullet in his brain, then plant him deep. When I'm big enough.

Only weeks after that confession the old priest had died, on the island, in the fields, still planting his miracles. John Burton had not confessed his grievous sin to another, aware that none would give him the reply that he desired.

Then go home, my son, and kill the murdering bastard.

He shuddered, blinked, shifting the window again into focus. Grey out, and the wind rising, the oak beating its branches against the roof. Still too early to start on the milking. His eyes roving the walls, found the small head and shoulder portrait of Liza, transferred from the sprawling old kitchen over the river to this small room, and his mind moved back to the day of her pathetic little funeral.

He'd gone to it. He'd stood at his mother's side, working hard at doing the right thing for the first months after his return. They'd opened up the other children's grave. Linda and Patrick's. His sister. His brother. He hadn't known them. Had he remained at home they may have been alive today – or never born. He barely remembered the baby who had been Bronwyn, only two when the fifteen-year-old boy had run from that house and hailed down a truck, leaving hell behind him. Leaving little Annie behind him too.

They had interred Liza's small white coffin in the early morning, in private. Ben had arranged it. Ben had taken the place of the oldest son. Little Ben, the decision-maker, man of the house. A good man. A lucky man. He looked like his grandfather. Ben had wanted no reporters at the funeral to pry, to spy on Ellie's grief, so he'd arranged the brief service for the early morning and by nine the white casket holding a seven-year-old's bones was buried deep.

Father Fogarty performed the service, and perhaps for a while the well-known ritual had grasped Johnny, carried him. He'd felt that old safe peace, that distancing from self once more, that splintered crutch to lean on. But words ended.

The stone, chosen in advance, had been paid for by Narrawee, in advance.

LIZA, LINDA, AND PATRICK. LOVED CHILDREN OF JACK AND ELLIE.

Ellie had her memorial service in the late afternoon. No pathetic bundle of bones to spoil it, just the large full portrait of Liza that had hung for nearly a quarter of a century over the fireplace in the old lounge room. Miss Tiny Tot, 1963.

Miss Tiny Tot, and a mountain of flowers brought to the church by the crowd. Most of Mallawindy, Anglican and Catholic, had been in the church, or leaning on the front fence. May Burton had driven up for the day. She'd brought her own flowers, and a flashy condolence card from Sam, who due to illness could not attend the service – or so she said. But John knew all about Uncle Sam. He'd been dead since 1967, his burned remains found in the sand dunes out at Dead Man's Lane. John hadn't spoken to May and she had not spoken to him, because she knew that he knew.

Ann had stayed away that day and Ellie hadn't forgiven her for that. But she'd wept over Sam's card. Kept it too. Ben had laminated it for her, had it framed. Now it hung over her bed – a large print of the baby Jesus in Mary's arms, the price written in gold on the bottom. And his words, that bastard's words written there in black.

The writing was too familiar. How had Ellie not known? Ben had noticed the similarity, and commented.

'They're identical twins, love. Of course they'd write the same.' Poor simple Ellie. His mother, the fool, the child who had never grown out of childhood.

To my dearest Ellie and family.
I know that wherever Jack is, he knows that Liza has come home to her family. He is at peace at last, Ellie. Be happy for him.
Love as always, Sam.

Jack Burton had always had a way with words.

Sam, Sam, the dirty man,
Washed his face in a frying pan,
Combed his hair with the leg of a chair
And told his mother he didn't care.

That verse was about the only thing his father had ever taught John. He'd sat him on the old kitchen table and kept it up until the two-year-old boy could parrot it. A pair of bastards, a perfectly matched pair of bastards, Jack Burton and Uncle Sam. Between them they had possessed all the vices of mankind.

Murder too. Jack had killed his brother when he'd caught him molesting Liza.

A near carbon copy of the two, John saw that pair of bastards every time he looked in a mirror. Couldn't get away from them. He feared them, or feared the genes he'd inherited from a paedophile and an abusive drunk, thus he murdered his inner self daily, as he killed emotion, fearing it, fearing life.

The wind was rising, moaning, mourning the Burton twins. Dead. Both of them. Murdered. Both of them. They'd got what they'd deserved. Both of them.

But what now?

Saturday now. Bronwyn's wedding at three. He'd have to raise some semblance of manhood today. He'd have to sit in the church at Ellie's side. Couldn't get out of going. He'd have to put on a suit and a tie, walk out of his separate *here* and into family, a false smile on his face. He'd have to see Ann, make hard conversation with her.

He rarely saw her, but they were bound together, hand and foot, by an old lie.

Somehow they managed to keep up a polite facade when forced to be in the same room. 'Pleasant weather, Ann,' he'd say, or 'Unpleasant weather, Ann.' 'We need the rain,' she'd say. 'How are the boys, Ann?' 'Growing,' she'd say.

Like Malcolm Fletcher and her husband David, these days John always called her Ann.

But he thought of her as Annie.

As little wide-eyed Annie.

Lost.

A light clicked on in the passage. It startled the thinker. He looked up as Ben, dressed for the cow yard, entered the kitchen.

'G'day. You're up early,' his brother said around a stretch and a yawn.

'I thought I'd make an early start,' Johnny Burton lied. Lied easily. Lied constantly. Annie had forced him to lie.

They had held each other the day he'd come home. They'd howled in each other's arms and talked and laughed, and howled again. It hadn't been too late for them. For a day, for a week, it hadn't seemed too late.

Now he rarely saw her, rarely spoke to her, couldn't, wouldn't forgive her for making him live a lie.

'Cold out. Probably too cold to rain.' Ben raked the ash from the old wood stove and set to with a twist of newspaper, a handful of twigs, building a tepee, placing the larger sticks of wood on top. He struck a match, held it until the newspaper caught, and flames crept up to the kindling, then licked higher. 'Feel like some porridge?'

'Sounds good to me.' Lie. What did it matter what he ate, or if he ate? 'Is Mum up yet?' What did he care if she was up or not? Just talk. Something to say.

'Let her sleep. Bessy gave her a pill to settle her down last night. I don't know what it was, but she's still dead to the world.' Ben measured rolled oats into a saucepan; he added salt and water. 'What a time for it to happen, eh?'

'Very bad timing for Bronwyn.'

'I don't know how Mum is going to get through it. She was a howling mess last night.'

'Yes.' But she'll put on her lipstick, plait her hair, close up her mind. She'll survive, Johnny thought.

Silence then, only the wood cracking, warming the old black stove, already sharing a breath of its heat with the tiny room where a small table stood hard against the one bare wall. Only three kitchen chairs. Space was at a premium. The sink was below a high window and beside it, too few cupboards were packed full.

No room for a refrigerator and the kitchen door, so the door had been removed years ago. The equally small dining room was across the passage. They never dined there. It was Ellie's room; it was where she sat her visitors when they came for afternoon tea. It was where she read her newspapers and did her crosswords.

'Annie and Bron are coming down at twelve. David will leave later. He'll drive straight through and meet us at the church.'

'Right.' Ben still called her Annie. Annie and Bron. Never Bronwyn. Pretty name, Bronwyn. Johnny had named her too, found that name in a book. *How Green Is My Valley*. At thirteen he'd liked that name. Liked the book too. It was still on the shelf at the old place. He'd read it again.

Wind in the vines moaning. Wind in the wires, adding their low, mournful whistle. John stood and walked to the sink, staring out at the gun-metal sky while rinsing his mug.

'I'll have to get down there before two, they said. Have to pick my suit up. You should have hired one, Johnny.'

'I'll do okay, Ben.'

'It's not as if we're on the breadline.'

'You forget, I've got a ready-made wardrobe.'

'Yeah.' Ben stirred the porridge. 'You're as bad as Mum, you know. You won't move on. Burn his clothes. They still stink of him. I don't know how you can wear them.'

'Waste not, want not, lad.'

The words were memory. The smell of porridge bubbling in this kitchen was memory. The small sandy-haired man making porridge was memory.

Big pots of porridge cooked each morning by Grandpa. And

there he was, his back turned, still leaning over his little black stove, stirring.

Get the bowls out, lads. It's a good brew this morning. It will stick to the stomach like glue.

The Burton brothers – so different. John tall, thick hair, dark but greying now at the temples, and Ben small and wiry, his sandy hair kept short. Three years separated them. Since their father's disappearance, Ben had been overflowing with drive and energy; Johnny was an empty shell.

He sighed and took two bowls from the cupboard, placing them on the table with the sugar. He took the milk from the fridge as Ben carried his saucepan to the table, ladling the heavy concoction evenly into the bowls.

'It's a good brew this morning,' Ben said with a grin.

'Stick to the stomach like glue, lad,' Johnny replied.

mother of the bride

~

'My goodness, what a crowd of them,' Ellie whispered. One glance through the telephone book was enough to prove that Smith was a common name, but Ellie hadn't expected all of them to be at Bronwyn's wedding. The Daree Catholic church was full of Smiths and ex-Smiths.

The Burtons were not so well represented. Only Bessy, her son Mickey, his wife Jenny, and her great-grandmother, old Granny Bourke. Why Bronwyn had asked her, Ellie did not know. Still, there was no understanding her daughter – daughters – and that was a fact. She'd never understood them, not when they were little, and even less now. She never knew what they were going to do next, and she'd found it better not to know sometimes. Like this rushed wedding!

Annie was seated in the row behind, with David, and she was wearing black! Johnny was on Ellie's right. He almost hadn't made it to the church. They'd picked him up from the Daree hospital at two-thirty.

What a day. The rain had started misting down ten minutes after she and the girls had left Mallawindy. It hadn't let up since. So cold in the old church too, but when they closed the door, if they closed the door, the crowd of Nick's relatives would warm it up.

Bronwyn had invited Kerrie Fogarty and she actually had a skirt on. It was the first time Ellie had seen her in a skirt. Not much of a skirt. Not for a wedding. Lord only knew why Bronwyn had invited her, but at least having Kerrie on the guest list had given Ellie the excuse she'd needed to invite her uncle, Father Fogarty.

Bronwyn hadn't wanted him at her wedding. She'd put on a turn, threatened to invite Mr Fletcher if Ellie asked their old priest. 'And I'll sit them side by side,' she'd said. 'You see if I don't, Mum.'

Bronwyn didn't even like Mr Fletcher, and well Ellie knew it, but she'd stuck to her guns and given him a late invitation. He'd turned up too, and was seated two rows back, taking up half a pew. Ellie intended altering the place cards at the reception – if she could get to them before everyone sat down. Father Fogarty and Mr Fletcher may have been born in the same year, but that was all they had in common. Always arguing. Every time they got together they argued, and they could become very loud about it.

Nick's family lived in Daree. Bronwyn had said that he had a lot of elderly relatives who were not up to travelling. That was the reason they were marrying in Daree. Not that Ellie could see many old ones. She glanced over her shoulder at Granny Bourke, resplendent in pink, hat and all. And the hat smelt of mothballs. She'd lay a bet that none of the elderly Smiths had made it to one hundred years old. Not that Granny was a blood relative, but since Bessy's Mickey had married her great-granddaughter, she'd sort of moved herself back into the family.

Ellie shivered, folded her arms, wishing she'd worn her old overcoat. Bronwyn wouldn't allow it.

The wedding should have been in Mallawindy – and it probably wasn't raining there. The whole town would have turned out to see Bronwyn; and Father Fogarty, who had baptised her, should have done the service. He wasn't happy at all. Ellie glanced at him. He was sitting beside Kerrie, at the opposite end of Mr Fletcher's pew. She smiled at the old priest. He nodded, but didn't smile back.

Then the organist changed tunes mid note and started on 'Here Comes the Bride'. And there they all were, flower girls and page-boys, and Bronwyn, looking so beautiful, like a walking angel – but with bare arms and shoulders. She'd catch her death of cold. And Benjie! He looked so handsome and proud. Ellie's eyes filled. This was her first wedding. Annie hadn't married in the church. She and David had gone to Sydney one weekend and Annie had turned up the next week with a wedding ring on her finger, married to a divorced man. Terrible, Ellie thought.

White weddings were so beautiful. A tear fell onto her jacket. She grabbed for her handkerchief as the bride halted her procession beside her.

'Don't you cry, Mum. You'll spoil your make-up.' Bronwyn lifted her veil and kissed Ellie, hissing between her teeth. 'See how they set it up? Half a dozen Smiths in front so I can't make a break for it through the vestry. Half a dozen more cutting off my bloody escape from the rear.'

'Bronwyn!'

Ellie shed no more tears. Bronwyn was no angel and never had been, and if the truth was told, Ellie doubted Bronwyn's reasons for the hasty marriage too.

It was a long service, and half of it in Latin. She loved the Latin, loved the whole ritual – not that she understood a word of it. But she had the book with the translation in it and Bronwyn and Nick's names on the cover. Not that she could read a word without her glasses. It would be nice to keep, though.

'Do you Nicholas Thomas Smith, take Bronwyn . . . ' At least that was in English. As was Nick's reply.

'Just call me the last of the good Samaritans,' he said.

There was laughter, and half of the guests continued to giggle. When Bronwyn handed the priest a bull's nose ring instead of the wedding ring and said, 'Put it through his nose, please,' everybody roared with laughter.

'What a terrible thing to say. Neither one of them has got one ounce of respect for the church,' Ellie whispered to Johnny.

He had his metal crutches on the floor beneath her feet. He'd dropped the crowbar on his foot this morning and broken a small bone. Mr Fletcher had driven him down to the hospital. What a time for it to happen.

And Jack . . .

Not that Ellie thought for one minute that it was his body they'd found. Not for one minute did she believe it. Not today. Of course it wasn't Jack. Who on earth would do such a thing? Lord only knew what she'd been thinking of last night. She'd let her imagination run away with her, that's all. And Bessy – it was almost as if she'd been pleased about it.

Yesterday. It had started out bad and everything that could have gone wrong had gone wrong after Bessy came down with her news about finding that body. The little brindle heifer had miscarried in the late afternoon and Ellie was petrified that she might lose more calves. One year they'd lost six.

It wasn't Jack's body. It couldn't be.

And that pill Bessy had made her swallow last night, and when she rarely even swallowed an aspro. She couldn't remember getting into her bed. Couldn't remember getting into her nightgown. All she could remember was Bessy drying her hair with the dryer, and making a tangled mess of it, then the cup of tea Benjie had made and the tiny little pill that didn't look as if it could harm a fly. The next thing she knew it was fourteen hours later, her bladder bursting and Mr Fletcher at her door telling her he'd left Johnny at the Daree hospital with a broken foot. Minutes later, Bronwyn and Annie had turned up and she hadn't even had breakfast or a shower.

And now the rain. What a day for a wedding.

Poor Jack. He should have been here to see Bronwyn. From the rear she did *look* like an angel.

But what if it was him?

She shook her head, shook the thought away. She wouldn't

think about him. She would not. Not today. As if he'd mix with criminals. As if anyone would . . .

Buried out near Charlie Owen's property. As Bessy had said, everyone knew about Vera Owen and Jack. Charlie Owen had split Jack's head open one night, and everyone knew he'd been threatening to kill him.

She looked up, swallowed and tried to force her mind back to the Latin. She glanced at Johnny. He'd know what the priest was talking about. She peered at his book, saw a picture of a bell and turned her page to catch up with his. He was listening to the Latin, his mouth moving, saying the words too.

My goodness. Fancy being able to talk a different language. Her son. How proud she was of him. How wonderful it would be if he decided to go back to the church. He might one day. Her son, her own beautiful boy, a priest! Wouldn't it have been lovely if he could have done the wedding?

Ellie had wanted him to give the bride away, him being the eldest, but Bronwyn refused point-blank – like she'd refused to let Ellie wear her overcoat.

'Benjie will give me away,' she'd said. 'He was the nearest thing I ever had to a father.'

The mouth on that girl! Lord only knew how she'd given birth to either of her daughters. Both of them were so determined. Just as well they had been girls and not boys or they would have turned into second Jacks. Benjie had more gentleness in his little fingernail than both of those girls put together. No Jack in that one. And he'd been that pleased when Bronwyn asked him to give her away. Just as well she hadn't asked Johnny as it turned out. His foot was in plaster.

She'd wanted to buy him a new suit for today, but he'd refused. He was wearing the one of Jack's he'd worn to Liza's memorial service. Annie had let the trousers down as far as they'd go, put false hems on them, and taken the waist in, but the suit jacket looked tight across his shoulders, and not as well as it had looked at Liza's service. All the heavy work he was doing was broadening his shoulders, Ellie thought as she brushed white fluff from his sleeve.

Jack had always dressed well. That suit had cost over five hundred dollars, and Ellie knew it. His clothing was one of the first things she'd noticed about Jack. She'd always been proud of the way he'd dressed, but spending five hundred dollars on a suit!

Jack's shirts wouldn't do up around Johnny's neck. She'd bought him a new shirt for today, but he was wearing one of his father's ties, the dark grey with the red and light grey stripes. It had always looked well with that suit, so that was the one she'd chosen.

Johnny hadn't wanted to come to the church. He'd told Ben to pick him up at the hospital on the way to the reception. But it wasn't as if it was a bad break, just one of the small bones, and the bruise of course; he had painkillers if he needed them.

'How's your foot, love?' she whispered.

'Fine.'

Nick said something, and she'd missed it, but everyone was giggling again. He and Bronwyn were probably a good pair. The first night Bronwyn had brought Nick to the house, to introduce him, he'd told Ellie that she ought to get her hair cut, that she'd look ten years younger with short hair. He'd said that if he were twenty years older he'd dump Bronwyn and run away with her mother.

And in front of Jack too. Was it any wonder that he'd . . . he'd . . . he'd taken a dislike to Nick. Poor Jack.

She caught the thought before it had time to form and crushed it. Today was Bronwyn's day and that's all she was going to think about.

The Smiths had organised the wedding and the reception. They'd hired an old hall miles from town, but Ben knew where it was. While cameras flashed, Ellie walked off to Jack's old car, her skirts held high. The rain had stopped but the sky was black.

'There will be some good rain before nightfall,' she said. 'I wonder if we're getting any at home.'

Johnny, already seated in the rear of the car with his crutches, nodded, then in silence they waited for Ben, one of the bridal group and long in coming. But he came with his map, and he led the Burton convoy to the old hall beside a disused football oval, ten kilometres from town.

'I hope it's a bit better inside,' Ellie said.

'I hope we don't get bogged,' Benjie replied and Johnny looked out the window, wishing he was digging post holes.

Bronwyn had been in a fiery mood when she'd arrived this morning to do Ellie's make-up, but she was smiling now and waving, beckoning Ellie and Benjie to join the wedding party again for more photographs. Side-on she almost looked – Ellie shook her head. It was just the way the wind was blowing her dress. Her interest still on Bronwyn's waist, Ellie dodged the mud and puddles and joined the group, stood where they told her to stand.

But why the rush, if she wasn't? She glanced at Nick. Some men could be too persuasive, and well she knew it.

Three weeks. Three weeks notice was all they'd given Ellie. Everyone in Mallawindy was talking about it. Bronwyn said they were rushing it because Nick's father had to go into hospital for a serious operation, but he was standing beside Ellie now, his hand on her shoulder. He looked well enough. He looked like an older version of Nick; those same cheeky eyes and grin, but bald as a billiard ball. Ellie didn't like men who looked at her like that, and she couldn't stand for them to put their hands on her. She moved away as the cameras clicked, then walked quickly into the hall, again looking for Johnny.

She found him and Mr Fletcher already seated so she couldn't change the place names. The hall didn't look as bad inside as out, thank goodness, and they had plenty of mats to wipe the muddy feet. There were pot plants by the dozen hiding the worst of the walls, and someone had spent the day blowing up balloons. They hung from every corner and over every window. And the long trestle tables looked a picture, they really did.

David walked in alone. He joined the men.

'They did a nice job with the decorations,' Ellie said. He smiled, nodded. He's going quite grey, Ellie thought, and no wonder. He looked as if he'd lost weight too, or maybe it was because he was standing behind Mr Fletcher. Then Benjie joined them, and David didn't look so slim.

The men got to talking about cars, and joking about David's new six-seater van, so Ellie wandered off, eyeing the tall flower and candle arrangements on the tables. Silk flowers. She hoped they wouldn't catch fire when they lit the candles.

The place cards were handwritten and set out in front of pink serviettes folded like fans, which must have taken someone a lot of time, she thought, peering closely at names, needing her reading glasses. She hadn't brought them; one of the arms was missing. Her bad eye closed, she squinted at a place card. It wasn't Elizabeth Burton, but Elizabeth Burkitt. Surely they hadn't made a mistake. Wandering alone then from table to table, just a little panicky, she continued her search.

'You're looking lost, dear. Come over and meet Nick's aunties. You'll be sitting with them.'

'I told Bronwyn to sit me with Bessy.'

'You and Ben are at the bridal table,' Bronwyn's new mother-in-law said. She looked to be years older than her cheeky-faced husband, Ellie thought, as she followed Mary Smith to a group of women who all looked the same.

'Didn't the boys do a wonderful job with the hall?'

'It all looks a picture,' Ellie replied.

Over a hundred Smiths and their offspring were at the reception, and most of the adults were introduced to her. She was kissed, had her hand shaken, and she tried to keep track of their connections to Nick. She could remember Mary Ruth because of her size, and she could remember Mary Aileen because of her hat. She said a word or two to each face, frequently adding, 'Doesn't it all look like a picture?' Occasionally she turned the phrase around. 'My word, it's a picture.'

She'd had little to do with the preparations, apart from making the wedding cake and giving Bronwyn five hundred dollars to put towards the catering, but not for alcohol. She'd stressed that. Someone else had paid for alcohol. There was beer and wine on every table.

'Who did the catering?' she asked.

'There are enough of us, Mrs Burton. We've got it down to a fine art.'

'You must be very proud of yourselves, I'm sure.'

Ellie's shoes were pinching by the time she took her seat between Bronwyn's new mother-in-law and Mary Aileen, one of Nick's aunts. She nodded towards the three-tier cake that didn't look anything like the three fruit and pumpkin cakes she'd baked two weeks ago. 'They did a lovely job with the cake. Who decorated it?'

'Mary Ruth.'

'Oh, the big one,' Ellie said then, aware she'd opened her mouth and put her foot in it, almost committed the unforgivable sin of stuffing her runaway mouth with a tiny circular sandwich, and before Father John Frances Smith had said grace.

The sandwich hidden in her hand and held on her lap, she bowed her head and wished again that Johnny hadn't left the church. But he'd always been the same, even as a little boy. Once he'd made a decision there was no going back for Johnny. She glanced across the table to where the Burton guests had been seated. Johnny was beside Annie. She hoped they'd be all right together. They were very strange with each other – polite enough, but strange. Not that it was Johnny's fault. Ellie had always found Annie hard to talk to.

Father Fogarty sat at the end of the table, Mr Fletcher on his left, Kerrie on his right. She was beside Jenny. Old Granny Bourke was between Jenny and Bessy so they could keep an eye on her. Mickey had been seated at the head of the table, then Johnny, Annie and David on Mr Fletcher's side. Bessy had already moved the flower arrangement and the candles from the table. A law unto herself, was Bessy, and wearing her old grey pantsuit again.

Ellie bowed her head while Father John Frances droned on and the sandwich filling oozed into her hand. She opened her palm, allowing the sandwich to lie flat, her hand held well above her dress. It had been a long time since she'd said grace before eating. Jack had refused to allow grace in his kitchen.

As if he'd end up buried in a shallow grave. It sounded so . . . so criminal. She flinched, shook her head. He'd been gone for over a year one time but he'd come home. He'd be back one day. One day.

The priest's words rumbling in the recesses of her mind, her thoughts turned to Benjie. He didn't look as if he was ever going to marry, and of course Johnny wouldn't. Bessy only had the one son but four grandchildren already; they all lived with her. Ellie rarely saw her grandchildren. Annie spent most of her time with Mr Fletcher, or at the shop with Ben on her rare visits to Mallawindy.

If Benjie had married, it would have been different, she thought. She would have had his babies living with her, but Benjie had never shown much interest in girls. All he ever did was work. Never went out.

Jack had wanted to go out and have fun when they were first married. Of course she hadn't been able to, being pregnant. After Johnny was born, they'd left him with Bessy twice and gone to the pictures. Then there was that time when Jack had decided they were going to move to Narrawee. Ellie hadn't wanted to leave her father and Bessy, but Jack had packed her bags and said that she was going. He was her husband after all, so she'd gone to Narrawee for over two months. Just left everything. Left the chooks and the cows to Bessy and her father.

Like a fish out of water, she'd been. The house was a mansion; the only place she'd ever felt at home was in the kitchen. And Jack's father! What a horrible old man. He'd ignored Johnny. Sam hadn't. He'd been nice – a real gentleman, but when he went and got himself married to May Hargraves, Jack had packed their bags again and they'd caught the train home to Mallawindy.

Since those months she'd spent in Narrawee, Ellie had had a soft spot for Sam; it was a pity that they'd lost contact since Jack went missing. Sad, really, how families grew apart, she thought, easing her heel free of her right shoe, wriggling her toes.

Too new, the shoes were killing her. She shouldn't have worn them today. Bessy had said she was a fool to buy high heels at her age; but they looked so smart, and she could tell that Bronwyn had been proud of her when they'd got her all dressed up for the wedding.

Annie had made her outfit. That girl was a magician on the sewing machine, there were no two ways about it. She'd chosen the material, paid for it, then made it the way she wanted to.

It wasn't really what Ellie had wanted to wear. Mothers of the bride wore chiffon. She'd always liked chiffon, and she had the money to buy nice things these days. She'd been planning to go to Daree with Bessy to buy her outfit, then Annie had turned up one afternoon with this one.

She looked down at her jacket, jade-green shot silk. And to the frock, long, a muted floral that picked up the jade green. It looked like something out of one of those expensive magazines. She liked it. She did really like it, and it was so smart. Too smart for a wedding reception in a football hall.

'Amen,' she said, noting the mumbling had ceased. Head still down, she popped the entire sandwich into her mouth then licked the filling from her fingers. Some sort of peppery paste. It reminded her of the sandwiches her own mother used to make for church suppers, neat and small, their fillings always holding a surprise. She chose a second sandwich, obviously cut with a small scone-cutter. The patience of the maker! And what a waste of bread!

Chicken livers. That's what it was. Chicken livers boiled up and made into a paste, a taste she had almost forgotten. She'd have to ask Bronwyn to get the recipe for her. After her marriage Ellie had thrown out the chicken livers. Jack had refused to eat any of the chooks' innards, and the day she'd made soup from their feet – my goodness, had he put on a performance!

With a shake of her head she glanced around the table. They were friendly enough, and noisy now, but Ellie had always been ill at ease with strangers, and today she couldn't get Jack and the little brindle heifer out of her mind. Just too young, that's all. She hadn't wanted her to have a calf this year, but fences and a river had never stopped Bessy's bulls.

Bronwyn had a lot of her father in her, a lot of his expressions. She was more like him sometimes than either Annie or Johnny, even though people said she took after Ellie, which she did around the eyes and the figure, but somehow her eyes had always had Jack's expression, sort of sarcastic, and her mouth when she was bored was so much like Jack's. She looked bored at the moment. And her hands, the way she held that cigarette. Jack all over.

She and Nick were going to Melbourne for their honeymoon. Nick liked the city. He'd lived there for a while. Itchy feet, that one. He'd moved to Warran when Bronwyn had moved there, years ago, but he changed his jobs as often as Jack had changed his socks.

Ellie flinched.

Black socks. They'd found one black sock still on the body. On Monday she'd have to go to Daree, look at it. She shuddered, bit into a third sandwich, filling her mouth with taste. This one was fishy. Smoked salmon. She didn't like it, but she got it down.

Mary Ruth from across the table commented on someone's frock.

'It's all a picture,' Ellie said, turning to Bessy's laugh and wishing she was sitting with them, laughing with Bessy, who liked a glass of wine. By the sound of her laugh she'd already had a few. Annie was opposite old Granny Bourke. They seemed to be talking. David had his arm behind Annie's chair, his hand on her shoulder.

She'd chosen a good husband, even if he was a divorced man. The loss of a child could draw a couple closer, or push them apart, and well Ellie knew it. But my goodness, pregnant again so soon!

68

Annie had been Ellie's fourth baby, Johnny already eight years old the night Annie was born. Poor little long-limbed wisp of a thing, she'd looked like a skinned rabbit. There had been less than eleven months between Annie and Liza when there should have been thirteen. They'd been too close. But she'd had a good space between Benjie and Liza, and six years between Annie and Bronwyn.

Jack had . . . hadn't been the same after Liza went missing – died, Ellie mentally corrected. After all those years thinking of her eldest daughter as kidnapped, it was still hard to think of her as dead. A shudder travelled from her scalp to her knees. What if the body they'd found was Jack's?

What if?

No.

But in all the years Liza had been missing, Ellie hadn't believed she was dead. And she had been dead.

She shook her head, shook it hard, and glanced at the glass of wine in Bronwyn's hand. She was drinking but not eating a thing and she'd always liked her food. She looked thinner around the face lately and her eyes looked different. And that dress, the way Annie had made it, sort of eighteenth century, fitted at the bust-line then flowing. Almost like a . . .

'My goodness,' Ellie said.

'They got a lovely lot of presents,' Mary Ruth said.

'My word, they did. And did you see the size of Mr Fletcher's cheque?' That probably wasn't the right thing to say. Ellie was reaching for another sandwich to stuff up her mouth when Bronwyn caught her eye, touched her left cheek. Ellie wiped at her face, removed a spot of chicken paste, licked her finger. Bronwyn nodded.

Why on earth they'd sat her in the middle of a mob of aunties, Ellie didn't know. Bronwyn was four seats away and Benjie away down the other end with the groomsmen. It might have been all right if they'd sat Benjie beside her, but they probably didn't want to sit him in the middle of all the elderly women, Ellie thought.

They'd stuck her there instead.

She waved to Benjie. He waved back.

That half-smile, his grey suit; from this distance he looked more like her old dad than ever. 'The living image,' she said, and mind-travelled back to her own wedding day. Back to sitting at the bridal table with Jack.

Three months pregnant she had been, and she hadn't been able to look at food, or look at anyone, anything. They'd gone to Albury for their honeymoon. Poor Jack. It hadn't been much of a honeymoon for him.

'A terrible time for you, dear. You are being very brave.'

'Pardon?'

'Finding your husband like they did,' Aunty Someone-or-other said, and Ellie jumped, almost knocked her plate onto the floor, but Mary, the mother-in-law, caught it.

'It must be dreadful for you and your family, at this time.'

Ellie was still shaking her head when another aunt overrode the first. 'At least the sun came out for a few minutes, Mrs Burton. August can be a bad month for weddings.'

'I don't know why they didn't put it off for a few months.' A long silence followed that comment.

'The girls did a wonderful job with the food, didn't they, dear?'

'They certainly did. It all looks a picture.'

'Will you have a prawn?'

'No thank you.'

'A glass of wine?'

'No thank you. Do you think I could get a cup of tea?'

'I wouldn't mind one myself. Mary Ruth, could you be a love and tell the girls to round up a cuppa for me and Mrs Burton? My word, but didn't your Annie do a beautiful job with the dress. You'd never guess she was – '

'Annie is very clever with her hands. How she finds the time, I don't know.'

'She's expecting too. It will be nice for the two of them to – '

'Could you pass me the cream puffs, please,' she said.

She didn't have to know anything she didn't want to know. And wouldn't know. Not today. She turned to Johnny, to Bessy, to the priest who had performed the service, sweating on the speeches now, wanting the speeches. Once these people got started they'd probably keep going all night and she'd be able to sit back and relax, not try to find the right thing to say. And she could take her shoes off.

forgive us our trespasses

~

As Bronwyn's wedding day wore on into night John's tolerance wore thin. He had cousin Mickey on one side, Bessy opposite, and Annie on his right. Malcolm Fletcher and Father Fogarty were warring verbally between cooling, or lubricating, their vocal cords with red wine. Mickey had been hitting the beer since he'd sat down. Bessy was giving the white wine a nudge and Bronwyn had supplied two bottles of stout for Granny Bourke, who was becoming louder by the glass.

'So how many is that now?' Gran asked.

'The last.' Ann had been patient with the old dame but patience, like tolerance, wore thin.

The table of misfits laughed, except for Malcolm and Father Fogarty.

'Terrible about your first one,' Granny said.

Ann ignored her. She turned away, pouring an inch of wine into her glass then offering the bottle to John. He took it, emptied it. A juvenile Smith waiter replaced it immediately.

The doctor at the Daree hospital had given John a packet of strong painkillers. Not to be taken with alcohol. It was on the packet. He'd held off taking them, but as he toasted the bride and groom he tossed two pills down with the wine. Then he toasted the bridesmaids and the bride's mother. He toasted Granny's snore, and the glass she managed to hold on to without spilling a drop, then toasted her blessed exit to the back seat of Mickey's car, and he doubly toasted the non-return of his raucous cousin.

He did a lot of toasting, toasted the body they'd found near Daree and his was the only glass raised. As he drained it his eyes strayed towards his mother, noting the paleness of her skin and the occasional sheen of perspiration on her brow; he also noted the colour of her hair against the jade green. She looked more like the old Ellie tonight. Up close, the lines of Mallawindy suns were visible, but tonight, beneath candlelight, they had been smoothed out. She looked young again.

And the shade of her jacket. It, or the wine, had brought back memories of a jade-green frock she'd worn when he was five or six. Worn it to a fancy dress party at the shire hall. He'd been dressed as a pirate, with a black patch over his eye and a rag parrot, complete with glued-on rooster feathers. Ellie had made it and pinned it to the shoulder of his costume. He'd won first prize. One pound. He could still feel the envelope in his hand, still remember dancing with his mother, then later, watching her glide around the floor with other partners.

And watching the door, waiting for –

The girls had badgered Ellie into doing her hair up in the old double plait she somehow wound like a two-tier crown around her head. It framed her face, balancing it and bringing back its own memories. She'd always worn her hair in the double plait when he was young. Just him and Ben and time to believe that things might get better in those days.

Bron or Ann had pinned a scrap of fabric and a tiny cluster of jade roses behind the plait. Yesterday Ellie had been determined to wear her black hat, but she'd settled for the flowers, or been browbeaten by her daughters into accepting them.

The girls dressed her, re-creating her for special occasions, as if trying to make her fit the image of a mother they held within, an image they forced her to assume for a day or an hour.

As that bastard had.

Dead.

Her fading eyes looked green again tonight. Someone had done her make-up, plastered it on, covering sun and age spots, darkening her brows, highlighting her eyes. Interesting what an artist could do with a good canvas, he thought. Ellie was such a canvas. She had a high brow and wide eyes. A tall, slim blonde once, the years may have stolen an inch from her height but she was still slim enough, and the high heels she wore tonight more than compensated for that lost inch.

Because he hadn't seen his mother's gradual aging, he could remember the beauty she had been, and he could see it tonight. He could see a lot tonight. This wasn't Ellie of the faded dresses and the shrunken sweaters she wore in the cow yard. This was the one his father had created with the frocks he'd brought home from his trips. He'd dressed her in those early years. He'd bought the jade-green frock, he'd bought the shoes and sheer stockings and the golden earrings.

I've got nowhere to wear them, Jack. We could have used that money . . .

Jack had given up on Ellie. He'd continued to bring home his parcels from Narrawee – pretty dresses, fancy shoes – but all for Liza. Everything had been for Liza.

Johnny refilled his glass. Ann looked at him, then to where he was looking.

'She still scrubs up well, doesn't she?' she said.

'Little dabs of powder, little puffs of paint, make a girl's complexion, something that it ain't,' he said.

'Bron did her make-up. I told her we should go into the make-over business.'

Silence again. They shared many silences. Johnny had given this sister life, and his love, perhaps attempting to balance the love his father had lavished on Liza. For a while it had been them against the world. When he'd heard that the skeletal remains of Liza had been found, he'd come running back for little Annie, unaware of what he'd find when he got there. He'd found a woman, determined, and strong, a woman with a husband.

He'd gone home that Christmas Eve convinced that one way or another he was going to rid Mallawindy of Jack Burton. Since the day he'd found Sam's burned bones at the old Aboriginal burial grounds out at Dead Man's Lane, he'd known why his father had spent half of his life at Narrawee; he had played two roles, his own and his twin brother's.

John knew that he should have gone to the police back then, but a boy's loyalty is strong, and frequently misplaced. To protect Ellie, he'd kept his silence. Hadn't wanted to break her childish heart. Maybe he'd been lying to himself. Maybe he'd never had guts enough to go to the police.

Cowardly little bastard.

That Christmas Eve his father had been the one who ran, but John had known where he would be found. There were things he'd had to do in the city, so he drove the hire car there, then continued on to Narrawee where he'd found the white stone mansion unoccupied. For two nights he'd slept in his hire car, waiting for his father to arrive.

As a youth John had once spent a day sharpening the old wood axe, convinced he could split his father's head wide with it as easily as he might split a small block of wood. He had honed the worn blade of his mother's carving knife to razor sharpness one evening, convinced that he could cut out his father's heart and feed it to the pigs. In Narrawee he'd had neither knife nor axe, but his bare hands would find a way to rip that bastard apart.

Jack Burton had not shown his face, nor had May, so John had returned his hire car and caught the bus to Warran and to Ann. She had taken his case and placed it in the spare room, so pleased to see him, eager to spend time with him.

It was after David had gone to bed that he'd broached the subject of his father. 'I know he's not at Narrawee, Annie, but he's somewhere. Find May, and we find him. We've got him.'

'They're at the flat in Toorak. I drove him there that night,' she'd said. And his world crashed, and out of the wreckage came anger, raw and red and aimed at his sister.

'You drove him down there?'

'I thought you would have guessed.'

'That night? That's where you disappeared to?' She had nodded, held a finger to her lips. 'In God's name, why, Annie?'

'I don't know why, but I did it.'

'He's going to pay.'

'And what do we gain? More months with reporters hanging around our doors. Him in jail, or back in Mallawindy when the cops don't believe you. Forget him.'

'They'll believe us. Have you still got Sam's ring?'

'It was Sam's ring. Sam is wearing it again. Let it end. For me, for David, for all of us, let it end here.'

'I want justice, Annie.'

'Don't confuse justice with revenge. They're different, Johnny.'

'Call it what you will, I want it.'

'And what does Mum do when you expose her puppet master?'

He hadn't been thinking of Ellie. Hadn't wanted to think of her, but the words woke a place in him that had been sleeping. He had no memory of what he'd said next, but when he was done, she'd smiled, shaken her head.

'And I thought priests were big on forgiveness of sins. Forgive him his trespasses. He's Sam – and a better Sam than the original. Forget him and get on with your own life.'

'What life? I haven't got a life to get on with. I just tossed it in. He's it now.'

'Then take your gun to town, Johnny. He'll be at Liza's inquest. Shoot him as he leaves the court and spread us all over page one again, then spend the rest of your life in a cage.'

'I've spent my whole bloody life caged.'

How did it happen? He didn't know, but too suddenly their

voices had been raised against each other and she'd closed the door, closed David's bedroom door.

'Please keep your voice down, and remember, you're not the only victim here. I have to go down to that inquest. Do you think I want that? Do you think I want those cameras on me again?'

'I just realised I don't know you, Annie. I don't know what you want any more.'

'I want to run. Every fibre in my body wants to get me into my car and just drive me to some place where I can wake up free, go to bed free. But I can't run. I'm pregnant, so I'm stuck here, just like you are, and I have to go on, just like you do.'

'You'll . . . you'll sit in a room with him at the inquest, and you'll lie for him?'

'I started it, so I have to finish it. It's just the old fairytale, about a gardener and a motorbike. It's just another Snow White and the seven dwarfs.'

'I don't understand you.'

'I don't understand me either, but it's not important.'

'It's important to me, Annie.'

'Your priorities are twisted. All I know, Johnny, is . . . is the day you came home, my world was ending. Mandy was dead and I wanted to die and then I opened the door and you were there. When I needed you, you came back to me.' Her hands covering her face, she'd looked at him from behind the fan of her fingers. 'Why are we fighting?'

'Over a mongrel dog that doesn't deserve to live.'

'And that's the reason I went to Mallawindy that night. I knew I had to get there before you – get him away from you.'

'You should have let me rip the bastard apart.'

She had reached out a hand to him. 'The only place inside me that isn't a numb ache these days is the little place I saved for you. I searched for you forever.'

He hadn't taken her hand. 'It's not me you'll be lying for at the inquest.'

'It's not for him! None of it is for him! Driving him to Toorak wasn't for him. It was making an end to it, that's all. It was giving you an out, giving Mum her missing Prince Charming. All I have to do now is get Liza home, get her buried, get her name on that bloody tombstone, then I've done enough, Johnny. Then it will be over.'

'Who are you?' he'd said.

'Maybe if you'd stuck around instead of running, you might have found out. Maybe I would have found out a lot sooner too.'

He'd had no answer for that. He'd walked to the spare room and picked up his bag. She'd followed him to the back door.

'Don't go. Not like this. Sit down and talk to me.'

'I can't stay here.'

'I did what I had to do, and you have to help me to keep doing it – wipe him and May and Narrawee from my brain. I have to if David and I . . . if this baby is to have a chance.'

'And what about Mum? I'm supposed to lie to her?'

'What about Mum? It's always about Mum, and I don't know her. I don't know what I feel for her any more, or if I feel anything.' She had looked at the door, at the walls. 'This house used to be full of Mandy. You should have known her, Johnny. This house belonged to her. Toys all over the floor, little giggles from beneath the table, little dresses in the laundry. She's gone.' Her fingers raked the hair from her face, her eyes travelling the floors, the walls.

'I can't look at Mum these days without feeling anger. She used to say to me that Mandy was Liza reborn. Every time she saw her. *She's Liza all over, love,* she'd say. Every time. And maybe she was like her too, but I wouldn't see it.

'But I saw it when she died. She looked like Liza when she died. Little red playsuit, blood on her golden curls. And . . . and do you know what Mum said to me, Johnny? *I'm so sorry to hear of your loss, love*. No kiss, no hug, no bloody nothing. *I'm so sorry to hear of your loss, love*. She lost about as much sleep over Mandy's death as she did over my life. So don't ever try to use Mum as a cheap weapon to bludgeon me with.'

'What happened to the little girl I left on the road?'

'You left her on the road, and life happened to her, and death happened, and years of searching for you happened. I didn't care what I might find either, just as long as I found you, knew you were alive, safe. I didn't expect to find a fifteen-year-old boy. I wouldn't have cared if you'd sold cars, ran a brothel, yet you expected to come back here and find poor little dumb Annie still waiting for you.'

'It's all gone. All changed,' he'd said. 'Hating that bastard is all that's left from back then. Everything else is lost. If I let him get away with what he's done I've got no reason to wake up in the morning. Can't you see that?'

She had walked to the sink, filled the jug and set it to boil. 'Have a cup of coffee with me. Sit down and let's start again.'

'Come to the police with me. That's all I want from you.'

'Look at me, Johnny. Inside I'm still that little kid and she's standing here still screaming out to you. For God's sake, listen to her!'

'Help me to put him away and I'll listen. He killed Liza. He killed his brother. He's a murderer, Annie.'

She had sighed then, swiped at the tears now trickling. 'Liza took a blow aimed at her rapist who was using her as a shield. Dad didn't want to hurt Liza. He loved her. The day Mandy died I understood what he has had to live with. He *loved* Liza.' The jug had boiled, boiled, turned itself off. 'Maybe a priest can't understand that sort of love, that sort of loss. You've probably buried little kids in the cold bloody earth and watched the mothers cry, blessed them and told them that their child was in a better place. What better place than safe in her parents' arms, Johnny? I watched Dad dying the day Liza died. I can still hear him crying.'

'He's not crying now. He's down there playing the toff, having a ball. He's got everything he always wanted. He's got that mansion, that property, and May.'

'And he has to look at that rose garden, that cellar every time he steps outside the door, and he has to do it stone-cold sober. May won't let him drink.'

He had laughed then. 'So he'll come back.'

'If he sets one foot in Mallawindy, I tell it as it was. He and May know it.'

'I can't live like this. I can't lie to Mum and Ben for the rest of my life. I can't do it, Annie.'

'Then find a way to do it. I have. I hide in this house all day, and at night I sleep in Mandy's bed.'

He'd left then. He'd walked away from her into the night. Six years on, their conversations were brief and polite.

'How's your foot?' she said.

'Better by the minute.'

Just words. He kept up his end. He found enough words, cold, guarded things, each one censored, checked before it was spoken. That's how he lived these days. Hiding self. Hiding knowledge. Losing self. No black suit and dog collar to hide him, or give him identity. No longer Father Burton, so who was he?

He watched Ann as she turned to David. She hadn't told him where she'd driven to that night. Like Ellie, David had grown accustomed to his partner's disappearances. She'd told him she'd argued with her father then driven away to clear her head, bogged the car out at the ten-mile. She'd told the same story to the police when they'd found the gun in April.

Destined to live a lie. But these days she was handling it better than he. On the surface she was handling it.

Johnny filled his wineglass and he toasted the dog that had dug up the leg bone.

Let it be over. Thy will be done.

Wine was flowing freely and for once he was having his share. He'd sleep tonight. One way or the other he would sleep tonight.

He raised his glass to Ann. She glanced at him, then away. Her face was all angles, still the eight-year-old face he had left behind, still the wild black hair, pinned high tonight. Half of it was pinned high but, as always, corkscrew curls escaped at ear and neck and brow.

He used to tie up her hair with rubber bands, try to keep it out of her eyes when she was a kid. She'd let him comb it. Refused to let Ellie near her with a comb after her return from Narrawee. Refused to go near Ellie, but she'd stayed close to her father – until he taught her not to. Six years old when Liza died, nearly eight when they'd found Sam's bones. Almost thirty years ago. She'd be thirty-seven come Christmas, hair still as black as coal. He leaned closer, trying to see grey amidst the black. If there was any, she covered it well. His own hair had shown a little grey at thirty-nine; at forty-four grey was winning the war.

He laughed, raised his glass again. 'To grey hair,' he said. No other glass was raised, so he drank alone. What else was there to drink to? The speeches droned on. Johnny filled his glass and drank to speeches, to the new bottle a Smith placed before him while his mind again wandered the past, then back again to the sister seated beside him.

She was wearing a black pantsuit, the top loose and long, her only colour red lipstick, large gold earrings and the long red and gold scarf. Maybe she looked her age. He didn't know. He couldn't see the adult. He could see Bron's age, Ben's, his own, but never Annie's – just the little kid with the wild hair he had left screaming on the road. Guilt had embedded that image in his brain and he couldn't get it out. Maybe he could wash it out with wine, but the more he drank tonight the more she looked like that little kid. Her little hands signing, 'I come, my Johnny. I come with you. I love Johnny.'

He was going to become a howling maudlin drunk in a minute, and he knew it. Quickly he glanced away, found Ben up at the bridal table. Never much interested in suits but, like Ellie, Ben scrubbed up well. Little Benjie, scared stiff of his father, yet he'd never left

Mallawindy. Always said he was going to be a farmer like Grandpa when he grew up. He and his partner Bob Dooley had inherited the shop when Bert Norris died, but at heart Ben was a farmer, and the image of Grandpa. John's eyes turned to Bronwyn, matching her big brother drink for drink.

'Bless me, Father, for I have sinned.' Bron had found him in the top paddock a month or so back and she'd wanted to talk. 'I'm pregnant, Father, and I'm going to sue the bloody doctor who gave me the antibiotics, and I'm going to sue the bloody dentist who bummed up my tooth in the first place. If I have an abortion, it's murder, Father, and if I don't have an abortion, life is going to be murder, Father, with a thousand Smiths fighting me through the courts for one more Smith. As you know, Father, the world is short on Smiths.'

'Lay off the Father bit, Bron, and of course you can't have an abortion.'

'You can take the priest out of his church, put him in a cow paddock with hay seeds up to his bum, but you can't take the church out of the priest, Father. So what do I do?'

'You've been living with Nick for six years that I know of. You're probably overdue to get married, aren't you?'

'Stuff marriage and happy families, Father – if you'll excuse my French. I've seen enough of them to last me a lifetime.'

Sisters. Three of them he'd known.

Liza. Miss Tiny Tot.

I'm telling Daddy on you. You wait till Daddy gets home, and you'll get it.

Daddy. He'd ruined the lot of them. Liza too. What might she have been without him? Just a normal wilful kid like Bron. He liked Bron. There had been no past to come between them. Only two years old when he'd left, they'd met as strangers. Bron had nothing against strangers.

Memories were rushing at him from all sides tonight, but the constant tension he lived with had gone. His neck wanted to give up the effort of holding up his head, so he rested his chin on the palm of his left hand, his right still occupied with his glass.

On Monday he'd drive his mother back to Daree and have a look at what they'd found of the bastard, and he'd spit in his eye socket. Would he recognise anything? What would be left apart from the teeth? Would he recognise the teeth outside that cruel, cynical mouth?

Have a go, you cowardly little bastard.

Maybe he'd tell the police that he'd finally grown up and had a go. Put the barrel to the bastard's head and pulled the trigger, then loaded him into the car boot and buried him. It might be a relief to go back into hiding, this time in a cosy cell. No cows to milk, no post holes to dig in there. They'd give him a big pile of rocks and a little hammer.

He laughed at the image, and faces turned to him as he stood – tried to stand. His foot stopped the laugh. He couldn't stand, couldn't drive to Daree with Ellie on Monday either. No foot to drive with. He looked at his fat plaster cast in its blue hospital-loan cotton shoe and he filled his glass, drank to his broken bone as David stood to retrieve the crutches leaning against the wall.

'Do you need a hand, John?'

'What I need is a toilet.'

With David steadying him, John manoeuvred the crutches beneath his arms. He stood head down, waiting for the walls to still or for the impetus that might move his one good foot forward then, David still at his side, he made his slow way to the door and through the mud to the old toilets where he struggled with Jack Burton's zip.

'We are an odd race, David. Conceived in drunken lust, born of the virgin Ellie; alcohol and milk runs through our veins, and it's a bad mixture. Warm it up a bit and it curdles. The Vevers in us begin to feel pain, but the Burtons don't like feeling anything, so they top up the alcohol content . . . which uncurdles the curdle and kills all pain.'

'Wine has always been Ann's happy juice.'

'Ann. I don't know your wife.'

'I'm not sure I know her brother tonight. Are you right there?' John was struggling with the zip, and required two hands. He released his hold on the crutch and David caught it before it hit the floor, wet with urine and tracked-in mud.

On their return to the hall, David remained standing. 'Are you up to another dance, Ann?' he asked, unimpressed by this reincarnation of Jack Burton and eager to get away from that table.

'The flesh is willing but the back is weak. Ask Mum. She loves to dance,' Ann replied.

Johnny had watched them dance earlier in the night. They were well matched on the dance floor. Maybe he'd envied them.

What was it that drew two people together? What was it that held them together? He turned to stare at Bronwyn and Nick and he smiled, wondered if they'd make it to their first anniversary.

He'd married a few score, spoken the words and blessed the rings. He'd advised a few score contemplating the union, or contemplating the dissolving of the union, but he'd never been with a woman.

He laughed, and poured more wine, drank to celibacy. He'd been perfect material for the priesthood. By the time he was eight years old he'd seen enough of the male animal rutting in the dirt to kill that urge. Raping, murdering bastard.

Lay down and play dead, you cold bitch.

He'd been three or four when he'd run to their room, afraid of the dark, and seen him on top, heard Ellie crying. He'd got a back-hander for his trouble that night and he'd never gone to their room again, but a year later he'd belted his father with a piece of firewood when he'd found him on top of her in the kitchen. Six or seven at the time, he'd seen Bessy's bull at the heifers. He'd known. He'd known too much.

Maybe that's what he'd expected to find that Christmas Eve. Time trapped. Ellie weeping in the dust, the bastard on top, laughing. He could have pulled him off, shoved the kitchen knife between his ribs, split his head open with the wood axe, blown him to hell with his own gun.

He laughed again and this time Ann turned to him, a question in her eyes if not on her lips. His laughter continued until she reached for the bottle of wine, poured a little into her glass then placed the wine out of reach.

His reach was long and he poured more wine while staring at the bride's table, where David now stood behind Ellie. He watched her smile, watched her wriggle her feet back into her shoes, willing to dance with a divorced man if it allowed her to escape the table of Smith aunties.

'She was born to laugh, born to dance,' John said. 'I remember that night at the shire hall, old Mrs Norris on the piano and her son, Bert, on the drums. Mum knew everyone in town. They all danced with her. She was laughing, happy. She used to have a beautiful laugh. Then that bastard walked in, stood at the door and stared at her. She closed her mouth and cowered, left her partner stranded and walked to the door. A flighty little bird mesmerised by a venomous snake.'

'Don't start on him tonight, Johnny.'

'I'm not starting. I'm finishing. I'm having a wake for the bastard. Join me.' She reached for the bottle, pushed it down the table. 'It's my party and I'll drink if I want to,' he sang, his face close to hers.

'You're making a fool of yourself.'

'No. You made me the fool, sister mine.'

Bessy was outside having a smoke. A silenced Father Fogarty had driven Granny Bourke home. Whether he got her out of his back seat or not was another matter. Father Fogarty and Gran out on the tiles all night? That would set the old town talking.

The thought tickled John's funny bone; his head tossed back, he roared with laughter, spilling his wine as he pointed his glass at cousin Mickey, dancing in his sleep, propped up by his wife.

At the far end of the table, Malcolm Fletcher, in deep conversation with Kerrie Fogarty, lifted his many chins to glare at Johnny; Kerrie lifted her eyebrows, smiled. His laughter dying as swiftly as it had been born, John turned to Ann.

She didn't want to be beside him. Her back was turned.

There was a time when she'd tailed him like a small shadow. He stared at her back, waiting for her to turn. She looked at her watch, at the dancers bouncing to the jarring, broken rhythm of some Smith band.

'She can still dance,' he said. 'He tried hard enough, the bastard, but he couldn't kill her, could he, and he couldn't steal her dance. She beat him.'

'He was no saint, nor was she. If she'd ever thought of anything other than her chooks and her cows, he might have been different. You're celebrating his death and everyone here knows it.'

'I am. I am. Won't you drink to a dead dog with me?'

Ann stood, knocking her chair over, her dark eyes wide. 'Did you . . .'

'Ask me. Go on,' he taunted her. 'Ask me, Annie. Say it. Did you kill him, my Johnny? Ask me, Annie. Did you blow his brains out, my Johnny? Did you bury him out the Daree Road? Come on. Where's your guts? Ask me.'

'Where's yours? You won't find it in the bottom of a bottle,' she said and she walked away, skirting the dancers and making her way to the bridal table, where she sat on Ellie's vacated chair.

By ten the numerous Smith offspring had escaped parental restrictions and taken over the function. Balloons burst as the older boys jumped, prodding them with drinking straws and safety pins. The crowd began to segment, and as the various Smiths gathered their own together to begin the sorting out of pot plants and dishes, the hall rocked to the thunder of children's feet and echoed with their screams. Malcolm Fletcher said his goodnights.

'They sound like a herd of bloody horses in hobnail boots. I think we'll take off. How are you getting home, Kerrie?'

'I'll grab a lift with your sister, thanks, Mrs Bishop.'

'We should get going too,' David said.

John lifted his bottle to the group as they left the table. After ten minutes, Kerrie Fogarty gave up attempting to talk to a weaving brick wall; she excused herself and found a vacant chair opposite the bride.

He was alone then, alone, the way he liked it. All alone at a long table with a half-full bottle and plenty more where that came from. He propped his foot on a chair, and his head on his hand and he watched Ellie. He saw her smile and walk to the dance floor with one of Bron's new in-laws, and he wanted to howl.

Then his eyes turned to the door, watching, waiting for the ghost of his father to return and again still her dancing feet.

the couple

~

Ann and David were barely out of town when the skies opened. Rain thrashed the car and the headlights hit the slanting stream and bounced back.

'We should stop. Let it ease off.'

'Too dangerous to stop here, and if we get off the road we'll end up bogged.'

Dangerous to drive too. This was kangaroo country, the forest tall, native scrub and wattle trees growing too close to the road offered shelter to countless kangaroos. A large roo exploding out onto the highway could do a lot of damage to a car and its occupants. Did they have enough sense to stay out of the rain or were they out on the roads tonight, celebrating the start of a delayed breeding season?

'There's another one,' Ann said. Thirty kilometres out, and they'd already counted fifteen dead roos. She sat forward, watching the road, four eyes safer than two.

'John was flying tonight,' David said.

'He'd taken two tablets and he wasn't supposed to be drinking. Thank God he's not driving home.'

'I doubt he's still walking. What got into him? Finding your father?'

'I told him he was celebrating Dad's death. That's what it looked like.' Five minutes passed before she spoke again. 'I've been thinking about Aunty May all night. She should be contacted before it hits the papers.'

'Ben said he'd called her – or tried to. She wasn't at Narrawee. He left a message on her answering machine,' David said.

'Told her Dad's body had been found?'

'He didn't say. Just that he'd left her a message.'

'When were you talking to him?'

'You were with Bron.' A road train roared by, spraying water and cutting their vision to nil. The windscreen wipers battled a while to clear it. 'He was worried about your mother, but I was amazed how well she got through the day.'

Ann's hands signed 'strange' but he couldn't see her hands, and he wouldn't have understood anyway.

'She looked well tonight,' he said. Still she made no reply, and he tapped her knee. 'What are you thinking about?'

'May's answering machine. Ben's message. Not a nice way for her to learn that . . . that someone she cared about has died.'

'Better than hearing it on the evening news.'

'I suppose so.' Too much traffic on the road tonight, and a too narrow road. David hugged the edge of the bitumen while some fool in a four-wheel drive tried to prove his vehicle was a mud-runner. 'Bloody idiot,' she said.

'Ben was saying he's been checking the newspapers. It got five lines in the Sydney *Herald*, but didn't get a mention in Melbourne.'

'It will once he's identified. They'll bring up the Liza business again. Poor May.'

'Why don't you try her at Toorak in the morning?'

'It's been too long. I've left it too long, David.'

'I'll give her a call for you.'

'No. No. Leave it to Ben.'

She hadn't seen May since the inquest. She'd walked away from her that day, and from her father – walked away and refused to look back, determined to wipe them from her life and from her mind. The last time she'd spoken to May was on the phone, over four years ago.

A sad call that one, May had been weeping and Ann didn't want to think about it tonight. Her hands playing, she opened her evening bag, closed it, she fiddled with the radio, pressing buttons, selecting, rejecting until she found some mellow music.

Johnny the stranger, seeking a new identity as Jack Burton's son, tossing the wine down as if it had come from the last grape crop on earth. Each time they met, she had to pack a part of herself away, place old love and vulnerability in some inner space, protect herself from him.

What if she'd asked her question?

Did you kill him, Johnny?

Didn't want to know the answer. Better to play the ostrich, bury her head in the sand. Just wait it out.

The music ended, and again she pressed buttons. They were approaching Mallawindy when David turned the radio off and flicked the headlights onto high beam. The rain had been left behind.

'I can understand to a degree what you must be feeling. Our parents are not perfect, but it doesn't stop us caring about them. It's natural that you'd feel upset by his death. Talk to me about it. Get it out of your head.'

'Kangaroo!' she yelled and David swerved, bracing himself for the impact, but the kangaroo lived to play chicken another day.

'I thought we were going to hit it,' he said.

'God,' she said, her hand on her womb. 'God. Why don't they learn, David?'

'Pinheads. Small brains.'

'You'd think they'd learn from old mistakes and near misses, wouldn't you? You'd think that when they get a second chance at life, that they'd breed knowledge of danger into the next generation, wouldn't you? They've been dodging cars for eighty years or more. Why don't they learn?'

'I doubt it's the smart ones that survive. I think it comes down to luck, my love.'

Only the rush of wind then, only the noise of the road to challenge the silence for the remainder of the journey.

Dee and Peter Williams, their neighbours, had the boys tonight. They swapped babysitting services. One by one, David carried blanket-wrapped bundles to their own beds. Only one eye opened.

'Lipe sayba,' Tristan the tyrant said.

'Tomorrow. It's bye-bye time now.'

'In dere. Lipe sayba, Mummy. In dere.'

Ann kissed him, tucked him into his cot and slid the rail high. It was a large cot. He hadn't learned to climb out yet. Not quite.

'Lipe sayba!'

'Shush. Tomorrow we'll find it. Hush now. You'll wake your brothers.'

'What's his life saver?' David asked.

'God and Tristan know, and maybe Dee. She said she couldn't get him to stay down so she let him watch television until he dropped. Do you want a cup of tea?'

'Not particularly. I've eaten too much. Did they say how long your father had been dead?'

'No more than – no,' she said, her eyes wandering the kitchen cum family room, unchanged since the house had been built. Same tiles on the floor, same clock on the wall, same fridge. A large room. Room to walk. She walked.

'Sit down and talk to me.'

'I feel wound up, restless.' She tossed the red and gold scarf onto the back of a chair and removed her earrings, released her hair from the band and her fingers massaged her scalp. 'Go to bed, David. It's been a long day.' He reached out a hand and she took it, looked at a chair, then shrugged. 'They'll be up and rampaging in five hours. Get some sleep while you can.'

'But will you?'

'I will, but later. I'll crawl into Mandy's bed when my legs are ready to lie down.'

That was her place when she was restless. Narrow bed with its hand-worked quilt, the revolving nightlight that made patterns on the walls.

He held her to him and kissed her brow. Perhaps she'd sleep in Mandy's bed. Perhaps she'd walk the silent house all night too, and tomorrow the half-moons beneath her eyes would be dark.

'It may not be him, my love. Have you considered that?'

'In a way I hope it is him,' she said. 'In a way. I know it sounds callous – and I don't mean it to, but he'd be at peace, David.'

'Try to stop thinking about him and get some sleep,' he said and left the room.

She walked. Walked to the sink, filled the jug, then shook her head. She didn't want a cup of tea. Didn't want to think about her father either.

She'd told her last lie for him and for May at the inquest. Pregnant with Benjamin at the time, she'd been ill, head aching, back aching all of the long day. And when it was done she'd walked away from May, vowing that from that day forward there would be no more Narrawee. For her, the property and those who lived there would not exist.

Then May had telephoned when Ann had been newly pregnant with Matthew.

'I know you don't want to speak to me, sweetheart, and I do understand completely, but I'm out of my mind with worry. Have you seen your father?' she'd said.

'You know he wouldn't come back here, Aunty May.'

'He's been drinking again and he's disappeared, Ann. I haven't heard from him in three months. There are things that . . . has your mother heard from him?'

'He won't come back here.'

'Where else would he go?'

'I don't know and I don't want to know. He's Sam now, and Sam has got to be your problem.'

'I can't report him missing, Ann. God knows who they'll find.'

'Will it never end, Aunty May? Will it never go away?'

'I'm sorry. I'm so sorry. Forgive me for troubling you, sweetheart.' May had wept then, and Ann had waited, waited for the tears to end. 'I miss you so much, my dear, dear child. I have no one if not you. No family. No one. I feel so alone. So afraid.'

'I'm pregnant again, and I'm happy about it this time. David is happy and it's been a long time since we've dared to . . . to hope. I'm sorry, but I don't want to know if he comes back or if he doesn't come back. And I . . . I don't want to be cruel to you, but please don't call me again, Aunty May. Please. It just brings it all back.' She had hung up and left May weeping.

So cruel. How had she become so hard?

Self-preservation, that's how.

After Mandy's death she had lost over a week of her life. She'd been at her baby's funeral, had been looking at the flowers and the small white coffin and then . . . then nothing. She'd been nowhere.

Like a one-dimensional shadow on the wall she'd watched a world she was no longer a part of. And when she had somehow rejoined the world from a hospital bed, she had no memory of how she had come to be there.

So much fear had followed that awakening. Blind, black fear. For weeks afterwards life in this house with David had felt like a temporary reprieve. For months she'd moved within these walls afraid to be alone, in fear of her own mind, and of the other one, the Little Annie she had always believed to have shared a part of her mind.

Fear had sent her back to Dr James, a Sydney psychiatrist she'd spoken to briefly after Mandy's death. She'd kept her appointments with him, and she'd learnt to speak to him of her fear, and of Mandy. He'd helped too, but there was so much she could not tell him, and in the latter months he'd known it.

You said that you had been watching the television with Liza just prior to her death, Mrs Taylor. Can you remember what you were watching?

She couldn't tell him about the midday movie, about a red-headed man on a motorbike who had stolen a little girl's dog, because she'd already told him that the gardener had ridden a motorbike, and that he'd had sandy-red hair.

Were you enjoying the film?

Yes.

Was Liza enjoying it?

She liked television.

Can you remember what it was that made you leave the house that day, why Liza went to the cellar?

No.

I believe you can if you try, Mrs Taylor. Try to remember.

She didn't need to try. Since waking in that hospital bed she had remembered the day of Liza's death in detail, but she could not speak of Sam and the new kittens in the cellar.

Time and time again Dr James had turned the conversation back to the television and to the gardener.

What was the gardener doing when your aunt left the house that day?

I don't remember.

Was he mowing the lawn? Pruning the roses? Digging?

I don't remember, I said.

Was he tall, short, thin, stout?

I don't remember!

Or don't wish to share those memories with me, Mrs Taylor?

It was her final appointment with Dr James that convinced her she must cut her ties with Narrawee. She'd spoken to him two days before the inquest into Liza's death.

You obviously loved your aunt. How did you feel about your uncle?

I . . . I had little to do with him.

How do you feel about him now?

I don't want to talk about Narrawee. Can we move on to something else?

You said you had been feeling restless, not sleeping well this past week. Do you think this might be due to having to attend the inquest, or possibly because you will see your aunt and uncle there?

I don't know. If I knew why, then I wouldn't be here, would I? Can we please change the subject?

We keep coming up against that same brick wall. I believe there are many unresolved issues associated with Narrawee and your uncle. And they will not be resolved until we can get beyond that self-constructed brick wall, Mrs Taylor.

I saw my sister killed, buried there. That's the wall and that's all.

You said that your aunt was gone for only a short period of time that day.

I was six years old. I was watching television and I didn't wear a watch. I don't know how long she was gone.

Do you consider it odd that the couple who manage the two properties were not aware that Sam and May had employed this elusive gardener?

Do you tell your cleaning lady when you employ a new receptionist?

Would you leave two young girls in the care of a casual male employee, Mrs Taylor?

I don't have two girls. I don't have – Will you stop this. Please.

Who killed Liza, Mrs Taylor?

Ann had not made another appointment, aware that sooner or later she'd scream out the truth of that day. So May Burton was as much a victim as she, but Ann could not cure the world's ills. During the months prior to Little Ben's birth it had been hard enough to live with her own ills and Johnny's, with David's. He'd had to go to work each day. He couldn't hide at home. Such bad months, those.

They'd gone down to the inquest and survived it, and since that call from May there had been no further contact.

Where had Jack Burton gone to after leaving Narrawee? What had he lived on? Had May given him access to Narrawee money, or had he been dead within days of leaving May? Murdered? Buried in that shallow grave?

Matthew was now four. There were twenty-two months between him and Benjamin, and she'd been in the very early stages of pregnancy the night May had phoned. If her father had left Narrawee three months prior to May's call, then it was almost five years since he'd been sighted. Had her father returned to Mallawindy? Had Johnny seen him and –

She couldn't complete that question.

Johnny hated him. Always had. The day he'd left home he'd attacked him. Ellie had pulled him off, dragged the weapon from his hand.

I'll call May tomorrow, she thought as she walked down the hall to Mandy's room. Tomorrow. Or maybe . . . maybe it would be better not to start it up all over again.

She stripped to briefs and bra and slid beneath the light quilt. The pillow was too flat. She shook it up and tucked it beneath her head.

Tomorrow.

No. She'd call Ben tomorrow. That's what she'd do. See if May had received his message, returned his call. If he hadn't heard, she'd give Ben the Toorak number. Yes. She rolled onto her side. That was the way to go. Call Ben. Leave it to reliable Ben.

He'd wiped Jack Burton from his mind, his life, twenty years ago. They'd lived in the same town, but never spoken. Always stronger than he'd looked, was Ben. He'd got up on the dance floor tonight with Bron, and then with the bridesmaids. Lucky, lucky Ben, no secrets to hold him to the past. Lucky Bron too. All of those lucky people who didn't have to live with lies.

Poor Johnny. It was her fault. Poor mixed-up Johnny.

She rolled onto her back again, pulling the quilt high.

Scent of Mandy in this quilt, in this room. Soft golden curls and blue, blue eyes. Perfect baby limbs. Swim like a fish. Climb like a monkey. So full of love, there had been no room for fear in sweet Mandy.

Mummy, what work does bees do?

Mummy, why does Tiddy have got one, two, free, four legs and a tail?

Mummy, can them stars all fall down sometimes and hit my head?

'Shush, baby,' she said. 'Sleep now. Mummy's here. Sleepy-bye time.'

The birds had gathered in the trees across the road to sing their early morning song before she slept, but small boys do not sleep late.

the never-ending story

~

Sunday 10 August

Jeff Rowan, in full uniform, knocked at Ben's front door on Sunday morning. Police work didn't allow for a day of rest, and these days he had work to do.

'I've got to get you down to Daree this morning, Mrs B, or they'll be up here looking for you,' he said when Ellie peered through a narrow gap.

'I'm going to church, and I'm late,' Ellie spoke around two long, fine hairpins. She had dressed hurriedly, having slept like a log last night, and without the aid of Bessy's pill. The boys hadn't woken her when they'd left to do the milking. She glanced beyond the lawman to the clouds, black with rain, her fingers twisting a single plait into a convoluted topknot, pinning it high while holding the door wide with her foot. 'It feels too cold to rain, doesn't it?' she said.

Jeff shrugged, watched her hands. The topknot seemed to weigh heavier today. 'So, what time will you be through, Mrs B?'

'I'll be home by twelve.'

'I'll pick you up at twelve then.'

'No thank you, Jeff.'

'Look, I'm not my own boss here, you know, Mrs B. I've been told to get you down there and it's no good trying to put off the inevitable. You've got to go and talk to them, like it or not. I'll give

Daree a call and tell them I'll have you there at half-past twelve.'

'Bessy will drive me down. She was going to take me tomorrow anyway. I can't see why they can't wait until tomorrow. It's not Jack they've found.'

'Well, let's hope your right, if . . . if that's what you're hoping. I'll talk to you again after church.'

Only a handful of people had braved the chill this morning, and Father Fogarty wasn't at his best. He was getting too old for it, Ellie thought. Bessy wasn't at her best either, which might teach her not to drink wine. She'd taken two aspros before they'd left for church. She took two more before they left for Daree, and two more when she got there. And after all that, the police wouldn't let her into the interview room.

They closed the door on Bessy then offered Ellie a glass of water. She drank most of it before allowing herself a brief, fearful glance at the three men who had followed her into the room. Only one was dressed like a policeman. The other two were probably the men from Sydney. They wore ordinary clothes, but they looked like Sydney police – or like Sydney police looked on the television shows she liked to watch.

Unaware that she never responded to any given situation without permission, most of their questions had to be asked twice before she'd offer a nodded yes, or a head-shaking no. She murmured a few times, 'I'm sure I don't know, officer.' Then the taller one stood, so Ellie stood and smiled, believing the interview was at its end.

But he took up a box, and from the box he removed two plastic-wrapped parcels.

Ellie had always loathed having her soiled linen aired in public places, but these men were flaunting some of it. They showed her a pair of underpants, sealed in plastic. They were Bonds, but the size had worn away. They could have been Jack's. She blushed a deep pink and she sat again.

They showed her a sock in a matching plastic bag. Her mouth

fell open and her heavy lidded eyes grew wide with disbelief. The sock was black, if impregnated with red earth. She reached out a hand to take it, then quickly drew the hand back.

'Jack always wore woollen socks. Nylon made his feet sweat. He always wore pure woollen socks.'

'It's pure wool, Mrs Burton. Probably Holeproof.'

Jack had liked Holeproof socks. They were expensive and he'd liked expensive things. She stared at the sock as she shrank low in her chair, her hand reaching for her apron pocket. No apron. No pocket today. She opened her handbag to touch her rosary beads, then, to prove she had another reason for opening her bag, removed a handkerchief. Her chin down, she closed her eyes and moved away to the side of her chair, twisting her handkerchief corner, unable to meet the eyes of the watching men. When they started again with their questions, her eyes remained down as slowly she told of the night it had all begun.

'Annie and Bronwyn drove down when they heard about the police finding Liza's body. Then later on, after we'd had something to eat, Bronwyn went over to Mr Fletcher's, our neighbour's house, to phone Nick, her husband. Since yesterday. They got married yesterday. Down here. In Daree. Nick's family live in Daree.'

'Bronwyn is your youngest daughter, Mrs Burton?'

'Yes. Well, Jack came home while Bronwyn was over there phoning. He got a lift home with Jeff, our policeman. Jack and Annie got into an argument, so I went outside to stand on the verandah.'

'A heated argument, Mrs Burton?'

'No, it was . . . was just . . . normal. For them. They were always arguing when they got together, which wasn't very often, thank goodness. I used to tell her not to argue, but Annie always had a mind of her own. Too much alike, they were, they never got along.' She wiped at her mouth with her handkerchief, glanced up, then back down to her handbag.

'So they argued.'

'Yes.'

'And . . . ?'

'Then this other car came driving up and I went out to the yard to see who it was, and then the house lights went off. I thought it was the lightning. There was thunder rolling around for hours that night. Anyway, I thought it had struck a power pole. It often happens and we get cut off for hours.'

'The car . . . ?'

'It was Johnny and David. Annie's husband. I didn't recognise them in the dark until David spoke. You could have knocked me down with a feather when I saw Johnny. I was so pleased to see him. He hadn't been home in years and years, you see. We just . . . ' Her hand shook as she picked up the glass of water. She drank in gulps.

'If you could continue, Mrs Burton.'

'Well, we sort of didn't come in for a while. Then we came inside and I started looking for candles in the sideboard. I always keep candles. It was David who noticed that Mr Fletcher's lights were still on, so he checked the fuse box, and he found out the lights had been turned off at the main. So we turned all the lights back on.'

'Your daughter and husband? Where were they at this time, Mrs Burton?'

'We didn't know where they were. Then I noticed that Jack's gun was gone.' She swallowed, considered the glass of water. It was empty. 'We started looking for them, calling out for them. Outside. We looked everywhere. Bronwyn came back, and Mr Fletcher came after her. We all called to Annie and Jack. Then Bronwyn ran over to Bessy's place, over Ben's bridge. They weren't over there. A bit later the rain came pelting down and I went back inside, and after a while the others came in. The rain was like thunder on the roof and we could hardly hear ourselves talking. Then Annie just came walking into the kitchen looking like a drowned rat, her hair plastered to her head, dress plastered to her back. I asked her where her father was, and she said, "Gone".'

'I went out to the verandah and called to him again, and Annie

101

picked up her purse and went out to her car. David yelled at Annie to get out of the rain. I thought she'd gone to get something from the car. She had Jack's briefcase in her boot, you see. The next thing I know, David is running off to his car because Annie is driving away.'

'He was gone about an hour, but he came back. Said he followed her, but lost her car down some track near the river. He said he nearly got bogged, his wheels were slipping and sliding in the mud. Those old tracks down near the river get very greasy in the rain.' For minutes Ellie sat unmoving, her green eyes dripping tears onto her lap. When the question came again, she shook her head, sprinkling her tears. 'I don't know anything else I can tell you, officers.'

'Mrs Taylor did not return to the house that night.'

'No. We waited for her. After David came back we all waited for about an hour. Mr Fletcher was there too. We all had a cup of tea and some Christmas cake, sort of expecting Jack to come back any minute. Then David drove home, because we thought that Annie must have gone home. To Warran. They live in Warran. David gave Mr Fletcher a lift over to his house. It was still raining. It rained all night. Johnny and Bronwyn and I sat up talking until after twelve. I hadn't seen him in over twenty years and he said to me that night that the best part of coming home was my Christmas cake. He's a priest, you know. Was a priest, that is. I'm sure he'll go back to the church one day. When he's ready.'

They nodded, waited.

'Well.' She shrugged. 'I was still thinking Jack would come back, and him and Johnny might – ' She swallowed, delved into her handbag for her rosary beads and the hand remained in the bag as she continued. 'I put clean sheets on the spare beds and we all went to bed. And that's all I know.'

'You didn't report your husband missing for some months, Mrs Burton.'

'But that would have been silly, knowing Jack. I mean, he was always away. Anyone in town will tell you that. It would have been silly to report him missing. I didn't know that he was missing.'

'Can you explain?'

'I mean . . . it's his family. They live in Victoria. At Narrawee. Where they found Liza. He used to spend as much time down there as he did in Mallawindy, you see. He hated Mallawindy, so I thought he'd just gone down there again.'

'You believed he'd gone without his car?'

'Yes, but I didn't know about the car until the next day. I told you, Jeff Rowan had driven him home that night because Jack had got into an argument with Mr Owen. I didn't know that his car was still up at the hotel until Benjie came home from his trip and he said that the car was still up at the town.

'We thought that was a bit strange, but then Jack never did drive when he'd been on the whisky. I thought he'd probably got a lift down to Melbourne with someone. He'd done that before, and there were a lot of strangers in Mallawindy that night – newspaper people and television people. They wanted to know about Liza. He'd been drinking with them at the hotel before he came home. He said they'd wanted to pay him to go on the television. I thought . . . thought they'd probably given him a lift down to do an interview. We watched the television for a few days, but he wasn't on it.'

She'd worn a hole in her handkerchief. Her finger poked through it now, and she studied the broken nail, the sandpaper skin. Terrible. She snatched her finger out and shrank lower in her chair.

'Bessy will be getting tired of waiting for me. We've got cows.'

She needed Bessy. She'd leaned on her all her life. Bessy had been nineteen when their mother died, and she'd stepped in, taken her mother's place. Ellie had never been able to lean on Jack. Jack had been her handsome prince who had come riding along on his borrowed bicycle that afternoon. A prince wasn't expected to get his hands dirty in a cow yard, wasn't expected to behave like . . .

But he had worn Bonds briefs and black woollen socks.

'He was wearing his best grey trousers and a white shirt,' she said. 'And he had a good watch. Very expensive. He always wore his watch. It was silver and gold, sort of woven together. Very heavy. Sam and May bought it for him not long before he disappeared. And he would have had his wallet with his licence. He always carried his licence and his cards. His bank account cards. They'd still be there. Plastic lasts forever.'

'Nothing else has been found, Mrs Burton.'

'He lived up in Sydney for twelve months after little Linda died.' Her chin trembled. 'We lost three of our babies.' She glanced at the desk where the sock and underpants lay and she shuddered, looked away. 'He had a very hard life, officers. He should have inherited half of Narrawee, but his father disowned him, you see. Sam and May got the property and the money, though they did try to make it up to Jack. They were always buying him things. Very good to us, they were.

'They paid for little Liza's funeral and bought her a lovely stone – with the other children's names on top.' She looked at the men as she drank again from her refilled glass. 'Everything just went on and on. I wrote to Narrawee to ask about Jack, but May said he wasn't there, so I thought he'd gone to Sydney, and that he'd come home when he was ready, like he always did. Then about six months after he left, Benjie got Jeff Rowan to check on the bank accounts, and Jeff found out that Jack hadn't been withdrawing any of his money. Not since the day before Christmas. So that's when . . . when we reported him . . . missing.'

She stilled her tongue but not her fingers. Her handkerchief was now almost in two pieces. She attempted to hide it, balling it in her hand. Her mouth open, her eyes wandered the room, eager to find escape from these men. She scanned the floorboards and the bruised legs of the desk, the walls. Hard plaster. Grey. Rough. She looked at the ceiling. Yellow. Smoke stained.

For two hours they kept her there, and for those two hours Ellie Burton repeated the same story, convinced she'd spend the night in a cell because of the insurance money.

'Everyone is talking about that insurance money. As if I paid the premiums on Jack's policy just so I could get money if he died. As if I was like that. It was like a bank account for our old age, that's all. We would have got what we paid in plus bonuses when Jack turned seventy. I don't want him to be de . . . to die. I wouldn't want to gain by his death. What do I need that much money for anyway?'

Her mouth was working and she didn't know how to stop it. Knowledge of police stations far removed from her small sphere of experience, she feared the scent of bricks and mortar, of aged male sweat, of stale cigarettes and mould. Fear, fatigue and cold feet loosened her tongue.

'He – Someone else will tell you this anyway, so it might as well come from me. He . . . he goes with other women.' The words, spoken in a rush, created a silence, and she hated those words hanging there in that silence, growing, accusing her of disloyalty, so she attempted to bury them beneath nervous babble. 'He's not responsible when he gets on the whisky, and he'd been on the whisky that night. That's why Jeff drove him home, because he'd been drinking with Vera Owen and then her husband Charlie – ' Her tattered handkerchief dabbed at a tear, wiped at her nose. 'Her husband, Charlie, is a truck driver. He's away a lot and Vera is . . . is . . . I mean everyone knows what she is!'

'Would it have been possible for your daughter to have returned to the house that night, Mrs Burton?'

'What?'

'Your daughter, Mrs Taylor, would it have been possible for her to have returned to the house that night?'

'I told you she didn't come back. We waited until after twelve for her.'

'You were in bed by twelve?'

'It was around twelve-thirty by the time we'd made up the beds.'

'Would you have heard her if she'd returned after you went to bed?'

'I didn't sleep very well. I kept listening for Jack and worrying that Johnny might hear him first. And little Liza, she was on my mind that night too. And Benjie. He'd gone off somewhere in his ute. I hardly closed my eyes that night, then I was out of bed by five-thirty for the cows.'

'But it would have been possible for Mrs Taylor to have returned to the house, between those hours, woken her brother, then returned to her vehicle.'

'She said she was bogged out past the ten-mile. It was a terrible night. No one would have been wandering around in that weather. She said she had to wait until daylight so she could see to get some timber to put under her wheels, to get the car out.'

'But she may have returned without your knowledge.'

'No. I would have heard her come back, for sure. I knew every noise in the old place. I would have thought it was Jack coming back and I would have been out of my bed like a shot.'

Shot was a bad word, and she wished she hadn't said it. Poor Jack.

'It isn't him that you've found. You're wrong,' she said, but her tears didn't know it. They were trickling silently now, large green eyes like overflowing pools let the water flow.

They brought her another glass of water and again showed her the underpants and sock.

'You are not able to identify the clothing, Mrs Burton?'

'No. No, it's not him you've found, officers.' Her nose was running. She sniffed.

'Can you say with certainty that the items do not belong to your husband?'

'No! I can't say that! How can I say that? They're Bonds.' The last word was a howl.

The detectives glanced at each other, and she wished she hadn't said that. Her tongue, like her eyes, was out of control, and these men weren't giving her time to think of what she should be saying.

'And you have been unable to recall the name of your husband's dentist?'

'He went to some place in Melbourne.'

The taller man shook his head and looked at his colleagues. 'Would you recall if he had root canal work done on the left eye-tooth, Mrs Burton?'

'What treatment?'

'Root canal.'

She felt her own eyeteeth with her tongue. 'He had a lot of work done on one of his eyeteeth. He'd had a terrible toothache for weeks and he wouldn't go to my dentist.' She wiped her nose, her mouth. 'I think they had to drill the nerve out.'

The city men had enough, and as much as they were going to get from Ellie Burton. They had verification of root canal treatment to one of the eyeteeth, a tentative identification of the garments found at the scene, and three possible suspects. They released Ellie to sob in Bessy's arms.

'It's not him. Why would anyone kill him, then bury him in his underpants and one sock, Bessy?'

Bessy had her own ideas on just who might have done that, but she wasn't saying anything. Not to Ellie. She'd had a few words with the young girl cop, though. She'd filled her in on some old gossip about Jack and Vera Owen and a tyre lever-toting truckie husband who had sworn to get Jack Burton if it was the last thing he ever did.

the central hotel

~

Tuesday 12 August

Tuesday awoke grey. Better that it had remained in bed. Soaking rain had begun falling at midnight and by three-thirty, the town mud was deep and red as blood. It stuck. Old umbrellas were found behind doors on Tuesday, dusty umbrellas; the women who carried them to town had little experience with the things that caught the wind and tried to fly. But the women's shoes, weighted with Mallawindy mud, held them to the earth. This town clung to its few inhabitants. It wouldn't let them get away.

Granny Bourke had got away near dawn; she'd slipped over on her way to the outdoor lavatory. There was a ladies and gents behind the bar, but for eighty-odd years Granny had used that old lavatory, and as she frequently sat there for an hour, it was a convenient aberration. That morning she'd slipped in the mud and snapped one of her sparrow ankles. Unconscious, wet and frozen to the bone when found by her grandson, he'd called Jeff Rowan and they'd dropped her off at the Daree hospital. The news was all bad, though it barely caused a ripple in the bar.

'She's had a good life. She went out the way she would have wanted to go. Independent old bugger,' Mick said. 'Oh, by the way, I seen the cops all over Charlie Owen's place when I was driving back.'

'At the house or where they found Jack?'

'At the house. The place was swarming with cop cars.'

'Poor old Charlie. Why did the crazy bastard bury him right at his own doorstep? That's what I'd like to know.'

'Because he's a crazy bastard. When's your gran's funeral, Mick?'

'She was still alive when we left her there, but they don't reckon she'll live through the day. Frozen to the bone, she was. Wet as a shag. Christ knows how long she'd been out there.' Mick Bourke's tone didn't echo his words. He pulled two beers and pocketed the cash.

Wet days were boom days at the Central. There was little work that could be done in the rain. By mid-afternoon the bar was full but the conversation hadn't altered.

'You know, whoever done Jack in, Charlie or not, he done it with a pistol or a small-bore rifle. It went in through the back of his skull and come out through the front of his head. The Sydney cops reckon they must have had him on his knees praying.'

'Who told you that?'

'Jeff. He told me this morning, on the way back from dropping her off.'

'Dropping who off?'

'Old Gran.'

'What happened to her?'

'Broke her leg. It will be the end of her, they say.'

'Poor old bugger. Ah well, look on the bright side, Mick – she's had a good life. Not many of us make the century.'

'Hey, did you hear about Charlie?'

And others entered with more current news. 'How about that crazy bastard? I hear they've took him in. We've had a bloody hit man living in town and didn't know it. It was a real execution-like hit. Pow, right through the back of the skull.'

Malcolm Fletcher stood in Jack's old corner, sipping his double brandy, listening as the growing group rehashed the news.

'So when are you paying up, Mick?' Joe Willis asked.

'What for?'

'Jack.'

'When they identify his corpse, Joe.' Mick Bourke turned to old Robbie West who had entered to get out of the rain. 'Did you hear about poor old Charlie?'

'Charged him with Jack's murder, eh?' Robbie sneezed, wiped at his nose, then grudgingly passed his coins over with the same hand. Mick scooped them into his till before setting to washing glasses, and his hands.

'I didn't know that they'd charged him yet. When?'

Malcolm listened again.

'That's what I heard, but.'

'Shit! They don't muck around, do they?'

'They was waiting for him when he got back with his truck. Took three of them to take him, so Vera was tellin' young Bob. He gived one of them a black eye, dislocated the other copper's shoulder and half killed the little bloke – so Vera was saying.'

'Got poor old Jack begging on his knees then *phitt*, a bullet in the back of the head. That's how they do it on television.'

'Charlie might be a moron but he's not bloody mad. If he done it, he would have tossed the body on his truck and dumped it in Perth. He wouldn't of put him so close to home.' A third voice bought into the conversation.

And a fourth. 'That brainless bastard? It's just what he would do. Everyone in the bar heard him say he was gunna do it one day.'

'If you're planning to kill some bastard, then you don't spread it around, do you?'

'I wonder who dobbed him.'

'Christ knows.' Many eyes looked at neighbours, accused neighbours. Heads turned to scan corners, to glower at Malcolm.

'They got a mob still out there, going over his truck with a fine-tooth comb.'

'He come from Sydney, you know. Both of them did. They reckon Vera was on the game in Kings Cross.'

'She's still on the bloody game, just that no one pays their bills.'

Laughter. Raucous. Beer swilled down as conversations over-lapped, interlocked. Voices merged, then hushed as new fuel was added, fresh from the street.

'His truck was full of drugs. The cops found a bloody pile of them.'

'Probably moonlighting for the Mafia, drug running. Probably got one of their hit men to do poor old Jack in. They import them, you know. Fly 'em in from some place to do the hit and fly 'em out before anyone knows it's been done. I guarantee that Charlie has got a watertight alibi. I bet the bastard's log book will have him in Perth the night it was done.'

'They don't know the night it was done, do they? How the bloody hell can they tell to the day when he was done in? They can't. Oh, I hear your old gran carked it, Mick?'

'Broke her ankle and spent half the night out in the rain. Hypothermia and probably pneumonia.'

'Wouldn't do her much good.'

'No. She had a good life, but.'

Malcolm left them to it. He waited beneath the other small shelter of the verandah with King Billy and his dogs while the rain slanted down, but the dogs scratched and King Billy cursed him, and every whitey who had ever walked. Malcolm left him cursing and his dogs scratching and he walked into the rain, playing chicken with a Falcon that wasn't obeying the speed signs. Wheels skidded and the Falcon thunked into a deep open drain. Malcolm proceeded forward, blinded by the rain on his glasses.

'G'day,' Ben Burton called from his rear counter as Malcolm cleared his vision with a white handkerchief.

'Little good about it, Burton. Any more news?'

'They've circulated his X-rays to every dentist in Melbourne. They'll check his DNA, but that takes time. I've got to give them some blood – me or Johnny.' Ben continued, counting notes to pay into the post office cum bank agency.

'I hear they've arrested Charlie Owen.'

'Yeah. They reckon they found a kilo of amphetamines in his truck. He always looks half zapped out of his brain.'

'They have him down as the local hit man at the Central,' Malcolm added.

'I'd like to know who set them onto him.'

'The body was discovered near his property. A logical assumption, perhaps.'

Ben shrugged. 'It's getting to Mum. She keeps on denying that it's him to everyone, but I think she knows he's dead. She'd be better off facing it and getting over it, I reckon.'

'There appears to be little doubt in the minds of our Sydney friends.'

'Mum recognised the sock and stuff found out there, and they're going on his left eyetooth. He got it root-filled back in the eighties. I remember when he had it done.' Ben slipped a rubber band around his notes. 'It's got to be him. And the fact that he hasn't touched his money since he left. He's not the type to live on air. And he couldn't be on a pension or they would have found him – unless he's using somebody else's name.'

'A possibility.'

'I can't see it. He was Jack Burton, and proud of it. He wouldn't scrounge around on a pension using another name when he's got thousands in the bank. He wouldn't do it. It's got to be him,' Ben repeated. 'Jeff reckons it is. Reckons it's just a formality – getting him identified.'

'Our young lawman has become a law unto himself, Burton. He confiscated my car keys and licence last evening.'

'I hear you took on Willis's bus.'

'Which is still on the road, I note.'

'Jeff's gone power crazy lately. He caught Bron speeding one night. She did her licence for six months.' Ben walked off to serve a paying customer. Malcolm turned to the bookshelves.

Chef-Marlet's latest had disappeared. He looked back to Ben as the customer left. 'They say the demised has been that way for some considerable time.'

'At least five years, they reckon. It's not the way I thought he'd go. I mean, this sounds like one of those execution murders.'

'Perhaps he became involved with some drug baron's moll, Burton.' He watched the notes slide into the calico bag. 'Have you spoken to your sister recently?'

'She rang me on Sunday morning.'

Malcolm nodded. 'I have some items in her care and no longer the means to retrieve them.' He had little interest in the items; his question was only bait, tossed randomly in the hope it might net him information on Ann.

'I'll run you down on Sunday, if you like. I usually drop in on Sundays.'

'I may have my keys back by then. Young Fogarty was kind enough to collect me this morning and will see me home.'

Ben glanced up, interested. He liked the no-nonsense infant mistress he'd driven home from the wedding. 'You're back at the school again.'

'O'Rouke is incapacitated. A pathetic fool of a man, that one.'

'Funny how his wife hasn't turned up anywhere. Mum said she saw her walking down the road with her handbag that day. She seemed normal enough – what I saw of her. She didn't stick around long enough for anyone to get to know her.'

'Three months in Mallawindy is more than enough for most, Burton.'

But not for everyone. They turned, smiled as Kerrie Fogarty walked through the door. Tall, lean, her blonde hair trimmed to within an inch of her head, she had a grin for everyone, and there were few males in town who could deny her a smile in reply.

'G'day Ben. Ready to roll, Fletch?' she said.

Malcolm picked up his loaded string bag and rolled. The young teacher and the old were at the door when Johnny Burton limped through, shedding water.

'Mr Fletcher. Miss Fogarty.' He swung by them, leaving a three-legged trail of mud and water to Ben's back room, where he helped himself to the key ring and its many keys. 'I need to borrow your ute, Ben.'

'What's wrong with the old man's car?'

'Mum's got the keys.'

'What's she going to do with them?'

'Toss them in the river, the last I heard.' John attempted to go around his brother but Ben stood his ground.

'What's going on?'

'You're not involved.'

'I am if you're taking my ute. It's a manual. You can't drive it with that foot, and anyway, I've got to lock up in an hour and my shop keys are on the key ring.' But Johnny was out the door.

Two women entered. Ben, who had inherited Ellie's preference for keeping family secrets in the family, walked back to his calico bag, pushing it deep beneath the counter. He wasted fifteen minutes trying to sell them a thirty-dollar dinner set, and ended up with a sixty-cent sale of chewing gum. It was almost five before he got to the telephone and dialled home, and he waited long for the phone to be lifted.

'Mum? Are you there?' He heard a sniff, a stifled sob. 'It's me. What's going on with you and Johnny?'

'Bessy told him that they've locked up Charlie Owen for your dad's murder,' Ellie wailed.

'They haven't got him for murder. They've got him on assault and possession of amphetamines. And what's it got to do with Johnny? He's taken my ute and shop keys and it's Dooley's day off. Can you bring my spare shop keys up? They're hanging behind my bedroom door.'

Ellie howled in his ear.

He'd heard her scream often enough and he'd seen her weep in silence, but never like this. 'Mum. Mum! Stop your howling and tell me what's got into Johnny.'

'He said Charlie didn't kill your dad that night. He said he was going to Daree to tell the police how he knows that Charlie didn't kill him that night.' Her words silenced Ben, and the cold wet Tuesday crept up his spine to his head. 'He knows something, love. And I don't want it to be – '

'Stop howling, and tell me what he said.'

'The police keep hinting about him and Annie, as if they think they've done something.' She wailed again and Ben waited. 'They kept asking me if Annie came back that night, and could she have woken Johnny without me hearing.'

'It's just questions. They've got to ask their questions.'

'Annie nearly shot him once. And she took his briefcase. Why did she take his briefcase? They asked me if your dad had a handgun in his briefcase.'

'You know he didn't.'

'I don't know what he had in it,' she wailed, and the phone hit the floor.

'Mum. Mum. Pick up the phone. Mum! Can you bring up my keys?'

The only reply was Ellie's wail, but from a distance.

He hung up and tried to call Bessy. She was engaged, probably passing on the news to the rest of the town. He dialled Ann's number and the call went to her answering machine. He was starting to wonder what he'd done to deserve the lot of them when her voice cut in.

'I'm here. In the flesh. Taylor's asylum. Head loony speaking.'

'All hell has broken loose down here, Annie.'

'Tell me about it.'

'Johnny has gone to the cops and Mum's cracked up. She's been heading for this since Friday and I can't leave the shop. It's Dooley's day off and I can't lock up here until I track him down or get someone to go down to the house and get my spare keys. I can't raise Bessy and Mum won't let anyone else in.'

'I'll toss the boys in the car. Give me forty-five minutes.'

'No. It's too far and too wet. What I'm calling about is the old man's briefcase. Do you know anything about it? Mum keeps going on about it. Did you take it that night?' Ben heard bellowing in the background, he heard Ann's footsteps, then her voice.

'Share the toys, Matthew.'

'I did share wiff him and he wouldn't share wiff me.'

'That's because he's smaller than you. We have to teach him how to share.' Footsteps returning. 'Sorry, Ben. They're on the rampage. I need to get out of the house, and I can tie them down in the wagon. See you soon.'

'No. It's late. I'll get hold of someone up here. Have you got his briefcase?' She made no reply. 'Annie? Are you there?'

'I hear you, Ben. Just. Every time I pick up the phone they start a war, and everyone I know has called me today; I'm just about ready to confess to his murder for a quiet life. Maybe that's what Johnny is doing.'

'I don't know what's going on with him. And I don't know what's going on between you two either, but it's as plain as mud on your face that something is going on. What do you know about that night?' Seconds passed and she made no reply. 'The night the old man disappeared. Do you and Johnny know something?'

'I know you should have rowed your boat to China, Ben, and I should have gone with you. If you feel like taking off I'll go you halves in a speedboat. Tristan! Puppy dogs bite. Are you a puppy dog?'

'I Darp Bada.'

'Well Darth Vadar doesn't bite his brothers. Go to your room, please.'

Ben leant against the wall, listening to the distant voices, smiling when there was nothing in the world to smile about. But there he was listening to Annie, and for some reason it didn't seem real. Annie, whose only voice had been her hands when they were kids. Hard to believe it was the same Annie, laying down the law to her boys.

'Go to your room. Now. Do you want Mummy to put you in your cot and close the door?'

'I det you wiff my lipe sayba.'

'Go. Run. I don't want to see that naughty face. Bedroom! Now!' Footsteps on tiles, a door closing. Footsteps returning.

Ben waited and looked out at the rain, his mind away in yesterday, at that serene white house in Mahoneys Lane that was once a place of peace, and the little girl who'd called him Unka Benny, who had kissed him all better, had held his hand and taken him to see her kitty. Not so serene these days.

Life and death. Who deserved what life dished out?

'Sorry, Ben. It's like living in a madhouse at times.'

'I can relate to that. Johnny is half as mad as Dad ever was, Mum is heading for a nervous breakdown, and I'm stuck with them – and I'm sick and tired of being stuck with them, and that's a fact and I don't care who knows it, Annie. I had Johnny singing drunk all the way home on Saturday night and Mum howling because he was singing drunk, and Kerrie Fogarty wondering what the hell she'd let herself in for. I spend my life pussyfooting around the two of them lately and I'm fed up with it.'

'I know. I know you are. I'll try to call Mum.'

'You won't get anywhere. She's left her phone off the hook. Those Sydney cops have been down here today. They asked me about his briefcase. I'm only telling you because you'll probably get a call from them tomorrow. I've got to get down to Daree and give them a blood sample – to check his DNA, which apparently takes weeks.'

'They called me but I had the answering machine on. Living in Bedlam has its advantages. Oh God. I think he's taken off in his spaceship. Got to go.' The phone disconnected, Ben hung up and dialled around until he found Dooley and his keys. He left him to lock up and he walked home in the rain. Ellie sat at the kitchen table, her head on her arms, sobbing for Johnny or Jack. He didn't know which one and he didn't care either. The cows hadn't been milked.

'If he's dead, then he's dead, and he's been dead for six years. Pull yourself together, Mum. I've got to do the cows.' He was changing his clothes when he heard the knock at his door; he flung it wide, ready to take on the police in his singlet.

Only Kerrie Fogarty. 'Is John at home, Ben?'

'John? No. Want another serenade, do you?' Sarcasm had never been Ben's forte. He didn't do it well and he felt his face begin to burn. The cow yard sweater was pulled quickly over his head, hiding his blush first and his singlet and freckled arms second. 'I've got to do the cows,' he explained. 'Nothing has been done around here today. They've all gone mad.'

'Mad cow disease?'

'Yeah.' He grinned and he wasn't sure why, because he sure as hell didn't feel like grinning. 'Johnny has gone off somewhere in my ute and Mum's bawling. You might be able to make her a cup of tea or something.'

'Can I tag along with you, give you a hand? I've served my time in a cow yard.'

He looked at her rain gear and boots. 'The mud will be up to your knees.'

'It will wash off.'

'Reckon you could fit into Mum's gumboots?' He didn't wait for a reply or invite her in, but collected his raincoat and two pairs of gumboots, then watched Kerrie undo her shoelaces and slide her feet into Ellie's black boots. They fitted well.

'We're off, Mum,' he called, closing the front door and leaving Ellie weeping at the kitchen table. Leaving her, her topknot tumbled, her thick plait hanging loose to the floor, sweeping the floor; a skein of fading silk shimmering with each heave of her shoulders.

his father's son

~

For forty-five years Ellie Burton had absorbed the blows life and Jack had dealt out to her. Few had got close enough to see through the cold armour she wore, and wore proudly, armour forged from crumbs the world and Jack had tossed to her, but Ellie had swept each crumb up gladly, had buttered it lavishly.

Butter melted. Her armour was crumbling, falling away, and Ellie Burton, hiding within, couldn't take life without her crumbs.

She didn't hear the ute return, nor the thunk of the crutches and the single footstep across the verandah. Johnny entered via the back door. He stood in the passage, watching her weep.

'I've seen you like this since I was two years old. I've watched you cry for that bastard, wait for that bastard.'

Ellie lifted her head, her swollen eyes shaded against the light with her hand.

'They let you go.' She attempted to uncross her leg, to stand, but the blood supply, too long restricted, had turned her legs to twin lumps of wood. She stumbled, fell to her knees.

He didn't move from the doorway to help her, but stood watching her try to pick herself up. She grasped the table, and a chair, she heaved, then released her grip and sank slowly back to the floor.

John's eyes were empty of feeling. Cold. Cold anger, colder rain had chilled his blood, and her tears for that bastard had driven anger deep, seeding his eyes with cynicism.

'Help me up, love.' Her arms reached out to him.

Still he would not move. Perhaps he feared he might hit her, as his father had hit her, that he might smash her head against the table, keep smashing it until she woke up. His hands clenching the crutches grew white.

'I thought you'd done it. I thought they were going to take you away from me too. I couldn't go on. I couldn't. I couldn't lose both of you.'

'Don't mention that bastard in the same breath as you speak of me, Mum.'

She wiped at her mouth, her nose. 'He's my husband.'

'He was a diseased dog and now he's dead.'

'He was your father!'

'It takes more than a high sperm count to make a father.'

She looked at him, her head shaking. 'I can't stand to think of him as dead, as murdered. I can't do it, Johnny. I can't.'

He made no reply, but his right hand left the crutch. It clattered to the floor as his fist slammed into the wall. It hurt, and the pain was good.

She howled anew for his pain and her mouth remained open as she shook her head, the plait swaying backwards and forwards, backwards and forwards, like a charmed snake.

'Did he . . . did he come back that night? Did you or Annie – ?'

'Kill the bastard? Didn't we have reason enough, Mum? What did he ever do for you, for any one of us, but make our lives a purgatory on earth?'

She leaned against the leg of the table, her own legs extended before her, and she rubbed at her calves, trying to force blood to circulate.

'Answer me tonight, Mum. What did he ever do for you?' His voice was loud. 'Answer me, Mum. I need answers tonight.'

'It's . . . it's not what people do.' She wiped at her eyes with her sleeve. 'It's . . . I married him in the chur – ' she began, then she looked up at her first-born, looked at his eyes and knew she needed a better excuse for Johnny. 'He loved me back then. You know he did. He used to call me his Sleeping Beauty. He used to buy me such beautiful things. You know he loved me back then.'

Johnny leaned on the doorjamb, as his father used to lean, and he stared at her, as his father had stared, tired, bored. 'Love? Was his brutality love, Mum? Did a roll in the dust turn you on?'

'Stop it,' she screamed. 'You stop talking to me like that, Johnny.'

He turned away, aware he'd gone too far. 'I'm leaving. There is nothing here for me. Where are the car keys?'

'There's nothing here for any of us,' she said. Perhaps it was her tone, perhaps her words that brought him back to the door. 'Nothing,' she said. 'Not any more. Nothing matters to me any more. Not the cows and the chooks. Nothing. It's like we're lost, love. It's like everything that should have been good got lost. All of my beautiful children, all of my beautiful hopes for my children just got lost.'

'Tossed in the gutter by that bastard.'

'I don't know what to say to you. To any of you. I tried to do the right things. I thought I was doing the right things, but I don't know if anything I've ever done in my whole life was right or wrong any more. I don't know anything, love.'

'Because he isn't around to tell you what's right and what's wrong, he's not around to belittle every move you make?'

'I don't know. I . . . I . . . it's like Bessy says, like I didn't let myself grow up. It's like, suddenly all the years of not growing are pushing me down, Johnny. I don't know who I'm supposed to be if he's dead. It's like . . . like I'm no one.' She wailed anew and he stood there, wanting out.

'Where are his keys?'

'Don't go, love. Don't leave me.'

'I've got to go. I'm going mad here. I shouldn't have come

home. This wouldn't have happened if I'd stayed away. Annie would have worked it out. She didn't need me.'

'I need you, love.'

'I'm just a convenient replacement for him. I'm just the shape, the shadow of that bastard, when what you need is the real thing. If he were to walk in this door now, you'd get up, wouldn't you? One way or another you'd run to him – or crawl to him, kiss his muddy boots while they kicked you.'

'He didn't have anyone but us.'

'And he didn't want us. It was Liza. All for Liza. So little love in that bastard, he had none left for the rest of us. He hated me from the day I was born.'

'He didn't. He was proud of you. He took you home to show to his father. It was his father that . . . that spoiled everything. Going to Narrawee spoiled everything. I didn't fit in there, love, and his father was a terrible old man.'

'So the father blames the son and the son blames the father, hate creating its vicious little circle that none can escape.'

'He would have been all right if Liza hadn't died.'

'He killed her, Mum.'

'Don't you start that again, Johnny.'

'He killed her.' She shook her head and he turned away. 'I couldn't fight him then, and I can't fight him now. You'll defend him with your last breath.'

'I just care about him. I don't want to think of him as dead, as dying in his underpants and one sock – dying with a gun to his head. He was so proud of himself and his Narrawee and his great-grandfather. If I think of him dying like that, like some sort of a common criminal, then it all gets too hard for me to bear, love. I just want to give up. I just want to lie down somewhere and sleep and shut it all out of my head and never have to wake up again.'

Poor old rag doll, tossed to the floor, to be walked on, kicked around, her stuffing knocked out of her, then tossed aside for a newer doll. Someone had to pick it up, prop it up, shake it back into shape.

He limped towards her on one crutch and she reached out a hand.

'My legs have gone to sleep. Can you help me up to the chair?'

'You've been asleep all your life.' He took her hand but one leg and a crutch could not support him. Somehow he was on his knees and her arms were around him.

A little boy, lost too long, and a betrayed old rag doll. They clung together and they wept. But his tears were too hard. In time they dried her own.

'Hush, love,' she whispered. 'You'll break my poor old heart with your crying. We'll be okay, you see if we aren't. We'll get over this. Don't cry, my beautiful boy.' Rocking him, kissing his face, she soothed him as she had soothed him forty years ago. 'Hush now, my beautiful boy. It's going to be all right. Remember what you used to say to me when you were little and I used to cry? You used to say to me, "Don't cry any more, Mummy. All your tears will run down to the river and make the water salty, then all the fish will die".'

'They're all dead. They're dead, Mum, and I can't make them live because I'm dead too. There's nothing left in me to give to you, to Annie, to anyone.'

'Oh, yes there is so. You're my beautiful boy. My own precious boy. And those fish aren't dead. We just let that old river get a bit too muddy there for a while. But it's going to be all right soon, and you will be too. We will be, my beautiful boy. You hush now. Those eyes were made for smiling, not for tears. Shush now. Hush, my boy.'

a long way to spring

~

Wednesday 13 August

The sky was grey; the trees across the road were grey. Life was grey today. No neighbour to stand yarning with at the side fence, no children set free to play in the back yard, just the sleety wind-driven rain, beating against the windows, trying to get in.

Not much to be said for motherhood on miserable days. Kids stir-crazy, mother with cabin fever, and the rat-a-tat of knuckles against the back door. Little boys, seeking something of interest, fought to be first out.

Ann caught Tristan beneath an arm and blocked Matthew's progress with an extended foot as she opened the back door.

Dee Williams and her large umbrella blew in with the wind, and the door was closed fast, the glass shuddering in its frame.

'Your C A T,' she spelt out. 'It's D E A D, Ann. A car H I T it. Didn't even stop, the callous swine.'

'What did she say, Mummy? Who didn't stop, Mummy?'

'The taxi,' Ann replied, looking at her neighbour then down to the small interrogator. Poor old Tiddy had been Mandy's cat. No more cat now. 'I'll settle the boys and B U R Y it.'

'What's B U R Y, Mummy?'

'Banana under raspberry yoghurt. What do you want, a video or some yoghurt?'

'I want *The Lion King*.'

'I want da bidio Lion Tin.'

'You can both have the video *Lion King*.'

Good old video. David's study was now the boys' playroom, complete with television and video player. Ann's sewing room held Tristan's cot and his chest of drawers. The house, once considered too large, had undergone radical shrinkage over the past six years. Even the family room/kitchen had shrunk a size.

The boys seated on well-separated chairs, silent and still, Ann took a garbage bag from the cupboard and her parka from the back porch, pulling the hood up as she walked with her neighbour to the road, walking slow against the wind, fine needles of rain in her face. Her back was aching today; a speedboat to China looked better than it had yesterday.

'Silly old cat,' she said when she saw it, wet, bedraggled, its mouth open, eyes open. She picked it up while Dee held the plastic bag wide, then Ann took the bag and the two women returned to the yard.

'Silly old cat. It used up the last of its nine lives two years ago. Cost us a fortune at the vet's when the last car hit it,' she said.

'I could take him down to the vet. He'll dispose of it, Ann.'

'I'll bury it,' she said. She found her favourite spade in the garden shed and chose a site between the bare apricot tree and the plum. Tall now, they'd burst into blossom soon, be covered in fruit come Christmas, if Christmas ever came. The earth was soft here, and the cat not so large.

She'd never liked it – or never forgiven it. Mandy had been chasing it when she'd fallen down the stairs. How many children tumbled down stairs and lived? Not her baby. Not sweet Mandy.

Bloody cat. Ann wouldn't have bothered with the metal pins and the seven hundred dollars two years ago, but David had bothered. He hadn't blamed the cat for Mandy's death.

So now it was dead, and no metal pin to give it another life.

'Let me do that. You shouldn't be digging.' Dee said.

'I'm fine. Fit as a mallee bull and twice as dangerous today. I've been stuck inside too long. It's nice to feel the wind in my face. With a bit of luck it might blow the rain away tonight. I've had enough of it.'

'It's been a bad time for you. Bad enough to lose a parent without it happening like this. It must be terrible for your mother.'

'Yes.'

'No more news?'

'No. They're checking the DNA. It takes a while.'

Dee knew better than to pursue that subject. They were friends, but not close. Ann, like Ellie, was difficult to get close to. Dee took the shovel when Ann stopped to stretch her back, and in silence they completed the soggy hole and placed the bag in, tucking the edges under before shovelling back red mud.

'Poor little thing. They drive too fast along this road. When we built here, it didn't go anywhere. We need signs, or speed humps.'

'It had a long life.' Longer than Mandy, Ann thought. And it was only a cat, not like when she'd buried old Mickey, her dog. Just a fat, self-satisfied cat that had it all, a safe house, meals all day, a warm bed in the laundry, but it had craved live food to torment and it couldn't get live food in her yard, because when it tried, she'd chased it with a broom, sprayed it with the hose. It had hated her broom, and her hose, spat at her each time she swept the floor, watered the garden.

Greedy things, cats. Cruel cynical eyes that never quite made contact with your own, she thought. Not like dogs. Dogs looked you in the eye, communicated. Honest, honourable people were dogs. Maybe she'd get the boys a pup – get herself a pup.

'Got time for a cup of tea, Dee?' she said, wearied today of her own and the boys' company. Wind and rain had never caged her before she'd had the boys. They caged her; not a lot of walking you could do with tiny ones in tow. It was all very well to play mother earth, populate or perish, but motherhood was wearing. Matthew, barely four, Tristan having a premature run-in with the terrible twos, and David always at work. Only minutes before Dee came knocking at her door, he'd called to tell her his computers had misplaced ten thousand; he'd be late home. Again.

Dee looked at her watch. 'Just a quick one. I'll pick the kids up today.'

'It's my turn.'

'You look worn out. How long have you got to go?'

'A little over six weeks. I'm usually pretty close to time.'

'I shouldn't have let you dig. Have a rest this afternoon. Put your feet up.'

'The doctor's wife giving advice now.'

Dee laughed. 'Live with them long enough and it starts to wear off on you. I've got to do some shopping anyway, so I'll pick the kids up and take them with me.'

They washed their hands in the laundry, and they spoke of the weather and the school and the town; they sipped tea, ate biscuits, kids' biscuits – chocolate teddy bears. At three-fifteen Dee left. She had three children; the last one, Jana, was in Benjamin's class. Frances, the middle man, had been a few months older than Mandy. He was ten. Her oldest was at high school.

Ann walked her neighbour out to the gate, then returned to check on the boys. The one thing these two agreed on was *The Lion King*.

'Best invention since the wheel,' she said as she sat on David's recliner and took her doctor's wife's advice, put her feet up on the footrest. Perhaps she might steal a minute of mind-numbing peace.

From its protective pillowslip Ann took a wedding gown bodice she was beading for some unknown Sydney bride; she unscrewed the lid from a plastic container half-filled with small pearls, then balanced it on the broad arm of the recliner.

It was an intricate design she and her needle worked. She could see what she wanted in her mind's eye and her mind's eye drew the lines before her needle. Ann had always looked on these bridal gowns as therapy; while her hands created, her brain slowed down, put its feet up too. The therapy part wasn't working today, but the panel was almost done when her doorbell rang.

'Damn it,' she said, capping the pearl container, safe from tiny hands. Two small faces peered from the study door, but visitors couldn't compete with undeserved videos.

Two men, two strangers, waited beneath the shelter of the patio. Ann knew who they were without their introductions or ID.

'Mrs Taylor?' She nodded. 'We'd like to ask you a few questions. May we come in?' the tall one said, his foot already inside.

She considered slamming the door on his toe, blaming the wind, but it probably wasn't a good idea. 'It's not a good time,' she said.

'A few minutes only, Mrs Taylor.'

The time has come, the walrus said, to talk of many things –

She sighed as she held the taller man's bloodhound, red-rimmed eyes. Then she stepped back, led the way to the family room and pointed to the chairs. But she stood, so they preferred to stand.

'As you were the last person to see your father alive – '

'Highly unlikely,' she interrupted his opening speech as she packed her sewing into the pillowslip, leaving it on the table with the colouring books and textas and a gumnut bubble pipe.

'If you could tell us again your movements on the night he disappeared, Mrs Taylor.'

'I signed a detailed statement six months after my father left and another one in April when his gun was found.'

'Bear with us. Refresh our memories.' The smaller man's voice was patronising. King Rat, lording it over a guilty mouse.

'I saw him down by the river, not far from Ben's bridge – the footbridge. There was a flash of lightning, a clap of thunder and . . . and I ran for cover.'

The words, repeated too often, sounded flat today, sounded like a lie, and these two men had built-in lie detectors. They weren't interested in flashes of lightning – not now, not with that body in its shallow grave, but they made their scratches on paper, scribbling *liar, liar.*

'In a previous statement you said that you then drove off in your car – to clear your head.'

'That's what I said.'

'It was still raining at the time?'

'Yes.'

'I believe your husband stated that you returned home after four on the following afternoon.'

'And as previously stated, I didn't look at the clock. I had a cup of tea and I went to bed.' Words read from a tattered old script, the actor having lost interest in her role.

'You said, I believe, that on the night in question you drove out the old river road, that your vehicle became bogged near the ten-mile, and that you waited until daylight before attempting to drive out. You did not attempt to walk out.'

'Too much mud to walk.'

'So you sat in your car.'

'Yes.'

'For eight or nine hours. And come daylight, you somehow managed to extricate your vehicle, but you did not return to your home until around four that afternoon. Perhaps you could tell us where you drove – after leaving the river road. Did you continue on to Daree or return to Mallawindy?'

'I continued on to the bitumen then drove blindly. I don't know where I drove. Almost seven years and three children have not improved my memory of that night. I'm sorry.'

'You drove blindly for many hours. From daylight until four p.m.'

'Apparently.'

'So you have no knowledge of where you were between daylight and four p.m?' She shook her head and drew her hair back, pinned it back, and all the while they watched her. 'Your mother stated that you and your father had a heated argument that night, Mrs Taylor.'

'It was one of our bad habits.'

'And your father disappeared shortly afterwards.'

'If you say so.'

'And you spoke to no one for a period of nineteen hours, from around nine-thirty on Christmas Eve to four p.m. the following day. Did you buy petrol, Mrs Taylor?'

'I filled the tank before driving to Mallawindy that night.'

'Where you took possession of your father's briefcase.' She waited, her head to the side. 'Your mother stated that she saw you place it in the boot of your car.'

Her heart rate had increased, disturbing the one in her womb. A future football champion, it kicked back. Ann turned to the sink, stared at a baking dish she'd meant to wash, ran water into it, then she sighed and turned back to the men. 'My mother may have seen me place my briefcase in the boot of my car.'

'She stated that the case she saw belonged to your father.'

'It's difficult to tell one from another.' She shrugged. 'I don't recall having my briefcase with me that night, or putting it in the boot. I may have.'

Both men were watching her as she placed a hand on her stomach to still the movement. Burying the cat may not have been such a good idea. She'd been uncomfortable since she'd made the tea. Pressure beneath her left rib and rolling pummelling on the right. She poured a glass of water and drank it, slowly.

'Did you return to your parents' house that night, Mrs Taylor?'

'Is there a point to that question?' The one in her womb lurched.

The larger man scratched at his armpit. 'Your brother, John Burton – '

'John slept in Mallawindy that night, but his hire car was parked here, on our front lawn, where it remained for three days after my father went missing. Ben drove him up to collect it.'

'So, let me get this clear, if I may, Mrs Taylor. You left the house in Mallawindy around nine-thirty. You did not return to your parents' home that night?'

'I did not. And for the record, I did not conspire with my brother

John to kill my father either, if that's where these questions are leading – and I can think of no other good reason for them.'

It was the wrong attitude, and she knew it. Smartarse answers were not the way to go. She should be playing the humble Ellie, the good housewife/mother. Maybe she should offer them tea, turn off the video, get the boys fighting again. That might get rid of her unwanted visitors.

She walked to the study door, glancing at her boys, away in cartoon land. Small demanding demons had become sweet angels, their wide eyes avid as they stared at the screen. Videos were a treat, and only allowed if they had been good, and they hadn't been good, but they were now. Through the window she saw Dee's car drive in, and children tumble out. Little Ben was growing so tall.

Quietly she closed the door and returned to the detectives. 'If you'll excuse me now, I have to go next door to get my other son.'

The smaller man barred her way. 'One moment more if you please, Mrs Taylor.'

His type always angered her. He reminded her of an old school inspector with his knowing sneer and his sniff, and his sly little eyes.

'Do you still have the briefcase in your possession?'

'I have my own briefcase in my possession. Naturally.'

'We'd like to see it, if we may?'

'Why not?' She walked towards the main bedroom.

'Do you mind if I accompany you, Mrs Taylor?'

'Please yourself. Don't fall over the boys' toys and sue me.'

On her knees in the bedroom she dragged the old black case from beneath the bed she hadn't slept in since Bronwyn's wedding. It wasn't her father's case, but the one she had bought many years ago, because it had looked like her father's. As a child she'd coveted his briefcase with its lock, and its little key. Such a good safe place in which to hide her secrets – as he had hidden his.

The smaller man smiled, pleased with himself. She attempted to walk around him but he reached for the case, and for an instant she felt the urge to give it to him, right in his sneering ratty little mouth, to send him tumbling out the door. Unleash old anger. Feel the satisfying smash of leather against that sneer.

The footballer within saved the moment. It kicked, did a cartwheel. Anger was no good for him.

Control. Think boys. Think David. Take a deep breath. Humility is required here. When a cop pulls you up for speeding, what do you do? As Bron had discovered, you don't tell him where he can put his ticket! Play the game, Annie. Play the pregnant mother. Breathe beneath anger and gain control. And when in doubt, smile.

She flashed her teeth, good teeth, white and strong like her father's, but her eyes were not smiling as she led the way back to the family room.

'Do you have the key, Mrs Taylor?'

'What use a lock without a key?' Her teeth flashing, she handed him her car keys.

'If you wouldn't mind,' he said, and the second man stepped forward to view the contents as she inserted the smallest key into the lock.

Only a bundle of letters addressed to Malcolm Fletcher, his publisher's return address on the envelopes. Only a newsletter from the Authors' Association.

They sifted through the mail, then glanced at her.

'I pick up Mr Fletcher's private mail from his postbox. I have his key.' She offered her key ring, offered the key. 'If he can't get up here to collect his mail, I deliver it when I go to see my mother. I've been doing it for years, since the eighties.'

They were studying the key, studying her as she gestured to the case.

'As the name suggests, it is my own. I've owned it since I was sixteen. I wrote my name on it the day I bought it at a Brunswick opportunity shop.' She pointed to a label on the inside of the lid. Her name was there. *Ann E Burton.* 'Forensic could probably carbon date that biro with as much accuracy as . . . ' Her mouth closed then, she waited, watching them pry.

The taller man picked up an envelope, glanced at it, then at her. 'You are speaking about the elderly fellow, the big – '

'There is only one Malcolm Fletcher in Mallawindy.' She took the envelope, placing it face down.

'You did not see your father's briefcase that night?' The detective's voice no longer sounded so certain.

'My memory of that night is not clear. We had just learned that Liza had been found dead. My mother was upset and confused. Take the case with you. If she saw me put a briefcase into the boot of my car then it must have been this one. You might like to deliver Mr Fletcher's mail while you're about it. It would save the boys and me a trip.'

'You've been very helpful, but perhaps . . . '

She emptied the letters onto the table, offered the case. The smaller man took it. 'If there is nothing else, then I have my son to collect next door.'

'We'll leave you to get on with it, Mrs Taylor,' the larger man said. 'We may need to speak again when we have a positive identification.'

They were out the front door, her hand reaching to close it, when the smaller of the two men turned. 'Your brother, Benjamin Burton, mentioned that your father was one of twins.'

'He was.'

'Identical?'

'Yes.'

'Is the twin brother still living, Mrs Taylor?'

She shrugged. 'Since my father's disappearance we haven't kept in touch.' Again her heart began its hard thump, thump, thump as she waited, her hand on the doorknob.

'The deceased's skull was found intact. An identical twin would have identical bone structure.'

'Of course.'

'Your brother has attempted to phone your uncle at the Narrawee property and at his city residence. He said that you may have their city address.'

'They had a flat in Toorak many years ago. I don't know if they still own it.' She gave them the street name, and the number, and the phone number she'd given to Ben.

'Samuel and May Burton?'

'That's correct.'

'When were you last in contact with them, Mrs Taylor?'

'Four, five years ago.'

They left, and as Ann returned to the family room, her hands were trembling. The police may not be able to trace Sam Burton, but it would surely be simple enough to trace his dental records. And find identical fillings, root canal work on the left eyetooth.

'Oh God,' she said. 'It's not over, Aunty May. You're going to be drawn into it too. You've got to be told what is going on up here.'

the lion king

~

Ann bathed the three boys at five, readying them for bed. She fed them baked beans and stewed apples at six then rewound *The Lion King* and set it to play again, because Benjamin wanted to see it right through. There was no argument. They never tired of it, and tonight she allowed it to buy peace. Too weary to sew, her hands were not her own tonight. Small pearls jumped from her needle, trembled to the floor to become lost on the tiles. Her back didn't feel up to searching for them.

After Ben's phone call yesterday, and his mention of her father's briefcase, she had emptied her own, removing her childhood treasures, her scribbled poems, packing them into a carton. Then last night, unable to sleep, she'd crawled from Mandy's bed and taken the carton down to the incinerator, setting a match to one aging page, watching it burn while slowly feeding the fire with the other pages.

She saved the gumnut bubble pipe Johnny had made for her seventh birthday. It had amused Matthew and Tristan for an hour this afternoon and the wind-up mouse that had long ago forgotten how to dance had been placed in their toy-box. An old handkerchief from Narrawee, her initials embroidered on its corner in blue, she had tossed into the washing machine. Mickey's bloodstained dog collar had been hung on a hook in the garden shed.

Perhaps one day she'd regret her dawn burning, but her childhood poems were gone now, their ashes blown away. Just yesterday's dust blowing on the wind.

Only this morning she had placed Malcolm's mail in the case. The idea had come to her when he'd called to say he'd be down on Sunday, with Ben. Thank God for him. Thank God for Ben. They had been her saviours.

Stress was eating her, fist-clenching stress that refused her sleep. She couldn't continue on without sleep, couldn't keep on walking the house at night as she had done since Bron's wedding. She needed sleep and the baby inside her needed her to sleep and David wanted her to sleep in his bed. He didn't understand.

But she couldn't do it. She knew she still spoke in her sleep – or little Annie still spoke. Stress always brought on the old dreams of the cellar. These days, she attempted to avoid stress, but since they'd found the body, stress and the dreams had returned.

No thought had been given to future consequences when she'd told her father to run that Christmas Eve. A moment of madness. A moment of pity.

'Mainly madness,' she admitted.

But that night it had seemed like the answer for everyone. Get him away from Johnny, get him out of Mallawindy, get him home to May. Give him a second chance.

He'd spent half of his life away, and he'd had a perfect excuse to take off on a drinking binge. His Liza, his golden treasure's bones, had been found beneath a rose bush at Narrawee. She'd told no one, other than Johnny, of her night drive. Had to tell him.

Poor Johnny, he'd been a seven-day wonder in Mallawindy, then everyone had returned to their own lives and Johnny had discovered there was nothing to return to. He shouldn't have left the church. He was not equipped for reality. Life was hard. Life was cruel out here in the real world.

Ellie had liked the idea of a priest son. Perhaps his leaving the church had been one of her greater disappointments. Ann had been

Johnny's greatest disappointment, and she knew it. Not much she could do about it. He'd driven down to the inquest. Ann had sighted him in the street, but not in the courthouse. Perhaps he'd planned to expose Jack Burton, or dispose of him. But he hadn't.

Not that day.

She shivered, shook her head. A priest, an ex-priest, could not bring himself to kill.

But he'd killed rabbits as a twelve year old. She'd watched him wring their necks. She'd watched him cut the heads off flapping fish, behead roosters with the wood axe. And he'd sworn to do it. He'd picked up Ellie's old black Bible on the day he had run.

If I ever set eyes on him again, I'll kill him, Mum. I promise you.

Johnny had always kept his promises.

Had her father returned to Mallawindy after he'd left May five years ago? Had he gone to the old house, found Johnny there alone? Had Johnny been devious enough to bury him close to an old enemy's property?

No. That wasn't the way her brother's mind worked. He would have gone straight to the police.

But did she know her brother these days?

The baby within rolled and her hand went to soothe it.

Since the inquest, the past had remained the past. Was it six years ago? Six years lost in babies, one after the other. She'd thrown herself headlong into motherhood. There was safety in numbers – safety in the camouflage net of motherhood. Little thought had gone into Matthew's and Tristan's conceptions. They had come and been welcomed. Now this one. It would be the last

Until the teacher's wife had gone missing, until they'd found the shotgun in the river, she'd kept her father and May in a padlocked compartment of her mind and refused to go there, refused to think of them, speak of them. Now the padlock was off and the compartment lid wide open, and she was back to lies and the old cover-up.

Lies were like rats in a crowded cage, nothing to do bar breed and bite.

Too much stress, and the boys respond to her stress by adding more. Stuck with them, within four walls, day and night, and that old wanting-to-run feeling had come back.

If she had told David where she'd driven to that Christmas Eve, she would have had his support now. She hadn't told him. And how could she have told him, unless she'd told him the whole story? And he couldn't lie to save his own life.

Couldn't tell him. Not then. Not now. Not ever. And the old invisible wall was back between them. She hated it, but couldn't tear it down.

Not yet.

If only Amy O'Rouke hadn't walked away then the gun might never have been found. If only the couple had decided to camp somewhere else, walk their dog in a different direction that night. If their dog had been on a leash then he wouldn't have found the grave.

Fate, or Ellie's God, had had a hand in this one. No one was safe from fate and Ellie's God.

Just have to keep on telling the same story, that's all – until Johnny cracks. And he will soon, and when he does he'll go off with a bang, she thought. He's built himself in with his invisible wall, it's wrapped him, trapped him, and it's so filled with that lie it has forced out the gentle Johnny of my childhood.

'I still love him. Or do I love only the memory of who he was?'

Tension in her head. Tension crawling in her neck. She shrugged her shoulders, stretched, turned her head from side to side.

The murdered required a murderer. That was the problem. She fitted the bill nicely. Missing for nineteen hours, and couldn't tell anyone where she had driven in those hours. Still, unless she'd had access to a block and tackle, she could not have disposed of a body. Obviously.

So who had assisted her?

Johnny. Obviously.

The police had made no accusations, but let them identify the body and they'd be back for their nice neat ending. They were not going to get it. She had no intention of volunteering for the position of the accused. She'd tell them the truth if it came to that. But having lied initially, was it likely that they'd believe her if she told them the truth now, told them she'd driven her father to Toorak that Christmas Eve? Probably not.

Would May back up her story? Almost certainly – and she'd end up in jail for her part in concealing the deaths of Liza and Sam.

'Oh, what a tangled web we weave when first we practise to deceive. I was too young, Annie. I didn't know.'

They had been clever, her father and May. Devious. They'd thought well ahead. Her father had never gone to a local dentist; always he'd driven to Melbourne, playing Sam at the dental clinic. His reputation as a drinker, his long-suffering wife in Mallawindy. And May Burton, strong-willed, independent pillar of Narrawee society with her gadabout teetotaller husband, Sam. Even the clothing they wore. Sam's jeans and sneakers, his long greying hair and moustache. Jack, the clean-shaven insurance salesman, well dressed, black socks, black leather shoes, black dyed hair. So different.

There had been no DNA tests when Sam's bones had been found in the sand dunes almost thirty years ago. No teeth to identify him.

Do they keep unidentified bones? she thought. What if they'd kept Sam's bones, and just happened to check the DNA, discover it was a perfect match for –

'Stop it,' she said. 'Stop it.' Repeating the words, she walked the room, shrugging her shoulders, stretching aching muscles.

Luck of the devil had led her and Johnny out to Dead Man's Lane that day. Luck or the devil had allowed her to find Sam's onyx ring, like a black and gold flower growing on a reed only a metre from where Johnny had found Sam's well-burned bones. Johnny had recognised the ring and he'd remembered his father scrubbing the boot of his car the day Liza was reported as missing. He'd remembered the smell of early decay.

What did you have in there, Dad?

A bloody mongrel dog.

A fitting description of twin brother Sam. Johnny had heard it many times, and if he hadn't understood that day, almost two years later, almost two years older, he had understood. He'd recognised the ring with its shoulder diamonds, and he'd read the inscription inside the ring. *Sam and May 1953*. How had Sam Burton's ring found its way to the sand dunes?

'Oh God, stop this!'

But her mind had slipped into overdrive, as had the one in her womb.

Shouldn't have buried the cat. Should have let Dee take him to the vet, let him do whatever they do with dead cats. Mass grave. Mass cremation.

Small bones in the garden now. One day she'd be digging, or David would be digging, and up would come Tiddy's skeleton.

Or maybe it wouldn't.

Shouldn't have buried it in plastic. Might stop it breaking down. The hole hadn't been very deep either. What happens to dead cats sealed in plastic when plastic doesn't break down? Cat intactus? Cat sludge?

'Do something. Wash the baking dish. Wash the floor.' But her back and the footballer didn't feel like work so she sat, her feet up, while from the study came the familiar *Lion King* soundtrack. She listened a moment and knew exactly how much time she had left to sit and think.

David would miss the cat. He had fed it, let it sit on his lap late at night while it purred its brains out. David's cat, after Mandy. It didn't – hadn't – liked the boys, hid from them, spat at them. Fat, spitting old cat.

And she was up again. Time enough for a fast shower before the video ended. She chose clean jeans and a shirt, then stood long in the shower, allowing the hot water to rain on her back, on her neck. She washed her hair too, towelled and combed it. It would dry wild, but she had no energy to blow-wave it tame tonight.

Late now. Where had the day gone? Gone where all of her days had gone since Saturday. No Bronwyn to pop in for coffee and a stolen smoke. She missed her sister. Six years between them but they were friends more than sisters. Bron's world had turned upside down. Poor Bron, she was unaccustomed to an upside-down world.

'We got used to it early, Annie.'

Standing then before the framed photograph of Mandy, her vision blurred. This was all she had left of her precious baby. A photograph. Golden hair, David's ocean-blue eyes and that mischievous smile that crushed her heart.

Mongrel, murdering cat.

Quickly then she walked away from it to the fridge where she opened the freezer, seeking something fast for dinner. Frozen steak. Frozen chicken. Frozen peas. She opened the lower door, certain she'd saved some chicken casserole. No casserole. A half tin of cat food. She took it out, tossed it into the kitchen tidy. Plenty of eggs. Ben still kept her supplied with eggs. A couple of rashers of bacon left. Beer and a half bottle of red wine.

The wine took her mind to Johnny and Bron's wedding. Wine had always made Ann happy, but it hadn't made her brother happy. The cork eased out, she tasted it, straight from the bottle.

Sour.

She forced down another mouthful, then a third.

'Mummy, *The Lion King* is finished and Tristan is asleep and Matthew is nearly asleep too.'

'We'll tiptoe them into bed.'

She carried the sleeping one to his cot and kissed his face, petulant in sleep. He had copped a few of his grandfather's genes. The line would continue. She tucked Matthew in with a kiss, and thought of his paternal grandfather, a gentle old man. She chatted a while to Benjamin, dark hair, dark eyes, but David's mouth and his smile. A beautiful boy. It was easier to give him his full name. He was the biggest. These days he didn't like being called Little Ben.

'When is Daddy coming?'

'He's going to be late tonight. He'll creep in and give you a kiss on the nose when he comes, and I bet you sneeze.' Benjamin giggled as she kissed his nose, and he made three mock sneezes. 'Bye-bye now, my handsome one. Sleep tight.' No stories tonight. They'd had their dose of *Lion King* violence and happily ever afters.

Back in the family room she poured a glass of wine, sipping it while staring at the old gumnut bubble pipe. Then her hand reached for it and she smiled at the memory of a young Johnny.

She had watched him make this bubble pipe. He'd hollowed out the gumnut and cut a hole for the reed stem with his pocket knife, then he'd filled the gumnut bowl with softened soap. Bubbles unlimited. Just add river water. Huge bubbles, purple and blue and gold, shaken from that pipe to fly away.

He'd taken her everywhere with him – to town when he delivered the eggs, to the forest when he'd set his rabbit traps, to the sand dunes when he'd gone there with Malcolm Fletcher's son. Johnny had been her teacher, his blackboard the dust, his chalk a twig scratching in the dust, and his hands, signing, talking hands. She'd had no one else to give her love to, so she'd loved him. But he'd come back to her a paper cut-out, his well-known features pasted over with a stranger's expressions.

At least he'd been real on the night of the wedding. Not so pleasant, but real, and very, very familiar.

She yawned, stretched her limbs. Maybe the wine was hitting some spot.

'Perhaps there comes a time when we all have to submit to our own genetic code, Little Annie, like it or not,' she said, and she forced down half a glass of sour wine.

grievous intent

~

Johnny Burton's week had been long, and it was only half over. Last evening emotionally draining, a migraine had threatened all morning, then hit hard mid-afternoon. At the moment it was taking precedence over his aching foot. He was supposed to keep the foot up, stay off it; he'd spent most of the day on it. Immobility led to thinking, the one thing that stopped his thinking was a book, but his aching head refused him this escape.

No more painkillers left in his packet. He'd swallowed too many in the last few days. No post holes to dig by torchlight, no seven-kilometre hikes through the forest. No peace at the mud brick house, so at seven-thirty he picked up his crutches and limped across Ben's bridge to the old house. It offered him silence and solitude in which to nurse his headache.

Much of the furniture had been left behind when Ellie had moved in with Ben six years ago. The battered old table was still in the kitchen with the old sideboard and the worn-out chairs, but the lounge room was empty, its unworn suite now cluttering Ben's tiny lounge room.

He had a choice of three sagging beds, one in the boys' room and two in the girls'. Those rooms had been wallpapered in some forgotten era. It was aged and brown now; one day he'd strip the wallpaper – but not tonight. The front bedroom was empty, apart from an old wardrobe. Ellie had taken her dressing table with her, and her bed, near new, expensive. Jack Burton had liked his comfort.

John often spent the night in the old house. He had accumulated a small stock of supplies in the bruised refrigerator; he had tea bags and coffee on the sideboard, sugar in a jam jar on the table. He lit the old wood stove, and within minutes it was throwing out its heat and the old black kettle began to sing its way to boiling. Same old black kettle, same old dented lid, same old battered frypan on the hob; it would still fry an egg. No one bothered him here, no one talked at him, forced him to find and make replies. No television choking him with canned laughter while Ellie sat blindly staring at it.

He leaned on the kitchen table, his eyes scanning the unlined walls. Scarred. He glanced at the cupboards with their red-checked gingham doors. The wooden doors of his youth had long been kicked in. Ellie had replaced them with fabric supported on elastic. Elastic stretched. Fabric gave.

A pot of tea made, he looked in the fridge for his bread. No butter but plenty of bacon grease. He smiled, remembering fried bread. After the nausea of a migraine passed, his stomach always demanded food, so he broke an egg onto a flat plate, beat it with a fork then dipped his stale bread in it. The bacon grease sizzling, he placed the egg-soaked slices in the pan and stood over it, cooking supper. French toast, topped with plum jam; they'd eaten it often when he was a kid. No money then, only a few cows, but Ellie had always produced a tasty meal.

He was eating the last crust when he heard the car pull into the yard and he wasn't fast enough on his feet to kill the lights. They came then, the long and the short detectives, approaching the kitchen from opposite directions. One to the eastern door, one to the northern.

'The doors are open,' he called.

Seated close to the stove he didn't rise when they entered. They

144

sat each end of the table, and they watched his every move and he watched the kettle, full of huffing, puffing steam, like his visitors.

He heard but didn't listen, until the smaller one said, 'Your father, did he own a handgun, Mr Burton?'

John picked up a crust, chewed it, then brushed crumbs from the sleeve of his navy windcheater, his eyes following the navy blue down to green drill working trousers, to his one muddy shoe and to his plaster foot, protected tonight by a thick sock and a plastic bag and his soiled hospital-issue cotton shoe. He stared at it.

'I have no idea what he had or didn't have.'

'If you could tell us your movements on the night in question, Mr Burton.'

John pressed his fingertips to both temples. 'My movements on that night were well documented when the shotgun was found.'

'We would appreciate your cooperation.'

He looked from one face to the other, and he smiled. 'I don't envy you your job. Wouldn't get to watch much television, I take it. And the boredom, the abject boredom of repetition. How many times do you cover the same ground?'

'As many times as is necessary to get to the truth, Mr Burton.'

'But the truth does not alter with each telling, sir. Truth remains the only constant. I can repeat my truth for you, but it will add little to your knowledge and considerably to my headache. Not a migraine sufferer, are you?'

'No, thankfully, Mr Burton. Now, you arrived home after your father and sister left the house that night.'

'I did.'

'You did not speak to your father that evening?'

'As I did not see him, I was unable to speak to him. You appear to believe that he died the night I returned to Mallawindy.'

'At this time we believe the body has been there for between five and ten years.'

'So, working on the assumption that he died that night makes me a convenient suspect.'

They did not deny his words. His head back, he looked at the smoke-blackened rafters while blood hammered in his temples and beat behind his eyes, then he stood, stumbled, leaning heavily on the wall as he walked to the stove where he picked up the old iron poker, weighing it in his hand. Bent, aged thing, black, he opened the firebox and with the poker stirred the coals, added more wood from the hearth before closing the firebox with that old lift and slam action, unchanged in thirty years.

The silence was new, and too complete. Not a cow in the distance. Not a dog barking across the river. They were waiting for his confession. It was a long time since he'd made his last confession.

Bless me, Father, for I have sinned.

As the smaller man stood, John turned to him, offering the old poker, pushing it at him. 'I used this on him one night. Knocked him out. Swung it like a golf club and got him over the right ear. Flattened him. He fell there, right at your feet.'

The monotonous computer voice of justice began, and John listened, a smile growing until the rendition ended.

'I was a few months shy of sixteen at the time and had planned my father's murder in great detail. I was an imaginative youth. The plan was to wait until he was seated. He should be seated. He was so much bigger, heavier than me. I was then to pick up this poker and use it to crush his diseased brain, smash it to pulp. The plan that year was to load him into my mother's laundry copper and boil him up for pig food. Pigs aren't particular. They'll eat anything. I was then to rake up his bones and pulverise them, toss them into the river. However . . . however, my mother would not allow it at the time.' Again he pushed the poker towards the smaller man. 'But do take it. Please. My intent to do grievous bodily harm is etched deep into its metal.'

The detective took the poker as he stared at the madman who stood before him, smiling, massaging his temples.

'There is a wrongness about this business, Mr Burton.'

'The wrongness you perceive, sir, is perhaps my total lack of interest in the whereabouts of a rabid dog who should have been put down thirty years ago. As stated before, I have not sighted him in thirty years, and should I happen to sight him in the next thirty, he may yet end up as pig slops. Arrest me for an unrealised dream, if you wish.'

They had no reply. Their suspect was limping by them, collecting his crutches from beside the old wireless where his father's gun had once lived. He leaned on the padded armrests as he spoke again. 'I suggest you speak to May Burton, his sister-in-law. She knew my father well.'

'His sister-in-law. Your sister, Mrs Taylor, mentioned a flat in Toorak.'

John lifted his head, turned to face the west. 'My sister, Mrs Taylor. Well, I suggest that you contact the flat in Toorak. I can state for a fact that my father was with May Burton in early '91. If she denies it, she lies.'

They made way for him as he swung by them and out onto the dark verandah, but they followed him.

He turned, leaned again on one crutch and looked down at his plaster foot swinging there. 'One more suggestion, if I may. Ask her for the name of her husband's dentist. It could prove . . . interesting.

'Can you enlarge on that, Mr Burton?'

John ignored the question. He made his clumsy way along the verandah, down two steps, and away into the night.

'We will need to speak to you again.'

From the dark John replied, 'Never fear, I will be here. I can't run at the moment and have nowhere to run to – should I feel the urge. Have a nice evening and turn the light out when you leave. Good night.'

where is the butter

~

'Sour vinegar,' Ann commented, draining the last of the red wine into her glass, drinking it down as medicine. 'And fly spray,' she added, her mind straying south to Mallawindy, to the eternal fly spray, to the flies by day and the mosquitoes by night and the frogs along the river who had feasted on flies and mosquitoes doused in fly spray.

And she thought of the one now limping towards the river, his crutches sinking in the mud. For a fleeting instant their minds connected.

'What happens if they charge us with his murder?'

Johnny Burton halted his progress, his eyes turned towards the west, and he saw her at the kitchen sink, a glass in her hand.

Ann placed the glass down and turned her face to Mallawindy, seeing him in silhouette against Ben's bridge.

Then the line was cut and two minds wandered away down separate roads.

'Innocent people are charged, jailed. Look at . . . look at . . . ' No example presented itself, so her mind flitted away to her briefcase. A flitting mind now. Better. Much better.

'You can fool all of the people some of the time, and some of the people all of the time, but you can't fool all of the people all of the time, Annie. Sooner or later, you get found out. But Mum will think it was my briefcase she saw. She didn't see me take it from the wardrobe. Saw me in the room, that's all. David believed me when I said I got bogged.'

She had been bogged out near the ten-mile. Bogged to the axles that night. Her father had dragged small logs from the forest to place beneath her wheels, and he'd pushed the car, pushed it while the wheels slid and skidded, his desire to get away lending him strength that night.

A cramp stilled her thinking. She felt her stomach, her palm searching the lumps, the bumps there.

Little Annie Burton, elective mute for seven years. How had she got to this day, this night? How had little Annie Burton become the wife of David Taylor, the bank manager? How had she become friend and neighbour of Dee and Peter Williams? How had poor little Annie Burton become mother of three raucous boys, president of the kindergarten committee?

'How did it happen, Annie?' she said. Again the baby kicked. 'Mother of almost four.'

More dirty napkins come September and she'd barely started introducing Tristan to the potty. It would be another boy – he'd looked the same on the scan, but as usual she'd told Peter Williams she didn't want to know the sex. Didn't want it to be a girl, that's why. Didn't want to carry it, live these last months not wanting it, not wanting its little dresses to replace the memory of Mandy's little dresses.

The wine had gone directly to her head, opening up old pathways she usually blocked with red road signs. *Wrong way. Go back.* All the road signs were down, the pathways open. She let the tears roll. No one to see her. Boys sleeping. David trying to locate his missing money. And why shouldn't she cry for precious, perfect Mandy? While she had lived, each day had been a wondrous thing. Life had reached forward into ten thousand perfect tomorrows. But she was gone. And now her cat was gone. And all of little Annie's poems, written over another lifetime, were gone. All of those yesterdays, used up, worn out.

Boy Johnny gone.

Little Annie gone.

Jack Burton gone.

She sniffed, hiccupped. Everything was gone, including the fly spray wine. Didn't like red wine, even the best of it, and this bottle hadn't been much good when David had opened it last night. He knew what wine did to her. It made her giggle, made her forget; it wasn't working tonight.

There was a dribble in the glass. Ruby red. 'A pretty wine.' She smelt it, sipped it, then wiped at her eyes with her sleeve.

Blood red were his spurs in the golden morn, wine red was his claret coat.

Blood red. Mandy's blood that murderous day. She had picked her up at the bottom of the steps, ready to kiss a little hurt better. Just grazed, blood on her hair. She hadn't known that the hurt had gone much deeper. Maybe she shouldn't have picked her up. Should have left her there, called Dee, called the ambulance. Maybe it was her fault that Mandy had died.

Gone. Just like that. One second laughing in the hot sun, chasing the cat, then . . . then gone.

Her palms wiped at her face, and her fingers ran through her hair. Still damp. She glanced at the heater, walked to it and turned it high, then she closed the heavy drapes and walked out to the back door. Cold and dark outside but no more rain. Stars trying to get out. Cold, wet earth and the night wind moaning in the wires, slapping at walls. A mournful sound. A door bang-banging somewhere. Probably the garden shed. She must have left it open when she'd gone in to get the pick and shovel.

Poor Tiddy in the mud in its plastic garbage bag.

She walked out to the yard where she slammed the shed door then continued up to the gate, flinging it wide for David, wanting him home, wanting to talk about something other than videos and bubble pipes and potties. He shouldn't be too much longer. She opened the garage door too, willing him home, and she stood a moment watching the road, the wind whipping her damp hair, tying it in knots.

No David.

There was a small door at the rear of the garage, giving access to a wine cellar David had dug into the clay beneath the house. No light in there but she knew where he kept his white wines. She chose the nearest bottle then climbed the spiral staircase to the family room.

No time to wipe the dust away, she eased the cork out, poured a glass, brimful. It went down fast, washing away the aftertaste of vinegar and fly spray. It wasn't bad either, not sweet, but not too dry. David liked wine and she didn't mind the taste of this one. 'Definitely fruity,' she said, half filling her glass before looking at the label. It was probably one of his good wines. Not that her palate could tell good wine from the not so good. Its main purpose was to follow the red wine straight to her head, straight to where she needed it to go tonight. A little wine might open up old pathways but a lot of wine would smooth out the old potholes with fuzzy pink dust.

'Will the world ever get back to semi-normal, Annie?' she asked.

Little Annie never replied these days. She'd taken off that Christmas Eve, left her shell to calcify or blow away.

'I didn't blow away, did I, because I refuse to blow away. I'll get through this too – one way or another – plenty more wine down there.'

Will Johnny get through it?

'I wasted years of my life waiting for him to come home, spent years searching for him, and now he's here and he's a stranger. Siblings who don't grow together have only blood to hold them, and what's blood, little Annie? It's spillable, that's what it is. And stop waving your wine around or you'll spill it too, and stop talking to yourself or the boys will hear you.'

She sipped again, mind-travelling to Johnny and to Mallawindy as she spoke on to Annie or her wine. Happy medicine. It hadn't made Johnny happy at the wedding but Ben said it had made him sing all the way home that night.

'I wonder if he's still singing?'

She looked at the telephone and thought to ring him, invite him down for a drink. She could be stuck here alone until midnight.

'I was once, Annie, and the computers had only misplaced a thousand or two that night.'

Then just like that, the glass was down and the phone was up and she pressed number one for Ben.

Four rings only, then, 'G'day,' Ben said.

'Head loony returning your call from Bedlam, Mr Burton,' she said. 'All is now quiet in ward ten. How is your ward . . . or is it wards?'

'Quiet.'

They spoke a while of inconsequential things, but that was what friends did, they spoke of nothing that became something, and when they'd filled ten minutes with the boys and the shop and Malcolm's lost licence, she said to him, 'Is Mum okay?'

'Better,' he said, which meant Ellie was listening in. No gain in pursuing that subject.

'How's Johnny?'

'He's got a headache, which is pretty much normal.'

'Ask him if he'd like to come down for a drink.'

'I think he's had enough driving for a few days. Tried to drive my ute yesterday but didn't get far. God knows how he got it home. The clutch is heavy as lead.'

'Then I'll just talk to him.'

'I don't think he's around. I'll have a look,' Ben said, and the line went dead. Ben the quiet, reliable brother; he hadn't run away.

It did no good to run away. It never worked – not for long. In the end all runners had to return, to go back for the self they'd left cowering behind in some dark corner and try to bring it back with them to the now. She drank again while she waited.

'He's disappeared somewhere, Annie. Probably over at the old place.'

'I wouldn't like to tackle that bridge with crutches. No insult intended.'

'Yeah. It could do with a rail and some new boards. Do you want him to call you when he gets in?'

'No. He probably won't anyway. Just tell him that I've been thinking about him. I found my old gumnut bubble pipe today and the boys have placed their orders for two more.'

'I've got plastic ones at the shop.'

'They've been through their plastic era. Anything old is new again, you know.'

'Oh, speaking of old. Remember the wild red poppies we used to find in the top paddock? He found one.'

'A wild poppy? Johnny?'

'In the far paddock where the pigs used to be.'

'How did it survive the pigs?'

'I don't know.'

'Did he build a fence around it, Benjie?'

'Yeah. Covered it with chicken wire too.'

'I thought they'd disappeared off the face of the planet.' Tears misted her eyes and she picked up her glass, emptied it fast, refilled it. 'But they haven't, have they?'

'Nope. It's got more buds too. I had a look at it this morning.'

'And they'll live to seed, Ben, and there will be wild red poppies there next year, and all the years of our lives. And one day soon, things are going to be fine again. They will be.' The tears were trickling again so she tossed the wine down, then sat down. That last half glass had hit the right spot. Her shoulders had relaxed first, now every muscle in her body was taking the hint.

'Are you okay? You sound a bit . . . a bit weird.'

'I'm fine. I'm really very fine now. I'm also very drunk, Ben, so I'd better go.'

'Who are you drinking with?'

'Just me and little Annie. Give Johnny my love, but take seventy-five per cent of it for yourself.' That silenced him. He wasn't accustomed to declarations of love, but she did love him and she'd never told him, and what if she died tomorrow of a hangover and never got to tell him? 'And tell him we're glad about the poppy, and even gladder about the fence, but now we've found the guts to make another call. Bye, Ben.'

She disconnected with a finger, then dialled again and got a Telstra recorded message. She listened, frowned. She used to know that number. Used to ring it often. It took four attempts to get it right. It took a call to directory assistance, but when the phone finally began ringing, she knew it was the right number. It had that rich, Toorak, well-fed cat purr. Wide-eyed she waited, her glass in her hand. What was she going to say to May?

No one answering. The phone rang out and she was left listening to the beeps. No answering machine there. She shrugged and dialled the Narrawee number.

Ringing. Ringing. Five. Six. Seven. Eight. Then the ringing stopped.

'May Burton speaking.'

Ann swallowed hard, poured more wine, suddenly sober and not liking it.

'Hello. Is there anyone there?'

'It's . . . it's Ann. I was sitting here, thinking of you, and . . . and I thought I should let you know – '

Then she heard him.

She heard him!

What did you do with the bloody butter I tossed in that trolley, May?

is dad there

~

It was him! Ann's womb lurched, and the words she'd planned to speak scattered as her ears strained, but in Narrawee a hand had covered the phone.

Then May spoke again. 'Ann. Is it really you, sweetheart?'

Nothing she could say to sweetheart. Her heartbeat swimming in wine, her head swimming in wine. Silence.

Then, 'Is Dad there, Aunty May?'

'Yes. Yes, he is, dear. I'll get him for you.'

Just like that.

A muttering of two voices; a long muttering while Ann held the phone pressed hard against her ear, straining to hear every breath, every murmur. Cold now, freezing cold; and his voice was on the line and she grew colder still. Shivering, shuddering cold. Mind-numbing cold.

'What is it?' he said.

'Why didn't I know? I should have known.'

Silence on the other end of the line. Then, 'Have they identified me yet?'

Humorous bastard, but she wasn't in the mood for humour. Her heart was hammering and the one in her womb was pressing down, down, down. Her hand shaking, she lifted the glass, gaining courage from it, and she gained enough.

'Just thought you might like to know that I have absolutely – absolutely – no intention of being charged with your murder.' No reply to that so she spoke on, choosing her words carefully, speaking them slowly. Concentrating. 'So, you would be well advised . . . to do whatever you can do to end this little farce. Or . . . or the other little farce will end right here.' She waited for a reply, but heard only his breathing. 'So, that's it. That's all. I hope you find your butter. Goodnight.'

And she hung up. And she shook, and her heart beat in her head and throat and stomach. And her glass was empty and she tried to sip directly from the bottle. It connected hard with her front teeth.

'Shit!' Her tongue checked for breakages. No cracks, no chips, thank God. Bron had paid over a thousand dollars to have a broken tooth capped and fate had thrown in an abscess and a pregnancy.

Is Dad there? It had sounded so normal. Is Dad there? She looked at the bottle. It was half full, or half empty, so she poured more into her glass, which made the bottle two-thirds empty. She drank again. Shivered. Cold. Freezing.

But oddly relieved.

He was alive.

'Is Dad there?'

Normal people said those words every day, but she had never said them before because she wasn't normal. Never had been. Mother, wife and kindergarten president. All abnormal.

'Is Dad there?' She glanced at the closed doors, at the windows. What if the ratty little cop was hiding outside? What if they'd planted a bug and they'd been listening in?

'I've blown his cover.'

So they weren't his bones. So whose bones were they?

So what did it matter? They were not his. It altered everything. He wasn't dead. He wasn't a skull with a bullet hole through it, wasn't old bones bleached white in a shallow grave.

Huge absurd relief. And her bladder near bursting.

Her fingers gaining support from the wall she walked to the

bathroom, then returned the same way, feeling better now, very inebriated but better.

'Why do I feel so . . . so relieved? Because Johnny didn't kill him? Not that I thought he had, Annie, but I thought he might have.'

She laughed then, her fingers checking out the underside of the table, her eyes scanning the room for a bug. Or maybe they'd put one inside her phone, while she was getting the briefcase. That's what they did in the movies. One cop stayed with the guilty party while the other one planted the bug. Eyes circled the room, looking for a bug.

'Don't know what a bug looks like, so I don't know what I'm looking for, so it's not much use looking for it, is it? Why do they call them bugs? Because they look like bugs, like flies on the wall? No flies tonight. Ah, but a daddy-longlegs spider in the corner.'

It was moving too, so it was no bug, unless it had electronics in its legs.

She sipped from the glass and giggled into her wine, blew bubbles there, continuing to force a little down, sipping and giggling until she heard the car drive into the garage. Then she tried to kill the giggle, to find lost self-control, but the world suddenly seemed to be a very funny place.

Such a huge relief. She needed to tell someone. Crazy.

She wanted to phone Johnny and tell him. He was the only one she could tell. Couldn't tell Ben. Couldn't tell David. No one she could tell. That was the worst bit, no one to celebrate with – except Johnny.

Celebrate? Johnny wouldn't want to celebrate.

Weird stuff going on inside her tonight. 'Admit it,' she said. 'You didn't want him to be dead, because if he was dead, then something . . . something would be lost, and no chance ever to find it. Admit it.'

Crazy. Too much wine. Too many old potholes smoothed out on those old roads. Head full of dust.

What do I tell David? Oh, by the way, the cat is dead but Dad is not. Or, the cops were here today looking for Dad's briefcase, so I gave him a call. Or the other way around. By the way, the cops were here today and the cat is dead.

I can't tell him that Dad is not dead, because it was Sam who I spoke to tonight. So, Dad is still dead, but Sam is not – even if it is the other way around. Except Sam wasn't ever supposed to be dead.

I'll have to ring Johnny. Have to let it out to someone or my head will spin off its cogs. She looked at the phone, stood, but the ceiling moved so she sat down again. Tomorrow. First thing tomorrow. I'll do it face to face, drive down and see him, and see my wild red poppy. Tomorrow. First thing in the morning.

'Is Dad there?'

She'd never spoken to her father on the telephone. Never. Not once. He had a nice voice, from a distance.

'I had to wait until he was dead before I got to hear his nice telephone voice,' she told her wineglass. 'There's something symbolic about that.'

Then David's footsteps were walking up from the garage so she swallowed her smile with a gulp of wine as she looked at the door, and when he opened it, she nodded, very seriously, while her eyes laughed on.

He kissed her cheek, seeing the laughter, seeing the bottle, and knowing where the laughter had been born. 'What's the celebration?'

Valiantly she composed her mind as she attempted to coerce numb lips into forming controlled speech. 'Did you find . . . the money?'

'It wasn't money. Just a figure, and we found it. Someone hits a wrong button and all hell breaks loose. The boys are asleep?'

'Hours ago.' Head down, she watched the table, watched the light moving on table and bottle as David moved around the room.

What do I tell him first? The cops, the cat or the case? Forget the call. She swallowed a giggle but it bubbled up with a wine burp.

'Excuse me! Did you . . . eat, David?'

'No time.' He glanced at his chair, no cat sleeping there. 'Where's Tiddy?'

'Dead,' she said, and the giggle exploded. He looked at her, not believing. She tried to stand, to explain. Couldn't make it to her feet. 'I'm sorry. I'm really very sorry. It's just . . . just, what is dead somehow got mixed up with what isn't. It's just – oh God, I'm so sorry for laughing, David.'

He waited until the laughter subsided before trying again. 'Is the cat dead?'

'Yes. It is. A car. Dee found it. It's buried. Down the back. In a plastic bag and I don't think I should have put him in a plastic bag. Non-biodegradable.' But all control was lost. Too much wine, the red and the white warring, had turned both stomach and her world a rosy pink.

He stood before her, not amused. 'What have you been up to tonight?' No reply. 'You've had enough wine, I know that much.' He reached for the bottle, but her reflexes were still good enough. She snatched the bottle, holding it behind her as she stood. 'Have you eaten anything, Ann?'

'I said that first.'

He sighed, took off his jacket and adjusted the heating. The bottle in hand, she walked to the refrigerator, where she selected two eggs, brown ones. She'd always liked the brown ones the best.

'It's like an oven in here,' he said.

'My hair was wet,' she explained, trying to close the refrigerator with her shoulder. The two eggs, balanced in one hand, toppled off, smashed onto the floor.

'Sit down. You're a disaster area. Sit, Ann. I'll do it.' He tried to take the bottle from her hand. She held on tight to the neck but allowed him to guide her around the broken eggs to her chair, to sit her down. 'What brought this on?'

'Just the phoney old world.' *Phone* set her giggling. She watched him clean up the spilled eggs with paper towels while she poured more wine into her glass.

'That's one of the Chardonnays. Did you drink the entire bottle?'

'No, I left the bottle. Fill it up from a cask. Give it to Bob and Enid next time they invite themselves to dinner. They won't know the difference.'

'Ann Taylor, the comic drunk. What happened here today?'

'What do you want first – the cat, the cops, the case, or the call?'

It set her off again so he gave up and crept into the boys' rooms, pulling up quilts, kissing small heads. He hung his jacket and when he returned she was leaning on the table, her head in her hands. He sat beside her, one hand on her shoulder.

'Tell me all about it.'

'The cat, kids, cops, case or call?' Two fingers pressed to each side of her mouth held it safe from smiling.

'You'll suffer later.' He reached for her glass.

'Get your own.'

'Is the cat dead, Ann?'

Her lips trembled. 'No confusion with the cat.' Only a small giggle, a bare shuddering of her shoulders. 'It is buried.'

'How did you bury it?'

'Shovel.'

There would be no sense out of her tonight. From the pantry he took a can of baked beans, from a cupboard he selected the smallest saucepan and he returned with them to the table.

'What does a bug look like? An elet . . . electronic bug that the cops plant? Does it look like a bug?'

'I have no idea. Will you have some beans on toast?'

'I ate the boys' leftovers. I'm sick of the sight of beans.'

'If you continue drinking, you'll be sicker still. Hand it over.'

She shook her head as she stood unsteadily, the bottle in her hand, and walked towards the bathroom, laughing because the narrow doorway moved out to bump her, then the walls of the passage got in on the game, tossing her from side to side.

'Shush. You'll wake the boys – and leave that bottle here.'

'It's my security blanket. Can't go anywhere without it,' she yelled.

He heard the bathroom door close with a bang and he let her go. He showered in the upstairs bathroom. Fifteen minutes passed before he noticed the silence and went searching for her. He found her slumped on the floor beside the toilet.

'Come on. Up you get. You can't sit on cold tiles.'

'I keep running to the toilet every two minutes so I may as well stay beside it. And I feel sick too.'

'I hate to say I told you so.'

'You love to say it. Anyway, I was sick already. I've had a sickening day.'

'Cats get killed every day. Is that what set you off?'

'No. It was . . . it was . . . more the undead.'

'Have they found your father's dental records?'

'I found the originals.' She covered her nose and mouth with cupped hands, looking over them at him. 'I found my original vegetable knife when I was digging the cat's grave too. It must have gone out in the mulch. The handle is still intact but the blade is rusty. It's terrible burying things.'

'Knives?'

'Cats, dogs, bodies. Must take hours and hours to dig a hole big enough for a body, mustn't it? They were here today.'

'Who?'

'Those Sydney cops. One's got bloodhound eyes. Woof, woof, he said.'

'We knew they'd find your father sooner or later. Isn't it better to know that he's dead? Better for your mother. Once this is all over, she'll be able to get on with her life.'

'That's first-rate bullshit, David. People don't get on with their lives when they're all screwed up. They just keep screwing around and around and around in the same old screw holes, can't get a grip on good wood to dig in deeper. Anyway . . . anyway, who says he's dead except the bloodhound and his weasel mate?' She looked at him, then down to gaze at her reflection in the toilet bowl, and she waved her hand to her reflection. 'Hello, little Annie. How's life down there? It's bad up here. Want to swap places for a month or two?'

'It's gone on too long. You've all lived with it for too long.'

'And you don't know the half of it. You talk about what you know nothing about as if you know what you're talking about, David, and it's no use me talking about it to you anyway.'

'I understand about the loss of a parent. We know it will happen sooner or later, but it's still a shock when they go – and particularly when they die violently.'

She raised her finger to make a point. 'Yes, but that's the other half of the problem. You might understand about loss, but what we're into tonight is anti-loss and fossilised lies.'

'Fossilised lies. That's a new one.'

'No. It's a very old one, that's why it's fossilised. They are the ones that become a part of your core; there for all time, because they're a part of you, and there's not a bloody thing you can do about them except . . . except wear them and call them ornaments. Turn them into an art form, David. Live with them. Polish them up every Monday while you wipe the dust away.'

'I thought you'd given up dusting.'

'I have. Yesterday's dust is no worse than next week's, and there's more of it to wipe up – so it's more satisfying wiping it up, isn't it? Logic. The same goes for cobwebs.' She waved a hand at cobwebs and the world. 'Oh, and there is a daddy longlegs in the family room. You'd better move him down to the garage before Matthew sees him. How can two brothers be so different? Tristan likes spiders. He loves all the bad guys. The witch in Snow White, and Darth Vader. Anyway, where was I before the spider?'

'Dusting fossilised lies.'

She stared up at him, and for a moment her eyes mirrored Ellie's quizzical expression, but only for a moment. 'Anyway, the cops think that Johnny and I bumped him off . . . Dad. They think we buried him that night. I know they do, and he could clear up the mess in five minutes, but he's – ' She looked at him, closed her mouth, then opened it again. 'Speaking of messes, Tristan had diarrhoea today. Did I tell you? Probably not. It starts with a D. Doesn't fit in with cat and cop and case and kid – '

'Perhaps we should try to sort out the cops and the case before we start discussing diarrhoea.'

She sat, head in her hands, elbows resting on her knees. 'Maybe they did plant a bug. If they did then the game's up.' She frowned as he sat beside her, squeezing in beside the bath. 'They would have heard every word if they'd put it in the phone.' She stopped abruptly, hiccupped and grabbed at her stomach.

'In the phone?'

'That's what they do on television.'

He had no idea what she was on about, but he kissed her, remembering her at sixteen when she'd wiped herself out on spiked punch. She was a mad drunk, each glass seemed to deduct five years from her mental age. Tonight she was a raving six year old. But he loved her anyway. He looked at her hair. Black fairyfloss tonight. She rarely allowed it to dry untamed. He looked at the long legs and the one shoe off and the one shoe on, and the long toes. Then he picked up the wine bottle.

A centimetre remained. He tasted the wine, rolled it on his tongue, swallowed it, then emptied the bottle, closer to Ann than he had been since Bron's wedding, his thigh against her thigh, his shoulder against her shoulder, her hair tickling his nose when he turned. The years had not dulled his need for her. He kissed her brow, lost beneath the wild hair, kissed her wine-flavoured lips, and she sighed, rested her head against his.

'Did he have a temperature?'

'Who?'

'Tristan. Diarrhoea.'

'I hope not, the rabid little coot. He almost bit Matthew's finger off. He's too much like you.'

'Me? I don't bite.'

'Matthew is too much like you. I think I'll have to teach him to bite back. And don't do that,' she said as he kissed her again.

'Why not?'

'Because.'

'That bug, eh? Big brother watching.' His arm slipped around her shoulder and her head fell against his, rested a while.

'I'm . . . I'm a liar, David. I'm a cheat.'

'Who with?' he said, lifting her chin, kissing the speaking lips.

'You wouldn't believe me.'

'What did you do with the boys while you were out cheating?'

'They watched *The Lion King*. Twice.'

'A long session, eh?'

Nice to sit close to him. Nice to talk. She wanted to tell him about her father. Her briefcase was empty, so why shouldn't she empty herself? Not so easy. Mightn't be anything left in her if she did that. Couldn't ever empty that place. Mandy might get emptied out too, and she wasn't going to let her be gone. She wanted to turn her face to him, to kiss his smiling mouth, make love, which could blot out the world more effectively than wine, and no hangover either. Wanted him. Wanted him, but she pulled away, tried to struggle to her feet. Too hard. She gave up.

'I think you'd be better off in bed.'

'Incapable . . . at this particular moment. Can't go anywhere without it,' she said, patting the seat of the toilet. 'It's my security blanket.'

He prised her free, lifted her. Waves of nausea rose with her and she swung away from him to the toilet bowl, where her stomach gave up its rosy-pink froth. 'What a waste,' she said. 'Was it one of your expensive ones?'

'Two of them by the looks of it.' He stood waiting, damp cloth in his hand, and when she was done, he handed her the cloth, flushed the toilet.

'I'll replace it when I get my cheque. If I ever get another cheque. I'm a kept woman, David. I haven't got any time to sew. Everyone wants a piece of me these days, and there's nothing left for me. If they'd locked me up, I would have had time, wouldn't I? I could have made a fortune in jail. Come out in twenty years time a rich woman.'

'No wine in jail, and what in God's name possessed you to down a bottle of wine on an empty stomach?'

'It's not empty. I'm bigger than I was with Tristan, and I'm sick of being big, and sick of napkins and wiping little bums and breaking up little brawls. Motherhood stinks sometimes – and I smell like a cross between a winery and a public loo,' she said, weaving by him in the limited area and stepping into the shower recess, turning the cold water on full blast.

'You're supposed to take your clothes off to shower, Ann.'

'Kill two birds with one stone.'

He adjusted the water, testing the heat with his hand while she stood there in jeans and shirt, watching him.

'Your eyes hurt me too much, David. They're her eyes.' He shook his head, and her hand reached blindly for the soap. It slipped from her grasp to the floor. She studied it a while, then her eyes sought his again.

'I'm sorry. I'm sorry. I love your deep ocean eyes, and I miss her. I still miss her.' She thumped her breast with her fist. 'It eats me. It eats the inside of me. Every day. Every hour.'

'I know, my love.'

'I know you know.' She looked down at the wet shirt now moulding her high pumpkin belly. 'I don't want it to be another girl.'

'I know.'

'I know you know, and I know you know that I do want a little girl. I do. It's just . . . it's just . . . it might stop me from missing her, and it makes me scared, like the last part of her might get away from me.'

He shook his head, wordless now. They never spoke of Mandy, never had been able to. She'd gone and they'd closed up that place, never to be reopened.

'I'm sorry,' she said, leaning against the tiled wall. 'I've got a pain, and I don't know if it's in my heart or my back or my stomach.' She looked down at the soap, stooped, then changed her mind. 'I might not get up again if I lean down there. Could you get it for me, please?'

He reached in, picked up and handed her the small bar. He watched her lather her face, and her hair.

'You're far too thin. That baby is taking the strength out of you.'

'Parasitic little growth. Him on the inside, them on the outside, I'm all sapped out.'

He turned off the water and handed her the towel. She blotted herself, her clothing, wrapped the towel turban fashion around her hair, and he went to the bedroom for a gown.

She was standing where he'd left her, dripping water onto the floor while studying her face in the mirror.

'Get out of those wet clothes. You'll catch a cold.'

'That's my problem.'

'And you are my problem, and tonight a drunken one.'

'Go and eat your beans – and turn the heater up.'

'I don't feel like beans.' He kissed her.

'That's not a good idea.'

'But it's nice,' he said softly. 'You taste like a cucumber, cool, picked early while the dew is still on the vine.'

'A pickled cucumber, vinegar seeping out of the pores. A screwed-up cucumber, not much good even for bottling.'

His fingers worked on wet fabric, attempting to undo large buttons, but her hand caught his, pushing it away.

'I don't know what I'm going to do, David.'

'You're going to get out of those wet clothes and get the hair dryer, and dry that hair, then you're going to bed. My bed.'

She took the towel from her hair and stood a moment, combing the wet mass back with her fingers. 'Listen,' she said. 'You can hear her in this room. Listen.'

'It's just the wind in the wires. Get into your nightie.'

'It's not the wind. She's out there, chasing her cat. It's out there with her tonight.' A finger to his lips, she said, 'Shush. Listen.'

And he listened and almost heard baby words in the wires, and he didn't want to hear. 'Where's your hair dryer?' he said.

She reached for it and he plugged it in, turned it on. It killed the sound of the wind in the wires.

'I wish so much. I wish I could . . . say so much to you. Just say everything and get it out of my head.'

'Say it.'

'It's like . . . in the end it goes on too long so you can't say it, and you'd hate me anyway if I did.'

'Try me.'

'Promise me that you won't hate me, that you won't tell anyone? Ever. Spit your death and hope to die?'

He stood brush in one hand, dryer in the other, speaking above the noise. 'You've done enough spitting for both of us tonight. Consider me spat.'

'You can't ever break a promise. No matter what happens. Promise you'll come and visit me on visiting days and bring the boys if they lock me up for his murder?'

'I promise. Every Sunday, maybe on Wednesdays. If I can get the day off.'

'He's not dead, David. He's in Narrawee.'

'How do you know?' He turned off the dryer and looked at her face, trying to see into the dark eyes.

'I know.' She rested her face against his. 'I just know.'

'Just a minute. Just one cotton-picking minute, please. How do you know?'

'It would have been good for Mum if it had been him. She could have given him a good Catholic funeral. Stuck his name on a tombstone. RIP.'

'You're sidetracking again. Is your father alive?'

'Physically. Not technically.'

'Concentrate, Ann.'

'That's what Johnny used to say. Concentrate. That's what he said the day I found Sam's ring. Whoops.' She claimed the hair dryer and turned it on to high, pointed it at her hair and the black curls flew. 'He found a wild poppy on Monday and he built a fence around it for me and he put chook wire over it for me so the cows can't eat it. I'm taking the boys up there tomorrow to see it.'

'Ben has to go to school tomorrow, and you're going to have a hangover.'

'So? That's a good reason to take a sickie.'

'We'll take them up to see your poppy after school. I'll finish early and come with you. And what ring were you talking about?'

'Nothing. Anyway, they can't blame me for his murder when he hasn't even been legally murdered.'

'No,' he said, finally giving up. 'Not unless it's all been done legally, my love.' He turned off the dryer and he led her by her hand to their room, holding her against him as he stripped off the still-wet shirt, eased the saturated jeans down.

'I used to think he was a basically decent man once. Very basically. I mean at his base, at his very core. He used to talk to me when I was little and I used to sit with him and try to dig down deep. I used to think that if I could dig down to his core then I might find the rotten bit and dig it all out so he'd be good . . . like . . . like when Ben and I used to dig out the stink weeds in the paddocks so the cows didn't eat it. It used to make the milk taste off. Horrible.'

'You talk too much.'

'You know, if someone had tried to do that years ago, before it got its roots down too deep, then they might have been able to dig down and get out all the bad bits. But even if it's too late for her to dig it all out, she knows everything. And she is a good person, David. She's a very good person. She'll make him do it, won't she?'

'I'm sure she will.' He was no longer attempting to follow her ramblings. So familiar, the touch, the scent of her flesh. He kissed her.

'Your kiss is like . . . like rain on the dry dust of a paddock. And your breath is a cool breeze, heralding the end of drought in a land where the sun has ruled for too long, where the grass is grey and the greenness too long gone.'

'I love you.'

'I don't know why.'

'I've missed you.'

'I miss you too, so don't work late. I go stir-crazy on wet days. Can you give me a job at the bank? I won't lose your money.'

His lips traced a pathway from ear to lips. 'Are you well enough?'

'For a job at the bank?' His hand explored the rise of her stomach, resting there. 'Oh,' she said. 'Him. He's just mistletoe on a gum tree. As long as the host lives, so does the mistletoe.'

wind in the wires

~

She was sleeping when David glanced at the bedside clock. Ten-thirty, and he hadn't eaten since two. Hungry now, but at peace, he moved his arm from beneath her shoulder, brushed the bare shoulder with his lips. She didn't move, the rhythm of her breathing didn't alter, so inch by inch he moved away. As he stood, she murmured and rolled over to his side of the bed.

In the kitchen he opened a can of beans, heated them in the microwave and ate them on hot buttered toast. He read the paper, drank his tea then, near midnight, crept back to the bedroom and slid in beside her. She turned to him, reached out to him, and he gathered the warmth of her back into his arms and he slept, and he slept soundly for the first time in a week.

It was near dawn when he rolled over and found himself alone. Wide awake instantly, he listened. Only the wind in the wires. He lay listening to it, and listening for movement, then he swung his feet to the floor and checked the bathroom.

Light was showing beneath the family room door. He smiled. She'd grown hungry too, he thought, but when he opened the door he saw her grasping the back of a chair, her teeth clenched.

She glanced at him. 'My hangover is having contractions.'

'Practice pains?'

'Probably.'

'Not positively?'

'They've been practising for a while,' she replied, straightening as the pain eased. 'I was going to make a cup of tea and some toast.'

He filled the jug, plugged it in. He set bread in the toaster. 'How long have you been up?'

'A while. They'll stop in a minute.'

A wicked wind rattled the back door. He locked it, then walked back, and they spoke of the wind while the jug boiled and the toast popped, while he took two mugs to the sink and tea bags from the canister, while he poured the water, his eyes rarely leaving her face. Then he saw her grip the chair and he forgot about the tea.

'That's a bad one.'

'It's not due for weeks. It will stop. I had pains for the last month with Tristan.'

'Sit down,' he said.

'It's better if I stand. He's riding my spine and digging his boots in.'

He added sugar to her tea, he buttered the toast, and she took a bite, a sip of tea then placed the cup down.

'I don't think he's practising, David.'

'Have you got anything packed?' She shook her head, and he walked to the bedroom where he pulled on trousers and a sweater.

She was watching the clock when he returned to the room, shoes in hand, and he looked at the clock, tied his laces, drank tea until the minute hand ticked over and another one began. He saw the pain return too soon, and he went for her overcoat and shoes.

'We can't leave the boys.'

'Dee will watch them.'

'God.' A prayer, a moan. 'What a night to be born. I hate that wind. It's screaming. I hate it.'

One button dialling their doctor neighbour. 'Peter,' he said. 'It's David. Sorry to disturb you but we've got an impatient baby on the way.' And the phone was down. Before the next pain hit, he had her buttoned into her overcoat, had her at the back door, an easier descent to the car than the staircase.

'Wait there out of the wind. I'll bring the car around.'

She'd never done as she was told, not the child nor the woman. She followed him to the drive, her hair whipping her face.

'All the baby clothes are in the bottom drawer of – ' Nauseating pain closed her mouth, her mind. He stood at her side, holding her, supporting her until the contraction eased. ' – Benjamin's wardrobe,' she said.

Then Peter and Dee Williams were running from their yard. 'How close are the pains?' the doctor called.

'A minute – two. I don't know. Very close.'

'Why didn't you call me sooner?'

'I woke only a moment ago. Ann was planning to produce it in the kitchen.'

'Silly woman. Get her in the car. I'll follow you.'

The hospital was five minutes away. David left Ann refusing the wheelchair.

'Do as you are told,' he said. 'I'll settle the boys in with Dee, then I'll be back.' He drove the empty roads home, and together he and Dee wrapped the boys in blankets and carried them next door.

'Daddy,' Benjamin opened an eye. 'Why are we here?'

'Mummy's gone to get our new baby.'

'Are we getting another boy?'

'We'll know soon. Be quiet, Ben, you'll wake the little ones. You help Aunty Dee if Tristan wakes up.'

'Will Mummy be a long time?'

'Not too long. Sleep now. I'll see you in the morning.'

A black night, studded with the pale yellow glow of streetlights. No stars, no moon, only an evil howling wind prowling the night streets, searching for spoil.

What the hell had he been thinking of last night? He hadn't been thinking. Hadn't considered the baby. But they'd made love late with the three boys, who had arrived close to the expected date.

The boys. Always lumped together as one. Always the boys. They'd chosen the name for another boy. He'd be Liam John. No name for a girl. They'd had their girl. There was still a gap in his gut, a raw unfillable hole when he thought of Mandy. Time and the boys could not fill it. There were tears, too, that still came at odd moments. In the garden when he watched a bee busy at his labour. Little dresses in shop windows hurt his heart. Little girl's hands held in larger hands. These things always brought back memories of Mandy, her moist little hand in his own.

Nothing was ready for a new child. They'd need Mandy's room for this one, if Ann would give it up. Unless they put Benjamin and Matthew in together, create a greater bedlam.

From time to time they had made tentative plans to repaint Mandy's room, to replace her curtains, but how could they touch that sweet memorial, the white walls with their cut-out fairies pasted there? The bed with its pretty bed cover. All frills and fuss and little-girl things. Mandy's place, not some stranger's.

David's return to the hospital was unhurried. He parked the car out front and looked at the bleak morning rising out of a black night. A bad morning for a birth, and it was far too early. Still, six weeks was nothing these days. Miniature babies were born three months early, and many lived. Peter Williams knew his business. The town was lucky to have him.

Have to go in, he thought. Stop feeling guilty and go to her.

He'd been at her side when Mandy was born. Hours of labour, hours of pain he had not been able to ease. And then that new life's lusty wail.

Never would he forget the sight of her tiny crumpled face, or the sound of that bellow. And Ann. She hadn't wanted a child so soon after their wedding – and had made it plain. Until she'd heard the wail, held the red-faced mite. An instant three-way love affair.

Benjamin's birth had been different. In the months after Mandy's death, that pregnancy had become fate's mockery. For two years they'd been trying for a second child but it had not been until after the funeral he'd learned there was to be another. How could they plan for another baby, hold another baby in their arms? How could they ever dare to love another child?

A very different birth, Benjamin's. An easy birth, as if the tiny boy had known he must not make a fuss with his entrance into their lives. A different wail too. A plaintive little whimper, then silence. And a different feeling when he'd first held his son.

No instant love affair that, but love had grown as the tiny being had grown into their lives, making a place for himself. His own place. He hadn't tried to fill the space that still bore Mandy's name.

Then Matthew had come along. A bigger baby, he'd taken his time arriving. He had looked a little like Mandy at birth; his wail had been a little like Mandy's. They'd been brave enough to want him, brave enough to love again.

Tristan the tyrant pushed his way into town two weeks early, barely waiting for the doctor to arrive. He'd taken one look at the world and decided to take it over. A born dictator from day one, frustrated by his immobility, he'd howled until he'd found his crawling legs at six months, walked at nine months, and God help everyone since.

And now, God willing, there was to be another.

David knew he had to go to Ann, but there was so little a man could do at this time. Just another minute to collect his thoughts, to shift his mind away from last night, of making love while that baby voice had whispered and chuckled in the wires.

Then the winds had risen, driving her tiny voice away.

He shivered, and the shiver travelled his spine and back again. Trees bowing low. Leaves flying, early birds up and complaining, a few cars moving now on the main road. David breathed deeply of the cold air, then he walked through the doors and down the passages towards the labour ward he had come to know quite well.

poor bloody jack

~

Thursday 14 August

Eight hundred kilometres south the birds were also rising, as was Jack Burton. He crawled from his blankets, wearing the skin he'd been born with and nothing else, and he sat a while looking for his Bonds size 18 briefs tossed onto the floor a bare five hours ago. He found and stepped into them, and into blue jeans he'd also discarded onto the floor. He pulled on cream woollen socks and a pair of sneakers before zipping his fly and hunting for his polo-necked sweater. It was tangled up with the bedding.

He and May had argued last night and he'd slept alone, or hadn't slept. Too much on his mind to sleep last night. His head was a bastard and always had been. It never turned off. Only the whisky had turned it off.

There had been a dozen or more messages on the answering machine when they'd arrived back at Narrawee yesterday. He'd listened to them. He'd known that they'd found his corpse. And he'd wanted it, wanted it for his own. May had started nagging him to return Mummy's boy Benjie's calls.

'Let it slide,' he'd said. 'We'll be in Singapore in a week.' They spent a lot of time out of the country.

Then a car had driven up to the front door. He'd recognised the driver and taken off like a scalded cat.

One thing led to another after May's visitors left. He knew that he'd tossed a tub of butter into the trolley at the supermarket and he hadn't seen May toss it out, but she had, the determined little bitch. He liked butter and he hated bloody margarine, but all she ever bought was margarine.

'It's easier to spread, Sam, and better for you.'

That last phone call had got her howling. She'd tried to call Ann back, and he hadn't wanted her to call Ann back. In the end he'd ripped the cord out of its socket and pitched the bloody phone into the yard so she couldn't call Ann back, and he'd gone to bed in the spare room. He could live without bloody telephones. Nobody called him.

Once clothed, Jack made his way down to the kitchen where he scratched around for coffee and a bowl of cornflakes, which he ate as he walked the room, the radio speaking softly. Nothing about his death on the news, only a pair of anti-comedians, telling unfunny jokes. He told them what they could do with their humour and turned them off, had another bowl of cornflakes.

Bloody cornflakes. He craved eggs on toast, a bit of bacon. Couldn't have it, could he? Eggs were full of cholesterol and so was he. A cigarette taken from his packet, he lit up, inhaled. It was the best smoke of the day, that first one. Sucking scalding coffee and cigarette in turn, he stood at the window, his mind nicotine travelling.

When he was a kid a year had been forever. Santa Claus gone home to the North Pole was damn near forgotten by the time he came back again, but in adulthood that same year took wing and flew.

The previous six years had flown, but not this last one. Not for poor bloody Jack Burton. The minutes of 1997 plodded, its hours dragged and its days crawled by on crippled feet. What was wrong with it?

Didn't want to let him get away with the subterfuge. Didn't want him declared dead. Wouldn't allow it. This bastard of a year had slowed time to give the cops and insurance investigators a chance to find him. And now they thought they'd found him.

Three weeks into January and 1997 had started putting the boots in. He and May had had a raging row about nothing and he'd taken off for Toorak, emptied their joint account before she could, and holed up at the flat. By March he'd drunk himself into hospital and it had frightened Christ out of him – if he'd ever been in him.

Bloody hospital. They'd treated him like a bit of dog's meat left too long in the sun. When they let him out May had driven him home to Narrawee, her tongue, once coated with honey, stripping the flesh from him. She'd kept it up for weeks, had worn him down to the stage where he'd got to look beneath the strips of flesh to his bare bones, and beneath his bare bones to his treacherous bloody liver.

He was scared of dying. Not that he believed in the hereafter, but he didn't want to find out that he'd been wrong about it either, didn't want to find old Satan waiting for him with his red-hot pitchfork, so he'd stayed dry through April. Scared dry. He'd been dry now for five months, because May had cut him off without a bloody cent. She'd had the locks changed at the Toorak flat and she'd closed their joint account, the only one he'd been able to help himself to without her signature.

It was for his own good, she said, the power-crazed little bitch. Like the bloody margarine. 'It's for your own good, Sam.'

'Bloody Sam.'

So there were days when the sun shone, when he looked out at the property and called it his own. Life looked halfway to possible on those days, but they were balanced by the black days, the soul-crushing dark days when he looked out at the land and saw grass and stock and he knew he didn't own a bloody thing.

It was May's grass, her stock. She ran the bloody place – her and her manager. She could sign the cheques without his signature, but he couldn't sign them without hers. That was the way it had had to be when he'd spent half of his time in Mallawindy, and that was the way it would be until he died.

He lit a second cigarette as he left the house by the back door and made his way around to the cellar where he stood for minutes, looking down into black, feeling black. It had started yesterday when the little bitch who walked like Ellie had turned up with a bloody husband, Nick, the smartarsed bastard. What the hell did they think they were doing turning up here?

And that phone call last night. It had brought it all back home, taken mind, if not body, back to Mallawindy.

'Shit,' he said, and he pitched his butt into the wind and turned on the cellar lights.

They'd put in good lights a few years back, four fluorescent tubes that flooded every corner with white light.

Birds squawking in the trees, a flock of cockatoos screeching overhead, the world was waking up to join him, so he closed the cellar door on the bloody world and walked down to the ghosts.

Come Christmas, Ellie would collect a quarter of a million, he thought, which she'd get whether they proved the body was his or not. She was probably wishing the year away. In four and a half months she'd be a rich widow.

'A bloody good catch, cold bed or not,' he muttered as he took up a wide-necked jar, carefully unscrewing it. 'Must be thousands in my trust accounts too, just sitting there, untouched.' The thought of the thousands he couldn't get his hands on made his head itch. If he could get up to Sydney, he could raid his accounts, live like a king for twelve months.

'Drink myself to bloody death and take my own pitchfork with me. Get the bastard before he gets me.'

But he couldn't raid his accounts and he knew it. He couldn't get his hands on Narrawee money and he couldn't touch his own money, couldn't even raid May's purse these days. She used plastic. Paid for everything with her card and had the money automatically transferred from her account each month.

178

'Bloody cards for supermarkets! Everything linked into the bloody banks, and she won't even buy a man a tub of bloody butter.'

The cops were probably linked to the banks by computer. They'd get him if he tried to make a withdrawal, then Ellie couldn't claim the Daree body for Jesus, and wouldn't get her insurance payout. Cops were smart, smarter than they'd been thirty years ago. Technology had caught up with poor bloody Jack Burton and left him high and dry.

'Bone bloody dry.'

He'd wanted a beer last night. Just one, and bugger his liver. One lousy beer wouldn't hurt him. He'd explained to May that he could control beer. Always had been able to. It was the whisky that blew his fuse. One bottle of beer to have his own private wake for poor old Jack.

'Mean dictator little bitch.'

He took a cloth pad from the jar, squeezed it, then he dusted the surface of an old cabinet before wiping the sponge across its aged surface.

The wood drank the shellac and before his eyes, it came to life. 'Jesus,' he said looking closely at the grain. 'Jesus, look at that. It's coming up well. Bloody beautiful timber in it. English oak. It's got to be.'

For an hour he worked there in silence, the sponge dipping, wiping, each coat of shellac enriching the wood. He should have been wearing gloves, but he wasn't. He looked at his hands, stained yellow.

'Murdering bloody hands.'

His hands had always been clean in Mallawindy. He'd kept them clean, scrubbed them raw with Solvol, picked his nails clean with a sharpened match. He stood, staring at his stained hands, at his ragged nails.

'*What hands are here? Ha! They pluck out mine eyes! Will all great Neptune's oceans wash this blood clean from my hands? No; this my hand will rather the multitudinous seas incarnadine, making the green one red,*' he quoted.

His usually well-shaped fingernails looked like a workman's. The high point in his life these last months had been spent in this cellar, reclaiming old furniture. Poor bloody Jack had come down to this, to working with his hands because he had nothing else to fill his days and his head. Nothing on television to watch. And May wouldn't even buy him a cake of bloody Solvol to wash his hands clean. Not for inside. If he wanted Solvol, he had to wash his hands in the laundry with old Harry, the hired help.

'A man has been driven mad by her, and by bloody hair hanging around his collar, by the bloody moustache prickling his bloody nose, and his bloody beard hiding his poor bloody face.'

It was all his too, and all grey. Grey-headed, grey-bearded old bastard, and May had mirrors hung on every wall to keep forcing the fact home to him.

Old. On his last legs. Satan sitting down there rubbing his hands in glee while he sharpened up his pitchfork.

Jack had been indestructible once, thought he'd live forever, or long enough to get what he wanted out of life. All he'd ever wanted was his name on the title to Narrawee. That's all. It wasn't much for a man to want, but he couldn't have it, could he? So the land was his, or Saint bloody Sam's, the perverted long-haired bastard who stunk of perfumed liquid soap and had bloody head lice.

Jack scratched his head, raked at it, then checked what was left of his fingernails, expecting to see head lice jumping there. He looked closer. He put Sam's glasses on, checking out a suspect. Only shellac and sawdust.

He knew his head was seething with lice. He itched. Itched day and night. And the little bastards had crept down to the hairs on his chest too. It itched. His back itched.

'One bloody big itch.'

He lit a cigarette and took a fast step back from the shellac, which was more methylated spirits than bug residue. This place would go up like a bonfire. Old wardrobe, old tables, antique couch, rolls of carpet, picture frames. He spent a lot of time down here with the rest of the junk May had been saving for a rainy day.

'Manipulating, using, mean-minded little bitch.' He liked the look of old frames. 'Might start on them next,' he muttered and ground his cigarette into the floor.

The rain was pouring down again. He could see it thrashing the small ground level window, spattering earth onto the glass. May and her manager would be smiling.

'Stuff the bloody rain,' he yelled. 'I hope your bloody bulls drown, die of footrot. Ah!' he snarled and his sponge dipped and he smoothed on another coat of shellac.

He liked wood. Liked the smell of it. Liked rubbing down worn-out surfaces to get to what was underneath. He liked the smell of shellac too, and he stared now at a two-litre can of methylated spirits, considering it as a possible pick-me-up, a possible entrance into the forgetfulness of foggy days. Fast days, those had been, racing days, their birth and death in the bottom of a bottle of Jack Daniel's.

He licked his lips, ran his tongue over his teeth and laughed, thinking of the cops trying to track down those teeth. His dentist was in Collins Street, and the name on his file was Samuel, as it had been for thirty years. May had put a bit of money into his teeth in the past few years. He'd snapped one of the front ones in half, so she'd bought him two new capped front teeth for the Christmas of '95.

And why not? She'd put a king's ransom into the house, and she paid old Harry, her gardener, a fortune to forest the place with flowers, make it into a showpiece. So poor bloody Jack was her showpiece too, her performing pup. So let her pay to keep his snarl intact.

He never laid a finger on the earth. Crops refused to strike if he looked at them. Plants curled up and died if he walked by. Sullen, wet, resentful earth, it hated him, and the wet old trees whispered about him, pissed on him, and his bloody father's ghost hooted at him when he wandered the land at night. That bastard knew he was Jack, and knew that Jack's name would never be on the title.

But when he was out, when he was in town, the property was

his, and the Melbourne solicitors and accountants thought the property was his. He was the only Samuel Burton they'd seen in thirty years.

He straightened, stretched his shoulders, his neck. The winter chill had crept into his joints this year, and winter hung on, determined to wear him down, kill him with old age. He needed heat and some of Ellie's curried chicken soup to sweat the aches out of him. Chicken soup and a feed of her sago plum pudding, lost beneath fresh cream. A few fresh eggs fried in butter, served on thick toast, made against hot coals. And a slab of her bloody pumpkin cake with a plaster of scalded cream on top.

She could cook, he'd say that for Ellie. She could make something out of nothing and have you asking for more. May lived on dry hash and rabbit food; his taste buds were shrivelling for lack of use, or old age had hit them as well as his liver. Nothing tasted like it used to – even the cream he sometimes smuggled into the trolley at the supermarket didn't taste like cream.

Almost sixty-bloody-seven. Three years away from seventy. He shook his head. He couldn't, wouldn't believe it; might as well be dead once you hit seventy. Maybe he should hang himself from the rafters and get it over and done with.

He'd come face to face with his age in America that first year. It had crept out of a hotel mirror in New York and king-hit him. He hated America for that. Refused to go back there.

He'd worn his wig and fake mo for months after he'd run from Mallawindy, and he'd kept his head low playing the role of teetotaller Saint Sam, complete with his fake halo. Knowing that Jack was hiding beneath that wig and mo had been enough to keep him sane. Sleeping each night as Jack, then putting on his Sam-face each morning had been an extension of the old role he'd played since Liza and Sam had died. He could do it, and did it well. He'd got a kick out of it back then, and if his audience didn't applaud, they'd been convinced.

May had applauded. They'd been happy for a while.

'Like a pair of bloody old honeymooners, we were. Sex on the bloody floor in front of the fire. Sex for breakfast, and better than eggs on toast.'

He'd sat through the inquest in his wig and mo. He'd handled it, but he'd sweated when the black-headed little bitch had started talking. He never had known what that one was likely to do next. May hadn't been too certain that day either. She'd clung to his sweating hand. Two hands, clasped, welded together with liquid fear.

But the little bitch had stood up there and spoken of a man who probably had an English accent, but it could have been Scottish or Irish. When you're six they just sound different. Not Australian, she'd said. And Jack had almost believed her. She couldn't guess at his age, she'd said, but she thought he was older than Uncle Sam, and he'd had sandy-red hair. She remembered that. He'd ridden a motorbike with a sidecar. She said she had watched him bury Liza in the rose garden, but remembered nothing after that. She couldn't remember him locking her in the cellar.

There had been many questions but her story had not altered. Just the image of the man. And his voice. No. He had not spoken as if English had been a second language. It was some sort of English accent.

The psychiatrist she'd seen after Mandy's death had said his piece, and the old copper who had run the search – eighty if he was a day, and eager for his moment of glory – hadn't been able to remember what he'd eaten for breakfast that morning.

They'd called Samuel Burton's name then, and Saint Sam had released May's hand to tell his tale. He'd been away at the time, in Queensland. He'd driven day and night to get back home. He knew nothing of the day Liza had disappeared, but he'd retold the tale of the Englishman who had come to their door looking for a job. Crow. Ted Crow. He'd been on a working holiday around Australia.

May copped the worst of it. She'd said her piece, admitted leaving the girls watching television while she'd driven to town for bread.

'There had been several cases of meningitis in town. I was petrified. I kept the girls home from school. Sam did the shopping. I was afraid to take the girls into town. My friend's son had been left deaf by the disease. The girls were in my care and I made a bad decision I'll regret until my dying day.'

They'd questioned her on the length of time she'd been gone from the property and doubted her reply. A child murdered and buried in the time it had taken May to drive into town, buy bread and return home, but they gave up when she broke down and howled.

David had done his fair share of staring that day. He hadn't seen much of Jack, and had never set eyes on him sober, so he'd been taken in by gentleman Sam in his wig and his mo and halo, his sibilant Ss. He'd shaken his sweating hand when the day was over, but Ann had walked away, walked away fast with May tailing her, begging her to wait.

Jack had sighted his own discarded car in the car park, and he'd known that Johnny Jesus was in town. Hadn't seen him, but later that night the car had been parked for an hour at the Narrawee gates. May had panicked; she'd sat on the telephone until she'd got two cancellations on a ten-week tour leaving the following day. Canada and America – she wouldn't have cared if it had been to Timbuktu.

Piebald at night when he'd taken his wig off, when they hit American soil, Jack pitched his wig to buggery and May had given him a haircut. No black then. Only the grey left, and a greyer grey than the wig.

He wasn't Jack hiding beneath a wig and mo any more, and he wasn't bloody Sam either. He saw his great-grandfather in the hotel mirror that night, old Samuel standing there with age and death staring him in the eye, so he'd escaped May and gone on his first bender with the money a pawnbroker had given him for his watch. Got a bit for it too. He might have stayed away long enough to miss the morning bus out, but he'd been mugged, and the mugging little bastards had put the boots in, letting him know just how bloody old and decrepit he was.

The New York cops got him back to May, sore enough, sober enough to fake it. He told her he'd gone for a walk, sightseeing, that the muggers had taken his watch as well as his wallet. She'd still believed him back then.

Ten weeks of trains and buses had been enough to grow a good beard and moustache, and the dinner tables at night had given him freedom to have a few glasses of wine. He'd done all right, lost his halo but not his sainthood.

It had taken longer to grow hair down to his collar.

'It's safer,' May had said when he'd fought her for the old short back and sides. 'For the moment it's safer to look the way you've always looked, Sam.'

Bloody Sam.

For weeks after their return to Australia, he'd stayed in Sydney alone, and had a ball, then for two months they'd lived at the Toorak flat. He'd spent his pocket money wisely, had a beer or three when she wasn't around, and sucked mints when she was due home. He'd got away with it until she deemed his hair, if not him, fit for Narrawee.

And he'd left it too late. Without realising it, he'd let the nagging little bitch gain the upper hand.

'Poor hen-pecked, grey-headed old bastard.'

Hen reminded him of chook shit country, and Ellie. A lot of things reminded him of Ellie lately. His youngest, the wild little bitch Bronwyn, had reminded him of Ellie. She had her walk, her legs, her build. She and her smartarsed husband had arrived at the door only minutes after he and May had driven in with the groceries. He'd seen her as she walked from the car, and he'd gone to ground. Hidden in the cellar while his liver ached. May entertained them, and left him starving in the cellar, and no bloody butter for his toast when she let him know it was safe to come out.

How old was that youngest one now? Seven years younger than Liza. 'Bloody near thirty-one,' he said. Born a bare month before

Liza and Sam had died. 'Shit,' he snarled, then shook his head and smoothed on a coat of shellac.

His hands working independently of his mind were those of a perfectionist. They'd surprised him, those hands. There had been a time years ago when he'd believed in them. Time had stolen his belief, left his murdering bloody hands lost in a limbo of waiting. Poor bloody things, they couldn't do much now. They could still lift a bottle, hold a pen, forge his brother's signature, and push sandpaper. Couldn't run the property. Didn't know how. But they worked on, his hands, and his brain worked on, and never the two did meet.

. Mallawindy. He couldn't ever go back. Even before they'd found his body, he'd been aware that he could never go back. The best he could hope for was that Ellie might give him a good Catholic funeral, buy him a decent tombstone with her insurance payout, and stick his name on it.

'Two hundred and fifty thousand! She'll give half of it to the church, you see if I'm wrong,' he told the can of methylated spirits. 'Bloody Catholic church. Got money coming out of its ears – it doesn't need my bloody money.'

For years he'd worked, on and off, for AMP, and during one bad month back in the eighties, he'd sold himself a big policy. Had no intention of keeping up the payments, but Ellie had liked the idea; she'd paid up every month.

'It's like putting money in the bank, Jack. We'll get it back when you turn seventy.' He could still do her voice, that nasal country tone.

'Bloody seventy. Bloody Mallawindy – sprawled in the dust like a worn-out harlot with her legs spread wide.'

Narrawee wasn't much better these days. Like every other town in Australia, it was dying while the cities choked on cars and people. Narrawee had been a world when he was kid. It had possessed a life, a personality; it thought it had a future.

Melbourne sucked the life from this town. Good farmland was

186

being sold off in five-acre lots to Melbourne's more affluent retirees. Hobby farmers. They built their own mansions, determined to outdo their neighbours. They built tennis courts but they were too old to hold a racquet. They kept horses they didn't ride. Poor old Samuel Burton would roll over in his grave if he could see his town today. He'd built it, naming it after his property. The Burtons had been someone back then.

Jack lifted his head, straightened his shoulders and sucked in his stomach. Old Samuel, his great-grandfather, had stood tall until the day he died.

Then he heard May's running footsteps, and his shoulders sagged and his stomach sagged. As the door opened he saw her silhouetted against the light, her umbrella high. For minutes she stood there, looking down.

'You spend too much time in here, Sam. It's not good for you.'

'Depression is a state of mind, induced by self for the self-satisfaction of wallowing in self-pity. Get used to it.' He glanced at her to see if his words had hit home, then his hands smoothed another coat of shellac on the cabinet barely recognisable now as the battered old workbench he had dragged from a corner only weeks ago.

May placed the umbrella against the wall and walked downstairs to his side, where she stood, watching his hands.

'It has come up well. That's the old one that used to be in the hall in your mother's time, isn't it?'

'It came over with old Samuel. Two of the drawer handles have gone.'

'There's a lot of junk in one of the old tin trunks. They could be in there. We never threw anything away.' She walked the cellar until she found the old tin trunk, and she opened its lid, squatting there, searching for minutes. 'Take it up to the garage and I'll go through it for you.'

'I'll look when I'm ready.'

'Please yourself.' She stood, wiped her hands on her handkerchief.

'I don't know how you can stand to work down here. Why don't you take the cabinet into the garage?'

'Because I choose to work here, May.'

'It's not healthy.'

'Don't like the fumes? Or the ghosts?'

'Don't start that again.'

'Can you still see them lying there on the floor, May?'

'Stop it! Every time you wallow in your guilt, you force me to wallow in it with you. Is that what you want?'

'Come on in, the wallowing is fine.'

'You're killing me with your moods. I'm trying. I'm trying as hard as I know how to make this work. You won't let it work.' He stepped back studying the finish on a cabinet door. 'I give you access to money and what do you do? You go off drinking. Do it again, Jack, and it will be the end of you. And well you know it.'

'What do you care?'

'I'm finding it more and more difficult, I can promise you that.'

He picked up the can of methylated spirit, shook it. 'They say it goes down well with a dash of cordial. Got any cordial in the house or is it fattening, May?' The sponge again in hand, he wiped another coat of shellac across the cabinet with smooth, easy strokes.

'You need professional help, Jack.'

He smiled. She'd called him Jack. 'Good idea,' he said. 'Join me up to the local AA, or I'll get myself to a psychiatrist. Spill my guts to him. Think he'd keep it under his hat?' She walked away, and he called after her. 'What I bloody well need is to hear you say my name. That's what I need. Do you know how good it sounds?'

For minutes she stood halfway up the stairs, watching him work. She had no reply. She knew what he was going through. She also knew she had to wipe that name from her mind.

'I've got to go into town. Do you want anything?'

'Yes. A couple of pounds of butter, a crate of Jack Daniel's, boss, and a cake of Solvol for the bathroom.'

'Do you want anything!'

'No, boss. Not diss boy. He don' wan' nuttin. You lockem him in, boss. You takem metho with you, boss.'

'Stop it, you fool. Do you need cigarettes?'

He turned back to his cabinet. It wasn't the first piece he'd reclaimed, but it was going to be the best. Stooping low he peered across the glass-like surface. In silence she watched him until he straightened. 'Bloody beautiful wood, isn't it?'

'It is. It is. It would sell for thousands in the city.'

'You can have it for five hundred bucks and the keys to Toorak.'

'I'm going now. Do you need cigarettes?'

'Can I come with you, boss, and have six dollars to buy my own?'

'Which one of you?'

'The pervert, of course. I'll discuss my antiques with Mrs Lamont.' He wiped on another coat of shellac.

'You really do a wonderful job on them. You really do.' He made no reply. 'I remember the day you brought home that little table you made for your mother, when you were fourteen, or fifteen.'

'It's at Toorak.' He looked at her, then back to the pad. Cotton wool wrapped in fine sheeting. It had been made as he had been taught by the trade teacher. Just a kid then, eager to learn. He could have been anything, done anything. Back then. 'I need some more sandpaper.'

'What grade?'

'Superfine. No. No. I'll go in. Something to bloody well do. We'll have something decent to eat in town.' The pad dropped into the shellac, the lid screwed down, as he'd been taught in the school room, he washed his hands with metho then wiped them on an old cloth before following her up the steps, closing the door on his own haven, his own little hell, giving it back to the ghosts of Liza and Sam for an hour.

May was upstairs dressing when the phone rang.

'I thought I'd killed the bloody thing,' he muttered, washing his hands in the downstairs bathroom, pumping liquid soap into his palm because it made less mess in the basin than Solvol – so she said. She didn't have to clean the bloody basin. She paid a woman to do the cleaning, paid old Harry to ride around on her lawn mower. She paid painters, and bloody carpet layers, spent money like water and wouldn't even buy him a bar of Solvol. He ignored the phone.

'Pick that up will you, Sam,' she called from above.

'That bastard is still dead, May.'

'Will you pick the phone up?'

'Why isn't the answering machine on?'

'Because I'm waiting for Maxine to call me back.'

'Bloody Maxine. I'm not playing social secretary for bloody Maxine Parker-Jones.' The ringing stopped.

'Thank you very much for that,' May yelled.

'A bloody pleasure. Anything else I can do for you, just ask.'

'It wouldn't have hurt you to pick it up.'

'Wouldn't have done me any good either.' Then it rang again, so he picked the bloody thing up just to stop her complaining. He stood listening to the STD beeps, and knew it wasn't Maxine Parker who had married Herb Jones – liked his money but not his name, so she'd added a hyphen, like his youngest. Mr and Mrs Burton-Smith.

'Mr Burton?'

'Who wants him?'

'Am I speaking to Samuel Burton?' a stranger's voice asked.

'So they tell me.'

'Sergeant Robertson, Mr Burton. Your nephew suggested that you may be able to assist us with our inquiries.'

Jack's liver quivered, his shoulders crawled and he needed a drink. Nephew? Bloody Bessy's Mickey. Thirty-odd years ago Jack had named a retarded pup for that hangdog-eyed little shit. And what the bloody hell would he know about anything anyway? Didn't have enough brains to come in out of the rain, that one – but his mother did. His stomach, his shoulders shivered. Bloody big-mouthed Bessy.

He needed a whisky. Since he'd heard that they'd found his body, he'd felt that old urge for a whisky. Since the little black-headed bitch had called last night his head had been screaming out for a whisky.

Then he realised who he was supposed to be, and it wasn't nephew Mickey Bishop who'd dobbed him in. It would be Johnny Jesus.

He drew a breath and attempted to raise Sam, all fake concern and bullshit over his twin brother's not so recent demise, but he'd been caught on the hop by liquid soap and he hated pumping the crazy shit. Anything May wanted, she had to have it. Didn't matter what he wanted. He was an also-ran in this place.

'We have been unable to trace your brother's dentist, Mr Burton.'

'A bit late for dental work, isn't it?'

The cop wasn't amused. 'If our information is correct, you and your brother were identical twins.' Jack made no denial and the voice continued on about forensic and positive identifications while Jack lit a cigarette.

He was trying to raise Sam. He coughed, but perverted Sam was slow in coming this morning. It was one thing to play the bastard for a day, a week, a bloody month, another entirely to live him, day in, day out, year in, year out. It didn't get any easier.

'Still so hard to realise he's dead,' he said, looking for Ss while taking Sam's glasses from his breast pocket, putting them on. It helped sometimes, but not this morning. He was Jack and today he felt like Jack, black as bloody original sin. He ran a hand through Sam's long hair, he tensed his jaw, then relaxed it into Sam's. He sniffed his hand. It smelt of Sam. He sniffed at the hand holding the cigarette. Overtones of Sam with a bit of Jack's nicotine. The bastard hadn't taken up smoking until after he was dead; Sam's hands had always smelt like a woman's.

'Yes. Yes. We've been away. Heard the news last evening. The shock. Not functioning at all well at the moment. Where exactly did you find the body, Sergeant?'

'Approximately twenty kilometres east of Mallawindy. He had been buried in a shallow grave.'

'Sad news. Very sad. He didn't bury himself, I take it?' Sam's hissing Ss were coming.

'As you say, Mr Burton.'

The policeman spoke on while Jack raked at his scalp and, as always, checked his fingernails for movement. He felt an itch near his eyebrow, and knew the little bastards were migrating south. Then his beard and his mo began itching. He scratched. Listened and scratched. Eaten alive by bloody head lice. He looked closely at his nails while the copper waited for a reply, but Jack wasn't too certain of what had been said.

How could you tell nits from dandruff? Nits were eggs. Eggs didn't crawl.

'Mr Burton?'

'Yes. So, you're treating his death as a homicide, Sergeant?'

He'd preferred the suicide theory. Ellie wouldn't get the insurance if he'd suicided, and he didn't want her to get it. She'd get his trust fund, though. There was no justice in the bloody world and never had been; she'd end up with the lot and he didn't have enough in his pocket to buy a packet of smokes or a bottle of louse shampoo.

'The black woollen sock and the briefs found on the body have been tentatively identified by your sister-in-law as those worn by her husband.'

'Have you been able to ascertain the cause of death?'

'A small calibre wound to the rear of the head.'

'Shit!'

That one got away. Shit! he thought. Poor bloody Jack, executed and buried in his underdaks. He almost felt sorry for himself.

West of Daree. West of Daree. Who was west of Daree? He

searched his mind, allowing memory to travel that road. He tracked the farmhouses, saw Jim Watson's place, Harry Docker's, then he had it and his chin lifted while a smile broke across his features. Buried in his underdaks might suggest Jack had died in bed, and Vera Owen had a welcoming bed out the Daree Road. Charlie had surprised him in it one night, sleeping like a babe. And the bastard had brained him with a tyre lever. Maybe it was payback time. Maybe the day wasn't going to be a total write-off after all.

Then Sam came. Just like that. The voice lifted, his Ss became a sibilant hiss, and his vowels became more rounded. 'I assume you've spoken to Charles Owen? I believe he owns a few acres in the vicinity.'

May was behind him.

'Who is it, Sam?'

'Jack,' he snarled, but quietly, then altered his tone. 'It's concerning brother Jack, my dear. Sergeant Robertson is on the line.' He liked doing Sam's Ss, he'd mimicked them from childhood.

'We are holding Charles Owen for questioning, Mr Burton.'

'Has he been charged?'

'What are you doing?' May hissed.

'Doing my best to assist the police with their inquiries, my dear.' He cleared his throat and lit a cigarette from the butt of his last, standing the old butt on its end on May's telephone table. 'Oh, and I believe the eldest son, John, arrived home shortly before my brother went missing. There was always bad blood between Jack and his son. Just between you, me and the gatepost, Sergeant Robertson, I wouldn't trust that one as far as I could kick him. An ex-priest – '

May snatched up the cigarette butt, replaced it with an ashtray, then attempted to relieve Jack of the phone, but she'd nagged him to pick the bloody thing up and she wasn't going to get it off him now. He was having fun. He was starting to enjoy himself for the first time in weeks. He held the phone high, well out of her reach.

'You wouldn't happen to have heard Jack mention the name of his dentist, would you, my dear? Didn't go against my will and pay any of the unprincipled swine's accounts, did you? I know how fond you were of him.'

May had dressed for town, her make-up smooth, her frock expensive; appearances were deceptive. The little bitch trod on his foot, ground it into the floor, choosing the site of the perennial corn that still dogged his smallest toe.

She didn't fight fair. He paled, and his voice paled. 'She doesn't know,' he breathed, hopping, dragging the shoe from his foot, tossing it across the room to hit a small table and send it and a vase of flowers crashing to the floor, water darkening the pale carpet.

May retrieved the vase, unbroken. She placed it on the mantelpiece, collected her scattered flowers, and his shoe, which she aimed at him.

Bloody-little-wild-cat-bitch, he mouthed. He was easy to lip-read.

Not a tendril of her champagne blonde hair out of place, agile, slim as a girl, a well-born lady, but the language she mouthed back from across the room was not that of a lady. Always a fast learner, May.

'When did you last see your brother, Mr Burton?' the distant voice continued, unaware his words were falling in the midst of a battle zone.

'Some years ago. Six and a half to be precise.' May had picked up the cracked guts of the phone, held it poised to throw at him – and she'd do it too. 'I'll pass the handpiece to my wife.' He got in his last Ss, dropped the receiver onto the floor and left her to it.

Ten minutes passed before she placed the phone down, then she began in earnest. He'd heard it all before. He replaced his shoe, tied his lace and leaned against the doorframe, raking at his scalp with his fingernails until she drew breath.

'Shot in the back of the head with a small calibre handgun, May.'

'And you told them to speak to John! And that other man. Who was Vera Owen? He said Jack had been involved with a married woman, a Vera Owen. What in God's name are you?'

'I dunno, May. Finish telling me and we'll both bloody well know, won't we?'

'You're a womanising conscienceless miscarriage of nature, and no better than your father. You're worse than your father ever was. You make him look like a gentleman. And I can't take any more of you. I will take no more of you, Jack. Get out of my sight.'

'I was going anyway. I can't bloody stand living with you, you manipulating bloody rabbit-food-eating little bitch.'

'You can't go, you insane fool.'

'Make up your bloody mind then.'

'He wants you up there. He knows that you and Sam were identical twins.'

'I know he knows, and how do you think he bloody well knows?'

'John.'

'And that blackmailing, black-headed little bitch. She didn't waste any time.'

'What did you expect? I wanted to call her back last night. Sergeant Robertson said they were holding Charles Owen on other charges.'

'He bloody nearly killed me one night. Split my skull open with a tyre lever. I hope they hang the bastard.'

'I'm going to call Ann.'

'She doesn't want to know you.'

'She doesn't want to know *you*! You are the reason she stopped coming here. What did you expect her to do? Call you Uncle Sam?'

'I expect bloody nothing from nobody, and that's all I ever get, May. And it's almost eleven-a-bloody-clock. I thought we were going to eat in town.'

'I've got to clean up your mess. And on the new carpet too. You are the limit, Jack. How did you get to be like you are?'

'Dead easy. Blame the old bastard. He screwed up my life.'

'You're like a spoiled six year old, always blaming someone

else. Your father has been dead for damn near forty years. You can't blame him forever, and you can't blame Sam forever either.'

'I'll blame who I bloody well like. Blame you too, you nagging little bitch.'

'Do you ever stop and think of the consequences of your actions? Have you ever once in your life stopped to think of anyone other than yourself?'

'I try not to. What's for lunch?'

'It's too early. Make yourself a coffee.'

'I ate my bloody cornflakes early, didn't I?'

'Then make yourself a sandwich!'

'There's no butter and I don't want a bloody sandwich. I want steak and chips at the restaurant.'

'Your cholesterol is sky high.'

'I like my cholesterol high. It's about all that is these days.' He walked out to the kitchen muttering, 'A poor bloody dead man will fry himself some bread, that's what he'll do.'

He was heating his margarine in the frying pan when the phone rang again.

'That will be Maxine,' May said. She spoke for only a minute but when she walked to the kitchen, tears were trickling. 'Ann,' she said.

'What the bloody hell does she want now?'

May shook her head, wiped at her tears. 'She's in hospital. She's had another baby. Oh Jack, she said to me that she was sorry. That poor little girl said to me that she was sorry. Sorry for what?' He dropped his bread into the fat, listened to it sizzle. 'God, Jack, after what we have done to her, she says she's sorry?'

'Don't start on that again.'

'We're going up there. Today. You're going to Daree, to do whatever the police want you to do.'

She stood there, her eyes leaking while he flipped his bread over, got the jam from the fridge and sat down to eat.

She sat by him, her head on the table, and he placed an arm

around her. 'Come on. Stop your bawling. I'm a bastard and you always knew it. She's all right if she can make a phone call. The kid is all right?'

'It's very small, and it's another girl, Jack, and she named it ... that's what's killing me. It's killing me, Jack. She named her Bethany May.'

the sand dunes

~

Friday 15 August

Jack had spent the morning in Daree, kowtowing to the Sydney detectives, then he and May had driven up to Warran, booked into a motel and had a decent lunch there. He would have preferred to eat at a pub, but he didn't feel too confident about walking into a Warran hotel. He'd spent a fair amount of his time in most of them, and been tossed out of a few.

It was two o'clock before they drove to the Warran hospital. May wanted him to go in with her, to look at the granddaughter – or great niece, depending on which one he was supposed to be. And he'd been planning to do just that. As May had said fifty times or more, Ann had called them; she'd opened the lines of communication, so now it was up to them to keep those lines open.

So he'd breeze in and front her. He'd planned it all morning, practising Sam's fake expression of concern. 'Lovely to see you again, Ann Elizabeth,' he was going to say. 'Sad news about your father.' That's what he'd planned to do on the eight-hour drive last night, what he'd planned when he'd woken before dawn in a strange bed, what he'd planned while driving to Warran, and to the hospital. But ten metres from the hospital entrance, he'd stilled his feet. Backed off. Chickened out.

His lack of fear had served him well in his youth, but fear was like a nest of lice in his guts. He couldn't face those eyes. They'd kill him. She had Ellie's big round eyes, but hers were black as coal. She'd always shielded them from him behind a film of accusation, and they'd accuse him again today.

Bastard, they'd say. Murdering bastard.

He looked at his hands. They were clean. He'd scrubbed them clean last night at the motel, scrubbed them with Solvol, bought at the Daree supermarket. Scrubbed them before they went to the cops this morning too, and made a bloody mess of the motel's hand basin.

They'd taken a sample of his blood and a bit of his hair, they'd X-rayed his skull, his teeth, his jaws. He was probably ticking today, probably giving off radium fumes. Then, when the technical mob had done with him, the cops had started in. Hours he'd been with them, and he'd played Sam, played him to perfection until every vessel in his brain had gone into atomic mode, threatening the big bang.

Fear was a killer. So were X-rays. His head was aching like a bastard. Maybe if he had a heart, then his heart was aching too. Maybe he wanted to see that kid, born early like its mother, with black hair an inch long – like its mother. All Burton, the husband had said when May had called him last night from the motel.

Another one of the long-limbed, black-headed little buggers, that old Celtic strain that refused to breed out, Jack thought as he drove slowly down the main street, massaging his neck, turning his head from side to side, striving to ease the ache. His heart had been thumping like a dying motor since he'd driven away from the hospital. Maybe he should have gone in. If you're going to have a heart attack, the best place to have one is at a hospital.

Too familiar, this town. Back on his old turf, his old stomping ground, it was becoming increasingly difficult to deny Jack. He'd known Warran well, known a few Warran women in his time too.

A beer and a couple of aspros, he thought. There were aspros in the glove-box. He reached across, and his heart lurched, choking him.

'Bloody world attacking from without and cholesterol attacking a man from within,' he said, doing a left-hand turn. 'Ah, you're already dead, you poor godforsaken bastard, so you can't die of a heart attack, can you? You're one of the undead; a bloody zombie.' He snatched the packet of aspros, peeled three from the foil and tossed them into his mouth as he turned out of the street and onto the road that led to Mallawindy.

Jack had grown accustomed to seeing green paddocks at Narrawee; the land here was brown with last year's grass, but already there was a haze of green showing through. Give it a week of warm days and these paddocks would be green again, green for a while. The only time this country was fit to live in was in spring.

He passed a truck. It looked like Jim Watson's. Driving on automatic now, he raised a hand, an old habit, then quickly withdrew it to scratch at his scalp. May had checked his head again last night and she'd laughed at him, laughed at his bottle of louse shampoo, bought when he'd gone out for Solvol and cigarettes, a twenty-dollar note in his pocket. He'd used his shampoo before he'd showered this morning but it hadn't done much good.

One day he'd get the lot of it cut off. Couldn't yet, not while the coppers were hanging around asking questions. He had to be unquestionably Sam, the long-haired S-hissing bastard with the pigtail.

Sam had never worn a pigtail, but he did now. Jack's hair was worn longer than the old wigs; it had to be longer so he could tie it back, get it out of the bloody way. Without his rubber band he looked like Big Chief Running Bear with a beard. But he didn't look like Jack. Jack had kept his hair black with the help of a bottle; he'd worn it short, brushed straight back from his brow. Jack had been clean-shaven.

'Poor bloody Jack.'

When he'd heard the voice on the answering machine, mummy's boy Benjie, telling Aunt May that they'd found the body, he'd wanted it buried wearing his name. Couldn't have it. The teeth and jawbone of the corpse had been found intact. It wouldn't match his – unless his old man had bred a third son on the wrong side of the blanket. 'What a bloody lark,' he said. 'The old bastard would roll over in his grave if he found out he'd given me an out.'

Laughter kept him going for a few kilometres. Maybe it eased the tension in his neck. It or the aspros he'd swallowed were making inroads into his headache.

The car he drove was near new, a big silver grey Ford. It ate the few short kilometres to Mallawindy, and when he saw the town seeping out of the landscape, he felt nauseated, hating what he saw and knowing he shouldn't be there.

'Suppurating sore on the backside of buggery,' he said.

He should have stayed in Warran or better still, stayed at the motel in Daree, let May drive to the hospital alone. He glanced at the old scar on his wrist, then pulled down the sleeve of his sweater. Should have put a bandaid over it before he'd gone to the cops, but if they'd questioned the injury, all he'd have to show them was Jack's twenty-four-year-old scar, legacy of the night he and old Rella Eva had played chicken with a train at a level crossing, and lost the game.

'Poor old Rell. It's a bastard of a world, Rell. You're better off out of it.'

He glanced to the left as he drove through town. He glanced to the right.

BURTON AND DOOLEY'S EMPORIUM.

Forced to stop at a pedestrian crossing, he squinted his eyes, trying to see through the newsagency door, but King Billy was hobbling across the road, three dogs limping behind him; he and his dogs had known Jack well. His face shielded with a hand he watched the dogs stop, sniff the air. Perhaps they smelt him. He'd kicked a couple in his day. King Billy stilled his feet to eye Jack's luxury car and to swear at its driver.

'Piss off,' Jack mouthed, driving around him, then around the block and through town again.

'A bloody man is stark raving crazy,' he said, but he needed to see someone he knew. Bill Dooley, old Robbie West. Anyone. The town looked dead. The plague had been through and killed every bastard in it. King Billy excluded.

Jack saluted him – or his dogs, then drove on, looking at his peppercorn tree in front of the Central Hotel, wanting to pull into the gutter and push the old door wide, be himself again. But he wasn't himself. Couldn't be himself.

'You're no one,' he said. 'You're nothing but a nothing, you're not a thing at all.'

His watch checked, he made the turn into Dead Man's Lane, a fitting place for the undead to go, and for half an hour he toured the tracks through the sand dunes, looking left at the rough bark of the gums, looking right at the river, choked with fallen trees. He parked the car and walked the dunes, and he cursed, and he remembered while the sun slowly crept across the sky.

He thought of Ellie and of the one in hospital; he thought of May. She'd been on a high since they'd left Narrawee. She'd got her Ann Elizabeth back. She'd got a kid named for her, and David had said he'd be taking the boys to the hospital to view their new sister, that he'd meet May there at two. She'd spent fifty dollars this morning on junk, determined to buy the little boys' hearts. She should have had her own kids. He should have moved to Narrawee back in the sixties. Should have done a lot of things.

May would be finished with her visiting, but she had the motel key. She'd be full up with the one in the hospital. Four kids in six years. Five kids in ten. The little one who had looked like Liza had been dead for around two weeks that night. That bloody night.

Run, Dad. Go out to Dead Man's Lane and I'll find you there. I promise you. I promise I'll get you home to Narrawee. Run, Dad. Run!

He'd thought the game was up and he hadn't been able to raise a run, but he'd walked, walked through the storm willing a bolt of lightning to strike him dead. It had tried to. He'd kept to the trees and the riverbank, just walking and thinking it was all over, and wanting it over; he'd walked the dunes knowing she wouldn't come, knowing that he'd fall down on the sand and dig himself in, die of pneumonia.

He'd been sitting on wet sand, scooping out his hole, when he'd seen the blink of old Satan's eyes against the black backdrop of Hell. In the distance though, too bloody far away. Twice he'd watched those blinking eyes before he'd raised energy enough to stand, to walk towards them.

Crazy little bitch; she had always kept her promises.

Sobered by the rain and the walk, an exhausted and dripping wet rag, he'd tried to open the passenger side door.

'In the back,' she'd said. 'We'll go around the river.'

'You'll get bogged.'

The old timber trucker's road had been a sea of mud – mud to the axles. He'd been right too. He'd pushed her out of a bog, ten miles out, almost given himself a bloody hernia doing it, then they'd ploughed on again, the Holden pushing through, damn near bush-bashing its way out behind Daree. He'd had a new respect for Holdens since that night.

She'd stayed on the back roads, bypassing the towns when she could. Nothing he could say to her and no energy to say it. She'd been silent too, her concentration on the road, until they hit Albury, where she'd filled the tank. They'd stopped at a self-service place with one sleepy bloke in the office.

'Stay down,' she'd said as he'd opened the car door.

'I've got to take a – '

'Self-control is good for the soul. Practise it.'

Capable little bitch. She drove like him. A stark raving mad woman behind the wheel, but she'd taken him to a public loo, driven around the block twice before stopping, opening the boot and tossing him his briefcase, hitting him in the gut with it, knocking the wind out of him in more ways than one. He hadn't considered his case, hadn't been thinking further than the moment, the escape. She had. All Burton, that one. Burton smart, always had been. A Burton to her bloody bootlaces.

Locked in the toilet, he'd opened his briefcase and dragged out Sam's lightweight slacks and his red knit shirt. He'd combed his grey wig and tugged it on, tugged it level, then he'd glued on his mo.

Like Superman, Jack had made a few quick changes in his life – in the airport toilets, his car parked in the long-term car park. In the city. Always had to get rid of his car when he'd driven down by day. The nights had been better. He'd parked it in the Toorak garage.

He'd been trying to clip the heavy gold chain around his throat as he returned to the car that night. Hated the thing. Had to wear it. Hadn't liked Sam's glasses either. Not then.

'Where are your clothes?' she'd said.

'In my case.'

She'd opened her purse and then taken Sam's onyx ring from it, handed it to him.

'You've still got that bastard of a thing?'

'Long live Uncle Sam.'

'The perverted mongrel dog – '

'That's your cross. Wear it.'

A tough little bitch. She wouldn't give an inch. He'd wanted her to stop at a roadhouse out of Melbourne, buy a feed of chips.

'Stop thinking with your stomach,' she said. 'We've wasted too much time already. May is probably at Toorak. When we get to the outskirts, call her.'

He'd done as he was told for once in his life, he'd called Toorak. May was there. 'It's Sam,' he'd said. 'I'm coming home. We should be there in under an hour.'

Melbourne traffic had been on the move when they arrived; May was waiting at her front door, but Ann refused to get out of the car.

'Thanks,' he'd said to her, aware that he should say more; what was there to say? It had all been said, said and done too many years ago.

May had tried to kiss her. 'How can I ever thank you?'

'By making sure he never sets foot in Mallawindy again. I promise you – I promise both of you, if he ever goes back there, then I tell it exactly how it was in the cellar. I promise you.'

'He won't go back. You have my word on it. Our word on it. Thank you. Thank you for everything, Ann. Thank you, my dear, dear child.'

No reply, just a squealing U-turn Jack would have been proud of. He and May had stood together, watching her car out of sight.

'Shit. Shit.' He sifted sand through his fingers, sifting out a beer bottle top. Probably one of his own. He'd spent many nights sitting on these dunes, cursing his brother's name. 'Shit,' he said, and he lifted the bottle top to his nose, sniffed it, then pitched it. 'Shit.'

Sitting, swearing, he sifted sand until the sun fell down behind the trees. Still he sat, staring at the western sky as it turned from blue to mauve to purple and gold, sat until two rabbits came out to eye a dead man, their ears high.

It was near dark when he drove away to tour the town, look at the old place. No lights showing. Deserted. Ellie would be living in her old man's house with her sons, running around after them like she'd run around after her old man.

'Bloody kids. Too many bloody kids. Always put them first, and her bloody old man. She'll be happy now with her mummy's boy Benjie and her Johnny Jesus. She'll be happy now.'

He turned, cruised back, parked his car on the verge of the road while he took out his cigarettes, struck a match and watched the small flame burn, felt it lick at his fingers. Familiar, these night noises. The river rustling by. Hardly a river, just a snag-riddled stream for most of the year, twisting, turning, still fighting the will of the dusky gods who, in some forgotten Dreamtime, had charted its course west.

Made a muck of it, didn't they, he thought. Never big enough, it hadn't gone far enough to do much good. It seeped underground, crept out into reed-infested billabongs; there was little left of it by the time it got to Mallawindy. But it had a smell of its own; a mud and fish smell, mixed with honey and eucalypt, chook shit and cows. Old essence of Mallawindy. It hung in the air tonight.

Essence of Ellie.

'Trapped by her, you stupid godforsaken bastard,' he said.

A door slammed behind him and he swung around to face it. Light filtered out, framing Malcolm Fletcher's shapeless bulk.

'Christ! Is he still alive?'

The cigarette stubbed out, Jack started the motor and took off, spraying gravel; he hit the brake and did his skidding U-turn. 'A bloody man is a maniac. That's the one bastard who'd recognise me with a black face and a boomerang in my hand. How the bloody hell can he still be alive? The obese old bastard has got to be hitting eighty.'

Jack was back at the Warran motel before eight and, May waiting, her eyes worried, her kiss of greeting given only so her nose could pick up the scent of whisky.

'I'm clean.'

'Where have you been, Sam?'

Bloody Sam. She was halfway to convincing herself that was who he was these days and he didn't like it. He lit a cigarette, wanting to stir her, pay her back for her suspicious kiss, for her Sam. 'I went down to see Ellie.'

And she bit, like he knew she would. 'You fool. You hopeless fool.' She stood before him, her face red. 'What in God's name possessed you to do a thing like that?' For minutes she ranted and he sat in silence smoking up the unit. 'What did . . . did she – ?'

'She didn't say much. *Where have you been for so long, love?*' He did the nasal voice; an actor born was Jack Burton. '*I've been worried sick about you, love. Oh, by the way, the old brindle cow had twin poddies.*'

May swallowed, waving his smoke away with her hand. 'You didn't go there.'

'Do you think a man's a total bloody maniac?'

'Don't make me answer that.'

'Then leave it alone. I think I'm dying. My head is crawling on the inside and lousy on the outside. Lay off me tonight, will you?'

'But you did go to Mallawindy?'

'I bloody well told you I did. I went out and spat on Sam's grave.'

The power struggle would continue until one of them died. May had held all the cards for too long and she wasn't going to give them up. She fought like a fiend, but she fought him with words, not tears. He could stand words. Many were the nights they warred, but only with words.

'Who saw you there?'

'A few rabbits.'

He didn't mention Malcolm Fletcher. He didn't want to think about that snooping old bastard who should have dropped dead twenty years ago, died of diabetes, been stomped on like the bloody old slug he was. Always pulsating around someplace, sticking his nose in where it wasn't wanted. Always behind you, listening. Always in front of you, derisive.

I shouldn't have parked there, he thought. Should have thought. Shouldn't have lit a cigarette. How long had the old bastard been watching before he opened his door? He was dangerous, and Jack was worried, and when he was worried, he preferred to blame someone else.

'You promised me you would never go back there.'

'Leave a bloody man alone tonight, will you? I've been through enough today. I did what you wanted me to do, didn't I? Gave them my blood, let them shoot me with their bloody X-rays, gave them the bloody hair off my head. What do you expect from a man? Some perverted cockroach you can crush beneath your bloody stomping little foot?'

'What if someone had seen you? You're a fool, Sam.'

'And you were hiding behind the door when the milk of human kindness was handed out. You push a man too far with your bloody demands and your questions and your bloody Sam. Shut up with your bloody Sam.'

'What else do I call you? Tell me that. You do what you want, and to hell with everyone else. You promised you wouldn't go near Mallawindy and that's exactly where you went. Your promise is not worth the breath it is given with, Jack. And you left me stranded at the hospital. I had to walk back here without a coat.'

Jack. He'd dredged one out of her. He wouldn't let her forget who he was, and while she knew who he was, Jack lived.

'I told you to take your bloody coat with you, didn't I? I offered to get it out of the boot for you, didn't I? If you'd listen to me sometimes instead of thinking you know every bloody thing all the bloody time then you bloody well wouldn't have had to walk home without a coat, would you?'

Safer territory, coats. Safer ground. And they both knew it.

'Go and have your shower and cool off,' she snapped.

'Where are we eating tonight?' he replied in like tone.

'David said they do a good meal at the club.' She took clean underpants and shirt from the case, tossed them at him. He caught the underpants and walked to the bathroom, leaving the shirt on the floor.

'You frightened me tonight, Sam. You frightened the life out of me. I didn't know what to expect. I've been sitting here since five, sick to the heart with worry that you'd come back drunk.'

'Don't bloody call me Sam!'

'I've been calling you Sam all day. Ben, your son was there. He's a lovely boy.'

'He's a mealy-mouthed mummy's boy little poofter and always has been.'

'Stop that! He said he remembered . . . Sam.'

The shower was running, the bathroom door left wide open. His voice rose to compete with the splashing.

'He probably had to dodge the bastard too. Hang on to his pants when Uncle Sam came visiting. Maybe that's what's wrong with him. Maybe he didn't hang on hard-a-bloody-nough.'

'Stop it, Jack. For the love of God, will you let up on it?'

'It's the only way I can get you to say my bloody name. I've got to fight you for it every time.'

'Be reasonable. If I call you Jack in private, it's going to come out one day in public. Be reasonable about it. I've got to stop calling you Jack, and well you know it.'

'Just for tonight, May, for Christ's sake call me Jack. Just for tonight let me hear my own bloody name. And dig me out a half a dozen of those Panadol extras. My head is like a nest of bloody stinging hornets.'

on the scent

~

Thursday 21 August

The wind and the rain hadn't left much behind. Three white camellias and a few reliable little violets had lifted demure faces to this morning's sun, which hadn't wasted time in creeping up on Mallawindy. By tomorrow the garden might be looking for shade.

Malcolm wandered his gravelled paths, selecting, rejecting until he had a small posy. He hadn't been to Warran in over a month, but he was dressed for visiting today, and as sober as a judge; not that he'd ever had great faith in the sobriety of judges. He wound a rubber band around the stalks of his posy, washed his hands, then slipped into his new jacket, the tailor-made dark grey with silver buttons he'd worn to Bronwyn's wedding. Quite sporty. It had set him back eight hundred dollars, but it concealed some of his bulges.

Monday's Warran *Advertiser* was still on his bedside table, the headlines screaming:

IDENTICAL TWINS' MOLARS NO MATCH. BODY NOT JACK'S
Samuel Burton's X-rays when compared with those taken
from the body found near Daree prove conclusively
that it is not that of the missing Jack Burton,
a police spokesman said yesterday.

The slim paper came out on Mondays and Fridays; it was full of items of no interest. Malcolm rarely kept newspapers for more than a day – except this one. It had Bethany's birth notice in it. He loved the mother, thus he loved the as yet unsighted new daughter.

He'd glanced at the full-page write-up on Jack Burton and his twin brother, but it was old news to Malcolm. He had seen the dead man smoking, he had recognised his tyre-skidding U-turn, and he'd checked the skid marks in daylight, always envious of how Jack could turn a car by hitting his brakes and allowing the rear of the vehicle to slew in a half circle. The old teacher had never attempted it himself, though many of the town hoons had perfected the art and now coloured the roads with their rubber.

So, with Jack no longer dead there would be a few in town eager to collect their winnings. Malcolm had placed fifty dollars on his nose, but he'd allowed a decent interval to pass, not wishing to look too eager for his winnings.

'Fifty dollars at five to one.' He rubbed his palms together, soft pink palms, then he clapped his hands. He'd be delighted to take a little of his own back from young Bourke's mean pocket. This morning the world was looking brighter, and not all of it due to the sun. His car keys and licence were again in his pocket.

After a mild confrontation with a passing bus, Malcolm had blessed his ten-year-old Falcon. It was of solid construction; its steering wheel a captive between hands, thighs and belly, the car had taken the jolt then continued on, in a near straight line, until all four wheels had come back to earth in the middle of a boxthorn hedge.

Then Jeff Rowan, the town dictator, had arrived on the scene and offered his breathalyser, and at a time when air was still at a premium. Malcolm had, of course, refused to blow, and for over a week now he had been without wheels.

'Ah, the power of my distant solicitor,' he'd quipped when licence and keys had been handed back at his door.

'You're a danger to yourself and everyone else on the road. I'll be following you, Malcolm. Every time you look in your rear-view, I'll be behind you, and next time you refuse to blow, I'll run you in. One wrong move and you've done your licence, and I'll see that you don't get it back.'

'I believe the term is police harassment, Constable.'

This morning Malcolm drove sedately to town, his posy of flowers on the passenger seat. When he parked in front of the Central Hotel, beneath *his* peppercorn tree, it was ten past eleven. Unable to absorb his smile he fronted up to the bar and Mick Bourke reached for a small glass.

'Never before lunch, thank you, Mr Bourke. I have come for my winnings.' Malcolm's puffy little hand was out, but Mick Bourke had other ideas. Though Jack was no longer dead, it appeared that he was not yet alive.

'Not today, Fletch. The cops still reckon he's a goner. With all the publicity he's had, they reckon he would have turned up, or the insurance blokes would have got him. They've circulated his dial all over Australia.'

'I have seen him quite recently, Mr Bourke. I believe the money is mine.'

'Yeah, but you got fuckin' pink elephants running loose down your end of town,' young Bob West commented from his corner.

'Oh, nothing so common, Mr West. The pink elephants with hobnail boots are waiting around some near corner for you, I fear. Good morning.' Malcolm left. He drove to the cemetery, one eye on his rear-view mirror.

Alcohol had not touched his lips while his wife and son had lived. He never came to their graves with the smell of brandy on his breath, thus his visits to the Mallawindy cemetery were rare, and always morning visits.

JOHN KELVIN FLETCHER, BORN 1954. DIED 1968.

His bright and beautiful son, who had grasped the world by its tail, had been stolen from him by this town. So fast. A healthy teen-ager one day, and dead within the week. Filthy, diseased little town.

And his wife. JILLIAN MAREE FLETCHER.

Always of nervous disposition, poor Jillian had taken her own life. She'd jumped from the Mallawindy bridge with enough weights tied to her dressing gown belt to hold her down. No one had seen her jump, but the river, cleaner, clearer back then, had given her up the following morning – unlike Amy O'Rouke. From the bridge Jillian's dark hair and her pink dressing gown had been visible to a drover herding his flock of sheep across the bridge.

Malcolm had sucked on his first bottle on the evening of his son's funeral. He had taken up the brandy bottle his wife kept in her pantry for cooking and medicinal purposes, and found it to be very good medicine. Then he'd slept for the first time since his son had died. Not until awoken by the then local lawman, Bob Johnson, had he been aware that Jillian was not beside him in the bed, but had wandered away in the night carrying the two flat irons they'd used as doorstops. The three days of waiting for her funeral was all it had taken to alter Malcolm's status from sober husband and father to childless widower with his bottle.

Poor, grief-crazed Jillian. He should have seen it coming, should have found some way to comfort her, but his own grief had been too blinding.

A month after they'd arrived in this town she'd begged him to leave, pleaded with him to take her home. 'No colour,' she'd said. 'It's grey. It's all grey, Mal.'

Heat and dust and flies and fools, and he the greatest fool of all. A foolish move, coming to Mallawindy. And he'd known it. Perhaps he would have taken her home. Perhaps he would have, in time, but his boy had revelled in the freedom. How he had thrived, for a time.

Determined Jillian. She'd slipped the belt of her chenille gown through the flat iron handles, knotting them tightly so her fingers might not change her mind and she'd climbed through the railing and drowned in six feet of water.

Malcolm glanced at her stone as he placed the small posy down. She had loved flowers. He never came here with an empty hand, but not once had he bought her flowers while she lived, bought her some colour. So much more he could have done to help her make the transition. Sad, really, how we need to lose those near to us to realise just how dear they were.

He moved to his son's grave. No flowers, but a groan escaped his throat. He closed his eyes, pressing his fingers to them as he thought of his son. So tall, so fine, and if not a conventionally handsome lad, he had epitomised perfection in Malcolm's eyes. A miracle, born of two plain and lonely people who had married because it had seemed like the correct thing to do at the time. Both unattached in their mid-thirties, mismatched certainly, but their embarrassed fumblings had somehow given their boy a brief life.

Malcolm felt an internal blush begin. He'd been a late starter in the sex stakes, his only experience with women gained in his unlit marital bed. Each lusty scene in his novels had, to a greater or lesser degree, been taken from his own limited marital experience. A shy lover, Jillian had refused to remove her nightgown, had never allowed him to see her unclothed.

As he stepped back from his son's grave, he heard the movement of gravel behind him, and for a moment believed it was Jillian rolling over, turning her back again.

Then that voice. 'Good morning, Mr Fletcher. We've got a lovely day for a change.' Ellie Burton had three children sleeping in this place.

'Mrs Burton.' He replaced his glasses. 'Yes. Indeed it is a lovely day.'

'I suppose you heard about it not being Jack that they found,' she said.

'Indeed I did,' he said. 'Indeed.'

She looked well this morning, due obviously to the fact that her absconding husband was no longer only a collection of bones. Malcolm watched her walk down a gravel path to a stone and place flowers there.

LIZA, LINDA, AND PATRICK. LOVED CHILDREN OF JACK AND ELLIE.

All in together, he thought as she placed her palm on the stone, smiled, then she saw him watching and turned her smile on him.

'There's something . . . something comforting about knowing where they are, isn't there?' she said.

'Indeed there is, Mrs Burton.' He found conversations with this woman difficult, so he usually agreed, whether he agreed or not.

'I asked Father Fogarty if I should . . . could put Jack's name on the stone. It might make it easier for me to accept that he's . . . gone.'

Malcolm nodded. A very strange woman. Didn't want her husband found dead in his underpants and sock, but apparently she had no problems in burying him. He shook his head and stood on, his eyes roaming this sad little place.

A hundred and fifty years ago the Catholic and the Anglican dead had been well separated, but necessity moved them closer each year. People kept dying, would continue dying, until only a gravel path marked their religious dispute. Mallawindy's forefathers had not been far-seeing. Perhaps they hadn't expected the town to survive, and thus produce such a field of the dead. No doubt if the ghosts walked, there were some rare old brawls at night between the orange and the green, sleeping toe to toe.

Ellie finished with her praying, walked back to join him in no-man's land.

'Are you on foot, Mrs Burton?' He pointed to his car.

'Oh, you've got your licence back. That would be lovely. Thank you very much, Mr Fletcher. It's a long walk from town, but it was such a lovely morning, I had to come out and see them.' They walked to the metal gate together. He held it open for her, saw her seated in his car. 'Young Jeff says that with all that publicity last week, it's pretty unlikely that Jack is going to come back.' Perhaps she wanted him to disagree. He kept his silence. 'He said that finding the gun in the river, and knowing how fond Jack was of his father's gun, that it's pretty certain . . . '

He couldn't tell her what he had seen on Friday night. The

match struck down on the box, the movement of the hand holding the cigarette, the silhouetted angle of the head. He hadn't seen the face. Had not needed to see it. That fast escape. That tight-screaming U-turn on the narrow road, the gravel flying. Malcolm had seen it all before, and too many times, to be mistaken.

'And his bank accounts too. He hasn't made a withdrawal since before that last Christmas. I think that's what's got me convinced. Benjie's convinced. He said that I have to accept it. And as he keeps on saying, Jack never had any money in his accounts. He was always waiting for the next payment to go in. I mean, what could he be living on? Benjie said he wouldn't find work at his age, and he's probably right, although Jack was a very good salesman. But, as he says, even the younger men can't get work these days.' Still Malcolm kept his silence. 'And Father Fogarty too. He says it would be better for me to realise that Jack isn't coming back this time.'

Father Fogarty probably had twenty dollars riding on Jack being dead, Malcolm thought. The old reprobate had been known to wile away many an hour in the hotel, watching the races with more interest than the average onlooker.

'Jack hated cemeteries, you know. He didn't come to any of the children's funerals. He wouldn't want to be here, but if I put his name on the children's stone – sort of look on it as Bessy did when Bill died – she had him cremated then spread his ashes in the river, you know, but she got him a nice little brass plaque in that new wall.' Ellie pointed to a green lawn, and a brick fence that went nowhere.

Malcolm nodded.

'I've been thinking, Mr Fletcher, that not finding his body is . . . is maybe God looking after him, so he doesn't have to end up out here.'

Or Satan, Malcolm thought.

'He was Church of England, you know. He wouldn't change, but he let me baptise all the children Catholic – except Annie. She would have been baptised that day – if she hadn't spoken. I'll never forget that day as long as I live. It was a miracle, and no two ways about it, and I don't care what anyone says.'

'Yes. Certainly. Indeed.' The cemetery road was narrow. Malcolm considered attempting a doughnut turn, but thought better of it. He did a careful three-pointer and drove away, one eye on the rearview mirror.

'Father Fogarty said it wouldn't matter, I mean, Jack not being Catholic. I mean, adding his name to the stone . . . on the Catholic side. It's not as if he's – '

'Rightly so. Rightly so, Mrs Burton.'

'I don't know what I should do, I really don't. I wouldn't do anything until after Christmas, of course. It's seven years this Christmas.'

'It is indeed.'

'Johnny says not to do it. He says it would be desecrating hallowed ground. He refuses to believe that his father is dead. And he says it like he knows he's right too. I always had the feeling that him and Annie knew more than they were letting on about that night, but the two of them are like clams wearing padlocks.'

Clams wearing padlocks? He nodded. Maybe there was hope for this woman yet. He liked that line and tucked it away in his memory bank to use, perhaps, on another day. A good image that one.

'We all believe what we wish to believe, Mrs Burton.' He made a careful right-hand turn onto the highway and proceeded on. The police van cruised by, heading out of town. Once it was out of sight, Malcolm increased his speed.

'He would have come forward, wouldn't he? He wouldn't have let me go through all of this worry.'

Malcolm found it impossible to agree with that one, so he turned the conversation away from Jack. 'John. He has cut his ties with the church, Mrs Burton?'

Ellie looked back towards the cemetery, waved a hand, blew a kiss.

'Yes. Yes he has, Mr Fletcher. Completely. He refuses to set foot inside a church door. Except for Bronwyn's wedding. And if I didn't know better I'd think that he broke his foot that morning trying to get out of going to that too.'

'What does he plan to do with his life?'

'I'm sure I don't know.' She peeled away a broken fingernail, levelling it with her teeth. 'I'm sure I don't know. He told me a while back that the church was just a hole he'd crawled into – like an injured rabbit going to ground, he said, and he said that one hole was as good as another as far as he was concerned. He's a worry to me, to tell you the truth. And with his broken foot, he can't get away from the house much. We're tripping over each other all day. I don't know what I'm going to do with him.'

'There are times, Mrs Burton, when we all need to first go back before we can go forward. And sometimes, having gone back, we realise what little we had to go back to.'

He was speaking from experience. Too many hours lately had been spent in the classroom, filling in for Norman O'Rouke. And he'd be back there again tomorrow. Too old for it now, he was out of touch with youth. Still, today he was free of the Wests and the Dooleys; Thursday was sports day and young Kerrie had roped in a dozen parents to assist her. Malcolm was on his way to Warran to view the new arrival, and the trio of tyrants.

'Have you viewed the new granddaughter, Mrs Burton?'

'Not yet. Benjie was going to drive me down on Sunday, but we had two cows calving, so we put it off. I should have gone down with Bessy on Monday, but I've been so busy, Mr Fletcher. Benjie saw her the day after she was born. They called her Bethany, you know. Bethany May.'

'Yes. Yes. I am on my way there now. You would be most welcome to accompany me.' Responsibility for another life usually kept his concentration on the road.

'That's very nice of you. I suppose I could go. I'd have to let Benjie know where I've gone, though.'

'Certainly.'

218

'Annie is home, you know. She up and left the hospital on Saturday night, Bessy said. Wouldn't stay away from her boys, and it's far too soon. They've kept the baby in for a while, because of its size, but she goes up there every day to feed it.' She sighed, then added, 'It's lucky she's near the hospital, really.'

'Yes.'

'She was born early, you know. Annie, I mean. I had to leave her at the hospital for months. She'd start picking up and then she'd have a setback. I think it might be right what they say these days on the television. You know, how you need to bond early with a baby. I never thought she'd live, Mr Fletcher, to tell the truth. I suppose I just sort of left her to God and the doctors, and expected every day I'd get word that she'd died. She was two-and-a-half months premature, just a little scrap of a thing barely three pounds. Bethany was almost five pounds. It makes a lot of difference to a baby, those few pounds.'

'I'm sure it does.'

'If not for Johnny, Annie would have died the night she was born. You know he held her all the way to the hospital? They said it was because of the hot night and that he'd held her to his warm little chest that had saved her life. He told the matron at the hospital that she had to keep her alive and that her name was Annie Lizabeth.'

She drew a deep breath and bit at a fingernail. 'Poor little thing. She was so different to the others when Jack brought her home. So skinny and her little face looked so old; she used to just sit there, watching everyone with those big black eyes of hers. My goodness. My goodness. Where have all of the years gone to, Mr Fletcher? It seems like only yesterday.'

The car had stopped in front of Ben's shop, but Ellie made no move to get out. Malcolm had never known her so talkative.

'It's funny, but I could always see the other children as grown up, as married, having their own children, but I could never see Annie as a mother. But my word! And isn't young Tristan the wild one?'

'Hopefully he will become tamer as he grows older, Mrs Burton,' Malcolm said.

'I don't know how she's going to cope with the four of them when she gets the new baby home. She'll have to lock that baby away from young Tristan.'

'She has a good husband.'

'Oh, yes. Yes she has. He's so good with those children, I'll say that for him. He is a divorced man, of course. Not that I've ever held that against him. I get on quite well with David. He's very respectful – and a very good dancer, you know.'

pride in achievement

~

'A jerry hat trick, Mr West? I realise your grasp of the English language is far in advance of the other students, so can you enlighten them on the meaning of jerry hat trick?'

'You, you fuckin' jerry hat trick old dickhead.'

'Ah, ah. We see the light, Mr West. We see the light. Geriatric: GERIATRIC.' Malcolm spelt the word as he wrote it on the whiteboard in large red block letters, which was less effective than large letters gouged into the old blackboard with chalk. He missed his chalk, the squeal of which had sometimes been enough to cool his ire – or quell a riot.

'Which differs considerably in meaning to a jerry hat trick. Can you give me the meaning of a common hat trick? Forget the jerry.'

'Fuck off.'

'No. Not quite. Anyone? Can anyone give me the meaning?' Hands went up in his fifth and sixth grade rows. 'Miss Dooley. Enlighten our friend, please.'

'In cricket. Like when a bowler gets out three in three balls.'

'Stupid moll,' the pinheaded bastard in his grade six row sneered, and Malcolm had had enough for one morning.

The mentality of old Robbie West's grandson was not dissimilar to that of his son's. Malcolm had handled them. He'd taught a few

221

to read and write. He sighed and made his slow plodding way to the six grader, on whom he tested out the concealed elbow jab to the ribs. And he had not lost his touch but, unlike his predecessors, this West kicked back, with big boot and mouth.

'Fuckin' touch me again and my father'll fuckin' do you.'

'Ah, so you do have a father, Mr West?'

The barb missed its target. Children these days knew more, but much less; however, their ears were still sensitive appendages, and the West ears, ever large, offered an excellent grip. An car in hand, Malcolm marched the kicking beast to the verandah, where he continued to twist the ear until the West stopped kicking to scream. Quite satisfying it was too, until the infant mistress saw to the somewhat swollen ear's release.

Kerrie dismissed the senior students for an early lunch then sat on Malcolm's table explaining the likely repercussions of corporal punishment, of manhandling students. Malcolm nodded, his attention divided between his smiling lecturer and his half cup of brandy, which, to the uninitiated with a poor sense of smell, might have been mistaken for weak black tea. Kerrie's nose was good. She picked up his trusty green thermos and gave it a shake.

'I could get into trouble for this too, Fletch – even if I could use a nip.'

He didn't offer a nip, but reclaimed his thermos and topped up his cup. 'Where is the fool of a man this week?'

'That body they found at Albury – they think it's Amy. He's gone down there, and God knows when, or if, he'll be back. And I've had it, Fletch.'

Malcolm said no more, but he thought of his own wife, and he thought of his days in the classroom after Jillian's death, the small thermos filled morning and afternoon. Better to give up perhaps, take to one's bed and weep – as O'Rouke had done. Let someone else carry the load. Perhaps. He had chosen a different method.

He glanced at his thermos, weighed it in his hand. A trip home may be in order.

That afternoon Kerrie moved her brood into the seniors' room for a pictorial lesson, via video. Freed for an hour, Malcolm sat at his table, his attention divided between Kerrie and his tea cup.

A pleasant girl, artless, her face bare of make-up, she'd been covering for O'Rouke since his wife disappeared, but the strain was beginning to show. The West's mouth flapping, again or still, she spoke to him, once, thrice, assuming he had a brain.

'Leave the room please, Robert.'

'Make me, you lezzo.'

Kerrie turned her back, turned the volume higher and the West turned up his own.

Unreasonable anger stirred in Malcolm's gut. His blood boiled with anger. How was one supposed to teach these days? How was one expected to control the out-of-control? What this bastard of a being needed was a sound clip under the ear.

'Outside, West!' Malcolm bawled.

The infants cowered and the junior mistress gestured for him to give it up. But why should he allow this swine of a swine to control his classroom? Why should the Wests and their ilk be allowed to control the future? God help the world. God help this lass and others like her.

There were few in town Malcolm tolerated, even fewer that he actually approved of, but he respected this girl who had battled on alone for most of this year, and he wanted to murder the vile-mouthed little bastard, certain, at this moment, that he could, without compunction, knock his pinhead off and peg it to the school fence by its ears.

He stood and waddled to the whiteboard. No multicoloured chalk missiles awaiting his pleasure. He'd tossed a lot of them in his time. He picked up the whiteboard cleaner, a near relative of the old blackboard duster. It had a solid plastic base. Able to locate the West by its noise, Malcolm aimed the whiteboard cleaner.

And, my word, he had not lost his accuracy!

For three long minutes the class was convinced he had

committed murder. Blinds rattled to the ceiling and the watchers groaned at the abrupt loss of a video, while five pinheaded, big-eared, big-footed Wests emerged from various seats to bewail the loss of their relative. By the time Kerrie had stemmed the bleeding and taped the wound, the beast of grade six was stirring into open-mouthed silence.

The juniors moved back to the safe confines of their own room, the seniors dismissed, Kerrie telephoned Jeff Rowan. It appeared that the silenced one could require transportation to Daree and a stitch or two or three.

'From a plastic missile?' Malcolm was amazed, if somewhat chastened.

Later, seated at his borrowed table, shamed into sham submission by the lawman but still in possession of his licence, Malcolm retrieved his trusty thermos from the table drawer and poured the last of its amber contents into his tea cup, catching all the drips; he spread his thighs, leaned back and sipped.

He had missed teaching when he retired, or thought he had until dragged back into harness by O'Rouke's absconding wife. Malcolm thought of the body found near Albury, which led him to thinking of the skeleton with its full set of teeth, not as yet identified, which led him to thinking of graves and his son's grave, and of Ann's sweet Mandy, which led him to Ann's boys and to the minute girl child he'd viewed yesterday in the hospital nursery.

He had visited with Ann, alone, after Ellie Burton left to do a little shopping. Young Benjamin at school, the tyrant sleeping, Matthew at playgroup and peace in the house. For an hour Ann had been his own. A wonderful hour. And for the first time in many a year, Ann had spoken of the future, of one day returning to study.

'So motherhood isn't necessarily a life sentence, Burton?' he had said.

'I think it's a part of the learning process, sir.'

Always 'Burton'. Always 'sir'. Was he friend, father or teacher to this girl, this woman?

There had been a wholeness about her yesterday, too long missing. Pregnant last week, slim as a reed this week. Jillian had spent three days delivering their son, and three years recovering. Poor Jillian. These days he thought of her often, and of his son, of the baby he had held and dreamed for.

Malcolm shook his head, shaking memory away. Babies had little personality, but the wisp, Bethany, had frowned at him yesterday, recognised him. So new, yet her eyes had been old, as if her premature birth had left intact the memories of her every former time on earth. What a world she will inherit, he thought. A world ruled by Wests.

Until three-thirty Malcolm sat in the empty classroom, sipping, thinking, until the electronic bell jangled, releasing him to waddle up to the Central for his daily refill. Safer to leave his car parked at the school today, out of view of the town dictator. And his heart needed the exercise. He'd seen his doctor yesterday.

'Walk,' the man had warned him. 'Walk, and cut your food intake by half or you'll be dead inside twelve months.'

'Promises, promises,' Malcolm had replied.

the teachers

～

Sunday 24 August

There was a determined knock on Ben's front door the following
Sunday morning, and in the kitchen, lounge and dining room, heads
lifted, ears listened. Friends and egg buyers always came to the
back door. Only salesmen, the police and Jehovah's Witnesses
knocked on the old front door, but salesmen didn't come on
Sundays, the police had stopped calling, Ellie's church didn't
approve of Jehovah's Witnesses, and she was running late.

'Get rid of them for me, will you, Benjie love? Give them some
eggs,' she called from the bathroom.

Ben left off printing out his shop accounts and walked to the
front door where he found Kerrie Fogarty, studying the mud brick
wall.

'G'day,' he said. 'What can I do for you?'

'What are you offering?' She grinned her cheeky boyish grin,
and Ben returned the grin as he swung the door wide. He liked
Kerrie. He cut her hair every six weeks and he wished it grew faster.

Scared silly that first day, embarrassed to be so close to a female
head, he'd held back. 'Shorter,' she'd said. 'Short back and sides,
Ben. Like you do the guys. More,' she'd kept saying. 'Run your
clippers up my neck. I haven't got time for combs.'

She had no time for lipstick either, or dresses. She lived in jeans and boots, or baggy shorts and leather sandals. She was wearing her shorts today. The sun was out and warm, and her legs were long.

'Actually, I was hoping to speak to your big brother. Is he around?'

'Yeah. He's reading. Come through. Watch that bottom step,' he warned, leading her down to a dark and narrow passage, past the steep staircase that led up to Ellie's room in the roof.

'What a funny little house you've got,' she said. 'When I first came here I used to call it the gingerbread house. Didn't know who owned it then, and every time I passed by I expected a cackling witch to beckon me in with her crooked finger. It's got real character, Ben. What's something like this doing in Mallawindy?'

He liked his house too. Always had. He'd known it well until he was five years old, until his grandfather had died and the house was sold. Then, around nine years ago, Mr Mack, the buyer, had died amid the chaos of his back bedroom, and no one had missed him for a week. The house and land had gone to auction and Ben had bought it for a song, hoping Ellie would move back.

She'd helped him clean it up and put it back the way it had been in her father's time, but refused to move in with him. It had taken Jack's disappearance and Johnny's return to move her from over the river.

'Mum's grandfather came out here from Germany when he was fourteen, back in the late eighteen hundreds. He built it. Started off with a couple of rooms and just kept adding bits, then because he'd built the roof so steep, he decided to put a room upstairs. Only trouble is, he hadn't left anywhere to put the stairs. Watch your head, there.'

'The little house that grew up.'

'Yeah. He made the bricks himself out of the riverbank. Clay and straw, plus a bit of cow manure. So my grandfather always told us.'

'I can't smell it.'

'Only on wet days.' They were still grinning when Ben ushered her into the dining room, where Ellie stood ready to make her escape.

'Oh, it's only you, Kerrie.'

'G'day, Mrs Burton. Just telling Ben I like his house.'

The newspaper opened to the crossword, Ellie closed it, self-conscious about her spelling, always a little threatened, a mite apprehensive, when around educated people. 'Sit down, Kerrie. Ben will make you a cup of tea.'

'Not today, thanks. I'm here to see John, actually.'

Ben walked to the double doors separating lounge from dining room. He swung one wide. Johnny, still seated, looked past his brother to the infant mistress.

'G'day, John,' she said. 'How's the foot?'

'Miss Fogarty.' He nodded, annoyed by the interruption. 'It's improving daily.'

'I like your shoe.'

An oversized sneaker, cut to fit, now covered his foot. He forced a brief smile as his eyes urged her to come to the point of her visit.

The three Burtons coexisted within these dark little rooms, but when together in any one of them, the room appeared crowded. Kerrie stepped down to the lounge room to perch on the arm of a well-stuffed couch, and Ben backed off, backed off to the kitchen to his accounts, but he listened in to the conversation.

'I've just heard that Norman O'Rouke is in hospital. His mother called, said he won't be coming back, and I can't let Fletch into the classroom again tomorrow or I won't have a school. Uncle Joe said that you had done some teaching, John. I was wondering – '

'My goodness.' Ellie was at the front door waiting for Bessy. She walked back to the lounge and stood at the double doors. 'What's happened now?'

'Fletch? He um . . . sort of did his block with young Robert West.'

'I meant to Mr O'Rouke.'

Kerrie turned to her. 'You knew they found that dead woman

near Albury? The police came for Norman and took him down there to identify her. He didn't come back.'

'I saw it on the news. About finding the woman. Was it his wife?'

'I think it must have been. His mother didn't say one way or the other. All she was interested in was her Norman and his breakdown. They've got him in a nuthouse . . . psychiatric hospital. Anyway, I was wondering, John – '

'You've got time for a cup of tea, Kerrie.'

'No. Not now, thanks, Mrs Burton. Another day, though. I'll come back and have a proper look at your house.' Again she turned to John. 'I was wondering if you're qualified to teach, John?'

'Not as qualified as Mr Fletcher, and with less patience these days,' he said, ending the conversation.

'I doubt that . . . greatly. Very greatly. We could have been in serious trouble on Friday. I could have been in serious trouble. He threw the whiteboard cleaner, could have knocked young Robert's eye out.'

'Fletch always had a thing with the Wests,' Ben said, joining Ellie at the double doors.

'Jeff knows about his thermos too. I had to do some fast talking. Anyway, the department will get me a replacement but I can't contact them until tomorrow and the kids have had a bad year. Norman's had too much time off, and the temps we've had have been in and out . . . like – '

'Bulls through the milking shed,' Ben said.

Kerrie nodded, grinned. 'And about as much use. It'll take them a day or two to get someone else up here, and I just thought you might be interested, John. Just for tomorrow, or a few days max. I want to keep the kids in school if I can. We've got six who are supposed to be going to high school next year. We've let them down badly.'

Johnny wasn't adding to the conversation. His book was closed but a thumb kept his place, and his expression suggested he was eager to return to it.

'You'd be qualified, wouldn't you, Johnny? You said you used to teach at some boys' college in Brisbane,' Ben said.

John looked at his brother, cursing him silently but not denying his words.

Ben moved into the room. Kerrie, when standing, looked him in the eye, but she was seated now; he could look down at her head, and he knew it intimately, knew her small neat ears, and the two gold studs she always wore, the long slim neck. She'd be coming in soon for another haircut. This pleased him, and he smiled as he looked beyond her head to John and his book.

His brother rarely left the property; he refused to take any money for his labour, wearing the working clothes Ellie bought for him, or his father's discarded trousers, the hems let down by Ellie, who was no seamstress. Since his accident he read day and night, replying only briefly when spoken to.

'Would you be interested in helping me out tomorrow, John? That's why I'm here. I'd be eternally grateful. I can't ask Fletch again. I dare not. Robert West ended up with two stitches in his head.'

John frowned at the ones determined to break into the space he'd managed to build around himself. The atmosphere in the house had lightened since the Daree body had altered its status from Jack Burton to John Doe. Ellie was happy, Ben was relieved she'd stopped howling, but for John, for him, it meant that Jack Burton was alive again, living in comfort at Narrawee. It meant that he now had to begin mentally murdering him again – and waiting, waiting for him to show his face in Mallawindy.

'It would be good for you, love,' Ellie said. 'It might take you out of yourself, being with the children, teaching again. You could wear the suit you wore to Bronwyn's wedding.'

The book closed with a snap. John considered a fast reply to the negative, a faster escape to the old place, but his reply became lost on the way out. He placed his book on the couch as he glanced at Kerrie.

She was watching him, her head to one side, her teeth chewing on a hangnail. He knew she was in her mid-thirties, but today she looked like a lanky kid who'd landed in a hole but wasn't complaining about it. An organiser, that one. Her eyes were a deep grey, flecked with blue – too hard to hold, so he looked back to the cover of his book.

Les Miserables. Fit company for him these days. He'd picked it up from the old bookcase yesterday. Hadn't read it in years, and he wanted to read it now. The distant past had been trapped between its worn covers and he preferred the past. He'd been planning to spend the afternoon wallowing in the ancient sewers of Paris. Not to be. They wouldn't let it be.

'I can't handle the boys, John. Some of them are as big as me. They need discipline. And they need a male teacher with a bit of self-discipline – and one big enough to look as if he means business. You sort of fit the bill.' Still John made no reply, but Kerrie wasn't ready to give up. 'Someone smashed two windows in the senior room last night. It was probably the Wests, giving me a warning. If I get Fletch back, they'll burn the school down tomorrow. I wouldn't ask you to do it if I wasn't desperate – if the kids who want to learn weren't desperate for help – but I am, and they are, John. And you're the only one in town I can ask. Beg. Kiss your smelly shoe.' She grinned, and for a moment his mouth attempted to return the grin. He controlled it, rubbed his eyes instead, rubbed his brow as he looked at his misshapen shoe.

'My movements are somewhat restricted, Miss Fogarty.'

'I'll pick you up at your door. I'll drop you home.'

'He can drive Jack's car. He only needs one foot for it. It's an automatic,' Ellie said.

'Three against one. It appears that I am outnumbered. I'll give it some thought, Miss Fogarty. Can we leave it at that for the moment?' That answer might buy him time.

'Kerrie. Call me Kerrie. Everyone does. Miss Fogarty always makes me look over my shoulder for my maiden aunt, and she was an old tartar if ever I met one – although the older I get the more like her I become . . . never know when I'm not wanted, and refuse to take no for an answer.' She grinned at Ben, then she stood. 'Can you let me know by six tonight, John? I'll have to contact the parents, get them to keep the kids home if you can't make it. Or . . . or get Jeff Rowan in to give them a tour of his jail.'

'We'll get back to you by six,' Ben said.

'Thanks.'

'Oh, there's Bessy. I'm off, loves. Take some eggs with you, Kerrie. You do eat eggs?' Ellie said

'Thanks. Yeah, but another time. Thanks in advance, John, in hope. If you can just give me a couple of days until the department gets its head together and gets me another temp. Three days, tops. I'll call them first thing in the morning.'

John nodded. He stood. Taller than his father, slimmer than his father, his grey slacks loose and worn, their half-centimetre hand-stitched hems barely brushing his odd shoes. Not as well pressed as his father.

'I'll call you by six,' he said as the infant mistress disappeared into the passage, then he took up his crutch and left the house by the back door.

the gun

~

Malcolm had served his time in the army. He'd fought the Hun – with a pen and ink, which had not been his choice of arms. Back then he'd wanted to get out there, shoot the swine and save the world for old England, but always a little chubby and never the sporting type, he had only seen the ravages of war, the totals of war, and the lands after the bombs had done their work.

He'd had friends in his childhood, his boyhood, but so many of his generation had been lost to war. Fresh-faced boys, with mischief and laughter in their eyes, had left old England's shores to return to it with the eyes of old men.

Saved from the worst of it, Malcolm had stayed on in the army when the fighting ended, travelling with his pen and ink. He'd bought a German rifle in France, and a handgun in Germany. Back in England, he'd got onto two grenades, building up quite an arsenal which he'd had to leave behind when he'd packed up for Australia. But the handgun had travelled the oceans, packed beneath hand-embroidered tablecloths in Jillian's hope chest.

He unwrapped the gun now. First the red cloth, then the oil-cloth, then the brittle old oiled paper. Each item he placed separately on the table until the gun was in his hand.

And he loved it, loved it as he had the day he'd purchased it. A treasured toy, owned from near boyhood, he loved the smell of it, the weight of it in his hand. He opened an ancient matchbox that had lived for fifty years beside the gun, and he poured two bullets into his palm. They weighed heavily. Gently he tossed them, listening to the click-click-click for seconds before rolling them onto the table like dice.

Hard to believe that death lived within each of those bullets. Tiny things, with eternity waiting patiently inside. His handkerchief out, he polished the bullets first and then his gun, as he had done a thousand times, as a young man, as a husband, as a father and as a fat old fool in his dotage.

His feet were swollen this morning. He'd barely managed to force them into worn slippers. His fingers were stiff with fluid, and every bone he possessed ached.

One should use these bullets, he thought. One into the temple. End it fast, Malcolm. Better to be in control of the moment than to die alone here, rot for a week in your own bed.

But he had two bullets. One would be wasted. Perhaps one should be used to blow a hole through Jack Burton. The bastard was playing dead and Malcolm knew it.

'One for his heart, and one for my head.' He inserted the bullets and aimed the gun at a shadow on the wall.

Perhaps it was a game the boy in the fat old man played. Just another scenario, replacement for the tales he could no longer complete, but he sat now, writing this one mentally in minute detail. And it had a satisfying resolution. His publisher liked satisfying resolutions.

'Don't move, Mr Burton. I have a gun on you. This is for the children you wasted, and for my son, and for me. This is my war and I shall win it.'

Then he saw Jack Burton's old car come to a halt out front. Quickly Malcolm wrapped his gun. No time to take the bullets out, he pushed it into his cutlery drawer. He snatched up the old matchbox. It went into his pocket as he walked to his front door, his heartbeat rapid.

'Burton?'

'Might I have a few minutes of your time, Mr Fletcher?'

'You may. Come. Come.' John followed his old teacher through the hall and into the kitchen. It was the first time he'd been inside the house, and once there he appeared ill at ease.

'Sit,' Malcolm said. 'A cup of tea perhaps?'

'Thank you.' Leaning crutches against his chair, John sat.

A houseproud spinster would have felt righteous in Malcolm's kitchen. He liked a place for everything and everything in its place. Busy now at neat cupboards, he allowed time for his visitor to state his business. As he took spoons from his drawer, the red-wrapped parcel got in his way. It was definitely not in its correct place. He fumbled beneath it, found a spoon, then quickly tried to close the drawer. It jammed on the gun. He repositioned it, slid the draw in gently.

'You've been spending some time back at the school, Mr Fletcher?'

'Indeed I have. The faces of Mallawindy youths have undergone little alteration; I can still pick a West from a Dooley, but the vocabularies have taken a turn for the worse, I fear. It has been an eye opener to me, Burton. And you? What are your plans – apart from farm labourer, fencing contractor.'

John looked at his shoe. 'I find physical labour cleansing. I miss it.'

'Cleansing? Digging in Mallawindy dirt?'

'There are worse occupations.'

'Indeed. Indeed. However, I admit to seeing your crowbar work as a criminal waste of a brilliant mind, and of your years of study.'

'No study is ever wasted. Isn't that what you used to say? No book ever written should be scorned.'

'I used to say a lot of things, Burton, however, I have had time recently to reconsider that one. Still, one man's poison is another man's meat. Do you have any plans to return to your former calling?'

'Some of us are called. Others enter the church seeking sanctuary.' John shrugged, glanced at Malcolm, then away, and he looked more like Ann than his father. So young still. A life ahead of him. Malcolm envied him his youth.

'You'd be in your early forties?'

'Not so early.' John looked at his hands, at his nails. They had grown long in his two weeks of inactivity. He had not inherited his father's hands, or his well-shaped nails. He had Ellie's hands, if somewhat magnified. Broad palms, flat nails. He linked his fingers, then looked up to his former teacher. 'As a thinking, reasoning adult, I know I can't continue digging post holes for the next twenty years, but I don't often think as an adult these days, Mr Fletcher. I don't often think. Or I try not to.' John sat forward on his chair.

Malcolm waited for more as he set out cups. Old cups, Jillian's cups. She had loved this set. One by one he'd broken them until only two of the original eight remained.

'The years have kept passing while I've been waiting, hoping that some new beginning might present itself.' John drew a breath, held it, and the older man stood, teaspoon in hand. 'I used to teach, Mr Fletcher. In Brisbane, then on the island for many years. I enjoyed teaching. I felt . . . felt more worthy in the classroom.'

'I must admit, I have never been able to think of you as one of God's black-suited messengers, preaching damnation to the masses.'

John Burton held the older man's eyes now. 'No. Nor I. That's one of the reasons I ended up on the island.' He drew breath, held it. 'A proposition was put to me this morning by Miss Fogarty.'

Malcolm nodded. He smiled his tight little smile that barely made an impression on the mass of his face. 'Ah hah. I see now what has brought on this visit. You, no doubt, thought you might be stepping on my toes by accepting her proposition?' John shrugged, nodded and Malcolm patted his broad expanse of stomach. 'Difficult to tread on my toes these days, Burton.' He looked down. 'Difficult to see them too, but no doubt they are still there as they continue to find the toes of others. Do feel free to accept our Miss Fogarty's proposition. You may save me from a mild case of murder.'

Murder. Ten minutes ago he had been planning a serious case of murder. He thought of the loaded gun in his drawer, and a shudder shook his profusion of flesh. Must remember it is in there, he thought. A blind grope for a knife might find a trigger and waste a bullet. I must remember to remove it. When he leaves.

He stood eyeing the drawer, his mind wandering. Was he capable of taking a life? One could not, in all conscience, fire a bullet into the most deserving of flesh – unless the life-taker was prepared to donate his own life to the cause.

He reached for a packet of imported biscuits, studied the pack, which required a knife to slit it open. He looked at the drawer he did not wish to open, at the bench, seeking a tool. Only his fingers to work on the cellophane, but they broke through and the biscuits were arranged neatly on a plate. All the while his mind was working.

Closer to eighty than seventy. Little to look forward to, apart from a fast heart attack, or slow disintegration. Not a soul would miss him.

Ann. She would mourn his passing. His readers might, but they would mourn Chef-Marlet, not Malcolm Fletcher. Who was Malcolm Fletcher these days? Just a lonely, fat old fool who spent too much time talking to himself. Why had he moved his family to this lucky country? To see them die? Or had he been sent to this hole in hell for a purpose? Why had he brought the gun with him, wrapped in his wife's prized tablecloth? Why, if not to use it on the extermination of vermin? He was rubbing his chin, his mind far away, when John spoke again.

'I enjoyed the children, Mr Fletcher, enjoyed watching a child's mind open and grow. I had forgotten how much I enjoyed it until . . . until Miss Fogarty's visit.'

Malcolm's attention returned to his visitor. The jug had boiled. He poured water into the small pot.

'Some are born to the profession, Burton. At one time I believed I had been born to teach. These days – ' He glanced at his cutlery drawer, coughed. 'What you achieved with Ann in those early years was quite exceptional.'

John nodded. 'She taught herself, once given the key.'

'But isn't this what we aim to do, to offer young minds the key to question, then set them loose on the path of life in quest of their own answers?' He poured the tea, placed the cups on the table, offering milk and sugar, biscuits. His visitor refused the biscuits so Malcolm dispatched one. He sat munching, stirring his tea, creating a whirlpool in the cup.

John added sugar, stirred slowly. 'I lost my direction, or took a wrong turn too many years ago and left no footprints behind to lead me back. I was a priest who had no real belief in God.'

'I consider myself a part-time atheist, Burton. Even as a child I was not a true believer in the old man with the white beard; still, the longer I live, the more I am inclined to think that there is something greater than man. Some great universal plan for all. A big computer, perhaps, deleting, adding, moving us around at will. Allowing man to progress to a certain stage then pulling the rug out from beneath his feet, watching him stumble, pick himself up and start all over again. It's just a game, Burton, a computer game and we the small cartoon characters scuttling madly around obsessed by our own importance.'

'Until we're bowled over like tenpins.'

'Yes. And fight as we may against it, that old computer in the sky finally gets us where it wants us, to do the task it has pro-grammed into its electronics.'

'You were sent here to find Annie. To turn her life around.'

'Perhaps. Or perhaps not,' he said thoughtfully, his eye on the cutlery drawer. 'I admit, Burton, that I saw more for your sister than motherhood. She has an exceptional mind, which is now buried beneath baby mush and napkins. I saw much more than that for her.'

'His genes didn't marry well to Mum's. They created a breed of misfits. We want to own the world, but end up malcontents, milking cows.'

Malcolm lifted his glasses and stared at his visitor. A long silence followed, then he asked, 'What is it between you two?' John glanced at him, then away. 'As a child, she was obsessed with finding you. I spent much time with her in the months after she began speaking again. She said one day that she had to find you because you would remember all the things she had forgotten.'

John made no reply. He sipped his tea, his eyes down, then he placed the cup on the saucer, a fine delicate thing, hand-painted flowers interlinked with gold. 'Siblings grow apart,' he said. 'We . . . too much time had passed. We have nothing in common these days.'

'Or too much in common, perhaps.' Again Malcolm stared at his visitor, his old eyes magnified behind thick lenses. Then it was out. 'Your father? Perhaps you are both aware that he is alive, Burton?'

Johnny Burton stood abruptly, forgetting his foot. He stumbled, grasped at his chair, his face grown pale.

Malcolm ate a biscuit, his gaze still on the younger man. Now he knew he had not been mistaken. Now he understood Ann's refusal to discuss her father's surmised demise. Although he had convinced himself that the man in the car had been Jack Burton, he had not been entirely certain until this very moment.

'I sighted him quite recently, Burton,' he added. His visitor's eyes were down, studying his odd shoe. How transparent, Malcolm thought. He looks like a guilty boy caught stealing his neighbour's apples. Both he and Ann knew that their father was alive! Ah, but where was the bastard hiding out, and why were they covering up for him? What was his game, their game? And where to go from here? A step back may be in order. A tight smile, a sip of tea. 'A biscuit, Burton? One less for me.'

John glanced at him and at the diminishing pile of biscuits, then away, but he sat again and he drank his tea, his face turned to the window. Denial came slowly, following the flush of blood creeping up from his neck settling in cheeks and brow. 'Sam and May were in Warran a week back.' He drank tea, then turned and went on quickly. 'Annie called me. She said they'd driven up to see the baby – to see Bethany. They would have passed through town. You may have seen the brother.'

Malcolm shrugged, pointed with his cup to the old Burton place. 'I think not. I watched him light a cigarette, Burton. Not ten metres from my front door. I have spent many years of my life watching your father, documenting his bad habits.'

John glanced at his old headmaster, then away. Another biscuit-munching silence followed. Malcolm had dispensed with two before John turned back to him.

'I'll guarantee you one thing, Mr Fletcher – if I ever set eyes on my father again, I won't need to consider my future. The courts will look after that for me.'

Malcolm nodded, his gaze on the single biscuit left lonely on its plate. He thought of his doctor, offered the biscuit to his visitor, and when it was refused, he sent it down to his gut with its mates.

'I would have hoped that the old computer in the sky might have had a more worthy quest for you than breaking rubble on some chain gang. Better the crowbar, Burton. Better the crowbar,' he said, his hands rubbing together, shedding biscuit crumbs as John stood, preparing now to leave. 'It may have been his brother Sam. Yes. Obviously it would have been the brother. Twins, perhaps, have similar mannerisms.' Better not to confront the issue. Let the guilty boy keep his apples today. He smiled, not wanting his visitor to leave. 'So, shall you tame the Mallawindy rabble – teach a West to read?'

John was at the door. 'As you say, it is just a computer game. One program closes and another one opens and leads us to where it may, Mr Fletcher. Why fight it?'

'Why indeed, Burton? Why indeed?' He prodded his glasses higher on his nose, and glanced over his shoulder to his study. 'Speaking of computer programs,' he said. 'You wouldn't be familiar with these . . . these personal computers, would you? Windows 95? Microsoft Word?'

'I couldn't keep up with the average ten year old these days, but I used to know my way around them. They use computers at the school?' John limped back.

'No. No. Yes. I do believe they have one or two, but it is my own beast I speak of.' He coughed and gained his feet, then he turned away, spoke to his sink. 'Would you mind stepping through to my study for a moment?'

John collected his crutches and followed his old teacher into a room unlike the rest of the house. The walls were covered with framed portions of naked women. He moved closer, recognising the pictures as book covers. He'd seen a few, wrapped around books in Ben's shop.

'My inner sanctum, and not for everyone, Burton. Definitely not for everyone, but I believe you have a mouth like a padlocked clam. Yes?'

John turned his frown on the older man.

'Yes. So. It is as you see.' He coughed. 'Your sister has been more than helpful in the past; she has spent much time in here. And kept her lips sealed, I might add. It goes without saying that I expect the same silence from you on this matter, Burton.'

John's eyes had wandered back to the framed covers. He counted nine of them. He limped to the bookshelves. Rows of each book, solid stands of red and black and gold. Coll M Chef-Marlet.

There had been times in the last six years when John had doubted his sanity. So it was proven. His sanity had flown. But a madman can lift a hand, point a finger, ask an insane question.

'Not you?'

Malcolm lifted his many chins, pursed his lips and nodded.

'You? Him? You're . . . ' John pointed to the bookshelves. 'Him?'

'Coll. I am indeed he.' Malcolm selected a copy of Number 1. 'My first-born and my favourite. Do take it.' He pushed the novel at his visitor. 'I receive free copies from my publisher but, for obvious reasons, I cannot give them away.'

John took the book, but continued to stare at the man. 'You?

Coll M Chef-Marlet? You wrote that – ?'

'Lewd smut. Yes. And don't stand there gawping, Burton. We do what we do and no apologies given. Life is too brief for apologies.' He stripped the cover from his computer, baring its face. 'Forget Chef-Marlet. This is why I brought you in here. That confounded machine haunts my life. Ann was attempting to instruct me in its usage, but her knowledge of its internal organs, as with her time, is limited. I attempted to turn three chapters into one and they became stuck somewhere in its gut. The arrogant bastard of a thing will not give them back to me.'

But John Burton was laughing. Years had passed since he had laughed. He could not remember the last time he'd laughed like this, but he leaned against a bookshelf now, bellowing with laughter, choking, crying with laughter.

'Very amusing. Yes, indeed, Burton. Well may you laugh, but it pays admirably.' Malcolm nodded and muttered as he reclaimed his book, placing it possessively on the shelf. 'Come. Come now. I did not invite you in here for your amusement. There is work to be done.'

the schoolmaster

~

John Burton leaned against the brick wall, surveying the school-yard. Empty now. The last ball bounced on the verandah, the last bike gone from the stands, the last squabble placed on hold until Monday.

And he wouldn't be here to hear that squabble.

His eyes roamed the small bitumen square and the dusty playing area. He'd played there a lifetime ago. His feet had walked him to that same school gate for six long years. Much had altered since he'd walked away. New school. New basketball ring. New fence between the playground and the headmaster's house, but old clay, old peppercorn trees, the same tall weeds surviving against the fence with the lunch bags and lolly papers, hair ribbons and half-eaten apples.

The headmaster's residence hadn't altered at all. Cream weatherboard, green roof, twin red brick chimneys, verandah up front, half-verandah at the rear. Small windows, green frames. Johnny had been inside that house; mentally he mapped it, seeing the interior as it had been in Malcolm Fletcher's time, in the time of Malcolm's son. He'd also been a John, which had led to confusion in the playground, so they'd called him John F, until some wit had added a K. Nicknames had been a part of life in this schoolyard, so John Kelvin

243

Fletcher, fresh from England, had become JFK. The name had carried over to the Daree high school.

He'd been a close friend, and one of too few Johnny had made in his lifetime. He'd invited Johnny to his house where he'd had his own room, his own desk, his own books, and Johnny had envied the life he'd possessed, envied him the future, planned for him by his father, the headmaster. He'd envied JFK's new racing bike too, on that day they'd gone riding out at Dead Man's Lane. A Saturday.

And John Fletcher had been dead by the following Saturday, struck down by encephalitis. So much for envy. That was the week the world had ended for Johnny Burton. That was the week . . .

John shook his head and took up his crutches, making his way to the fence where he picked up an empty cigarette packet and wondered which sixth grader had tossed it there. Not his problem. No more playing at schoolmaster. His plaster was coming off tomorrow and it would be back to the post holes and paintbrushes and long empty days.

A removalist's van had been parked in front of the residence for most of the afternoon. Norman O'Rouke would not be returning. Old news to Kerrie and John. Two weeks old. O'Rouke was being replaced by a senior mistress, Ms Glen White. She'd be in the class-room come Monday. She had three daughters, but would not be moving them to Mallawindy until the school residence had been 'made habitable for human occupation'.

'She's going to share my flat for a week. I've got two bed-rooms,' Kerrie had said.

'She sounds . . . ' John had sought a suitable description.

'Tough. And I hope she's as tough as she sounds. They're doing the bathroom, putting new floor coverings down and splashing on a bit of paint as soon as Norman's furniture is gone.'

Maybe John would miss his days in the school room. He'd enjoyed the last two weeks. He'd had a place to go, a reason to put on a shirt. He'd bought a pair of jeans and a sweater. Maroon.

Standing there, playing with the cigarette packet, he watched two men wheel a refrigerator out to the van. He watched them load it then return for a piano, and he wondered who'd played it and how they were going to get it on board. The police hadn't been able to trace Amy. Her mother lived in Lilydale, a Melbourne suburb. She said she hadn't heard from her daughter, but Amy's body had not been found. The dead woman, found in Albury, had been identified as a Sydney prostitute.

'Like two fish out of water,' Kerrie had said today. 'Amy was this faded tropical goldfish wanting to swim upstream. Norman was one of those grey sucker fish, always sucking onto her fins, holding her back. He wasn't much older than her, but from a distance he looked like her father.'

And the new teacher, Ms Glen White? What would she be? 'Another fish out of water?' John had asked.

'I'm hoping for a six-foot shark with razor teeth, something you couldn't kill with a bazooka,' Kerrie had replied.

An interesting girl, she didn't spend a lot of time wondering if what she said was right or wrong. She let it rip and hang the consequences. He'd miss her. Miss the lunches they ate together. Miss the laughs.

She had urged him to apply for the job permanently. 'I like your style, and your size. You're too big to tangle with, John. Go for it.'

He had the qualifications. More than enough. He'd done his years at the university in Brisbane, then taught in a secondary school there for two years, and at a primary school on the island. Spent most of his life studying something. Over-educated. Over-qualified for the job, but not for life.

'You're home-grown. You know the parents, and that's half the battle when you're dealing with some of these kids.'

He'd let it slide. Shouldn't have. Too late now.

He watched a wardrobe leave the house, saw O'Rouke's mother guarding it, and he smiled.

'Don't you scratch it. It was Normy's grandmother's. Watch what you're doing there.' Raucous little woman, she had to be eighty – another Granny Bourke in the making. He and Kerrie had been eating lunch on the verandah when she'd marched around the corner, mouth already in motion.

'A gummy shark, that one.' Kerrie's mind still on fish. He'd laughed. The old dame hadn't a tooth in her head.

Malcolm Fletcher had awakened John's laugh, and in recent weeks it had claimed its freedom. He was working his way through Chef-Marlet's novels – now that he knew the author – and his laughter sometimes disturbed the mud brick house in the dead of night. Not that the novels were particularly humorous – a little black humour, perhaps; but it was the thought of his old headmaster having written those words that tickled the funny-bone.

No one to laugh with, though, about the old man's secret. Except Annie. She and her little ones had driven down on Sunday. They'd been drinking tea, eating Ellie's pumpkin cake, when he'd said, 'Have you read Chef-Marlet, Ann?'

She'd turned to him, held his eye for a full ten seconds. 'You don't read that smut, Johnny?'

'Bron reads them,' Ben had said. 'She's sweating on Number 10, but by the sound of it, there isn't going to be a Number 10. The rep was up here last week.'

Ann and Johnny knew more than Ben and the rep, but they said not a word.

Secrets. Were they to be bound forever by secrets? He sighed then and looked towards his car – his father's car, now registered in his name. Time to go home. Didn't want to go home. Didn't want to get in that car and drive. Always got the urge to keep on going when he got behind that wheel. Just go.

Go to Narrawee and get rid of one secret.

He shook his head and turned his eyes again to the men at work and he let his mind roam back to Malcolm's son. Only a month between him and JFK. Both close to their sixteenth birthdays the year the world had ended. Too old to play games, but he and his mate had played at archaeology most Saturdays, riding out to the sand dunes, Annie sitting on the bar of his bike, JFK toting their digging tools.

They'd found an old Aboriginal burial ground and had been digging there for weeks. Not acceptable these days, but back then no one had considered old bones as part of a lost culture.

He'd taken Annie everywhere with him, as much to get her away from Ellie as from her father. His mate hadn't cared. John Fletcher had liked teaching her, liked looking at the sign language book and finding the signs for new words. She was signing well, and reading his lips too well. In the eighteen months since her father had brought her home from the Melbourne hospital, John had been her teacher.

She'd been making a sand castle close by when he and JFK started their dig that day. They unearthed charcoal first, then burned bones. When they'd found a portion of a metal zip fastener, they knew these bones hadn't been those of some ancient black man.

Then Johnny had seen Annie pick something up from a clump of reeds. He'd seen her look at it, grasp it in her hand, hide the hand behind her back.

'Show me,' he'd signed.

'No thing.'

'Bottle top?' he'd signed.

'No thing.' And she'd cried.

He'd taken her wrist, opened her hand and seen the ring.

'Where did she find that?' JFK had dropped his tools. 'That's a good ring. Those are probably diamonds on the sides.'

Johnny had known it was a good ring. Known the man who had worn that good ring too. He'd stared at the shoulder diamonds, flashing fire in the sunlight, and they had burned his eyes while a ghost walked over his grave.

Vision of his father in the flashing fire. His father scrubbing the boot of his car. Smell of disinfectant. Smell of decay.

What did you have in the boot, Dad?

A dirty mongrel dog.

Stink of rot.

Dirty mongrel dog.

Uncle Sam?

Uncle Sam's ring in his hand, the smell of disinfectant and decay in his nostrils, he'd picked up the burned zip fastener. A heavy-duty zip. Uncle Sam had always worn jeans. Then he'd dropped the ring into his pocket and taken up the shovel to search for more. Uncle Sam had always worn a heavy gold chain at his throat.

The voice, his mate's voice of sanity: 'We probably shouldn't touch anything else, Johnny. We probably should get Constable Johnson out here, shouldn't we?'

'You get him. Ride in and tell him, but don't say anything about the ring. It's Dad's.' First lie. Stupid lie. Why? 'Annie must have taken it off the dressing table. She'll get into trouble if he finds out.' Second lie. Why?

And too quickly he'd taken the ring from his pocket and slipped it onto his middle finger to hide the inscription.

Sam and May 1953.

He'd spoken to Annie when they were alone. 'You have to tell me where you got it, Annie. You have to tell me what happened when you were in Narrawee.' She could hear when she wanted to. He hadn't heard of elective mutes in those days, but he'd known she wasn't deaf.

'Tell me,' he'd signed. 'Uncle Sam ring. Where Annie find ring?'

'Forget,' she'd signed, and she'd cried.

'Tell me, Annie love. You have to tell me.'

'I like forget, my Johnny.'

He'd taken her home, and he'd gone back to the sand dunes, riding beside his mate in the back seat of the police car. They'd shown Bob Johnson their find. And the zip. Hadn't mentioned the ring.

It was late when Johnson drove the boys home, and John had been late for dinner. He'd walked to the kitchen door and stood watching his father gnaw on a chicken drumstick. So big, Jack

Burton had dominated that table. Gravy on his lips. Roast chicken, mashed potatoes, pumpkin and green beans on his plate. John could see it today as clearly as he had seen it back then. A colourful image to hold on to for so many years.

'We found a body out at the sand dunes,' he'd said, his eyes watching his father's face. It had paled. He'd dropped the drumstick and stood abruptly, walked from the room, walked away from his plate of roast chicken.

Little Annie watching, reading faces, her fork playing in mashed potato and brown gravy. Big dark eyes like pits. Angular little face tight. Little mouth moving. One large front tooth and a gap.

But no time to think of her that night. He'd snatched a handful of coins from the egg money jar and he'd ridden up to the post office where he'd placed a call to Narrawee. Had to know. Had to be sure. Then he'd tell. Then he'd go to Constable Johnson and tell what he knew.

May had picked up the phone.

'I want to speak to Uncle Sam, please. It's Johnny,' he'd said.

'John? I'm sorry, but Sam isn't here.'

'I know he's not there. Dad . . . Dad . . . ' He couldn't say the words. 'I found Uncle Sam's ring up here, Aunty May. I think Dad – '

'Don't.' That's all she'd said. 'Please God. Don't do anything, John. Please God, don't say any more.' And she'd hung up.

Mr Ponsford had ridden down the next morning with a telegram: 'Jack. Call me. Urgent. May.

She knew. She knew Sam was dead!

Madness.

And Annie hiding from him. Running from him. Crying. Annie knew.

He'd gone to the willow tree, to where he'd watched her hide her golden syrup tin, and he'd opened it, placing Sam's ring safe inside. No one touched her golden syrup tin. Ellie wasn't interested, Ben was trustworthy and Jack Burton wouldn't have gone hunting around the river for it. Johnny had looked at her treasures, brought with her from Narrawee, and at the scraps of paper, folded small. And he'd read her little poems.

And he'd read:

Daddy went to Narawee to get his Liza and get me
but he cort her in the sella playing with the derty fella
when he tryd to kill him ded, he got Liza's head insted
so he put his golden trezzur with the flowers to bloom for ever.

May knew. Annie knew. Now Johnny knew.

'Where is it?' That night the murdering bastard had dragged Johnny into the grain shed. 'Where is it? What did you do with the ring?' He'd taken off his belt, white with fear or rage, and he'd used his belt.

It hadn't got him what he'd wanted.

'You killed him. You brought him up here in the car boot and you burned him out at the dunes. You killed Liza too? Where did you burn her?'

'You don't know anything about it. You don't know a bloody thing about it.'

'It's your fault that Annie has gone like she is too. You'd better kill me too, because if you don't I'm telling Constable Johnson.'

'Then tell him, you disloyal little bastard, and see if I care.'

But John Fletcher was sick. He was in hospital. And Johnny's head was on fire. He thought he had encephalitis. Thought he was going to die. Ellie fed him aspros and told him he was delirious when he spoke of Uncle Sam and Liza's murder.

Then John Fletcher died. And Johnny cried.

Couldn't talk. Not to Annie. Not to Ben. Couldn't talk. Not to his mother. Couldn't talk to Bessy. Decided to do an Annie. Never open his mouth again. Couldn't think. Couldn't sleep. The encephalitis germ hadn't killed him, just killed his mind. For a month he didn't go to school. Spent his days planning, walking, planning. Spent his nights fighting his father. Spent his nights sharpening the axe, honing the carving knife.

Then that last day. His father drunk, taunting Annie, showing her photographs from Narrawee.

Annie screaming.

'If you can scream, you can talk, you shamming little bitch. Talk to me. Talk.'

Ellie screaming at him to stop.

'Talk to me. I don't need any more bloody guilt.'

Johnny's mind eaten away. Only red inside now. Only hate and fear and his own guilt. He'd picked up the old black poker. Used his father's head as a golf ball. He'd finish the screaming.

Tried to finish what he'd begun too, but Ellie wouldn't let him. She'd fought him for the poker, and he couldn't fight her. His fight wasn't with her.

For the love of God, Johnny. What's wrong with you lately?

He killed Liza, Mum. He killed Uncle Sam.

You dreamt it. You were sick. You're acting like a crazy boy lately. You don't know what you're doing any more.

He killed them, Mum, and Annie knows it. I could prove it to you if I could find her tin.

Little Annie, standing, head-butting the wall. Little Annie, crying soundlessly. Little Annie's golden syrup tin gone now from the fibre cave of willow roots. Sam's ring, gone with it.

If you keep on like this, they'll put you away, Johnny.

He killed them, Mum, and Annie knows it. That's what's wrong with her.

You've got to get away from here, or someone is going to die. You've got to go, Johnny.

And he'd gone. Almost sixteen. He'd gone, Annie on his heels.

I love Johnny. I come. Little hands signing.

Go back, Annie.

Little legs running. *Go away far. We take bad ring. Go far over sunset.*

And she'd given him Sam's ring, warm from her hot little hand.

He'd hailed down a truck; it had taken him south, where he'd wandered, picked fruit, worked for a week or two then wandered again, sleeping rough but staying close to home and to Annie.

He was going to go back. He had the ring. He was going to go back. When he was big enough. Never big enough. That was the trouble.

Then one morning he'd looked in the mirror to see if he was big enough and he'd seen the bastard staring back at him. And that evening, he'd drunk two bottles of beer and he'd become the bastard. That was the day he'd started running from himself, and he'd ended up in Brisbane, cold, hungry, lonely. He'd crept into a church, slept the night on a polished pew. Next morning a young priest found the dishevelled, broken boy, no soles in his shoes. Soulless.

The long black garb had covered this man. Only the face. Only the hands. Face bland. Hands clean.

How do I become a priest, Father?

Have you eaten recently, lad?

The old building, a classic from last century, sun glinting on coloured windows, high up, untouched by the filth outside. A priest might live, breathe, move within this clean and perfect world, that reality could not violate.

Outside, outside of this place . . .

Johnny had not wanted to step outside again. To be his father's son again.

How can I learn to be a priest, Father?

Do you have parents, family to support you?

I want to be a priest.

Breakfast, perhaps, and a shower, a change of clothes. Then we'll talk about it.

The church had paid for a haircut. The church had given him clean clothing, and shoes. He had not given the church his name, but he'd found work in a supermarket, and at night he'd sat again in a classroom, lost in his books, hiding in his books.

He'd completed form five, and packed shelves, waited tables for a second year, made hamburgers in the school holidays, mowed lawns. And when the results of his final exams came out, and his name had been amongst the top ten in the state, he'd returned to that church and handed the priest his results.

How do I become a priest, Father?

The Catholic church claimed him that day. It guided him, paid his way, filled the empty hole in his life. It allowed him to hide from self, to cover self beneath the black garments of anonymity. But the garments were gone now. Only a maroon sweater and blue jeans, a striped grey and white shirt. Only one casual shoe and a black sock to cover his plaster.

What now, Johnny Burton? What now?

So the seasons altered once more. September's page on the BURTON AND DOOLEY EMPORIUM calendar, a fluffy kitten, its mouth open in a yawn, gave way to a basket full of puppies. The paddocks were green, and the lambs fat, the cows were heavy with milk while their new calves nibbled grass and sucked mush from buckets, memories of the warm teat and the suck of bliss only a dream now.

Ms Glen White came to the school on that Monday morning in September, a new broom sweeping clean, but she left two weeks later, on the day the September school holidays began. She had three growing daughters to consider, and she didn't consider Mallawindy worth considering as a long-term situation.

Got out fast. Ran before the removalists had time to move in her furniture. Packed her case and skedaddled home to Mum and her girls.

So the old school residence remained empty, and when the nights grew warm, the town youths came with their girls and their spray cans. Newly painted walls made a fine canvas for graffiti, and on the new floor covering, placed down for Ms Glen White and her girls, Jeff Rowan found condoms and worse.

'Drug problem in Mallawindy' the Daree *Gazette* reported. Jeff Rowan was not yet ready to allow his tiny town to disappear again into dusty anonymity.

on the dotted line

~

A sometimes gentle month, October, summer in waiting, gathering her heat in readiness to scorch the land. But not yet, not today.

May and Jack had left Daree at seven-thirty. They'd be in Narrawee by mid-afternoon.

'That's a nice looking property.' May sat in the passenger seat watching the land skimming by.

'Yeah.' A fourth-generation landowner, Jack was no farmer. Land was land was land, and bulls were the raw material of roast beef. May ran the two properties, her own, Hargraves Park, and Narrawee, giving orders to her manager as one born to it. Jack was the tail that wagged behind her, but a more relaxed tail today. Christmas was now visible on the horizon; the year had begun to move again. Only two and a half months and black Jack would be dead.

For thirty years now he'd signed his *S J Burton* beside May's signature. Nothing would alter.

His mother had taught both him and Sam their early letters; they'd had a similar hand and it hadn't been difficult to forge his brother's signature. Just painful. It was still painful, but there wasn't a lot he could do about that pain.

As a boy he'd believed that one day the Narrawee property would belong to him. That dream had died the day of his father's

255

funeral. Narrawee had been willed to Sam, then to the children of Sam. The property would only fall into the hands of Jack should his brother die without issue. And Sam had died without issue, died by his brother's hand, and like the stinking corpse of an animal, he'd been burned to prevent the spread of his obscene disease.

May was also thinking about Sam, her mind wandering forbidden places as she watched the land glide by. Liza and Sam. Sam and Liza. Nightmare day of screaming and madness.

Sam had raped his seven-year-old niece. Had she called in the police, a jury may very well have found Jack innocent of his brother's murder. Perhaps his name might have one day been on the title to Narrawee. What father would not have done what Jack had done that day? What madness had taken possession of her mind, and why, in God's name, had she not seen that dark side of her husband?

But her marriage had not been as most. Nine hours after she'd walked down the aisle to her handsome Sam, she'd learned that he had no desire to share her bed, though he'd sat on it for hours attempting to explain his feelings.

'You're my little sister, a cherished sister, May. I can't . . . '

Nineteen at the time, and an innocent nineteen, her wedding night spent at a Melbourne hotel, a slow boat waiting to take the happy couple to England in the morning. What was she supposed to do? What was she supposed to feel? Her mother dead for five years, her father in his seventies, her friends envious – no one in the world with whom she could discuss sex, or the lack of it.

She hadn't wept or argued. She'd sat on the bed beside him, looking at her new wedding band. Hadn't asked why he had married her. She knew why. Two power-crazed old men had wanted that marriage for years. It would join not only the two oldest families, but the properties, Narrawee and Hargraves Park.

And what a property to own.

Since her eighth birthday she'd wanted to live in that white stone mansion, to be the queen of Narrawee. At ten she'd planned to marry both Burton boys. At thirteen she'd decided to marry Jack, but he hadn't waited around for her to grow up. Sam had waited.

That day of magic. That wedding gown. That magic night of dancing in her new husband's arms. Sam had been a wonderful dancer. And the drive to the hotel and her white virginal nightgown with its blue ribbon threaded through lace and her fearful expectations unrealised. Perhaps she felt relief.

'That's okay,' she had said to him. 'I feel a bit the same way tonight.'

'We can have a wonderful life, May.'

'Yes. Yes. We will.'

What else could she say? She certainly wasn't going to run home to her father, face her friends and the town and Sam's father, who Jack had always named John the Bastard, and rightly so. Her pride, fear of her father-in-law, would not allow it. Anyway, Sam would probably change his mind once they were far from that domineering old man.

Of course he would.

So they'd steamed away on what was to become the most wonderful holiday of her life. The sights she'd seen, the places she had been, dancing each night with Sam, so close to him. But when they returned to their cabin, Sam slipped into the top bunk and she into her own. He was the most handsome man on the boat, good company, intelligent; what more did she want? As the months passed she found she did want more, and found herself remembering Jack's vindictive words on the morning of her wedding: 'He's a perverted bastard, May. Run while you still can.'

On their return to Narrawee, she and Sam had slept in separate rooms; John the bastard had his say about that. May claimed it was her choice and Sam had shown such gratitude.

He was a thoughtful partner during those first years. They'd travelled and both loved the theatre; he'd bought her extravagant gifts and when they were in public, he'd introduced her as his queen of Camelot, but in private he suggested they have separate relationships.

'No,' she'd said. She'd begun to watch him then. Watching his every move became her obsession. She watched him when he was with other women – and with men.

A child of the thirties, a teenager of the forties, May had certainly heard the words applied to men who were assumed to be less than men; in what way they were less, she did not know. Sex, natural or perverted, was not discussed in respectable circles, and she dared not visit the local library and ask to borrow a book on the subject.

She hadn't seen Jack in three years, then one afternoon he'd turned up in a taxi, with no money to pay the driver. John, the bastard, had refused to pay, but May had her own money, her own property too; she'd buried her father that Christmas. She had paid for the taxi, made lunch for Jack, so pleased to see him, so much to talk about.

'No kids yet, May?' he'd said.

'Sam isn't ready.' That was her stock answer for those who asked that question.

'He was ready for kids at sixteen,' Jack had stated, his eyes holding her own.

She hadn't understood his words, but she'd looked away from those all-seeing eyes, and down to her wedding ring. For no logical reason her eyes had spilled over. And he'd kissed her, not a brotherly kiss either. It had set free a flood of emotions and a torrent of tears and words. She'd told him that she was a married woman only in name.

'You must have known what you were getting yourself into, you silly little bugger. He's a bent bastard and always has been. The only reason he wanted you was for a cover. May Hargraves, proof of Saint Sam's unquestionable respectability. That's all you are to him, May, a pretty little cover. I warned you.'

'Stop it, Jack. He's not like that. He's not . . . not – '

'The old man might be a bastard but he's not stupid. Go and tell him you're a virgin, three years wed. See what he thinks his precious son is.'

Should have. But she hadn't. Why?

Because the golden band Sam had placed on her finger had made her mistress of Narrawee. It had given her freedom. Mrs Sam Burton could work in the paddocks with the men. Mrs Sam Burton could learn all there was to know about this land. She lived a life unknown to her married friends. Many were the nights she slept in her old room, and many the days spent at the side of the man she had hired to manage her land.

Mrs Sam Burton dealt with the Narrawee workers too – sacked one on the spot one day because he had dared to put his hand on her.

Twenty-three at the time, and he a handsome thirty. Robin Crane. She would never forget his name. Too attractive, and she had been attracted; Sam had employed him. In hindsight May believed he'd handpicked Robin to father a child. Sam wanted her to bear a child if only to silence his father's questions.

'Get your things and get off my land,' she'd said to Robin Crane that morning.

'Sam might have something to say about that, May.'

'My name is Mrs Burton to you. Now get off my land.'

He'd gone, and thereafter not one of the workers had called her May. She'd shown them all that day. She'd shown Sam too that she was more than Narrawee breeding stock put to stud with a passing bull. And when John, the bastard, desperate to see a child of the marriage, called in his own doctor to examine her, she'd refused to submit.

'Look to your precious son,' she'd said – and suffered for that remark until the womanising old swine had died in 1960.

That was when the rot had set in. She'd believed that Jack and his shy Ellie would move back to Narrawee with their children – children she might share – but the old man had got in his last hit from the grave. He'd altered his will, left the property to Sam.

'I want a divorce – or an annulment, Sam. He's dead, and I'll no longer continue with this farce. I want a normal marriage. I want children.'

'As I've said many times, May, your children will be my children. They'll inherit this land.'

'No,' she'd said. 'No. My children will be my husband's. I want a divorce.'

He'd gone to the solicitors that day and he'd put the property into joint names. She'd considered it a bribe, and told him so.

Time proved it a necessity. With access to unlimited cash, Sam purchased the flat in Toorak; he'd spent weeks there, leaving May and his new manager to run the property, leaving May to sign the cheques. He'd flown overseas alone, spent months in Queensland.

May assumed he'd gone off to be with other women. Then, on a rare trip to Toorak, she'd finally met one of his male friends, a vile creature who had raised the hackles on her neck. And a girl, a waif of nine or ten. Her eyes had made May's heart ache.

'The child,' she said when the two had driven away. 'Who was that child, Sam?'

'Dennis's wife's niece. She adores him.'

'Does she?'

'Dennis is like a father to her. What are you suggesting now, May?'

'God knows,' she said. 'God only knows. The little girl looked so afraid.'

'Her mother died recently. Dennis and his wife are considering adoption. We should consider it, May. You know I want a family.'

'I don't . . . no,' she'd said. 'No.'

'We have so much love to give, we have the money. We could give a child a wonderful life.'

'I don't know.'

It was not until Ann and Liza had come to stay that May had begun to see Sam as a father. He'd taken the girls riding, he'd bought them a pony, spent his days with them, read them stories each night in bed.

He was a good man, and so gentle with the girls. Liza loved him, she followed him around like a little puppy.

Then came that night, Ann and Liza tucked into their bed, when May had raised the subject of children. 'You would make a wonderful father, Sam. We could have our own. There are . . . there are . . . ways. There are doctors who could . . . help us conceive our own child. I don't want to raise some little stranger. I want a little girl who looks like Ann Elizabeth, a son like Johnny; Burtons, Sam, Burtons for Narrawee. If I were to make an appointment in Melbourne, would you at least consider it?'

What a fool. What a gullible fool she had been. Not until the day of his death had she known the brand of Sam's love of children. Not until after his death had she understood fully.

Ann comatose in hospital, May and Jack had made their base in Toorak and spent hours each day beside Ann's bed. May had been alone at the flat when the innocuous brown envelope was delivered. She had opened it and removed a magazine.

Pages of children and unspeakable perversions.

She'd vomited on the page, and the guilt she'd felt at the part she'd played in concealing her husband's death had been washed clean away by the vomit. She forgave herself that day, and forgave Jack his every past sin, his every future sin, and she'd begged for his forgiveness. That night she had crawled into his bed. In her mid-thirties, he was her first and not so gentle lover, but she forgave him that too, and she held him inside her praying that a child might come out of desperation.

They made love often after that night, gaining courage from each other to face the new day of questions.

Jack had been born for the stage. He'd screamed abuse at her in front of the children's hospital one day while television cameras rolled. He'd threatened to kill his brother, naming him a protector of perverts. He'd cursed May for employing the Englishman they'd accused of stealing Liza away. The next day he'd played the gentle Sam in his greying wig and moustache, seated at her side, his hand on her shoulder, protecting her while they spoke to the same television crew.

None had questioned his performance. And why should they?

These two faces of Jack were opposite sides of the same coin. It was as if he had become Sam as he'd donned his clothing. His voice, his mannerisms had altered. He was Sam, her husband, and a better man.

The city had been an easy place for one man to become two. A month of fear, of lies and tears, then Jack, and the now silent Ann, had returned to Mallawindy, and May had returned to Narrawee; the double bed she had never shared was suddenly cold and wide.

She learned to lie so well that first year. Sam could not live with his guilt, she said. He could not stand to be at Narrawee at the moment so he'd gone away for a few months.

In the years after his father had died, he'd spent months away from Narrawee. May and the manager had managed. 'Sam is looking at properties in Queensland, or in Tasmania. Sam has flown over to New Zealand.' What fine stories she had concocted; what a fine lie she had lived.

But when she'd needed Sam in the flesh, she'd sent a letter to Jack:

Dear Jack, Ellie and family,
I hope you are all keeping well, and that Ann has improved. The weather here has been delightful these last weeks. Sam has been spending his days in the garden. It is looking a picture. He said to tell you that he would like to see you on the 14th, Jack. He has some business he wishes to discuss with you.
Love, May and Sam

The world so much larger in the sixties, Mallawindy so far away. For years she and Jack had kept up the charade while making plans that would see Jack's name on the title to Narrawee. Perhaps Sam would go overseas and disappear. But how would Jack get home?

Perhaps Sam should drive into the desert, lose himself forever in the immensity of this land. May would follow, a day behind. She'd drive Jack home.

Too many cars on the road, or not enough. Too much fear of discovery.

Or a motorbike, perhaps. Yes, buy a motorbike and Sam could carry it on a covered trailer, then Sam disappears and a leatherclad helmeted rider returns. Who would know?

Bike licence. What if there was an accident? What if the rider began drinking? What if the police stopped the rider? And who buys the bike? And who registers it?

So get a fake licence. Set up a fake address.

Desperation had given them nerve enough to hide the deaths of Liza and Sam. Years on, neither one had sufficient nerve to apply for a dead man's birth certificate, to approach a police station and apply for a bike licence.

So many plans had been made, spoken of in great detail, but always a problem emerged, with no way across it to a solution. All too difficult.

'Let it slide, May. Let it slide,' he'd said. 'Give it another twelve months.'

So they'd let it slide while the years had slid on by – until Ann had taken their fate into her hands that night and Jack had been the one who had to die.

Now it was too late. He was destined to sign Sam's name forever.

'Forty-odd kilometres from Albury,' he said.

'We might stop for a coffee, or an early lunch, then drive straight through.'

'Did you tell them about your will?'

'No need for them to know,' she said. 'They get on well, Jack. You have two beautiful daughters and I envy them their closeness. We made the right decision.'

They'd made a new will, a joint will, leaving May's property to Bronwyn and Narrawee to Ann. May had given the instructions and Jack had signed on the dotted line.

'Poor bloody Jack,' he said. 'Couldn't even sign his own will, have a say in where his money, which isn't his money, will go to when he croaks.'

'Who else would we have left it to?'

'Your cousin,' he said, and he smiled that same old boyish smile that could once have charmed the drawers off a nun.

'Him! He'd sell it for hobby farms as quick as look at it.' They drove on in silence, May's mind again wandering, but this time to Ann's children.

'Bethany was smiling today. She's barely two months old and tiny, but a bright little button if ever I saw one. Her big black eyes followed everything. Matthew, the second oldest, has got the blond curls. He's a little like Mandy. Just a little. I took some photographs.'

'She was the image of Liza, you know.'

'There was a definite similarity. Certainly the hair.'

'I saw her once. "Is you a bad man?" she said. She was her mother's daughter. She could pick 'em, May.'

'A delightful little girl with a beautiful nature. Fate is cruel, Jack. She'd be going on ten now. Young Benjamin is six years old already, and growing into a fine looking boy. He's very tall for his age. He has the dark hair and the Burtons' dark eyes, but oddly enough they wear David's expression, and he's definitely David around the mouth. A very interesting mixture, that little boy.'

'Benjamin. After Ellie's old man. I notice she didn't name one of them Jack.'

She knew how to divert his moods. 'Oh, and I meant to tell you, Ellie's sister and her daughter-in-law called in for a cup of tea. They'd been shopping in Warran.'

'Bloody Bessy? I bet she had a rare old time running me down.'

'Not at all. Not a bad word was spoken about you, except to tell me that Ellie is having Jack's . . . your name added to the children's tombstone after Christmas.'

Since the birth of Bethany, May had been telephoning weekly, and three times now they'd driven up. Jack drove no further than Daree, remaining in the motel room, watching daytime television until May returned. He didn't go near Mallawindy.

This time they'd slept one night at the motel, and with the trip up too fresh in his mind, the return journey seemed long. He knew every curve, every tree, every hill. Too many years spent travelling this road. But he drove easily, keeping to the limit. May didn't like speed. Didn't like a lot of things he liked.

So come Christmas, he'd have a tombstone. Maybe he'd feel better for it. Give it another two months and the seven years would be up. The courts would declare him dead. Dead and buried.

He'd be Sam then, and Sam could have his hair cut. It wasn't much to look forward to, but it was something.

They stopped for coffee and a light meal in Albury, then May took the wheel for the last lap home. Jack sat back, pleased to be going home. He was growing accustomed to being dead, and the closer December came the fitter he got.

He hadn't had a drink since April. It had been a bloody torment anyway. When he'd had it, he always wanted more. It wasn't worth the brawls it caused, and a bottle of Diet Coke felt much the same in his head as a stubby of VB. He drank a lot of Diet Coke.

Never a walker if he could drive, May had got him walking again. Each night now, she dragged him out for their constitutional, and though he might complain out of habit, he walked with her, walked for kilometres. He felt fitter than he had ten years ago, and today his sixty-seven years were not weighing on him so heavily. They'd shared a water bed at the motel last night and one thing had led to another. Sex had been pretty much a once-a-month exercise these last few years, but it always left him feeling younger, stronger, and it was bloody good exercise for the heart, better than wearing out shoe leather, he'd told May last night.

'I asked Ann and Bronwyn to come down and visit us, to let their children run wild in Narrawee. I want them to know the land while they're young, fall in love with it. It has missed children, my dear,' she said. 'In our youth, the old house was such a noisy, happy place, and it can be again. Bronwyn's baby is due around Christmas.'

'She's only been married a couple of months.'

'At least she got married. Half of them don't bother to these days.'

'The breed won't die, May.'

'She's proud of the Burton name. Calls herself Burton-Smith. She was saying today that she refused to marry Nick unless he added the Burton name. Still working – she says she'll take a few days off when the baby comes, then take it to work on her back. An interesting daughter, very you – and quite a character. She said she'd come down one weekend, after the baby is born.'

'I move into the cellar, do I?'

'You can go to Toorak – but I doubt she'd recognise you if you worked at it.'

He held up his wrist. 'She'd know that bloody scar in ten seconds.'

'Yes. Yes. You could wear a bandage, or one of those splints Barbara Dean wears. She's got arthritis, wears them on both wrists now. I was talking to her the other day.'

'Little blue-eyed Barbara Dean. I cringe every time I hear her name.'

'I'll swear she doesn't even remember. She must have been only a tiny thing – she was six years behind me through school.'

'I remember. I remember her little face and I remember that perverted bastard's face.' His anger rose quickly.

May knew how to cool it. 'I know, Jack. I do understand, but to get back to our previous conversation – '

'Jack?' he said. 'You always were a devious little bugger, May, a determined little bugger too. Refused to believe that there were things you couldn't fix.'

'We'll see.'

She liked to dream, but he knew what he knew, and he knew that

that black-headed little bitch and her kids wouldn't set foot in Narrawee while he was alive. His kids had inherited his memory, his inability to forgive.

'The bad times will soon be over. Wonderful times lie ahead for us and for Narrawee. One day there will be children there again and they'll run wild in the rooms, and they'll use the old oak table as a slide. Just as we did. Remember?'

'I remember. And I remember being thumped on the bum for doing it.'

'I missed out on the thump, so my memories are more fond.' She reached across and quickly kissed his cheek.

'What brought that on?'

'The water bed. As you say, wonderful exercise for the heart. And your refusal of the wine list at dinner last night. Thank you, Jack. Do you know that today I am at peace with life? For the first time in far too long I am at peace with life. Do you feel it too?'

'No.'

'How I'd love you to see, to know, Ann's children. That little girl. And Tristan. He's so wickedly adorable. You could not help but love him. He reminds me of that old photograph of you.'

'I was never adorable, May.'

'Oh, yes you were.' She smiled at his expression, then spoke again of the children. 'He wanders around with his dressing gown over his head, saying he's Darth Vadar.'

'Who?'

'Darth Vadar. Space anti-hero. A neighbour was looking after him one night and he refused to go to bed. She let him watch one of those old movies with her eldest boy. Now he goes to bed with his light sabre instead of his teddy. Don't underestimate the power of the dark force, he says, and it's so clear – when you know what he's saying. He's barely two years old and he can talk the leg off an iron pot.'

She was back on the kids again. They should be good for a hundred kilometres. He closed his eyes, his head back.

'What a handful for her. I don't know how she manages. But she does. And she's looking so well on it. She asked how you were.'

'Hoping you'd tell her I died in the night, eh?'

'Not at all.' She adjusted her sunglasses and drove on for minutes. 'She still cares for you. She gets a . . . a look on her face when she speaks about you. A look of sadness. God I wish I could get you two – '

'Stay away from that one, May. Stay well away from it.'

'Yes. Yes. You're right. I'm sorry, Jack, but I feel so good today, I want everyone else to feel it. It's over. It's finally over. Ann is fine. We're fine. Come Christmas and we can move on.'

'Can I have a haircut for Christmas, boss, and a large bottle of louse shampoo?'

'If you're good.'

'And a water bed?'

May laughed.

the phone call

~

Ann had been out all morning. At one p.m. she dropped Matthew off at the playgroup before meeting Bronwyn for lunch. So much to talk about these days. Bronwyn could now talk babies without throwing up. She was bottling Beth while Ann shovelled space food into Darth Vadar, complete with his hooded dressing gown. He refused to leave the house without it. Maybe he had a leaning towards the dark side of the Burton breed.

The conversation moved from babies to Mallawindy and to the old kitchen, finally having an overdue renovation. 'They're doing it properly, getting it lined, and they're putting in one of those modern kitchens. Some firm in Daree is doing it, Annie, and it's costing a fortune.'

'I like the old one,' Ann said.

'Yeah? A happy memory in every dent. You know I've got the feeling that Johnny is planning to move over there. He's paying for it.'

'Still teaching at the school?'

'And trying to make it permanent. He's like a different person these days.'

'He's certainly easier to talk to,' Ann said.

'But?'

'I don't know, Bron. Sometimes it's as if the last of the old Johnny is gone. He's reinvented himself so many times he's lost the real one.'

'About time too, the moody bugger.' She straightened, stretched her shoulders and eased her back away from the chair. 'You know, I can see him and Kerrie Fogarty getting together.'

Ann shrugged. 'Ben's rapt in Kerrie.'

'I know. He has been for twelve months. That's why I invited her to my wedding. Thought I might give them a nudge. But he's so bloody frustrating, Annie. Look at him with Judy Watson. I nudged and she chased – chased him up hill and down dale, and what did Ben do? Put his head down and ran faster.'

'Judy Watson is a fake. Kerrie . . . Kerrie is different. She came down to the house when I was there on Sunday. Ben was talking to her.'

'Yeah, but who did she come to see?'

'Johnny.'

'They're together every day. Proximity, opportunity, common interest. You see if I'm wrong, Annie.'

'The priest who came in from the cold,' Ann said and she bit into a sandwich. The conversation swung away then to May Burton.

'She's quite nice once you get past the plum in her mouth. What say we take her up on her offer, go down for a week?'

'I don't think so.'

'I might. When this one's out and bawling.' She patted the bulge beneath her maternity overall. 'Nick is all for it. He wants to meet Sam. He wasn't there the day we called in, and Nick can't believe in old Jack's sane identical twin. I mean, Annie, it is a bit hard to swallow. Jack's twin, into the restoration of antique furniture? Can you imagine Jack getting his hands dirty?'

'No.'

'I wasn't going to go in that day. I just wanted to see what the place looked like, but Nick's got the cheek of his namesake. Anyway, May treated us like long-lost relatives.'

'She always loved visitors.'

'You know, she said that Sam was in Toorak that day, but the dame at the supermarket – where we asked directions on how to get there – said Sam and May had been in only an hour earlier, said they'd just got back from Toorak. What's with him, Annie?'

Ann shovelled space food into Darth Vadar's small mouth and set to wiping up the spillage with a coiled pink serviette cum light sabre. She couldn't lie to Bronwyn.

'I mean, is he man or myth?'

'I suppose he's real enough, Bron.'

'She's always by herself when she comes up here. He never comes with her. How many times have you seen him? I mean, you spent a fair bit of time in Narrawee when you worked in Melbourne. How many times did you actually see Sam in the flesh?'

'Just the once. At the open day.'

'Yeah?' Bronwyn nodded and gently removed the teat. Bethany was sleeping. 'Am I supposed to shake her up and burp her or something?'

'She'll burp herself. One way or the other.'

'Do you use disposables?'

'Most of the time.'

'Nick's mother gave me two dozen of those towelling things. I told her they'd make great tea towels.' The bottle placed on the table, Bronwyn settled Bethany on one arm and emptied her coffee cup. 'It's cold,' she said.

'Cold coffee. One of the joys of motherhood. Unfinished sentences is another. Interrupted sleep.'

'Interrupted sex.'

'What's that?' Ann asked.

The waitress cleared the table and the sisters waited until she was done, then Bronwyn returned to a former conversation.

'Maybe he's a lunatic, Annie, and she has to keep him locked up in the cellar.'

'Who?'

'Sam. And May only lets him out on his good days. Or . . . or she hires an actor for special occasions.' She stopped short and stared at Ann, her eyes growing huge. 'That's it. That's it. That is it, Annie. I've solved the mystery.'

'What mystery?'

'Old Jack. That's where he went to.'

'When?'

'All the time. That's where he is now.' Bronwyn sat forward, her thighs spread, her eyes flashing. 'You just think about it for a minute. Think about June. You went there in June for their open day, and Sam was there. Right?'

'Right.'

'Well he was always away in June. Remember? I loved the June school holidays; rain, mud and all – because old Jack was never around.'

'He was never around, period, Bron.'

'Yeah, but that's what I mean. And that's what's wrong with Johnny too. That's the answer to everything, Annie. That's why Johnny ran. That's why he refuses to talk about Jack. He knows. Somehow or other he found out that the old man was a bigamist and he couldn't break Mum's heart, or something, so he took off.'

'Pregnancy isn't supposed to affect the brain, just the result of pregnancies. You've seen the photographs of Dad and Sam when they were small.'

'He had them done on a computer. They can do anything these days.'

'Ask Ben. He's met Sam.' She glanced at her watch. 'You're going to be late back to work.' Ann reclaimed Beth, placing her in the rear of the twin stroller.

'But can't you see what I'm getting at? That's where Jack has been going, all of these years. That's where he's been disappearing to. Remember how the letters would come – and always from May, never from Sam? Jack would pick up his briefcase and go. He's a bloody bigamist, pretending that he's twins. The first wife knew, but the second one didn't.'

'May and Sam were married in '53.'

'So . . . so reverse what I said. I'll bet you any money you like that he's down there now calling himself Sam.' Bronwyn stood, staring hard at her sister.

'Say bye-bye to Aunty Bron, Tristan, and tell her she'll feel worse when the baby comes.'

'Done unna ettimate da power ob da dark porse,' he said.

'And don't you underestimate me either, Darth.' Bronwyn replied. 'And tell your mother not to either. I'm inviting myself around tonight, Annie. Nick's going to see his parents and I think I might get a headache earlier rather than later.' She kissed Tristan. 'You know who he takes after, don't you?'

'May said it yesterday. Everyone says it. Even David, God help us.' Bronwyn laughed. 'And I wouldn't laugh about it either. You look as if you're having quads. Imagine four little Jacks.'

'I'd drown them at birth. See you tonight, Annie. We'll work out how we're going to expose him.'

'Come for dinner.'

Bronwyn nodded, waved, walked away. Ann sat on.

'So here we go again, Darth.'

'Done uner ettimate da power ob da dark porse.'

'I never did, my handsome one.' She sipped her coffee as she watched her sister's rounded form cross over the road, knowing that Bronwyn wasn't going to give up on this theory easily. And if she told Nick, he'd make it his one goal in life. Jack had pulled the gun on him once, and given him a two-barrel salute as he ran.

I'll have to tell her, she thought.

Tell her how much?

Her mind travelled back to yesterday, to Bessy and May. Both tiny ladies, but that was where the similarity ended. May in her pale yellow linen with her pale blonde hair. Bessy in her baggy trousers, legs spread, sitting on the back step, cigarette in hand.

'Jack told me so much about you,' May had said.

'And all bloody bad, I bet.'

'But he had great respect for your bull, Bessy.'

They'd laughed and for the first time in Ann's life, the two worlds of her childhood had merged. She had almost begun to believe in the impossible – May and Samuel. At Narrawee. The new Samuel mellowing with age.

Now this.

May, so careful with her choice of words, and so happy yesterday. She had told Ann that Jack had remained in Daree, but she'd dragged out the old virus for Bessy and Bron. Poor Samuel, always down with a virus, or out of town. And that was the major problem. Uncle Sam always there, but never there.

If he had the nerve to face Bronwyn, there was a chance he'd pull it off. Ann hadn't seen her father for eight years when she'd met Uncle Sam that time in Narrawee. She had been fooled. Fooled by his soft voice and his smile, and by his bandaged arm.

Came off a nag.

She hadn't guessed. She had not guessed.

But she'd had no memory of the previous Sam at that time, and she'd gone to Narrawee expecting to see Uncle Sam. Bron would go there expecting to see her father. She'd been in Mallawindy through all of the years, seen the letters from May, seen their father pick up his briefcase and drive away. She'd know him. He couldn't alter the expression in his eyes, couldn't alter old mannerisms. Bron would know him.

Better to tell her. Better to swear her to secrecy. The world was shrinking daily, and though Ann may never again visit Narrawee, Bronwyn and Nick certainly would. Sooner or later they'd come face to face with Jack Burton, then God help everyone.

May had spoken well of Sam yesterday, spoken about his reclaimed antiques, stored for fifty years in the cellar but now gracing the old rooms once again.

'The boys' great-grandfather brought a few of the pieces with him from Wales, but when the twins' parents moved back from Melbourne, they had their own furniture so they tossed what was considered to be old junk into the cellar. Samuel is quite the perfectionist when it comes to wood. I'd love you to see his work. I believe you would be impressed.'

Bridge-builder May, trying so hard to reconstruct that which had never been built, could not be built. No base on which to commence. Just . . . just blood.

It was almost impossible to believe. Jack Burton working with his hands, determined to put the old mansion back the way it had been in his youth. But people could change. If they wanted to. They could force change. Since Bethany's arrival, Ann had forced many changes. She'd put Mandy's photograph away, realising she'd been worshipping at it daily, as her father had worshipped before Liza's portrait. Life and love were for the living, not for the dead, and seven years had been too long to mourn her first baby.

She recognised much of her father in her own personality, but she fought it, fought his genes and his influence on her early life. A plant died if it was not given room to grow. Her father had refused to grow, to move on, but Ann had four good reasons now to move forward. Her past would not taint the lives of her children.

Mandy's room had been newly painted, the single bed moved into Benjamin's room, which was large enough to take the two beds. He was delighted with it. Now he could invite his best friend to a sleep-over. Little Ben, growing tall, developing his own personality. A brand-new person. A melding of the best of two families.

And Matthew, he adored his little sister. Gentle Matthew, so like David. Ann was seeing the boys as individuals these days and loving them more, because of Bethany. Mandy had not been replaced, but had taken her special place in that other time. Her room now smelt of Bethany, that sweet scent of white laundry and powder, of baby things and baby breath.

And Johnny too, the boy who had left her screaming on the

road, had also been placed away in that other time. The brother she spoke to in Mallawindy was the adult Mr Burton, teacher – the sometimes stranger. Perhaps he would marry Kerrie Fogarty, have his own children.

Ann knew he'd never come to terms with the part he played in their father's great charade, but he was beginning to forgive Ann her part in it. Other things on his mind these days. Was it Kerrie?

Malcolm Fletcher was also playing a role in his new life. Johnny spent most Sunday evenings with the old man.

Ann sighed, shook her head. She couldn't tell Bron and Nick the truth. Already too many knew. Far better to deny the bigamist theory, to laugh it off. Better if Bron had her baby early. A new baby and full-time job would leave little time for detective work. Better for all concerned to have Aunty May and Uncle Sam living safe at Narrawee, Uncle Sam dabbling in the restoration of antiques. Better for the boys and for Bethany too. Children were the sum total of those who had gone before them. Negatives created negativity, thus there would only be positives in her children's lives.

Better for Ellie too.

Bessy had let a cat out of a bag yesterday. She'd told Ann and May that Bob Johnson, a retired policeman, had moved back to Mallawindy, that Ellie had invited him to dinner after church.

Ann remembering Bob Johnson. She'd been twelve when Linda, the last-born Burton girl, had died and Jack Burton had taken off to Narrawee for a year. Bob Johnson had spent a lot of that year at the farm. He'd come with his saw and his hammer and he'd fix things, then stay on to eat dinner at Ellie's table. No doubt he'd read of Jack Burton's disappearance and returned to see how the land was lying.

Ellie was only sixty-two. She had years of life left to live – if she was allowed to live them. But if Bron ever learned that their father was in Narrawee, she'd tell Ellie, and no more the widow, it would be goodbye Bob Johnson.

Such a nice normal year that one had been. Bessy had bought a new sewing machine and given Ann the old one, and she had learned to make magic on it. It had been a year of growing. No fear. No fights. Bob Johnson seated at the end of the table on Sunday nights, and laughter all around. Ellie laughing too. And the card games after the table had been cleared. And Ben's utility. And old Mickey, the dog, sleeping his life away beneath the plum tree. A different year. Ellie had been so different that year. She'd found time to be herself, a self acceptable to Bob Johnson. If Jack Burton remained dead, Bob would not let Ellie get away a second time. Maybe that was why they were renovating the old place, Ann thought. Maybe Ellie and Bob were planning to move back over the river come Christmas.

Poor Ben. If Bron is right about Johnny and Kerrie, Ben will be left on his own to grow old alone. What a world, she thought. What a waste of a life. He should have had his own family. He'd loved Mandy, now he loved the boys and Bethany.

Tristan yawned, and she turned to him. 'Someone is sleepy, and he's been such a good boy for Mummy today.'

'I Darp Bada, Mummy. Darp Bada is a bad guy,' he explained.

She smiled and settled him in the stroller, rolled the pink serviette into an elongated coil and placed it in his hand. 'There's your light sabre. Now, sleepy-byes, bad guy. You've got a lot of space fighting to do tonight.'

'I det Maffyou wiff my lipe sayba. Pheeew. Pheeew. Pheeew.'

'I'm sure we can rely on that.'

She collected her handbag and manoeuvred the stroller out to the street where she walked and window-shopped but purchased little. That old feeling, that little Annie feeling, was back today. She felt a distancing from the other shoppers, and the sound of cars on the road was not so clear. Still, she could shake it off these days; she could kiss a sleepy face, tuck a tiny hand beneath a blanket, force her mind to deal with the present.

And it would have to be dealt with. Bronwyn would voice her hypothesis to her brothers. Ben would laugh it off. He'd known Sam, and still believed in him. But Johnny? Would he laugh it off, lie?

Warn May. That's what I have to do. Warn May and tell her to forget about her invitations. Let May deal with it. And speak to Johnny. Let him know what Bron was thinking. Prepare him in advance for her questions.

Her mind turned away from Bron to Ellie, who was having Jack's name added to the stone on the children's communal grave. She'd spent considerable time and paper in working out the words she might fit there. At each meeting, she read her new condensed composition, seeking everyone's approval.

John William Burton, [Jack] beloved husband of Ellie, loved father of John, Ben, Ann and Bronwyn. Resting now with – . The other names were already in place.

Ann had given this latest one her nod of approval, as she had given her nod to the other three. Only let it be done. Only let this chapter end. Only let Christmas come and go and get Bron's baby born. A large space between now and Christmas. A long space to get through.

At two-thirty she walked back to the playgroup to collect Matthew. He was full up with news, and he had a chance to pour it out too. Darth Vadar and Beth were flat out, sleeping in the twin stroller.

'An I drawed a bear. An I drawed a racing car.' Never a chatterbox, Matthew could fill a silence when he found one to fill. Holding on to the stroller handle, he walked beside Ann, her little ocean-blue-eyed boy, her self-assured little man who wore Mandy's curls. She kissed his curls as they walked on to the school, chattering together until Benjamin and Dee's bunch joined them for the long walk home.

'Why haven't we got your bus, Aunty Ann?' Dee's children preferred to be driven home after a hard day at school.

'Because six and one more make seven, Frances, and the van only holds six. Anyway, it's a beautiful day for walking.'

Eight months ago she and David had purchased a six-seater

four-wheel drive. These days a family sedan limited the size of a family. They were paying it off, but they'd made the final payment on their house. Money had never been a major problem. David was on a good wage, and unknown Sydney brides paid for the extras; Ann's wedding dresses sold quickly at the Bridal Palace in Sydney. They'd been calling lately, wondering what had happened to her. She'd told them she was on maternity leave.

Her gowns were magic creations, stolen from *Cinderella* and *Gone With The Wind*. They sold for a fortune, and she could make one in a week – used to be able to make one in a week. Hadn't made one in three months. Soon she'd get back to them. It was an odd occupation, though – hours of labour, then the posting away of her creation, never to be seen again. Malcolm Fletcher's creations were out there. He could pick them up, hold them in his hands. Maybe it was time to do something else, something that might expand the mind instead of turning it off – something that might take her mind away from baby mush and milk.

She thought of Michael, her old boss at the Melbourne advertising agency. He hadn't wanted to lose her. He might be happy to employ her again – at a distance. She had a computer and could have a modem fitted. These days most of her writing was done directly onto the computer, and saved on the *Ann* file with the taxable deductions. David was as free to read her poems as he was to peruse the annual lists of antibiotics, cough syrup and doctors' bills. Sooner or later there would be time to reclaim her life, so why not give it a kick-start? Contact Michael – if he was still in business. 'I will,' she said.

'Will what, Mummy?' little Ben asked.

'Have chicken and chips for dinner,' she said.

At the barbecue chicken shop, she bought a large chicken, chips and coleslaw for dinner, and a separate serve of chips to go, bribing her entourage on the long walk home.

Still addicted. Always addicted to salty chips, eaten hot from their paper.

'Maybe I should get a job in a fish and chip shop,' she said, and her small addicts agreed that it was a very excellent idea.

Back at the house she left the two little ones sleeping in the stroller and the two oldest playing with Dee's children. It was close to four-thirty when she set out the row of bottles and began mixing formula.

The phone rang.

'Damn it.' She reached for it, but changed her mind, allowing it to go to her answering machine, which was already flashing red. She'd been in demand while out walking the town.

Her attempt to breast-feed had lasted for six weeks. Breast-feeding always reminded her of Ellie – Ellie walking around with a baby dangling, serving Jack's breakfast while a hungry mouth guzzled.

'We are what we are and that's all that we are,' she said to a milk bottle. 'We do what we do, the best we can do.' Large hands, efficient hands, they worked on.

'Burton,' the disembodied voice spoke from her answering machine. 'Your uncle has been attempting to contact – '

She snatched up the phone. 'I'm here, sir.'

'Ah. Vetting the calls now? A dastardly practice, Burton.'

'My hands are full, sir.' She couldn't bring herself to call him Mr Fletcher. It sounded too cold, too distant. Fletch sounded disrespectful. 'At least I don't leave my phone off the hook, like some people I know. What did you say?'

'Samuel called.'

'Sam called you!' She shook her head, pouring milk into a bottle.

'He said he had left several messages on your machine.'

'Sam?' She capped the bottle. 'I just got in. I haven't had time to check it yet.'

'He gave me a city hospital number. If you have a pen handy, Burton.'

'What happened to him?'

'His wife was involved in a car accident.'

One hand reaching for a pen, she paused. The room had grown dark as a cloud passed over the sun. Little Annie stirred, sighed. Then the pen was in her hand and she shook her head, trying to absorb the old man's words, trying to reason with herself as she stared at the window and at the sun, a pale ghost beneath the cloud.

Malcolm spoke the number three times before she had it trapped on paper.

'What happened, sir?'

'He gave few details, Burton, but he was desperate to contact you. He said that his wife was asking for you.'

'I'll call her,' she said. 'Thank you. I'll call her now.'

And the phone was down, and Bethany stirring. Ann picked her up, not wanting her to disturb Tristan. She ran a bottle beneath cold water, sprinkled milk onto her wrist. Running water, splashing water, she stood there until she judged the temperature right, then, holding both baby and bottle with one hand, she dialled the hospital number.

'I'm inquiring after May Burton.'

It took some minutes before the voice returned. 'She's still in surgery.'

'Can you give me more information, please? I'm her niece.'

The speaker repeated her words. A computerised robot.

'Can I speak to a doctor?' Ann said. 'I'm in New South Wales. I want to know if it's serious. If I should be there.'

'Hold the line, please.' Ann held, tapped her foot. Held. Counted seconds, counted minutes – until a second woman's voice came on the line.

'Her injuries are extensive. We are hopeful. I'm sorry, but I can't be more optimistic at this stage. If you could call back in an hour she should be out of surgery.'

Ann looked down at the contented baby, her little mouth working hard on the teat. May had fed her a bottle only yesterday.

She had burped her only yesterday, and had her spit up on the shoulder of her frock.

'Could you give her a message, please? Could you tell her I am on my way? Or him, Samuel Burton – if he's around. Tell him to . . . tell him to keep her safe for me. I'll be there as soon as possible.'

She played her messages back then. One was from the Bridal Palace, and two from Sam.

Message for Ann. Samuel Burton calling. May has been injured in a car accident. They are operating at the moment. She asked for you before they took her in. I'll call back in half an hour.

Ann skipped to the next message. *Ann. Samuel again. May is in the Alfred Hospital in Melbourne. She asked for you. I can be reached at the hospital.*

Hours since he'd called and May still in the operating theatre. It was almost five.

'God. It's bad, Bethie. It's very bad.'

She played and replayed the messages, first seeking more information, then later, just to listen to that voice. It was Sam's voice. Very correct. More cultured than her father's. Hissing Ss. *Sssamuel.*

This was the illusive twin, trapped on tape. David had met him, had shaken his hand at the inquest. David, plus this recording, might convince Bronwyn, might silence her questions. Ann didn't erase the message.

It was close to five-thirty before David arrived home. She met him in the garage and told him of May. 'I have to go to her, David.'

'It's too late to start out now. Go in the morning.'

'I know he . . . Sam wouldn't have called Mr Fletcher unless . . . I think it's bad. I called them again five minutes ago. She's still in surgery. I have to go tonight.'

'It's late. It's a long drive and you're tired.' He looked at her and saw that old determination he had never been able to fight. 'But you'll go anyway, won't you?'

'I have to, David.' She returned ahead of him to the family

room. 'I bought some more disposable napkins today. And a chicken. Bron is coming for dinner. She'll help get the boys down.'

'We'll manage.'

'I've made up the bottles. If you need more, just follow the directions on the tin. I've made up a new solution for the bottles. Wash them well first.'

'I've been there, done that. I'll manage.' He followed her upstairs, where she tossed a few items into her bag. He followed her to the bathroom, watched her pull a comb through her hair, then tie the tamed curls high. 'Take my car and be careful. Stop for a coffee every couple of hours.'

'I'll try.' She kissed the boys, who tailed her every move, wide eyes questioning. 'Mummy has to go for a long, long drive tonight. She'll be back tomorrow before you go to bed. Be good for Daddy.'

They followed her down to the garage, David watching their every step on the stairs. Then Ann was behind the wheel, the motor running.

'She's a part of something else, David. I know you don't understand. I don't know if I do either. All I know is that I have to see her.'

'You're right. I don't understand. You didn't speak to her for five years.'

'One day I'll try to explain.'

'I wish you would. Take care, and don't speed. You know that your foot gets heavy when your mind starts to wander.' He kissed her through the window, saving her a reply, then with a wave of her hand, and kisses blown, she was gone.

The big motor wanted to fly, and once out of town she gave it its head. Farms flashed by, cars passed by with their spray of grit, trucks shook her vehicle with their wind draughts, but no car overtook her. She didn't look at the speedometer, didn't slow through Mallawindy. She filled up with petrol in Daree then drove on, and her mind went away, wandering the broad paddocks to the distant hills.

It went back, and back, and back to that other time. Back to the day it had all begun.

how many miles?

~

'How many more miles, Aunty May?' Annie and Liza were going to Daddy's Narrawee. Liza went there lots of times before with Daddy but Annie didn't go, and now she was going all the way to Daddy's Narrawee with Aunty May, and they were going to have a very exciting time, because Aunty May said so, and they might go to the zoo and see all the animals, and they might go to the beach and find some seashells too. Mummy had a necklace made of seashells from when she was little, and Johnny said that the shells came from the beach and they had little animals who live in there – when the shells were alive. Annie really wanted to see those little animals.

In the big back seat of Aunty May's car it smelt like Liza's brand-new red shoes from in the box, and Annie was sitting up like a big girl and the wind was making whistles through the window and it was a very long way that they had come. They even had dinner in a shop. And they had ice cream with chocolate on it and Uncle Sam bought a big bag of lollies so Liza would be happy and not tired.

'How many more miles, Aunty May?' Annie said.

And Aunty May said, 'Not far now.' Then she said *sweetheart*, just like Daddy said *sweetheart* to Liza. 'Not far now, sweetheart.

We go over Pretty Sally, then we turn off, and it's not very far at all.'

Sweetheart sounded good, like very special.

It was a long time more and then the car was at some big tall gates and through the gates and up the little road that was hiding in the trees and . . . and it was like Annie couldn't breathe, it was such a beautiful house, so magical a place.

'Do you live in there, Aunty May?'

'We do.'

'Is it like the Queen's palace?'

'It is my Camelot, sweetheart. Do you know about Camelot? About King Arthur's castle, and his big round table?'

'I saw it first. I saw it lots of times with Daddy. And I saw inside too and they've got a big tin full of biscuits with chocolate on them,' Liza said.

'Well I saw it now, Miss Smarty Pants,' Annie said, because Aunty May had called her sweetheart again, and she felt like she was a very special girl too. And anyway, Johnny sometimes called Liza Miss Smarty Pants. He just said it because Liza always said she was Miss Tiny Tot, so he just said, 'Miss Smarty Pants, more like it.'

Liza always got mad when Johnny said that and she told Daddy on him, but she couldn't tell Daddy today because Daddy wasn't here and nobody knew where to find him.

Inside the white Camelot palace was like . . . like so giant big and the rooms were all boooomy when you talked and there were special things, like pictures and carpet on the floor and a big boooomy bedroom for Annie and Liza to share. And there was a special lounge room which had a television, and outside was like fairyland, with only trees and flowers, and horses you could ride on.

Aunty May was a magic lady and she had lots of dresses so she just cut some up and sewed new little dresses from them on her sewing machine, a blue one for Annie and a pink flower one for Liza, and she made some pants too. There were new shoes from the shops and slippers, only for inside, because Aunty May had got a very new clean carpet.

It was happy times all the time, and even new dolls from the shop. They were the best part, because Annie got first pick and she didn't have to give her doll to Liza when Liza cried. Aunty May said so because Annie did what was told first-tell.

Liza didn't do things first-tell, and she asked all the time for biscuits, and she wanted Annie's slippers now because they were red ones like from *Wizard of Oz* and Liza said she wanted the red ones.

'No, Liza. You chose the green slippers when we were at the shop so you cannot have Ann's slippers, and if you can't be a good girl then you'll have to go to your room and stay there,' Aunty May said.

Liza didn't ever like 'no' and Aunty May said 'no' lots and lots of times.

'No more biscuits, Liza,' she said with her special strong voice. 'No more tantrums from you, Miss. No more television. It's bedtime.'

And even if Liza rolled on the floor and screamed and even if she kicked walls with her feet, she didn't make Aunty May say yes, because Aunty May wasn't like Mummy who just did anything so Liza wouldn't get her red face tantrums and get sick.

They drove a long way to the beach one day and found lots of shells and they went to the zoo one day and Uncle Sam bought big bags of lollies even when Aunty May said, 'No more lollies, Sam. They won't eat their dinner.'

Liza got lots of lollies, even in bed. Not Annie though, because she didn't do the all-over kisses when Uncle Sam tucked them in. She pulled her nightie down very tight and she only did what Aunty May said to do. Not Uncle Sam. Annie didn't like Uncle Sam anyway, because of how Daddy and Johnny didn't like him.

Johnny knew a poem about him.

Sam, Sam, the dirty man,
washed his face in a frying pan,
combed his hair with the leg of a chair
and told his mother he didn't care.

Annie wouldn't ever go in the cellar with Uncle Sam. She didn't like that cellar, because there wasn't any proper light in there, just the kerosene lantern light, which only made a little circle in the big dark and it was a very spooky deep-in-the-ground place.

'Uncle Sam has got the biggest apple in all the world in the cellar and he's keeping it for a good girl. Who is going to get the biggest apple?'

'Not Annie. It's mine. I have to get first pick because Daddy said so, because I'm Miss Tiny Tot.'

Liza always got apples and lollies when she went down there. And maybe Uncle Sam saw her do wee in there one day too, because Annie had to fix up her overall straps that were supposed to cross over at the back so they wouldn't keep falling off, and Liza didn't know how to do it. And she had a bare bottom underneath and she had on her sulky face, like she always got at home when she did something naughty.

And Annie said, 'You should do wee in the toilet, because you're seven, and you should wash your hands with soap after, like Aunty May said, Liza.'

Then . . . then there were even badder things in that cellar, even before that bad no-bread-for-lunchtime day.

Everyone was going to have a picnic under the trees with banana sandwiches and lemonade, and Annie loved banana sandwiches the best and Sam got back from the shops and Aunty May said, 'Oh, no. You forgot the bread, Sam.' But he was already working in the garden and Liza was screaming because she wanted the television on and Aunty May said 'no' again. And then . . . and then Liza just walked up to her and got her hand and she bit, very hard, so Aunty May's finger bled, and when she was washing it, and finding a bandaid to put on, well, Liza just ran into the lounge room with her outside shoes on and she turned on the television herself.

Annie did like the television a lot, and today the midday movie was just starting, and it was about a girl with a clever dog. They didn't have television in Mallawindy, just the pictures at the shire hall on Saturday, and they only went there two times when Daddy wasn't home.

'I give up,' Aunty May said, and she picked up her bag.

On the television a bad man had taken the little girl's dog and tied him in a bag and put him in the little car he had on the side of his motorbike.

'Wait right here. Don't move from this room. I'll be back in twenty minutes,' Aunty May said and she went outside to her car, because of the bread.

Then Uncle Sam came inside from the garden, saying about the cat. About that black mother cat.

'The old black cat had her kittens in the cellar. Come down, and you can hold one, girls.'

'Aunty May said that we have to watch the television and not move.'

'Then you can't see the kittens. I can't take them away from their mummy, they haven't even got their eyes open. Come on, girls. Who's going to see the kittens first?'

'Me. Me.' Liza didn't care that the little television girl's dog was in a bag and that the bad man was pinching him. She just went with Uncle Sam.

And it wasn't a long time, because the bad man was still riding away and the little girl didn't know about her dog yet, when Annie heard the old car come. It made that same old Daddy's-car noise, like vrooooom vroom-vroom, and the skidding noise Daddy's wheels made. Annie jumped up fast and went to look for Liza.

But Daddy came in the back door and he didn't know why Annie was there, and he yelled, 'What the bloody hell are you doing down here?'

'Mummy bought a new baby, and it is a girl and Johnny said its name is going to be Bronwyn, so Aunty May said for Liza and me to come for a holiday and go to the zoo and see the animals, Daddy.'

'Liza? Where is Liza?'

'I don't know, Daddy.'

But she did know. She knew about the kittens and about Liza doing wee and bad things in the cellar. And she knew that Uncle Sam knew about the bad things too, because when Annie started to tell Aunty May one day, well, Uncle Sam got all funny and he talked very loud and he picked Annie up and swung her around and around and laughed too loud.

'Where's that bloody mongrel dog?' Daddy yelled and he shook Annie, but she wouldn't look at him because it was her fault. She should have told Aunty May.

Daddy looked in the bathrooms and in the bedrooms, and the kitchen and he yelled, and he ran through the house and Annie ran to the cellar very fast to get Liza out.

'Liza. Liza. May! Where the bloody hell are you?' Daddy was yelling near the garage.

Annie could open the cellar door easy because it didn't get locked except with the key when nobody would be home, and so she opened it wide and she saw Liza doing rude things, like no pants on, and even Uncle Sam with his pants half on and –

'Liza! Liza!' Daddy's yelling getting closer.

And Liza and Uncle Sam heard Daddy because the door was open and it banged against the wall and Uncle Sam was trying to run upstairs and Liza was trying to put her red overalls on, only getting two feet in one leg of her overalls.

Then Daddy was in the cellar and Uncle Sam was walking backwards. Backwards. Slow. Down, down, down to the floor.

And Aunty May was coming home then with the bread.

Then –

Then –

Just screaming. Just everyone screaming. And Annie screaming. 'Don't, Daddy. Stop, Daddy.'

And Daddy punching Sam. And Sam picking up Liza. Holding her in front, like hiding. And Daddy's got a long piece of pipe, like for water taps. Hitting and yelling.

Awful terrible noise then. Smash!

And Liza on the floor. And still. Then Sam picking up the lantern and throwing it at Daddy, hitting him.

And all dark in there then, and Annie screaming and running back to the door where there is light. Black dark, like black night down there. And fighting and smashing, and Aunty May crying.

Then no more fighting. Only the black, black dark. Only the crying, and Annie wanting Aunty May but she's down there in the crying black dark.

Walking slow down, away from the light. Walking very careful. Down. Picking the bread that Aunty May dropped, feeling for the bread with her hand, picking it up on the steps and walking slow into the dark, where it isn't so dark, because there is a little window way up high that is making light on Uncle Sam. He's lying on the floor. Sleeping on the old carpet.

And Liza. She's not in the window light. Only her red overalls.

Daddy and May just standing there looking at each other and crying, grown-up crying, and it sounded like very bad hurting, crying. Annie wanting them to stop, walking to them, saying lots of words, like Mummy says when Daddy cries.

'I love you, my Daddy. I love you, Aunty May.' Patting them and saying lots of things to make them stop crying.

Then Daddy picking Annie up and crying and rocking her and Annie patting his face like Mummy does and his face is all wet with salty water. And Annie looking down over Daddy's shoulder at Liza and knowing that something awful, terrible bad happened because Daddy is cuddling her, not Liza.

And Annie saying, 'We have to make banana sandwiches. Make them get up, Aunty May.'

Aunty May crying louder and walking to the steps, sitting on the bottom step with her arms all hugged up tight around her, like trying to hold her shaking together. And Daddy putting Annie down with May. And the bread is all squashed because Daddy held Annie too tight, so it won't be any good for making sandwiches. Annie giving it to May, pushing it at May.

'Uncle Sam was being a bad man. Make him say sorry, Aunty May.'

'What are we going to do, Jack?' Screamed. 'What are we going to do, Jack?'

'Get her out of here and call the cops.'

Daddy lifting May, making her stand up. Pushing May, making her climb the stairs. Annie pulling at her hand.

Then all that light outside but Daddy still down in the dark, lost in the dark, except his little cigarette light that makes his face show up orange when he puffs.

'Get her out of here!' A screaming wild face.

Annie running from the door into the hot sunshine and everything looks just the same as before, all bright white light and the sun way up high and the house still looking like a magic Camelot palace. Sam and Liza are having a sleep, that's all. Aunty May will make it fixed up, because she always can make everything fixed. She's a very good lady.

Daddy walking out Liza all floppy in his arms.

'Get the cops, I said. Tell the bloody world what I've done, May.'

Aunty May not doing what Daddy says like Mummy always does what he says very fast. Aunty May just standing there, watching Daddy take Liza to the rose garden where there are millions of flowers. Then Daddy falling down on his knees like Mummy does in church. It looks funny. Daddy never goes to church.

And May, just staring at the cellar. 'He's booked on the six-fifteen flight to Brisbane, Jack.'

'Well, he won't be catching the six-fifteen flight, will he? He won't be raping babies in bloody Brisbane tonight, the dirty mongrel dog. Cancel his membership to the diseased dogs' club.'

'Think, Jack. Think.'

'Where is she?'

Annie backing away. Backing a long way away. Backing until her back is hard on the wall, and watching, listening.

'He has to go up to Brisbane.' Aunty May's words like thinking words again. Like we have to get things fixed up. Like this is hard to do but I can get it done. 'It's my guilt, Jack. It's my fault.'

'Ring the cops. I told you what to bloody well do.'

Cops were policemen. They put bad people in jail. They might put Uncle Sam in jail. And Liza.

'This is my world. Here. This is my life. I've got nowhere else, nothing else, Jack.' Then May looking around. 'They're working at Hargraves Park. There is no one here. They won't be here today.'

'She's bloody well here, isn't she?'

Then staring at Annie, staring at each other, like frightened faces, and looking around the paddocks. Just the horses and two crows on the lawn.

'Go and watch the television, sweetheart.'

But Annie not doing what she's told first-tell, just pretending to, walking along the house until they stop looking, then hiding behind the cellar door.

Aunty May with a shovel, pushing it at Daddy. Daddy digging up Uncle Sam's special Peace rose, and he's going to be very, very angry. May holding the rose up while Daddy makes the hole big – big enough for Liza.

Johnny dug a hole for the kitten when it was dead, and he put the dirt back in and Annie put some flowers on it.

May bringing the water pipe from the cellar and Daddy hammering it in with the back of the shovel.

Liza is always bad. She poked the kitten's eye out with a stick.

May stomping the dirt down, stomping all the dirt in Liza's eyes because she was a bad girl and if she didn't bite Aunty May and turn on the television, well, Aunty May wouldn't have got angry. And Sam is a stupid bad man. He shouldn't have forgot to buy the bread.

No one is thinking about Annie any more. No one knows where she is. She's the best hidey player, Johnny said. When they play hidey at home, no one can ever find her, and she watches them look

292

for her and she peeps out at them and giggles and sometimes they find her by her giggles.

She's peeping out at the roses, red ones and pink ones and yellow ones and orange and some with pink and yellow and orange all in together. Thousands of them, and her eyes are making them all go into like a carpet, like a magic carpet that you can fly on when you dream in bed.

Then Daddy is in the cellar and carrying out a big, big roll of old carpet, that's nearly too heavy for him. Throwing it in the boot of his car then running to the house. And Annie seeing May take the shovel into the cellar. Everything is so fast, but Annie is so slow to walk from her hiding place to the top of the steps.

Sam isn't down there any more, but she didn't see him come out.

In dreams people are there, then they are in another place. May is doing silly dream things too, like scraping up a bucket full of dirt from the cellar floor, like Johnny digging for worms so they can catch some fish for dinner. Then May is walking up the steps with dirt. And she must think she's got something except dirt in the bucket, because she starts to throw it on the garden, and then she changes her mind and digs a hole and puts the dirt in it.

And that would be a very silly thing to do if it wasn't a dream, so it must be a dream.

And Daddy. He's wearing Uncle Sam's clothes and looking very funny, so dream Annie giggles at him. What a silly dream she is having. When she wakes up she'll be in Mallawindy and she'll tell Johnny all about it.

Old crows caw-caw-cawing waiting for the crusts from the picnic while Daddy and Aunty May move lots of old furniture and boxes of apples to the wrong place in the cellar, move an old table from the wall right into the middle. And the old couch gets moved too. Mummy cat is watching them, her tail up, like she's very worried about her kittens.

'You can't take her with you.'

'I can't leave her here by herself, Jack.'

'You bloody left her before. You left her with that mongrel bastard – '

'Don't, Jack! Don't! The Murrays come to clean the house tomorrow morning. Ted comes here for his lunch.'

Annie listening. She likes Mr Murray's dog, because he's a very friendly dog.

'Then tell the bloody Murrays not to come here.'

'I can't. I never do. I'll leave them a note. I'll tell them we're dropping Sam at the airport, then the girls and I will be spending the night in Toorak. It will be all right. She'll sleep in the car.'

And Aunty May turning, seeing Annie and her voice changing. 'Doesn't Daddy look very funny, Ann Elizabeth?'

Annie nodding. Nodding.

'He didn't bring any clothes because he wasn't supposed to come here today. We won't tell anyone that Daddy came here today, will we? We won't say a word.'

'We won't say a word.'

'Promise, sweetheart?'

'I promise, Aunty May.'

In dreams you can't ask about things. In dreams you see funny things, like Liza trying to fly off the roof and landing in the river. One time Annie dreamed that. And like last night, dancing with some kittens, holding their hands and the kittens all turning into snakes. That was an awful dream.

She looks at the crows and they say caw, caw, caw.

'We better shut this door, Aunty May. Johnny said crows pick out baby lambs' eyes. They might pick out the kittens' eyes.'

And May staring at her. 'Yes, sweetheart.' Aunty May looking at Daddy, then back to Annie. 'I wonder who will look after the kittens for me. I have to go to Toorak for a little while.'

'You can't leave her in there either, you stupid bitch.'

'Get my car out, Jack. Get his wallet and spare glasses. They'll be in his room. Pack a case. There's money in the left-hand desk drawer.' Then her arm around Annie. 'Would you be big enough to look after the kittens for me, sweetheart? If Aunty May made you lots of sandwiches?'

'Banana ones, for the picnic?'

'You're stark raving mad, you bloody fool of a woman.'

'Do as I ask, Jack. Don't fight me. Ann is going to wait in the cellar with the kittens until I get back.'

'Uncle Sam isn't in there.'

'He's gone to Brisbane. Remember? We bought him a ticket to go on the aeroplane to Brisbane.'

'Did he go yet?'

'He's gone. Come. We'll have a look, just to make sure.'

And they looked, everywhere, in the old wardrobe even, and he wasn't in there.

'Did a taxi man drive him, Aunty May?'

'Yes.'

'Did he take Liza too?'

Aunty May shaking her head, her eyes, like thinking hard, then smiling, but not like a proper smiling face. 'Remember that man who came here on his old motorbike that day, sweetheart?'

'What are you bloody well doing?'

'A red herring. Leave it alone. Get the car out, Jack. Get it out!'

Mummy never talked like that to Daddy, and Annie was very frightened and she moved close to Aunty May, but Daddy went inside.

'What's a red hairy?'

'He's the man who cleaned out the fish pond. Remember? And we gave him some money. Now what was his name, sweetheart?'

'I don't know. The man on television was a red hairy, and he talked very funny, Aunty May. And he had a motorbike with a funny little car on it and he took the little girl's dog away.'

'Perhaps he took Liza for a ride on his bike.'

That was a very funny thing to say, so Annie just shook her head. But Aunty May did lots of talking about the man who came from England while she made sandwiches in the kitchen. And the crows knew about the sandwiches; they waited on the lawn for Annie to give them the crusts.

'One for sorrow, two for joy,' Aunty May said to Daddy, then she smiled her funny smile at Annie. 'Ted Crow. That was his name, wasn't it? Now I remember. It was Ted Crow, and he was older than Daddy.'

And later, sitting behind the old couch in the cellar with the kittens and Aunty May putting some kerosene in the lantern and making a little circle of light for the cellar, and kissing Annie and saying, 'I'll be gone for one dark time, and one more light time, and then I'll come back, sweetheart. I promise you. You mustn't touch the light, because it's dangerous, and you must be very quiet when Mr Murray comes, because they'd think I was a very bad lady leaving you all alone.'

'But I have to look after the kittens, don't I, Aunty May, 'cause I'm a big girl?'

'You're my very best girl in the whole world. Promise me you won't touch the light?' And the kissing, and the sharp, hard sound of the door closing, and the key going in and scratching, and the cars going away. Aunty May's car first, like purring, then Daddy's car with its big vroooom vroom-vroom, which was nearly like Red Hairy's motorbike on the television.

And quiet then. Eating a sandwich because Aunty May had made lots of sandwiches and they are all wrapped up separate, two for lunch, and two for dinner and two for breakfast and two more for lunch and then Aunty May would be back and that wasn't a very long time. Banana sandwiches are the best sandwiches in the world.

And wandering the funny old room with its window up very high inside but nearly on the ground outside. And finding Uncle Sam's bag of lollies and eating one and smiling because she could eat the whole bag full and didn't even have to kiss him to get one.

Sam, Sam the dirty man,
washed his face in a frying pan,

combed his hair with the leg of a chair
and told his mother he didn't care.

Saying that poem lots of times and saying *Mary, Mary, quite contrary*. And saying *Wee Willy Winkie runs through the town*. And counting to one hundred then eating another lolly, and counting to one hundred again, then eating another one.

It was very thirsty eating lollies and all the counting was very thirsty too. Lucky that Daddy had made the lemonade bottle-top loose.

And afterwards, after a long, long time, finding a really giant apple, the biggest one in the whole box, and biting it and the juice running down her chin. They are the best apples, the best in the whole world, and she got the biggest one and Liza didn't get it.

Liza is . . .

Liza is . . .

Aunty May left some books, and coloured pencils. Annie drawing pictures of five kittens and making the names, and writing the words in her best writing. Smoky and Spotty and Sleepy and Silly and Sucky. She liked making Ss. Johnny said she made very good Ss.

Sleeping then because she's all full up and heavy with apples and lemonade and lollies. And the dreaming on the old couch and waking up and it isn't even proper dark time yet outside the window and it is taking a very long time for the dark to come. Aunty May said one dark and one light and she promised.

Then dreaming again of kittens and they don't turn into snakes but they've got dirt in their eyes and Liza has got a big stick and she's digging.

Waking up fast and frightened because now it is proper dark time and the kerosene light is flickering and dying and flashing and dying because Aunty May didn't put in lots of kerosene. And then the light dying and no more flashing. And black dark. Silly Aunty May, she should have put in lots and lots and lots of kerosene.

Waiting in the dark, very quiet, like a mouse, only inside her she's not quiet any more. Inside she's like loud thump, thump, thump. Sitting on the couch like a big girl, but inside she's very, very little and waiting for the light to come back to the window.

And she has to do wee, very bad.

How come Aunty May didn't think about that? How come?

Waiting then for a very long time, then doing wee in the corner under the stairs and maybe it would all soak into the dirt and no one would know.

Everything got soaked into dirt, even blood.

Liza is . . .

Counting then. Very fast counting. Counting tiny star lights outside the window and counting apples in the box and eating more apples in the dark. Apples smell like they taste. Just the same.

Liza couldn't have any more apples, ever, because she's in the ground.

And shaking her head very, very hard. No she is not, Annie. Liza went for a ride with Red Hairy. On his motorbike.

But he didn't put her in a bag, like the dog. She just went to get some lollies. He will bring her back after, like the little girl on television will get her dog back after. In the end of television stories there is always happy ever after.

Liza shouldn't have bit Aunty May and run into the lounge room with her dirty shoes on. She should always put her slippers on inside.

And she shouldn't bite! Only puppy dogs bite, that's what Johnny said.

Liza is a naughty girl.
Her shoes were dusty brown.
She ran into the lounge room
when Sam came back from town.

Making up poems then. Making up lots of them and saying them, twenty times, until they remembered themselves. And trying to make a poem about Red Hairy, but Hairy just rhymed with berry and fairy and merry and good things, and Red Hairy wasn't good, so making his name Ted Crow, because Aunty May said his name might be Ted Crow.

Old Mr Crow, where did he go?
Into the trees with the birds and the bees.

And it is a very, very long time and the dark won't go, so sleeping again on the couch so her hand can touch the cat and it is warm and furry and purry.

Then it's a little light, but cold. Wrapping the blanket right around her, and lifting mummy cat up to cuddle her and get warm, but mummy cat wanting to go back to the kittens to keep them warm, so Annie curling up with the cat and the kittens and not dreaming at all.

And waking up and all the light has come back bright at the little window and soon Aunty May will come. One dark time and one light. That's what she said. And now it was light.

Eating two more sandwiches for breakfast and watching the window bars making stripes of light on the other wall, and soon Aunty May will come back and she'll open the door and the sandwiches aren't even nearly all gone yet.

Kittens sucking milk from mummy cat, and Annie putting some milk from the bottle into a saucer and watching mummy cat's pink prickly tongue clean it all up. And drinking lemonade that hasn't got any fizz in it and eating more sandwiches again, but the banana is all brown. And pretending it is her own picnic, but picnics are only good when other people are there, and banana isn't good when it goes brown.

Then wanting to do wee again, and doing it under the stairs, but needing to do the other one too, very, very bad, but she couldn't do that under the stairs.

The scared starting up again, big, because she really has to do it and it makes her tummy hurt very bad, like 'pendicitis that you have to go to hospital to get fixed from the doctor, like Benjie had to get his fixed. And you get stitches and you can't walk for a week.

And light for a long, long, longer time and Aunty May won't come, but a car comes and a dog comes too, and it might be Red Hairy come back with Liza, or the little girl's dog. And the dog, scratching at the door and barking, and Mr Murray yelling, 'Sit down, Cobber.'

Mr Murray is a good man. He's not a Red Hairy. He's just Ted and he is a working man for Aunty May and Uncle Sam, and his big girl and his Mrs Murray do all the work for Aunty May in the mornings, and they wash her floors and clean the bath and they are very good, so Annie doesn't have to hide from them.

Except Aunty May said.

But Annie wanting to yell out and make them open the door so she could go to the toilet, but she promised that she'd be quiet as a mouse. She promised. And you can't break a promise, because Johnny said.

Window, way up high. But she can climb up there. If she makes some steps up, she can climb up and watch for Aunty May's car. Getting an old chair and putting some wooden boxes on top of the chair and like building a cubbyhouse, like she does with Benjie, but Liza always pulls them down, though.

Miss Smarty Pants, more like it. That's what Johnny says and Liza gets mad. She breaks everything and she stamps her feet and she screams, and she bites everyone. And Mummy kisses her all better, not the everyone else who got bit. And she curls Liza's hair in rows and rows of fat yellow curls and she puts bows in her hair.

Not Annie's hair, though. Mummy says Annie's hair is too curly to curl, but Aunty May can curl it. She can make a hundred curls, more even than for Liza, and she ties some curls up top with a big blue ribbon and makes Annie look like . . . like a special girl . . . like an Ann Elizabeth girl.

Aunty May is a good lady and she'll come back soon, and she'll say, what a good girl you were, Ann Elizabeth, and she'll say sweetheart.

Sweetheart is nice.

Old Mr Crow, where did he go?
Into the trees with the birds and the bees.

And she's up on the wardrobe, because Johnny said she was the best climbing girl in the whole world, and she is too. And if she reaches right over, she can see Mr Murray's dog. It is a big shaggy red dog, big as a lion with curly ears. His name is Cobber, and Johnny said cobber means friend, so Mr Murray's dog will be her friend and talk to her through the window till Aunty May comes back.

What if she doesn't? Maybe she won't come back and open the door. Maybe she won't never, ever come back, but Uncle Sam will come back from Brisbane and he'll open the door and . . .

Annie doesn't like that big door and the big key that makes that hard sound, like a monster door. Like it is too heavy to open and it will never open. Maybe another dark time will come soon.

Liza is in the dark. Daddy put her in the dark because she was bad and Aunty May stomped all the dirt in her eyes. That's a very bad thing to do.

Annie gets too frightened with thinking, and her heart goes thumpity-thump. And she reaches over very far, so her feet are just on the wardrobe, but it is very, very rickety. And she's hitting the window with her hand. And the dog is coming over and he is looking at her like dogs always look when they don't understand something. Like with his head to one side, and his mouth hanging open, and his good dog eyes looking right at her eyes, like he's saying, 'What are you doing in there, Annie?'

She takes her shoe off so she can hit the window with its heel, and maybe break the window, and she doesn't care if she breaks it, because Aunty May is too long, and all the air is used up, and the thumpity-thump is in her ears so she can't hear the dog barking, because that's what happened in the submarine when everyone went to the pictures at the shire hall one time when Daddy was away. All the men's air got gone and they had to just sit down and get dead and she doesn't want all the air to be gone so she has to get dead and get put in the dirt.

And that man's name who cleaned the fish pond wasn't Ted Crow, it was Mack someone. And Aunty May is playing a trick on her. And maybe sweetheart is a trick too, and promises are tricks too, and Annie wants Johnny very bad, and her tummy hurts very bad and she cries.

Then she's not careful, because of crying too much.

And the falling and dropping her shoe and grabbing at the stupid rickety old wardrobe and . . . and . . .

Black.

And black air and the dog barking.

And, 'Lay down. What's got into you today, Cobber?'

Liza is in the dark too.

Aunty May won't never come back.

She said, one more dark, and one more light. Aunty May will come. She promised.

She tricked you, she tricked you. Aunty May tricked you.

and melbourne

~

Away with the old nightmares, only a small segment of Ann's consciousness had been on the road ahead. A red traffic light drew mind and car to a rapid halt somewhere in Sydney Road, Brunswick. Wet road, street lights glazing the bitumen with colour. A strange, still land, all of the houses sleeping, no cars crossing over, only the sad old ghosts flitting by.

She shivered, suddenly aware of the cold, aware of the rain, aware of how close she was to the city. The lights changed from red to amber to green, and still she sat, glancing to the right and left, attempting to work out which way to go.

Ten years of her life had been spent in the city. She'd rented a room in Brunswick when she was sixteen. This road looked much as it had on the day she'd stepped from the bus, her possessions stuffed into her small school case. Twenty years ago she'd walked here, walked for hours with nowhere to go until she'd found that little house in a side street, a sign taped to its front window: ROOM TO LET APPLY WITHIN.

Old Mrs Hadley, eighty if she was a day.

Come in. Come in. You look all hot and bothered, my dear. Would you like a cup of tea? I've only just made a pot.

Brunswick had given her immediate employment too. Twenty

years ago she'd caught trams each morning to a clothing factory where she'd stitched sleeve hems on shirts for two weeks before moving on to the office of an estate agent.

One house had led to another, one office to the next. She'd had few office skills at sixteen, but her typing speed had got her the jobs, and she'd been young enough to train. Then Michael had stopped by her desk one morning and asked her how she'd prove one loaf of bread superior to another.

Two courting pigeons had been outside the office window that day, billing and coo-cooing.

'Toss them some breadcrumbs and ask for their comments,' she'd said.

And that's what he'd done. The pigeon ad had run for years on television.

Two years later she'd moved upstairs, and when Michael had decided to go out on his own, start his own advertising agency, he'd hijacked her.

'Our minds are on the same planet,' he'd said.

Friends. Good friends, but only ever friends. It had been a good life. A free life – until Roger Wilkenson the Third had walked into their office one day.

A smattering of cars still on the roads but the trams had been put to bed. Ann followed the tramlines to town and past the hotel where Roger had stayed when he came to Melbourne.

Where did you come from? Did someone give birth to you or did you evolve from the ocean waves and the night wind, my lovely?

Memories. They were swamping her tonight. Where was Roger Wilkenson now? Had he found a wife to bear his children? Where was Michael, Mrs Hadley? All too long ago. Half a lifetime ago.

'God, how did I get to be so old, Annie?'

So long since she had been alone with time to think. Always a little hand tugging at her jeans, a little voice calling. What if she had remained here, had never gone home, hadn't married?

'What if?'

She was at the hospital before three a.m. She locked the car and hurried into the building. Hospitals. She could live without them. They raised goosebumps and memories, but tonight she shook off the goosebumps and found a guide.

A night sister pointed her to May's ward. One bed and many machines. Ann peered through the open door, then stepped away, again seeking her guide; she'd made a mistake. Elderly woman in that bed, gaping mouth, tubes feeding into her and from her – that wasn't Aunty May. Ann glanced with pity at the small shape of some damaged old woman, her identity lost with her hair and dentures, then she turned from the bed to a figure slumped in a chair.

Him?

So grey. Long hair. But surely him. His arm was held high in a sling, a white bandage covering his brow and one eye; pyjama-clad in green with grey stripes, a worn white hospital-issue dressing gown gaping open, his head back, jaw sagging.

So old. A snoring old man.

Daddy.

Ann drew a deep breath, lifted her chin then walked to his side. He didn't move. She stood for minutes looking down at the closed eye, the open mouth, at the years of lines at his throat, and her vision blurred. Then she breathed deeply again, once, twice, and she reached out, touched his shoulder.

Jack Burton sprang into wakefulness, his unbandaged eye terror-filled. Not since that day in the cellar had she seen such fear.

'Ann.' Just one word.

Had he spoken that word before? Black-headed little bitch, maybe. Shamming little bitch. Wild, black-eyed Burton bitch. But never Ann. Never.

'Dad.'

Silly little words. Where had they come from tonight? From the depths of a long night of memories and from the dark outside and the cold white room and the machines and the laboured breathing.

Oxygen tube to May's nose. Blood dripping into her arm. Electronics charting her heartbeat.

Both faces were now turned to the bed and to the small shell of May, so filled with life, so overflowing with vitality only yesterday. May, the organiser. May, the diplomat. May, who had learned early how to love and how to lie for those she loved, had learned early how to fix things the best way that she could.

Wordless, they stared at May. Nothing more to say. Their words had been spoken.

Dad.

Ann.

Nothing more.

May's hair had been clipped. Thin gauze covered the ridged raw flesh of her scalp. A head wound? What was hiding beneath the gauze, beneath the stitches, and beneath the white sheet?

She looked at one of May's hands and automatically sought the other. Only one hand. Where was the other, the other arm? Her left arm?

'She's all fight, that one. She'll make it.'

'How?' Ann reached for May's right hand. All that was left of her to hold. One single hand. The other was gone.

His reply was slow in coming. Perhaps he'd misunderstood the 'how?'.

'A transport. Coming towards us. A mob of spaced-out hoons trying to pass on a bloody sixty-kilometre curve. She didn't have a hope. She didn't have a bloody hope. We were almost home. Didn't have a hope in hell.' She watched a tear trickle, become trapped in his beard, watched it glisten there, watched it joined by another tear.

She had tasted his tears that day. She had patted his wet face with a tiny hand.

I love you, my Daddy.

But she shook her head. Hard. She freed her hair from the band, ran her fingers through it, determined to ignore his tears.

'Her head. Mandy – '

'Her head is okay. She said your name. Before they operated, she was talking. She knew what she was saying. Her head's okay. It's internal. The injuries are internal, but she's going to be okay. They took her arm off. Crushed. Had to cut her out of the car. The microsurgeon couldn't . . . couldn't do a bloody thing. But she's got the elbow. They've saved the elbow. She'll be okay. They've pumped gallons of blood into her. Hours – hours in the theatre. Eight hours. More. I don't know. I don't know. But she came out of it. They didn't think she'd come out of the theatre. But she came out of it. She showed the . . . ' He was leaning forward now and Ann watched a fat tear drop onto the bed cover, then two more.

She lifted her chin. His tears would not move her. They would not move her. She clenched her jaw, her teeth. She tapped her foot on the floor.

But how could she let him cry like this? How could she sit there and watch him cry? She couldn't. His tears had always hurt too much. She touched the back of his hand. A brief touch, and his hand turned, gripped her own, then as quickly released it.

'She's got to be all right,' he said, and he broke down, put his head on the bed and howled.

She moved away, afraid of the power of touch, of sympathy. Better it be withheld tonight. Let him hold his fear inside as she held her fear. In the morning tears may not be needed. Time enough in the morning to mourn for May's lost hand, her lost hair. In the morning. Just let the light come, let the sun flood this room and lend her strength. Let the morning come.

Jack turned his face when a sister glided in, adjusted the drip flow while Ann walked the corridors. She found a coffee machine and she made two steaming cups then returned to the room.

For half an hour then there was silence, but the coffee was hot and strong. It went down well and she went back for more. Sweet. One sugar for him, She remembered.

'She's holding her own,' a doctor said at four-fifty.

'What does that mean?'

'All we can do now is wait. You should be getting some rest, Mr Burton.'

Jack lifted his good hand. A swipe. Go to buggery, the hand signed. His lips could form no words. The doctor didn't understand. He saw a broken, aging woman in the bed, a woman without hair, without teeth. A problem to be fixed, if fixed it could be.

May would have hated this. May had always brushed her teeth in private. No one ever saw her without her upper denture. And no one should ever see her like this. But the doctor didn't care about hair and teeth. A car full of druggies had created this problem for him and he had to work it out. He didn't understand that his problem was Aunty May, and that she could make twelve small pairs of bloomers from a fine linen sheet and she could stitch pretty dresses and curl wild black hair, that she could cuddle and tickle and kiss and fix things. He didn't know that. But he wouldn't let her die, because that was his job. He was a fixer too. He fixed the broken, repaired the maimed. He wouldn't let her die. Not now. Not now that the world was finally getting back on track.

Ann glanced at the drawn blind, then at her watch. Bethany would be waking soon for her bottle. How would David manage today? He'd have to miss work. He rarely missed a day.

Johnny would be walking off to the school room in a few more hours to spend his day a wall away from Kerrie. She'd be good for him. In the short time he'd been with her at the school she'd done more for him than his family had done in six years. He needed a wife, children, a life.

But Ben. What about Ben? Poor Ben. He'd be pussyfooting around Ellie until the day she died.

She'd be waking. Up, dressed, and out to her paddocks, happy as a cow in clover. She'd be out playing bingo tonight at the shire hall, maybe taxied there by Bob Johnson instead of Ben.

Dear gentle Ben, what then? What if Bob Johnson became a permanent installation in Ellie's life? What then for my Benjie? He'd wasted his life on Ellie.

May's breathing slowed, then she gasped, and the two watchers at her bedside breathed deeply, willing breath into her lungs, and her lungs laboured on.

She wouldn't die. Not now, not with the two she loved best in the world guarding each side of the hospital bed. They wouldn't let her die.

For another hour they sat there while night, crouching like a hungry black beast outside the window, gave up and left. Jack stood then, he limped to the window and opened the blind, allowing in the weak dawn light. Stiff with sitting, he limped the sterile room while sisters and doctor again leaned over the bed.

Ann saw the hand move when they were gone.

'Dad. Her hand moved. It moved. Aunty May? Aunty May? We're here. We're here. We're with you.'

'Jack.' Barely a whisper.

And he was back at the bed. 'I'm here, May. Ann is here. She drove down last night.'

May sighed and slipped away again.

Seated on either side of her bed they shared that one hand, and sometimes their own hands touched and they pulled back, but that hand was all they had, and their hands, their fingers, crept back to touch it, to stroke it, both aware that May could not leave them while they pumped their strength into her, willed each breath into her lungs.

But too tired to hold up her head, Ann rested it on her hand. Perhaps she slept.

Jack kept watch, and he watched the curtain of dark hair shielding one closed eye, framing the contours of her face. The chin on the hand, determined Burton jaw. Large Burton hands. They had danced through her childhood, held a doll to her scrawny little breast.

It's mine, Daddy. My ticket was 48 and I won, Daddy. It's my dolly.

And he saw the other one, his Liza. Her hair the gold of Ellie's, but that was where the similarity ended. Foot-stamping, manipulating little bitch, that one, she'd had him wrapped around her little finger.

Give me the bloody doll.

And that little half-wild waif had handed him her dolly and he'd smashed its brains out against the wall.

He wasn't fit to live.

'Take me,' he said to Ellie's Jesus. 'Let her live and take me. Do something right for once in your bloody life, you useless bastard.'

'Jack?' May murmured.

'I'm here, May.' Maybe Ellie's Jesus had been listening.

The flutter of his fingers on her arm woke Ann. She sprang upright in her chair.

'She's awake,' he said. 'Look who's here, May. Ann is with me.'

'There's still time,' May said.

Perhaps he misunderstood. Perhaps he didn't. 'It's not too late, May.'

'Never. You're . . . you're hurt, Jack?'

'Not me. Poor bloody old Satan is shit-scared I'll do him out of a job when I get down there.' His finger touched her face.

Love there. Love in that finger, in that gentle touch. Ann had known that gentle touch, his hand on her chin, turning her face to the light, studying her face. A cleaner hand back then, a soap and cigarette perfumed hand.

She leaned over the bed, her eyes blurring, but she was smiling as she kissed her aunt's cheek, knowing now that May was going to be fine.

'My dear little girl. So far away. The babies?'

'All home in bed.'

'Love you,' May said. 'Love you . . . both. Love each other. For me.'

Then May Burton died.

alone

~

Tuesday 4 November

Jack couldn't take the empty house. Couldn't take the daily sympathy, couldn't handle the manager when he came to call, or the cleaning ladies when they came to clean. Couldn't eat the food the manager's wife brought over. Couldn't live like this. Didn't want to live. Wouldn't bloody live any more either. Nothing now to live for. Nothing left.

Fake bastard, that's all he was, and this was real. May was dead, cremated, her ashes spread on her beloved Narrawee.

Life had been coming together for them, old craving, old memories fading, but his moods were all one and the same now.

Black.

He woke up black and went to bed black and he cursed his life, a life wasted. He cursed every mistake he'd ever made and he thought of how it might have been had he married May when he was twenty, had he given her the kids she'd wanted. He would have grown with this place, learned, as she had learned to run the place. He didn't have a bloody clue about running a property. How the hell could he ever run the property?

Just a useless bastard. That's all he was and ever would be.

May had known this property. She'd given the orders. But May was gone.

Lonely. Soul-crushing loneliness. The never-ending days and the longer nights of his own cursed company. No one to sit with him. No one at his side to watch television. No one to look at the bloody paper and see what was on the television. No bloody milk in the fridge. No bloody food on the stove.

Nothing.

No one.

Almost three weeks had passed, and he'd spent each day of each week on his own. No ears in which to pour his pain. No one to see his tears. But when had there ever been anyone for Jack bloody Burton? Only May and that crazy little black-headed bitch who had refused to run from him.

Bastard. A cursed bastard. What had he ever done for her? But she'd come when he'd called. She'd bloody well come when he'd called. Dad, she'd said. Dad. She'd called him Dad.

Dirty filthy murdering bastard. That's what she should have called him. Dirty filthy bloody spoiling murdering bastard mongrel of a man.

If he'd been behind the wheel that day, he might have done something. Pulled the car off the road. Headed up the embankment. Hit a bloody tree. Something. He could have done something.

Dead. Fiery little May dead. It wasn't right. It wasn't real. But it was bloody true.

Everything he touched, he killed. Everything turned to shit in his hands, and always had and always would, because he was shit and that's all he'd ever be.

Ann had left for home after May had gone. He'd told her to get some sleep, but she'd taken no notice. Never had slept much – always wandering around in the dark, always sitting somewhere with her dog. Always watching him.

She'd driven down again for the funeral and stayed at the motel. He hadn't asked her to stay at the house. She would have refused if he'd asked her, and he knew it, and he hadn't wanted her to refuse, so he hadn't bloody asked her, had he?

'Love each other,' May had said.

Samuel Burton and his niece had sat side by side in the church, and at the crematorium, then they'd driven away in separate cars. She'd gone back home to her husband and her babies. His grandchildren. A nest of bloody little Burtons called Taylor.

May had taken photographs of them on that last day in Warran. She'd filled a roll of film with their small faces, and her camera had survived the crash. He'd dropped it into the chemist, got him to get the film out, develop it. Something unfinished he could finish for her; there was little enough he'd ever done for May, or for anyone.

He kept the photographs on the kitchen table, with everything else. He looked at them when there was nothing else to look at. The eldest boy had the height of the Burton strain, and the dark hair, something of his mother, and the youngest too, but it was the girl, that little black-headed bugger with black beetle eyes that got to him. She was of the old strain, God help her. The Burtons' mad bloody head was a hard load to carry.

They were all mad, the whole bloody bunch of them. Always looking for more. Always wanting something they couldn't have.

He couldn't take any more of his bloody mad head. And he didn't have to now. The cheques were his to sign. The shares, the investments, the bank accounts were his. The stock; each bloody bull in that paddock was his now. All his. He could sell the bastards to the butcher if he wanted to. No one here now to tell him nay.

'Blind paralytic drunk, that's what I need. Close it all out. Blind, blotto drunk.' He stood and limped out to the hire car the insurance company was paying for him to use. His back had been bruised in the smash, it was still bruised, his hand was still giving him hell; he'd lost a lot of flesh, and the sinew to his thumb had been slashed; they'd had to dig for it. He had a new red horseshoe-shaped scar dissecting his eyebrow and curving down the temple. His eye was still blood red, but they'd saved the sight in it.

Samuel Burton was marked for life. Might as well have the

bastard's name tattooed on my brow, he thought. No one could duplicate these scars, nor identify him by the old scar on his wrist – he had a five-inch skin graft running from the thumb, up the side of his hand, over his wrist.

May had fixed it. Her final action had wiped out Jack Burton.

But not his bloody cravings. He'd buy a bottle. Buy a bloody crate and shit on his liver. So poor, perverted bastard Sam had been driven to the bottle by his loss. So bloody what? Good enough for old Malcolm Fletcher, good enough for Sam bloody Burton.

It wasn't easy driving with one hand and the tips of three fingers, his thumb, taped in a splint, jutting out one side, but he took it slow, he made it to the licensed supermarket, and he dragged his bruised bones from the car and went window-shopping. Couldn't bring himself to walk in there and buy a bottle of whisky. He couldn't do that to May. Not here. Not in this town.

Nothing to stop him driving to the outskirts of Melbourne, though, and buying his crate. And that's what he did, but he settled for a bottle of Jack Daniel's. It returned to Narrawee on the passenger seat.

'I'm a bastard, and a drunk, May, and you always knew it.' He scratched his head, and pushed the long hair behind his ears. One hand couldn't gather the hair and bind it with a rubber band. May had been due to trim an inch off it. She hadn't trimmed it. She'd died instead. She'd promised to give him a short back and sides and a bottle of louse shampoo for Christmas. Bloody Christmas.

He hadn't washed his hair since the accident. How could he wash it with one hand? His other was refusing to heal; the slice of his bum they'd grafted to it didn't want to be there.

Back in the kitchen he stuck his head under the sink tap, used a palm full of louse shampoo on it and he stood there, head down, letting the water rinse clean before drying his hair on a tea towel. Using his damaged hand hurt like buggery, but he used it and managed to get most of his wet hair into a rubber band.

He had a collection of them on a doorknob now.

That's what Ellie had done with rubber bands. Stuck them on a doorknob. May hadn't liked it. She'd pitched his rubber bands to buggery, but he had a mess of them on the doorknobs now. The bills and his newspapers, delivered to his mailbox at the gate, were all held together with rubber bands.

He caught a glimpse of himself in the hall mirror as he walked by. 'Bloody old scarred, pigtailed, bloodshot-eyed poofter bastard,' he snarled, then proceeded on with his bottle and his glass to the dining room.

Unused, this room, except when they'd opened up the house and property for that one day in June, for his mother's birthday. He fought the top from the bottle, poured a good shot, then sat on one of the dining chairs. Too long away from the whisky, perhaps he was afraid, had to creep up on it slowly. He sniffed at it, placed the glass down. And the noise was too loud.

There was an echo in this room. Always had been. Hollow.

'Why bloody not?' he said. The words had no impact. They floated around him. Ghost words. 'Why bloody not?' he screamed.

Give me a push, Jacky.

Little May, on the table, on her stomach. He'd grasped her feet and pushed, and she'd slid all the way down the end, fallen onto the floor, then picked herself up and run back for more.

Give me another turn, Jacky, but not so hard this time.

Wild little bugger. Tough little bugger too.

Not tough enough.

'I should have been driving. She'd been driving for three hours. I should have taken the wheel. I should have been the one who died. She could have had her kids here then. Bloody little black-headed Burtons coming out of the woodwork. She would have been happy. She deserved to be happy.'

He stared at old Samuel's ultra long oak table, now veiled by a layer of dust. No May, no cleaning ladies to wipe the dust away. He looked at the chairs at the head and end of the table. Samuel's ornate oak carvers that little Jacky, Sammy and May had once believed to be the thrones of kings and queens. They'd sat on them and played Arthur and Guinevere. Bloody Sam had been Lancelot – the bastard who ruined their Camelot.

Jack walked to the head of the table now and he sat on his throne. Hard as the hobs of hell.

'King Jack,' he said. 'Supreme ruler of the ghosts, May. They're a mixed assembly tonight.'

Old Samuel Burton and his Jane's ghosts were sitting down one side. William, their son, and his Jessy beside them. Those two had died young, but they'd left two infant sons for Samuel to raise. Uncle Matthew, a consumptive two yards of pale bones, and Jack's father, John the bastard, who had married Elisa Hamstead, a tall and stately Melbourne lady. She had been the Burtons' first fine lady. She had bought class into the family, but she'd had no staying power. She gave up, gave in, died young.

They were all here, partying, and now May had gone to join the ghosts.

Bloody perverted twin brother Sam wasn't here. What the fire had left of that mongrel dog now lay in a nameless grave. Just another John Doe.

'And all he deserved. Better than he deserved.'

Jack shook his head, shook the memory of Sam and the funeral pyre and the gallon of petrol, and the stench of the burning away, and he forced his mind to old Samuel.

Big as a river gum, he'd been, and as tough. He'd made old bones, that one. One of the black breed who had wanted more.

He'd wanted more than his half-share of a few small fields in Wales so he'd come out here with his new wife and they'd carved these acres out of a foreign wilderness and named the property Narrawee. Aboriginal or Welsh, Jack didn't know. Nobody knew now. Nobody had bothered to ask old Samuel while he'd lived.

He hadn't been able to read or write when he'd arrived here. Someone else had done the writing, and the spelling. Old Samuel's tongue used to soften that second syllable, Narra*r*wee, he used to say.

'Nar*rar*wee,' Jack whispered. 'Nar*rar*wee.'

Old music. Sad music. The townspeople had given the music that old country and western nasal twang, the hard A. Yarra was Yarra after all.

Whichever way you said it, Narrawee now belonged to Jack. All of his life he'd wanted it. As a four year old he'd wanted it.

And it was his now. A thousand-acre property, and he didn't know what to do with it. May's land, Hargraves Park, was his too, and May's old house where the manager and his wife lived. All his – or bloody Samuel's, with his horseshoe scar.

To my beloved husband for his lifetime.

He'd been a husband to her, not Sam. He'd been her only husband, her only lover. She had to write Sam's name on her will. Couldn't get out of that.

To my beloved husband for his lifetime.

She'd made certain that he could never sell her land, and she'd known he wouldn't sell Narrawee, chop it up into ten-hectare lots for hobby farms. But what the bloody hell was he going to do with it?

When she was alive the manager had come down once a week, had coffee and scones with May. They'd worked it out between them, rotated their crops, sold their stud cattle and their bull juice. Jack didn't know a good bull from a bad bull. May had known. She'd had her books. Knew where every spoonful of bull juice had been sent. Poor bloody bulls. No jumping fences and swimming rivers for Narrawee bulls. These poor bastards didn't know what a flighty heifer was, but they'd impregnated a few.

He thought of Bessy's bull rampaging through the paddocks at Mallawindy, and he laughed as he walked to retrieve his glass, his eyes straying to the family graveyard, visible from this window. Much thought had been given to its site, chosen by old Samuel while his Jane lay in an earthen-floored hut, grieving over the loss of a daughter. Only a dream then, this white mansion on the hill.

Samuel had dug that first small grave in the wood paddock where the trees still stood undisturbed – in the western corner – and he'd planned this room around that graveyard, planned its long windows so his children's ghosts could wander in at night to play.

They'd lost three daughters and two sons to diphtheria, but they'd raised the middle son, William. He'd died in his early thirties, and when he was gone, old Samuel had placed all his hopes on the two grandsons. Matthew the beanpole, and John the bastard. Matthew had rolled over and died unwed, so John the bastard, Jack's father, inherited Narrawee. He'd given his fine lady, Eliza, twin sons in the first year of her marriage. He'd given her VD when they were ten years old.

Jack had learned hatred early. He'd hated his father.

His memories of old Samuel were good memories. Maybe he'd loved that snarled greybeard of a man. Big, and smelling of pipe tobacco and rough woollen sweaters, the soft Welsh lilt to his voice, he'd lived on at Narrawee until Jack was six years old.

You'll try to buy and sell the world before you're done, young Jacky Burton, but you won't ever sell my land, will you?

No, Pop.

Land is where we put down our roots, Jacky, and the Burtons need to have their roots well anchored. I transplanted late to this soil, but my roots have grown deep. You fight for this land, laddie. You fight until you die for this land.

'I fought for it, Pop. I fought for it with a bloody bottle in my hand.' Tears trickled then, trickled for old Samuel, and for May, and for his mother.

The old man had made his century, plus three, and John the bastard wouldn't even bury him on his own land. He'd stuck him in the town cemetery.

Even as a wet-behind-the-ears kid, Jack had known that was wrong. From that day forward, he'd made his mother call him Jacky, because Pop had called him Jacky and because John was his father's name.

Jack wiped at his eyes and lifted the glass of whisky, smelt it. He caressed the bottle, full of bottled dreams, and he thought of old

Samuel, and he thought of his mother, and he thought of May. Little cheeky-faced May Hargraves.

She had been an afterthought, born when her parents were old. She'd spent half her life sneaking off to Narrawee. Just a fence separated the two properties.

She'd come running over with a book one day, on the cover this picture of Camelot rising out of the mists, and she'd named Narrawee her Camelot. She'd had a large dose of wanting more, but she'd had the will to get what she wanted.

He'd probably loved her when she was four years old. He'd loved her strength, her guts, her fight. Competitive little bugger, she could ride beside him and Sam. Outride them, too, by the time she was twelve. He would have married her. Always thought he would. If his mother hadn't died, if that diseased mongrel dog –

'If.'

Life would have been different if his father had been different, but he hadn't been bloody different.

Jack had flattened the womanising old bastard the night his mother died, then he'd taken off with his old man's stash. Eight hundred pounds. It had been a fortune back in those days. He'd had a ball, too, for a few years, gone on the road with a bunch of actors he'd met at the university. He'd been good – made a great Macbeth – and he discovered early he was even better with a few whiskies under his belt to settle the nerves. Then one year they'd taken a play to Mallawindy, and he'd met Ellie of the sunshine hair.

He'd been planning to take off, run like buggery when he'd got her pregnant, but he'd married her instead. Her old man, eager to get rid of him for months, had no longer been so eager.

'Bloody old Ben Vevers. He only came up to my chin. Bloody bald-headed little two-bit runt with delusions of grandeur.'

Ellie had been sixteen. He'd blamed her for her youth and for the little bastard she'd produced six months after the wedding. But he'd dressed her in green and brought her home to Narrawee, planning to drag her out of her cow yard.

She could have grown here. She'd been young enough to educate, but John the bastard had laughed at her country manners and her country voice, and Jack had seen her too well through his father's and his brother's eyes. And he'd seen her beside May. That's what had buggered things up – seeing her beside May, and wanting May. That, and then May marrying that mongrel dog.

So he'd taken Ellie and her little bastard back to Mallawindy, and punished them for trapping him there. And that was the truth of the matter and there was no getting away from the bloody truth when there was no one else in the bloody house to hear anything different.

Bloody whingeing little bitch, she'd been. Cold little bitch. Fertile bloody little bitch with her bloody beautiful hair.

May should have known what she was getting into with Sam, but she swore she hadn't known. He'd been Jack's mirror image but they weren't the same. A crazy bloody partnership, him and May. Sam had liked little kids. Spent a lot of time pissing off overseas, but he'd stayed clean in Narrawee. Jack had threatened to kill him, to feed him to the dogs if he defiled old Samuel Burton's name in Narrawee.

'Sick bastard.' He dipped his finger in the whisky, looked at the dripping amber beads and dreamed on.

He hadn't touched May in those days. Maybe he'd wanted to, but he hadn't. Not in those days. That came later. That came after Liza and Sam died. It came when Ann was in the hospital, comatose. May had crawled into his bed one night in Toorak, afraid that Sam's ghost had followed them there. She was young enough to have kids, but he hadn't wanted any more black Burtons. Let the breed die out, May, he'd said.

He'd used a condom after that first night. Always used a condom – except with Ellie. Condoms were a sin with Ellie, and it had been hard enough to get her to lie down and play dead without coming at her wearing a rubber.

'Bloody brood mare bitch.'

He lifted his glass, smelling its contents. John the bastard had given the whisky a good nudge. Eliza's locked door couldn't keep him out when he'd been at the whisky.

He pushed the glass from him.

Ghosts all around him tonight. Ghosts and memories and guilt. Whisky wouldn't move the bastards, just open more doors, let more of them in.

Too much heartache. He didn't need tomorrow's headache. Carefully then he poured the liquid back into the bottle. He capped it, and took it to the kitchen. Left it on the table with everything else.

sydney

~

Tuesday 18 November

The whisky bottle, still full, haunted him more than the ghosts these days. He wanted it, but he couldn't have it here where Harry, the gardener, the bloody manager, or some other busybody might come knocking at his door. He didn't let any of them in, but they kept on coming.

His thumb splint was off and the skin graft looked like what it was, a piece of swollen red bum. His bruises had faded but his bones and his heart still ached and he had to get away, get out of the house or he'd blow his brains out. Had to go some place, drink and kill the pain.

He telephoned the property manager and told him to do what he liked. 'I'm taking off. Don't know where I'm going or when I'll be back,' he said, then he slammed the back door and drove away to lose himself in Melbourne.

He had a new car now, insurance supplied; it handled well. He took the road to Melbourne and, with no place else to go once there, he headed for the Toorak flat. It smelt stale, felt more empty than Narrawee. He left the car in the garage, walked up the road to a bar.

It didn't take much to make him feel better. Two beers to prime his throat and two whiskies to wrap a fog around his pain.

An hour or two spent in the stores had loaded him down with

plastic bags, a visit to a licensed supermarket had netted him two bottles, and by five he'd decided he wasn't going back to the flat.

A taxi took him to Spencer Street Station where he boarded the night train to Sydney. He sat up all the way, snoring, feeling no pain. A second taxi delivered him to a barber shop, which he left light-headed. He found a hotel he used to know quite well and booked a room for a week in the name of Jack Burton, Mallawindy.

He was going to drink himself to death, leave a suicide note and spoil Ellie's bloody fun. That's what he was going to do. He knew the insurance business well enough to know that they wouldn't pay up for a suicide.

Once inside the room he snibbed the door and from one of the plastic bags he took a bottle of Jack Daniel's, drinking greedily as he began shedding his outer garments.

Hotel rooms. They'd been home to him and his bottle when Mallawindy and Narrawee had been Hell. No ghosts to haunt him in hotel rooms. No one to see him.

Only a fly on the wall. It sat rubbing its front feet together thoughtfully. Perhaps it frowned, if flies can frown, as it watched him remove a small packet from one plastic bag.

Hair dye. Black.

Jack drank again from his bottle, and with each mouthful the veil of fog wrapping him thickened. He was feeling his way through a pea-souper when he changed his mind about the suicide note.

He'd go back. That's what he'd bloody well do. He'd leave a suicide note, but signed by perverted bloody Sam, leave it with Sam's clothes on Bondi beach, then he'd go back to Mallawindy as Jack. Claim amnesia.

And the bloody property would be transferred into his name!

'You stupid bastard. Why didn't you think of that before? Put the kybosh on her $250,000 and get my name on the title.'

Two small bottles in the packet of dye. He removed them, mixing them carefully, as per the instructions. He shook the

323

mixture, squeezed the liquid onto his remaining hair, read the instructions again. *Leave for half an hour.*

Dye trickled to his brow, it dripped to his beard, and the fly on the wall took flight, seeking a better view. It settled on the mirror to observe the combing through of the solution, watching it darken by the second.

New trousers dragged from a plastic bag. Grey. A white business shirt. He ripped off the plastic and the packaging, he removed the pins from the shirt's collar, shook it, then spread it lovingly on the bed. And he drank again and he laughed and he thought of Ellie's disappointment.

'But I promised to buy some new pews for the church, love,' he mimicked. Laughing then, bent double with it, he dragged new black leather shoes from their box and placed them beside his shirt. The black woollen socks, sealed in plastic, held him up, stopped his laughter. He snarled at the plastic, ripping his way into his pure woollen socks with his teeth, pitching the plastic at the fly on the mirror.

Jack filled his half-hour with his bottle, sloshing the whisky down, checking its level and the position of the hands on his watch, feeling better by the inch. But as the minute hand crept to the half-hour, Jack's head nodded to his chest. Tenderly he placed the bottle down, and he lay his head on the pillow. Slept. Slept for four hours.

'Shit,' he said when he saw the battlefield of black dye on bedspread and pillow. 'Shit!' he screamed when he saw his hair.

But the half-bottle of Jack Daniel's was beside his bed. He washed his mouth out with a worthy mouthful, then two more, and he made his careful way to the bathroom where he showered and washed his hair until the water ran clean – as per the instructions.

The fly braved the steam to laugh; Jack didn't laugh when he saw himself in the mirror. His hair was black. Dead flat black. It jutted out from his head in tufts, and his beard had a one-inch stripe down one side, from sideburns to mouth. One of his eyebrows was black, one side of his face a purple grey.

'A man looks like something out of a bloody Frankenstein movie.'

He closed his eyes, flattening his hair with his hands, and he looked again. He scrubbed at his face and eyebrow with hotel soap, and the soap got in his eye, and it cried. He took up his razor, scraping away his beard, and his face, protected from the sun too long was baby pink. He attacked his piebald moustache, squinting around the razor as he worked.

His bottle now forgotten, he showered again and he washed his hair with hotel soap, roughly towelling it dry, hoping some of the black might rub off.

The hotel towel remained clean but his hair felt like barbed wire.

'Holy bloody jumping Jesus Christ. You look ratshit, you stupid bastard.'

Slowly he dressed in his grey sports trousers. A little tight at the waist. His white shirt, his black socks and shoes were on and as he bent to tie his shoelaces, his trousers attempted to dissect him. But they looked good; looking down at them, they looked good. Looking down at himself, he felt like Jack again. His feet looked like Jack's, felt like Jack's. The bloody shoe was pressing on his little toe.

He drank from his bottle again, then walked to the mirror, his eyes partly closed. He shrugged his shoulders back and stole a fast glance at his reflection. And he didn't look so bloody good. One eyebrow cut in two by his red scar, the other brow a stubble of black in a purple-grey birthmarked brow.

He combed his hair forward. He combed it back. He wet it and combed it again, but hair given its freedom to stand on end hadn't refused the opportunity, and the fly now perched on the mirror saw what Jack could see. It flew off to hide its eyes behind the drapes.

A dye-stained hand ran over his smooth face and dye-stained fingernails played with his baby-pink chin. Nervous strokes.

'You look like a bloody madman.'

Slowly then he walked away from the mirror, kicking his jeans and casual shirt, his denim jacket, kicking the plastic bags. He lit a cigarette, puffing on it nervously, the ash falling onto the floor with everything else. He was hungry. He'd been planning to go to a restaurant, eat a decent meal, be young again, be Jack again.

'Stupid bastard.'

He couldn't go out looking like this. Couldn't leave the bloody room looking like this! For an hour he sat on his bed until his stomach forced him to pick up the telephone and call room service.

He ordered the roast of the day and coffee. A pot of coffee. He needed a bloody coffee. May had got him addicted to the shit.

The towel was wrapped around his head when he opened the door. No tip. Just a snatch for the tray, and a smart door close.

In the early evening he hit his bed and slept well, but when he awoke at six a.m. with a mouth like the bottom of a bird cage and a head like the inside of a European wasps' nest, he picked up his inch of whisky and pitched it at the fly on the wall, watched while whisky trickled.

What he saw that morning in the bathroom mirror sobered him. An ugly black-headed old bastard wearing Samuel Burton's new scars looked back at him. Wherever he went, those scars would go with him. How was Jack going to explain them?

'Bloody sympathy scars?' Wet, his hair looked bad. Dry, slept on, it was a disaster. Nothing for it but to take to his head with his razor, shave it smooth. 'Got you, you crawling little bastards,' he said to the lice. 'Try living on a bloody billiard ball. And don't bother moving south either.' The razor moved south and the eyebrows were gone.

He looked at the dye-stained bed and decided to do a runner, got as far as packing up his plastic bags, as far as the taxi rank before realising the hotel would send the bill to Mallawindy.

'Stupid brainless bastard,' he snarled, and he walked back, paid his bill with Sam's plastic.

That afternoon Jack took a room at an unlicensed motel that had clean sheets and a television set, a good supply of coffee and a comfortable chair. Bill Dooley, he wrote on the registration form. Goondiwindi, he wrote.

For the first week he kept to his room during daylight hours, watching television, living on coffee, saving half of his breakfast for his lunch. He watched *Days of Our Lives* and *Oprah*, watched the kids' shows and quiz shows, and ordered dinner at night in his room. He couldn't pay Bill's bill with his credit card, so he hit an autobank by night, paid cash and booked in for a second week.

His face was a gnarled stubble but his hair and eyebrows were not doing as well. It was this week that he discovered Chef-Marlet. He'd gone out to buy some clean clothes and he'd found a pair of sunglasses, wraparounds, and an Akubra hat.

Then he bought a book. The naked breast on it had got him in. He read it in a day and was waiting at the bookshop door when it opened for business the following morning. Safe beneath his hat and dark glasses, he bought Number 2. It had a naked bum on the cover, but he wasn't looking at the cover when he returned with it to his room. He was reading about Mack Curtin, a bastard people loved to hate. Jack felt sorry for him.

He'd been a voracious reader in his youth, but twenty years had passed since he'd been able to lose himself in fiction. He was wondering what it was about the novel that was getting him in when the bloody thing ended, leaving too many unanswered questions. So he went out for Number 3 and read on.

'When will you learn, woman?' Mack's voice was tired, bored already. 'Everything is your fault. Life is your fault. Bella Reva is more woman than you'll ever be with your pretty little blameless face and your pretty manners and your bloody cold bed.'

'You've brought her and her problems into my house before, Mack, but it's over now. I won't have her name spoken in this house. She's gone, Mack, and I'm glad she's gone, and I hope she never comes back.'

'Don't you try to come the big bloody property owner bitch on me again or I'll burn this one to the ground too, you mindless slut.'

His fist was raised, and his children moved to the eastern doorway as the fist swung.

Gretel cringed from him. Her lip cut by his first blow, her hands rose to ward off his next swing.

'Please, Mack. Don't, Mack. I'm sorry, Mack.'

Jack read faster, read through Numbers 4, 5, 6, 7, 8 and 9, while the billiard ball became covered in coarse sandpaper, and Mack Curtin was being pursued all over Australia by the cops. The silly bastard was wanted for a murder he hadn't committed – or probably hadn't committed, and Jack had to know if he got away with it.

On the Monday, on the dot of nine, he was waiting for the bookshop door to open. Once inside, he searched the shelves for Number 10. And discovered there was no bloody Number 10.

'Where is it?'

'It's coming soon,' the bookseller said. He didn't like the look of the scarred, aging skinhead who had forgotten his hat and sunglasses.

'Coming soon! The story isn't finished!'

'The reps say it should be out by February. Would you like to place an order?'

'Bloody February. A man will be dead by February.'

The bookseller looked now with sympathy at the bald head, the naked face, understanding, or thinking he understood. 'Been through chemo?' he said.

'What?' Jack wasn't into conversation. He wanted that book. He walked back to his room where he studied the covers of the scattered novels. He read the blurbs again, then turned to the last page of Number 1, staring at the youthful author's face, reading the brief biography.

A schoolteacher, Chef-Marlet was born in England. He moved to Australia with his family in the sixties and now lives in New South Wales.

It wasn't much to go on. But the moon face, those glasses, the stubby bloody little lump-of-putty nose . . . The dark hair put him off the track for a while, then he twigged and he sprang to his feet, pitching Number 1 at the hysterical fly who had stowed away in a plastic bag.

'You bloody eavesdropping, obese old bastard,' Jack said, his eyes wide. 'You slimy bloody slug of a man.' It was some time before he ran out of adjectives, and when he did, he picked up battered Number 1 and began reading it again, but more slowly this time.

Twenty days at the motel cost Bill Dooley dearly. Samuel Burton plastic couldn't pay for him either. Jack footed it to a bank and the dame behind the glass questioned his signature. He pulled out Sam's driving licence, and the dame questioned his photograph.

'I've been through bloody chemotherapy. What do you expect me to bloody well look like?' He flashed the skin graft on his arm, flaunted his scarred brow. 'It's in my bones. I've got a month to live. Do you want me to waste a bloody week of it standing here, for Christ's sake?'

She paid up and he paid the motel bill, then caught the night train to Melbourne. By ten the following morning he was holed up again at Narrawee, his answering machine flashing at him every time he walked by.

His head felt spiky, but his moustache and beard had done better, and his eyebrows were growing back. He'd do okay. So Samuel had had a haircut, and about bloody time. He had his scars now for identification. He didn't need his poofter hair and lice. Some primitive tribes shaved their heads when they were in mourning, so good enough for them, good enough for Samuel Bloody Burton.

The grey sports slacks had given him haemorrhoids and the business shirts had rubbed his neck raw. His feet, accustomed to spreading in canvas sneakers, hadn't taken well to leather, and for the first time in months the corn on his smallest toe was throbbing. He'd left the black shoes in the motel room, with his grey slacks, three filthy shirts and several well-used black socks. He didn't want them. Jeans moved with him, bent with him, and looked better with his sneakers.

No doubt they'd post the clothes to Bill Dooley, Main Street, Goondiwindi. A lot of Bill Dooley's dirty laundry was probably sitting in some dead mail department. Jack had used his name two dozen times or more when he'd gone on his benders, and Bill always left his dirty washing behind.

fletch.doc

~

Monday 8 December

Malcolm was gaining some control over the beast machine that purred like a lion ready to pounce and gobble up his labour. The trick was to name the file before hitting the Control and S keys every five minutes. This pasted his words onto the internal disc, took them out of the ROM or RAM or whatever it was and solidified them somewhere in bytes, to be called up again at his pleasure. Each day, just to be on the safe side, he also saved his work to a floppy disk, which was in fact quite rigid.

John had found the three lost chapters of Number 10; they'd been quite safe, down in the bowels of the beast. He'd found them in five minutes, using a search-by-date instruction. Once found he had somehow tethered and married them, then named the single file Fletch.

Six skeleton chapters had joined fletch.doc since that day. Not a lot in each, but they'd grow, Malcolm hoped. He was becoming familiar with the keyboard, larger than the confounded typewriter's, and not as touchy either. And the text, once you grew accustomed to it disappearing off the face of the planet, was quite wonderful. He could make it small. He could make it large, which he did. He also had control over the size of text in his . . .

'Hard copy,' he said.

There was something almost deviant about selecting the print command then sitting back while his printer whipped out five pages a minute. He loved watching the pristine pages roll into the printer and his words roll out. Never tired of it.

'Quite wonderful. A remarkable tool.'

There were games on it too, as he had discovered when Ann and her entourage had called in last week. She had been surprised by his progress and he, like a small child, delighted in showing off his developing expertise. Then young Benjamin had wanted to look at the games and the small boy had become teacher of the man.

'You have to try to fit all those blocks in, sir, and not leave any spaces.'

Sir.

'Ah, but how do we decide where they fit, Burt . . . Taylor?' he'd said.

A fine boy, that one. He'd grow into a fine young man.

Long ago Malcolm had claimed Ann as his own. He'd planned for her, dreamed for her. He could see her young face in Benjamin, see her hands and quick mind in her first son. It would be a fine thing to watch him grow to adulthood.

And sweet Bethany. She may well be a duplication of her mother. How wonderful it would be to see her grow, to watch a woman emerge from this small female cocoon. Already she wanted what she wanted when she wanted it, her determined little jaw working on the bottle, her little hands already speaking. Malcolm did not want the complication, but perhaps he was falling in love with her.

'Bethany.' He liked that name. 'Bethany Taylor.' It had a prophetic ring to it.

John was playing a large role in Malcolm's life these days. They spent many hours in deep discussion, and he'd read the three early chapters of Number 10. Malcolm could find no end for this novel as yet, so his fingers plodded on, hoping an end would present itself.

Hard, plodding work, this one. His characters refused to take off and run, to lead him a merry chase, but at least he had some words on paper and his phone was back on the receiver.

John had eaten dinner with Malcolm this evening. An interesting character. Assuredly his father's son, but with a depth to him and a pleasingly cynical outlook on life. A watcher of life, was John, as was Malcolm. They had much in common. But not the bottle.

Malcolm measured a portion of brandy into his glass, tipping it down to meet, to greet, the beef pot roast, and a very nice piece of beef it had been too. The vegetables had soaked up its juices and flavour. He enjoyed a tender beef pot roast.

No more classroom to fill his days now. Perhaps he missed it. John was completing a revision course in primary teaching. The department bogged down in red tape as ever, had taken their time, but after the constant stream of replacements they had posted to Mallawindy in the years since Malcolm retired, someone had seemingly recognised the value of taking on a home-grown ex-priest.

What was it that drove teachers to teach? Was it a fear of leaving that classroom, or perhaps a desire to control? A need to have some say in the future? What was it about this town that drove the teachers' wives away?

The single men had done better here. They had adapted – for a given time they had adapted, then run willingly enough. The married male is not an adaptable animal, Malcolm thought. Take away his dream, rip the carpet out from beneath his feet and he stumbled, fell, where a woman would find a reason to go on. Give her a child and she'd survive all odds for her child, but take away that child . . .

The observation of life was fascinating; watching the growth of those around you was a pastime like no other. He had spent some time spying on the Burton property last evening and through his binoculars, had seen Kerrie Fogarty's car arrive, and later he had witnessed two walkers and a brief kiss. It had pleased Malcolm well.

'A man with a quest,' he said. 'And your quest, Malcolm? One hundred thousand words and a title. And an end.' He only had twenty-nine and a half thousand. Still a way to go. Perhaps he'd get there. Perhaps not. But he was out of words for tonight. His cursor honed in on *File*. Carefully he chose *Close*.

Do you wish to save changes to Fletch.doc?

'Yes, you damn fool thing,' he said, clicking. His machine whirred, purred, double-checking his every move until it gave in and its face went blank.

Always at this point Malcolm felt fear, which increased his heart rate. Would his words be there for him in the morning? He shrugged, turned the machine off at the power point and took a step away from it, waiting for it to complain.

Silence.

He'd dredged out seven hundred plodding words today. There had been days in the past when he'd churned out fifteen pages on the old Royal. What a world he had known back then, his life spent in a wonderland of his own creation, words following him, waking him from his sleep, demanding to be set free. Such a pool of words to choose from back then. But the well was dry. And he was dry. He poured another brandy.

eggs

Dear Sam,

I am so sorry it has been so long since I have written to you.
I was very sorry to hear of your sad loss. May was a very nice
woman. I'm sure you must miss her very much.

We are all well up here. Johnny is now teaching at the school,
and looking so much better every day. Bronwyn is still keeping
well, and also Annie and her family. I hope you have gotten over
your own injuries, and are feeling better now. Annie told me you
were injured.

Half the reason why I am writing is to let you know we are
having a memorial service up here for Jack on Christmas Eve. I am
also having his name put on the children's tombstone. I know he'd
want to be with Liza, and I like to think he is now.

I'm going to get a new stone, and it will say: 'John W Burton,
[Jack] loved husband of Ellie, father of John, Ben, Ann and
Bronwyn. Resting now with Liza, Linda and Patrick'.

A ghost walked over Jack's grave. He dropped the letter, shivered,
then he picked it up and read on.

If you could get up to the memorial on Christmas Eve, it will be in the beer garden at the hotel. I know this is a bit strange, but my friend said that knowing Jack, it would be more suitable to have it there than at the church. As you would know, Jack was never a one for the church. Father Fogarty will be there to say a few words and as Granny Bourke said, Jack will be there too, and probably laughing at all of us. You would be very welcome to join us for the night, Sam. We've got plenty of spare beds at the old place.

All the best to you for Christmas. Love from Ellie and family.

'Bloody friend? What bloody friend? He's doing better than me, isn't he, getting you into a pub, you bitch,' Jack said, crumpling the letter, tossing it at the wall. But he picked it up and threw it onto the table with everything else. 'Couldn't write a letter to a lost dogs' home.'

May and Sam had always replied to Ellie's Christmas greetings with a cheque. He had to play the game out to the end. His cheque book was on the table. He wrote one for five hundred, then he ripped it up. She and her bloody friend would have his insurance soon enough. He wrote a second cheque, this one for one hundred, and he found a sheet of May's writing paper. *Merry Christmas to all, love Samuel.*

'Love?'

He'd loved her once. Loved May too. Loved his mother. Loved Liza. Maybe he'd loved that black-headed little bitch, but he'd hated her too – seen too much of himself in that one. Seen himself and tried to kill it.

Bastard. He flinched from a memory, ran a hand across his scalp.

Women. No man in his life to care about, or to care about him. 'Never has been – except old Pop,' he said as he stood and walked off to search May's office for envelopes.

He was folding the cheque and note when he changed his mind. He'd buy himself a decent tombstone. That's what he'd do. He had money. Money to burn. He wrote a cheque for five thousand, signed it, and added a PS to his note.

Please find enclosed cheque. I'd like to buy a new stone for Jack and the children. I will be out of the country over Christmas, so have a drink for him, for me.

Sealing that envelope made the hair stand up on the back of his neck. He walked to the television room and turned on the box, watching mindlessly. Spent a lot of time watching the bloody thing mindlessly, sleeping in front of it. At least it talked to him. But he nodded off while it was talking, slept through *Days of Our Lives*, and was dreaming of Ellie when the phone woke him. He woke sweating, breathing heavily – and un-bloody-satisfied.

'I said to do what needs doing,' Jack told the phone and his manager. 'Sell what you have to. Buy what you have to and send me the bills.'

'Can I come over and talk to you, Sam?'

'No.' His hair was growing, but slowly. Over a week now since he'd returned from Sydney. Hadn't left the house by day, but he walked the property at night, emptied the mailbox at his gate and twice he'd driven to the outskirts of Melbourne for a feed of take-away fish'n'chips.

'Old Harry has been around twice this week, Sam, jabbering about the garden.'

'Let it die,' Jack said. That gained him a few seconds' silence. He started to hang up the phone and he heard the voice again.

'Do you want me to organise someone to come in and cook you a meal – do a bit of washing for you?'

'No.'

'You've got to start getting out. People care about you. They're worried about you, mate.'

'Yeah. Right.' Jack wanted to laugh, wanted to howl at the 'mate', but he hung up instead and went back to the kitchen to hunt for food. The room looked like a neglected pigpen, as did his bedroom.

He'd lost weight in Sydney, and more since his return. His jeans hung on him, and he hitched at the waist now as he searched the pantry, the freezer. No sugar left. No bloody coffee. He made a cup of tea. Black. No bloody milk.

'Ah, shit.' Again his hand brushed his scalp. 'Bloody maniac bastard,' he said. 'What the bloody hell were you thinking of?' He took the cup to the table and sat looking through his bills, ten deep.

'Bloody manager. Got to pay him too. Can't post his bloody cheque, can I?'

Pen in hand he made an attack on the bills, piled high since he'd been away. He'd never had to worry about bills. In Mallawindy, Ellie had paid them, and down here May had written the cheques. But he wrote them today, and signed Sam's name, not once, not twice, but again and again, whittling the pile and his cheque account down.

'Bloody electricity,' he said. 'Bloody telephone. If a man didn't have a bloody manager, then he wouldn't need a bloody telephone, would he?'

He'd been signing Sam's name for thirty years, signing tax returns, adding his signature to May's on many documents, but he, or his hand, didn't want to sign it any more. He stared at the signatures. *SJ Burton*. It was the J buggering it up. J was for Jack and Jack's hand had always been heavier than Sam's. No wonder the dame at the bank had questioned his signature. He crumpled one cheque and wrote another, signed it, stapled it to a bill, then worked on.

The solicitors wanted to see him. He tossed their letter at the wall and considered his stomach. The bills pushed back to the general mess on his table, he stood and walked to the fridge.

Eggs. That's what he wanted. He knew how to fry an egg. None in the fridge. A tin of canned peaches in the pantry and not much else he could do anything with. May had been big on canned fruit. She'd stockpiled the stuff, and he didn't want any more canned fruit. He wanted grease. He wanted butter. And bread.

Frozen peas in the freezer and a lump of meat. A leg of lamb. He balanced it on his palm, considering it – until his hand froze, then he tossed the meat back in with the peas and headed for his bedroom, searching the floor for clothing fit to be seen in. He picked up three shirts, smelt them, chose the cleaner of the three. The others were returned to the floor. He looked down at his jeans and decided to buy a clean pair, a size smaller. He picked up his hat and his sunglasses, his wallet, car keys and the manager's cheque, which he dropped into the Hargraves Park mailbox before driving into town.

Sugar, milk, coffee, three loaves of bread and two tubs of soft butter, Solvol. He added a tin of apricot jam and a tin of fig, a large bottle of fake cream. He looked at the onions, tossed in three. Picked up a hand of bananas, a bag of potatoes, two packets of corn-flakes and three tins of condensed milk. Then he had to queue to get out of the bloody place.

Queue too close to the liquor department. Queue right beside a two-metre high stack of VB cans. Queue with six bottles of Jack Daniel's within arm's reach, and his hand reached. But he snatched it back, fixed both hands onto the trolley. He didn't have Sam's hair to hide behind now, but bastard Saint Sam had been a teetotaller. He could hide behind that.

'Nice to see you out and about, Mr Burton. And how are you managing?'

Jack unloaded his shopping onto the counter, tossing the cans and containers down while Saint Sam simpered his Ss and kept his eyes away from the grog.

'Just scraping by, Mrs Simpson. Just scraping by.'

'Time heals, Mr Burton. We don't think it will at the time, but it does. When I lost Martin I thought my world had ended.'

Until you found Clarrie, Jack thought, but he paid with Sam's plastic, poked in Sam's pin number, then pushed the trolley before him as he walked to his car. He unloaded his bags into the boot then walked into the menswear shop. Two pairs of jeans, three shirts and half a dozen pair of Bonds size 16 briefs and he was out on the street, walking by the butcher's shop. Steak. Steak and eggs for dinner.

Another bloody queue inside. More eyes to stare at his missing hair and eyebrows.

'Good morning,' someone said.

Jack glanced at the woman's grey head and he didn't know it. He looked at her hand and he flinched. 'Morning,' he said, his eyes staring at the plastic splints on the woman's wrists, then quickly away to the butcher.

'What will it be, Mr Burton?'

'Give me a couple of slabs of steak,' he said, and Sam added, 'And some sausages, please.' He didn't like sausages, but sausage started with an S and everyone in the shop was staring at his hat. Sam used to have long hair and he'd never worn a hat. Today he needed those sibilant Ss. And he could probably fry a sausage anyway.

The butcher was shaking his head. Something wrong with that order. Jack scratched beneath his beard as he met the butcher's eye. He was some blow-in from Melbourne.

'I've got a nice bit of silverside this morning, Mr Burton. It's easy enough to cook.' Sympathy in the pale eyes staring out from beneath the bushy brows.

They all looked at him with sympathy. The bastard in the menswear shop had shaken his hand, his pop-eyes watering. 'A lovely lady,' he'd said. 'The town will miss her smile, Sam.'

Jack had never had much sympathy, and sympathy hurt. He wished they'd all stop looking at him with their hangdog bloody eyes.

'How do I cook it?' he asked.

The women with the wrist splints smiled, but her eyes, her voice held that same sympathy. He knew her too. Didn't want to know her, remember the last time he was this close to her, but he did.

It was Barbara Dean.

He cringed internally. Bloody memory like an elephant. Why couldn't he go senile and forget? But he'd never forget Barbara Dean. He'd caught Sam molesting her when he was sixteen, and he'd belted the shit out of him. And here she was, bloody near sixty years old, riddled with arthritis and standing at the side of the man everyone thought was Sam Burton, telling him how to cook silverside when she should have been spitting in his eye, screaming 'pervert'.

'Pop it in your biggest saucepan with a good inch of water and a dash of vinegar, Mr Burton. But don't boil it too hard or it will go raggy.'

'Boil meat? In a saucepan?'

'Yes. But with the lid on. Add a touch of mustard and a dash of vinegar,' she said.

His face felt hot, and his spiked hair crawled beneath his hat. 'Thanks. I'll have a bit then.'

She smiled at him, then glanced at the offered lump of bloody red flesh on the butcher's hand, measuring it with her eye. 'He's giving you a nice bit there, Mr Burton. It shouldn't take more than two and a half hours to cook,' she said, and she smiled again and patted his arm. Patted the arm of the bastard she thought was Sam.

Nobody touched him.

Nobody.

Touch of forgiveness in that crippled hand.

He thought of the touch of that other hand in that grey dawn, on the morning May had died, and he wanted to howl.

The plastic bag of meat passed over the counter, he grabbed it, and too eager to get away, forgot that he had to pay. Halfway out the door he turned, like a lost bloody fool. And they were all staring at him with their hangdog eyes and if he didn't get a-bloody-way he was going to bawl.

His hand went to his wallet pocket, and the butcher said: 'Next time you come into town will be fine, Mr Burton.'

Jack put his head down and walked half-blind to his car, drove half-blind back to the house, where he howled. Walked and howled.

He'd taken on Sam's guilt and worn it as his own. And she'd forgiven him. Or maybe he was the only one who remembered that day. Little blue-eyed Barbara Dean and the bastard with his hand in her pants. Maybe his father had planted that image indelibly in his brain with the belting he'd handed out because bad Jacky had bloodied little Saint Sammy's nose.

Forgiven for what he'd never done.

He blew his nose and lifted his shoulders.

'You crazy bastard,' he said and he turned on the hotplate, found a dirty frying pan, added a lump of butter to it, and started looking through the plastic bags for his eggs.

He didn't have any eggs. He'd gone in there for eggs and forgotten to buy bloody eggs, hadn't he?

Fat and butter spitting at him and nothing to fry, he howled again for his eggs and for Barbara Dean. She'd never spoken to him before. But he'd never spoken to her either. Whenever he'd seen her, he, Sam, had put his head down and crossed to the other side of the street.

'Jesus Christ, a man's going mad.'

He tossed one slab of steak into the spitting pan and fried it charred and medium raw, but he hid the char and the blood between two slices of buttered bread, and it tasted all right too, with a dollop of tomato sauce.

'Jesus Christ.'

The solicitor phoned him at three. He had a $100,000 investment come due. They wanted to see him, but he didn't want to see them. He walked the house, walked until he tripped over one of May's old studbooks he'd tossed onto the floor. He sat and he read it, then searched out her farm journals, trying to fill his mind with words. He picked up a local newspaper, turning pages, and he thought of Chef-Marlet's Number 10, and he thought of Mack Curtin and he turned another page.

Pullets for sale. Ready to lay.

The ad ripped out, he took it with him to the kitchen, where he propped it between the salt and pepper shakers with Ellie's letter, his mind with Ellie and her fresh eggs.

That night he rang the number and ordered six chooks. It wasn't until he put the phone down that he remembered chooks had to be fed. He'd have an excuse to stay home now. He had to feed the bloody chooks. That had always been Ellie's excuse. Couldn't do anything. Couldn't go anywhere with him.

'I can't, love. I have to milk the cows, feed the chooks, get the eggs. I can't. It's a lovely dress, Jack, but I've got nowhere to wear it,' he said in nasal tones, his vowels flat. 'You know I can't wear earrings. They pinch my ears, love.'

'Couldn't, or bloody wouldn't. Couldn't or wouldn't.'

'Just let them loose,' Jack said to the chook farmer who delivered the pullets in a metal crate. Mallawindy chooks had roamed free. They'd always come home for their dinner.

'You'll lose them, mate. You need some sort of a run. Look, I'll leave the crate with you for a few days while you knock up a bit of a pen.'

The chooks were not laying, and were looking sick in their cramped quarters before Jack bought a roll of chicken wire and took up a hammer to build them a lean-to against the garden fence. He mashed his still fragile thumb and pitched the hammer to buggery; he was dancing, howling, when old Harry, May's gardener, came riding into the yard with his pup.

Harry took the wrist of the dancer, looked at the thumb. 'I vonce vorking in clinic. Ve vash him, tie him up. Ya.'

Past fighting, past arguing, Jack allowed him to wash the wound, bandage it and later, when Harry started ripping down the lean-to, Jack made no complaint.

'Ve no put him in missus garden. Ve making him good bird-house, behind tree. Ya. Make him for shade. Tomorrow. Ya. I vonce making birdhouse for my president.'

Seventy-odd, a bearded eccentric, his land of origin and native

343

tongue obscure, he worked slowly, but he worked and got the chook palace built, and while four of the pullets were still alive.

Jack wrote him a cheque. *SJBurton*, the J hard, large, and black.

Old Harry took it but stood on in the doorway, the pup at his feet. They watched Jack search for the least dirty mugs, rinse them, and make coffee. They watched him glance at the pup, add a dash of milk to one of May's best bowls then place it before the dog, watched him pat its head.

'What's his name?'

'Is Blooty-dok.'

'I can see it's a bloody dog. What do you call him?'

'Blooty-dok, come.' The dog left his milk and came.

Harry drank his coffee, washed his mug and looked around the kitchen. 'I see him plenty time in clinic. In my country after vaw. Man's head he go vhoooosh vith grief.'

'You go vhoooosh too. You've got your cheque. Go to buggery.'

Harry was moving newspapers from a chair. He sat on it. 'Ve talk. Ya?'

'I don't want to talk.'

'You grass is up-you-bum-to.'

Jack drank coffee, shook his head. 'I like it up to my bum. Piss off.'

'Is late for to piss off. Bike is notting light. Ve eat some dinner. Ya. Ve talk more. Ya.'

'I haven't got any dinner. Take your bloody dog and go, I said.'

The dog lifted its ears and walked to Jack, sniffed his shoe, then sat on it. Harry laughed and Jack patted Blooty-dok's head.

'I vonce cooking for six hunret man. Ve have beer. Ya. Then Harry cook.'

Harry had the beer, and in Jack's pantry he found an onion and a tin of ham. He found rice and frozen peas and a tin of tomatoes, and all three ate well in the kitchen. That night Harry and Blooty-dok bunked down in the cellar, and at dawn the ride-on mower was mowing, the pup barking, and when they still wouldn't go to buggery, Jack did.

to hell and back

~

The Toorak flat hadn't been robbed; these days, that was a plus. May had always been relieved to open the door and find the place as they'd left it. It was clean too. He walked a while there, looking at the old furniture that belonged in Narrawee.

Maybe he'd move the best of it back. Maybe he'd have old Samuel's bones exhumed, have them cremated and scatter the ashes over his beloved Narrawee.

'Nar*ra*wee,' he said. 'Why not?' He was standing before the portrait of Samuel. A proud old bugger, posed in his best suit, seated on his throne. Grey beard, grey hair. Jack lifted it down and carried it out to his car, placing it carefully in the large boot. It had hung in the entrance hall at Narrawee when he was a boy, and it would hang there again. He'd take that portrait home today and he'd look into taking the old man's bones home too.

The garage locked, he walked up Toorak Road, bought a clean shirt, then caught a tram to the city.

For more than sixty years Narrawee had dealt with the same company of solicitors and accountants. John the Bastard had worked for this group prior to inheriting the property, so he'd given them his business. The faces and names had altered through the years, but May had seen no good reason to take the Narrawee business elsewhere.

No May at his side when he rode the lift up. No May to prove he was his twin brother. No hair. But he had Sam's scars. He'd carry them to his grave.

A big firm, it took up most of the second floor, and he saw a girl shaking the hand of one of the solicitors, saw her hair. Slim as Ellie had been back then, hair like Ellie's too, gold by the bloody yard. He sat staring at the hair, willing her to turn around. She didn't.

He watched that hair to the lift, then it was gone.

No one commented on his hair, or lack of it. Handshakes for him in the office. Offered condolences. And papers to sign.

SJBurton. SJBurton. SJBurton.

And if the S grew smaller and the J and B larger, darker, no one in this office questioned it. He had been Sam in this place for thirty years. If he had a head for anything, it was for the business world. Had John the Bastard not been a solicitor, Jack may have taken law at university. Instead he'd taken medicine, and dropped out after that first dead body. He hated dead bodies. Hated death. And been dogged by it. He'd found his mother dead that winter morning. And the little one, Linda.

He shook the other dead from his mind, and listened again to the solicitor.

Since 1960 both Sam and May's names had been on the Narrawee title, but Hargraves Park had belonged to May. It would be Jack's for his lifetime, then it would go to Bronwyn. Narrawee would go to Ann.

'Jack's trust funds. They go to the widow?'

'The fund set up by your father was for your brother's lifetime. It ceases on his death; however, the second fund, from the estate of George Hamstead, goes to the deceased's wife, then to the children of the deceased. The money already paid into the accounts from the first fund, plus interest, will go to your brother's wife.'

Ellie and her bloody friend would be rolling in his money.

But he had Narrawee. He had thousands in shares. He had a brand-new Ford, insurance supplied. What else did he need?

346

A cook.

Old Harry could cook. Cooked for six hundred men, and he'd proved last night that he'd spoken no lie. That meal tossed together in minutes had been fit for a bloody king. Maybe he should let the old bugger hang around, mow his lawns, feed his chooks – and him.

They'd shared two bottles of beer, and they'd talked. The old bastard wasn't dumb; they'd talked for two hours.

This morning the cellar had smelt different. Smelt of old bloke sweat and tobacco. And dog stink. The stink of life. Just a room. For the first time in thirty years it had been just another room. The ghosts had cleared out.

'What?' Jack's mind was jarred back to the moment and to the solicitor.

'So what do you think? Are you interested in renting the flat, Sam?'

'No.'

'It's in a prime position. Good area.'

'I don't know. I'll probably sell it.' Then with a handshake they parted.

He was walking the city streets, not wanting to go back to the flat, when he saw that hair again – Ellie's hair – disappearing into a bar down the bottom end of Collins Street. He walked by it, one hand brushing his scalp. Then he turned, and walked through the door.

She was seated, her back turned to him, her hair bright beneath the spotlights over the bar – like a shower of sunshine, the hair cascaded free to her waist. He watched her hand lift, tilt the glass, empty it, push it back towards the barman.

'Vodka and tonic.'

Jack studied a shoulder, bare except for a slim lemon-coloured strap. His eyes followed the strap down. Slim legs crossed, a slim ankle in its light sandal, swinging. Liza might have looked like this. She might have been sitting at a bar too. Greedy little bugger. And he'd fed her greed.

He watched the second drink follow the first. This was a woman with a mission. He wanted a whisky but ordered a beer, and he looked around for a table, an ashtray. No ashtrays on the tables, but big ones on the bar. A cigarette lit, he sipped his cold beer, felt it wander its way down; and he felt at home, at peace. The stools taken, he leaned, sipping, smoking, watching the coot who sat beside that golden hair. Then the coot moved away and Jack took his beer and sat on the vacated bar stool.

She didn't turn her head. He waited until she pushed her glass back for a refill before he ordered a second beer.

'Carlton Draft, and a vodka and tonic for the lady.'

A long time since he'd bought a drink for a lady. Maybe he could find someone to talk to. Fill an hour. She turned to face him when the barman placed the drink before her, and she wasn't as young as her hair.

'I'm not for sale,' she said.

'I was buying the drink.'

She flipped her hair from her face. Lines around the eyes, her jaw not so firm. With the dim bar light and heavy make-up she looked forty-odd, which probably meant she was fifty.

'You look familiar,' she said.

'That line was old when I was a boy.'

'No. I know your face – but it was younger when I saw it last.'

'I've been at the solicitors. I looked younger before I paid my bill.'

She laughed then, a high girlish laugh, and she spilt her drink and she laughed while the barman mopped his bar, while he poured another drink, until she drank again and had to kill the laugh.

'I needed that,' she said. 'I just buried my mother. I needed that. What's your name?'

'Bill Dooley.' One more use wouldn't wear out the name.

'I didn't need that!' And she laughed again. He moved her glass out of danger. 'Sorry. Sorry, Bill, but I don't like your name.'

'What's wrong with it?'

'Everything. Have you got a dog? If you've got a dog, then we're finished.'

'What's wrong with dogs?'

'They wouldn't let me buy a vodka and tonic. Like the dogs of hell, they guarded that hotel door to stop me from walking through it. They used to sniff my skirt and eye me as I walked past. "This is it, lady," they'd say. "Get used to it".'

He nodded, emptied his glass, pushed it back, and she emptied her own.

'My shout,' she said. 'Anyway, I started walking one day, just stepping, one foot in front of the other until one of Hell's Angels stopped.' Her hand dived into her bag and withdrew a purse. 'Six hours on the back of a Harley and I couldn't walk for a week.'

'Due to the Harley, or the bloke riding it?'

'Bad joke, Bill.' Her finger pointed, made the point as she tossed her hair back. 'I'm not into smut humour. But for the record, it was the bike. He was only nineteen and he liked my hair.'

'I like your hair.'

'Mutton dressed as lamb. He got a fright when he saw my face. Marlon. Hell's little angel on his motorbike. He saved my life that day, but he smelt bad.' She opened her purse and removed a note, placed it on the bar. 'Ever noticed, Bill, how money makes you free? Are you free?'

'Free as a bird.'

'My mother set me free. Did I tell you?' He nodded. 'I had to come home for the funeral and to sell her house, but it doesn't feel like I've come home. I'm a stranger in a strange land.'

'Where do you live?'

'Live?' she said. 'Live suggests that you've got a life, got a home, Bill. I've lived everywhere. I had to keep moving, always moving. With him first. Then to get away from him.'

'Who from?'

'Him.' She flashed a hand, the wide scar of a missing ring still visible. 'I tossed it in with Mum. I got pregnant and she made me marry him, but now her solicitor is getting me a divorce. That's sort of poetic justice, isn't it? Anyway, I promised myself I'd drink six vodka and tonics today, and I'm doing it.'

'You're doing it, lady. What's the current count?' He pointed to her full glass.

'Five. If I count the one I spilt. You know, there was this old black guy who used to sit with his dogs outside that hotel. His name was Bill too – or Billy.'

'King Billy?' he said.

She stared at him, her head to one side. 'How do you know King Billy?'

'I stepped over his dogs a few times too many.' He bit his tongue, emptied his glass and his feet wanted to move him away.

'Mallawindy?' she said, her hand reaching, not wanting him to move away.

'Mallawindy,' he replied. 'Old Granny Bourke, a trout pickled in stout.'

'Bill Dooley and all of his little Dooleys.'

'Your accent isn't Mallawindy.'

'Norman was the schoolteacher.'

He considered the door, realising he'd given away too much. But outside, the world was lonely. He took out his wallet and found a card, glanced at it before placing it on the bar beside her drink, pleased for once to wear his brother's name.

Samuel and May Burton, Narrawee.

She focused on the small print, then turned to him. 'And where is your May tonight, Samuel Burton of Narrawee?'

'She died.'

'I don't like funerals.'

'Death stinks,' he said, and he touched the golden hair, because he wanted to. She looked at him as he lifted a strand of gold, and he allowed the curl to fall.

'Amy.' She offered her hand. 'Amy O'Rouke. Can I buy you dinner?'

'I've got to go home and feed the chooks,' he said, but he liked the hand.

'Do you sell fresh eggs at your back door, Samuel?'

'That's for next year.' As he placed his glass down and turned to go, she reached for his arm.

'I'm lonely,' she said. 'And I don't want to go back to that house. Surely . . . surely the only two people in the whole world who have been to hell and lived to tell the tale ought to have something in common?'

'It's not hell,' he said. 'It's just a malignant growth on hell's sunburnt bum.'

She laughed, and slid from the bar stool. Stood. Tall as Ellie. Slim as May. And she wanted his company.

Three beers gave him a lift. Six stopped the lift dead. He'd had his three. But he liked her laugh. Liked the sharp-featured face, and the colour of her dress. He looked out to the street. Day was ending and the Toorak flat would be empty tonight. He didn't want to go home either.

'I'm not going to beg, Samuel,' she said. 'But it's a long time since a man sat beside me at a bar and made me laugh.'

'I like your hair, Amy O'Rouke. Tonight it looks like a shower of sunlight in a dark and lonely world.'

funny face

~

Wednesday 24 December

A busy day this one, Ellie up to her ears in flour and eggs, baking trays clattering, the smell of her labour pervading every room. Johnny had made his escape early to the old place – not so old any more. The new kitchen was in, the walls lined and painted. He'd bought a new kitchen setting and cut up the old one for firewood.

No more schoolroom until late January, no more painting and no more fences to build, but he could read. He'd picked up *Dune* from the old bookshelves and last night become immersed in it, for the third or the fourth time, then left it face down on the couch in Ben's lounge room. It was close to five when he crossed over the bridge and crept in the back door to retrieve the novel.

In the front paddock Ann and her boys were playing football with Ben. For an instant, John considered joining them. Only for an instant. He passed by the kitchen and walked down to the lounge room. Today a plastic car crib had claimed his space on the couch, and from it Bethany hiccupped a greeting.

The book in hand he stepped closer to the overloaded basket – not much larger than the baskets he'd once filled with eggs then transported on his bike to the grocer to exchange for sugar and tea.

He squatted, at a distance, studying the tiny singlet and napkin-clad mite. Her bare feet were long, familiar, and occupied in kicking at the end of her cage, wanting out.

'You'll have the spine of a banana,' he said softly. She hic-cupped her agreement and lifted her arms to him.

Four months old, she near filled the container, but she wasn't complaining. Too much to see, strange furnishings and a colourful window where green glass in the three top panes turned the sky a shade it should never have been. She hiccupped again and this time an overflow of milk accompanied it. As he moved forward, reaching for the ever-present towelling bib, she offered him her silly little open-mouthed smile.

'Funny face,' he said, wiping milk from her chin and beneath her chin. She considered it a fine game and chuckled. He smiled. 'You're supposed to be sleeping, not laughing, and I'm not sup-posed to be in here,' he said, but she waved his words away, and one dark eye winked at him.

'Okay. I won't say a word about it – if you don't.' He gave her a finger to hold, and her strength surprised him. 'No biting. I can see your new tooth. Your mummy used to have one just like that.'

For minutes they played. Until he heard Ann return to the house, then he stood and again picked up his book.

'We're off now, Mum,' Ann called as she passed by the kitchen door.

'You are coming back with Bronwyn, aren't you?'

'Nick might drive down with her, Mum.'

'It would be nice if you could be there too, Annie,' Ellie said, and her old egg-beater got in amongst the yolks again and Ann stepped down to the lounge room.

'She spat up,' John said.

'That's her favourite after-dinner trick.'

'Her bib and singlet copped most of it.' He was standing back, but watching the dark-eyed mite who now gave her smile to her mother.

'Sicky old thing. When are you going to grow out of it?' Ann said, searching the baby bag that for six years had been grafted to her shoulder. She found a clean singlet and bib, a packet of baby wipes, a small sheet and a plastic bag. Johnny smiled, wondering what else she could draw from that bag. Ah, a disposable napkin. He watched her as efficiently she stripped the baby limbs, did a quick freshen up with baby wipes, then eased a white singlet over the head.

'She's got your curls,' he said, turning the book over and over in his hand.

'God help her.' Then she was up. 'Want to hold her for me while I change the sheet?'

'I'm . . . out of practice.'

'She's unbreakable.'

He glanced at the book, easier than looking at Ann, glanced at the tiny one with the fine black halo. 'Not too certain that I am,' he said.

'It's you or the floor. She'd prefer you.'

Uncertain of how the transfer had been made, he found himself holding Bethany, and too quickly he turned away, walked to the window while small hands decided his nose looked like an interesting toy.

Ellie's tame magpie warbling at the back door. Baking trays clattering. Distant voices of the boys. And Ben's voice. 'Kick it, Tristan. Kick it to Matthew. Good boy!'

Ben. He knew who he was, knew where he was going. Always had.

Where am I going? John thought. What do I have to take me there? A worn paperback novel.

And he already knew how it was going to end. And after this one he'd probably read *Dune Messiah* and he knew how that one ended too. Where was this tiny mite heading? Way, way off, into the great unknown.

With one finger he touched the soft baby knee. Such long legs. Long feet. So familiar.

The car crib fitted with a clean sheet, the soiled items stuffed and tied into a plastic bag, Ann stood on, staring at her brother's shoulders. Broad as her father's. And at his neck, shaped like her father's. Had she ever seen a baby in her father's arms?

Linda. On the morning she had died, he'd held her, his large hand patting her back. She could remember that day. Remember the loss, the empty stroller, the tears. And her father. He'd leaned over the cot and felt Linda's limbs, felt her brow, then he'd picked her up, wiped the vomit from her face.

He'd probably held the infant Liza. Ann could only remember her as the spoilt tale-telling brat. Whingeing Liza, her father wrapped around her little finger. Always waiting at the gate for him to come home, always running to him. 'Daddy. Daddy. Benjie and Annie won't let me play wiff them.'

It came out of the blue and she didn't know why. 'Did he ever hold me when I was little, Johnny? Ever?' No need for a name. Her brother understood. He shook his head, but didn't turn to face her.

'You held me, so it didn't matter if he did or not. One of my first memories is of you carrying me around.' No reply expected. None given. 'I'm so sorry. I'm so bloody sorry that I mucked it up for us, Johnny.'

He turned then, fast, and Ann saw his eyes were wet. She reached out a hand, touched his shoulder, and the tear escaped to trickle down the side of his nose. Bethany swiped at it.

'I told you I wasn't unbreakable,' he said, kissing the tiny fingers intent on exploring his mouth.

'We've been broken for a long, long time. She's a part of the healing.'

'Where have I been?' he said. 'What have I been doing?'

'Getting better.'

'Have I, Annie?'

For a long minute she packed her baby bag, then slung it over her shoulder and lifted the crib to the floor. 'We're like sick cats, you and me. We don't like anyone to see us when we're sick, so we crawl away into the bush to heal ourselves. Just one more day to go and we can crawl out again into the sunshine. It will be over. That's the way we have to think of it. That's the way it has to be. For Bethany, and for the boys. We are the past, Johnny. We don't matter, but they do.'

'I've been trying to tell myself that since dawn – trying to rub him out of my head. I can't do it. I think I want to. I think I'm ready to move on, but I keep seeing his face, laughing at all of us. He won. We let him win, Annie, and tonight he'll be having his own celebration.'

'Shush. She'll hear you.'

'And that's our major problem. It will always be "Shush, she'll hear you". We'll carry it with us until our dying day.'

'All he has won is a lonely old age and dirt and grass and a lot of bulls spreading a lot of manure.'

'In my mind he won't grow old. He's still in there snarling, "Have a go, you cowardly little bastard".' John tapped his brow with a knuckle. 'In there, he's still laughing.'

'I saw him at May's funeral and he wasn't laughing.' She pinned her hair back, stepped away. 'Maybe he didn't ever want us, but he's lost us now. He's lost May. If he has won anything, then as far as I can tell it's just a heap of bullshit and a cold stone mansion on a lonely hill – ' She fell silent then as Ellie entered with a plate of bite-sized egg and bacon pies.

'You've been thinking about Sam too, loves. I know he said he wouldn't come but I've just got the feeling that he'll change his mind.'

'He won't, Mum,' Ann said.

'No. You're probably right.' She offered the plate. 'These ones got a bit burnt at the edges. Want to test them for me?' Ann took the plate and Ellie claimed Bethany. 'My word, she reminds me of you. That hair and those black eyes, watching everything, just like you used to. Her mouth is different, though. It's more like Liza's mouth.'

'David's actually.' Ann spoke with her mouth full of flaky, melt-in-the-mouth pastry, as only Ellie could make pastry.

'Definitely David's,' Johnny said, and Ellie exchanged the baby for the plate.

'Did Bronwyn say what time Nick would be finishing work tonight?'

'I don't know, Mum.'

'She shouldn't be driving by herself. When is her baby due?'

'Soon.' It was already a week overdue.

The conversation ended as a herd of little boys entered from the back verandah. Ann strapped Bethany into her crib and John picked it up, carried it out to the van then stood watching as it and the boys were loaded in and strapped down.

'It's twenty to six. David said he'd be home early tonight.'

'Daddy dot a pwise,' Tristan said.

'A surprise, Tristan, and Daddy said don't tell Mummy.'

Ann turned to her boys. 'I bet it's a big fat chocolate cream cake.' There were three shakes of three small heads, and she laughed and turned back to John. 'Poor David. He's starved for cream cakes.'

'It's your birthday. I forgot. Happy thirty-seventh.'

'I'd forget it too, if I could.'

'A pity that we can't control time, Annie. Turn it back. Go back and undo old mistakes.'

She shook her head. 'I used to think so, but I wouldn't be brave enough to live it again. I don't want any single one of my days back, Johnny. I want what I've got now. This little tribe.' She opened the driver's side door, then turned again to her brother. 'Except . . . except I want you to become a part of my tribe again. More than anything else, I want that.'

'Sick cats. I like that analogy,' he said. 'Remember Bessy's old grey Persian, Smokey – the one that was bitten by a snake?' She nodded. 'Remember how it went missing for weeks, and they thought it was dead?'

'And it dragged itself back home one morning, and spent the rest of its life depositing dead snakes on Bessy's front doorstep.'

'Revenge is sweet.' John smiled, looked at the sun still high in the western sky. 'The sun will eventually go down on today, love, and it will probably rise again in the morning.'

'I'll give you fifty-to-one odds on it,' she said, and she slid behind the wheel, found her sunglasses and put them on before turning to face him. 'Come up tomorrow. Have Christmas dinner with us.'

'I . . . I could.'

'Could isn't good enough.'

'How about might? No promises.'

'Might, I'll accept. I never did like promises. They can get you into a whole heap of trouble. See you tomorrow, then. Around one.'

And she drove away while he watched her out of sight.

no more jack

~

Christmas Eve and lonely. All day Jack had driven. Hadn't known where he was going and hadn't cared. He'd eaten morning tea at a bakery in Yea, turned towards Seymour and taken the Hume Freeway north. Same old freeway. Same old trees. Same old hills. He'd hit Albury near twelve, and he'd seen the same old signpost shimmering in the heat haze, pointing vaguely off into the distance: DAREE.

So he'd made the left-hand turn, and followed the road. Same old dry grass. Same old paddocks. Same narrow road but bigger potholes. He had passed straight through Mallawindy, gone up to Warran and found that white house in Mahoneys Lane.

Six o'clock and the sun beating hard against the white bricks. Her Narrawee. She'd loved it too – couldn't have the original, so she'd built her own. Not so big, but the front door looked much the same. He was going to get out of the car and walk to that door, knock on that bloody door.

What would she do if he did? And what was he going to say to her if she let him in? Nothing he could say, so he parked out front and stared until his eyes watered.

No child playing in the yard. Probably down in Mallawindy, waiting for the party to begin. He waited in his car for half an hour, chain-smoking, until a Commodore drove into the garage.

Minures later a Toyota Land Cruiser turned up the drive and parked beside the Commodore. He heard the children's voices, her voice.

'Daddy beat us home tonight.'

'He might cook some of his spaghetti, Mummy.'

'Cross our fingers, eh, Ben?'

'I not like bisteddy.'

'You do so love Daddy's pisgetti, Tristan. Stop always being a bad guy or Santa Claus won't bring you any presents.'

'You tell him, Matthew.'

'I not like Sana Cause. He not a bad guy.'

Jack saw her for a moment as she reached for the tall garage door. Jeans and shirt, long wild hair framing that face. Kids all over her.

Then the garage door closed and she was gone.

Maybe she'd seen him, recognised him when she'd driven up, locked her kids away from him. Maybe she hadn't. She'd spoken to him the morning May had died. She'd spoken to him at the funeral.

But he couldn't knock on her door so he lit another cigarette and drove away, bought a bottle of Diet Coke and a ham and salad roll, ready to go, and he ate it by the river, just smelling the water and watching it flow.

It used to be green once. You could sit by this river and watch schools of tiny fish swarming at the bank. And birds, birds by the thousands – the iridescent blue of kingfishers, darting, ducking for their food. And snakes, they'd been thick along this river, kooka-burras watching them, and laughing from the trees. He'd sat beside this river one afternoon watching a kookaburra belting a snake's brains out on the limb of a tree, and he'd watched it until the two foot of snake had gone down that throat.

No kookaburras laughing tonight. No snakes either. No frogs croaking. It was all over, the reed-choked river was mud and snags, dying, and all the birds had flown.

The sun sinking low, he turned his car for home. Nowhere else to go. He'd drive through tonight, or book into a motel when he got sick of driving. What did it matter? Tomorrow Jack Burton would be as dead as that bloody river.

But he turned down the cemetery road at Mallawindy, and he wandered there until he found the grave. No new headstone with his name on it.

'She probably gave my five thousand to the bloody church; they'll stick my name on a pew and I'll have every bastard in town sitting on me,' he said.

Liza. Linda. Patrick. Who were they? Just names from another time. He read the names, spoke the names, trying to give them meaning. Seven kids he'd given life. Seven. The strong had survived his brand of fatherhood. The weak slept here.

'Shit,' he said. 'Shit.' And he walked away, not knowing why he'd come to this godforsaken place. He hated cemeteries. Hated the black hole, and the dirt that filled the hole.

Nothing here for him. No one here. Just a barren garden, growing grey stone, but tonight he wandered the garden, wandered until he found Rella Eva's grave, old Dave in with her.

'Sleep well, Rell. Sorry about that bloody train,' he said, squinting at his watch. Less than four hours to midnight. Jack had less than four hours to live.

Hot airless night. Hell's furnace doors were hanging on their hinges. Mosquitoes buzzed in his ears, bit, and he returned to his car, turned on the air-conditioning, slapping at insects, mashing two on his windscreen as he drove on down to the bridge, and over the bridge, and on to the old place he'd named Chookshit Country. No light showing there, but there was a glow from Malcolm Fletcher's house. He drove past it, turned, then drove back, parking his car on the verge of the road, far enough away from Malcolm's door, and he walked into a stand of trees and to the fence.

New. All new, the wires stretched tight. Didn't feel like castrating himself on wire, so he followed the fence to the gate, then wended his way across the paddocks to the river where he stood looking at the sagging footbridge that spanned the muddy water.

Bessy's ramshackle house sprawled to the east of the makeshift bridge, the old mud brick house was to the west. He was almost centred between those four houses – a dangerous place to be. Bessy would know him in the dark. And Fletcher; Jack wouldn't trust him as far as he could kick him.

He looked over his shoulder, knowing that he had to go back, get in his car and go home, but his eyes were drawn towards the mud brick house. No light burning there.

They'd all be up at the hotel partying, celebrating his death, working out how they were going to spend their $250,000 blood money.

He laughed softly, considered spoiling their plans yet, but across the river Bessy's dogs barked and Jack stilled his laughter. No light burning in her house either. He was safe enough down this end of town tonight. The whole bloody lot of them would be up at the pub. He walked to the footbridge, tentatively placing one foot on it, testing, testing. He took a slow and easy step, then two more, glancing behind him, before him.

Halfway across he kicked a protruding nail, stumbled. 'Shit,' he said, regaining his balance, muddy water barely moving below. Slowly then, he felt his way, slow stepping to that last board, then he was off at a run and down the dirt ramp to Bessy's land, his eyes searching for her, or her bull – one as dangerous as the other.

No movement. Dogs still muttering, rattling their chains.

'Bloody maniac,' he said. 'What are you doing coming up here?' Still he continued on, keeping close to the river and the slim cover of trees, creeping closer to the mud brick house. Until that last fence.

Wire not strung so tight here. Fences not so new. The wires whispered as he forced them down, stepped over. And he was in the orchard paddock.

Apricots on these trees. He could smell them. And peaches ripe and pink. He remembered those early peaches, and he reached for one and bit into it.

Sweet taste of Ellie.

Standing amid the trees he sucked on the peach, sucked it down to the stone, wiping the juice from his hands on the seat of his jeans, and smelling, just smelling the fruit and the land and the cows.

Smell of fecundity.

Smell of Ellie.

And he saw her, or thought it was her. Someone in the back yard, on their knees. Praying? Ellie had usually done it beside her bed – praying he wouldn't touch her.

Her back was to him, her hands busy in the earth. Two careful steps and he was behind the old fig tree, spread wider in his absence. He pushed in against the foliage, lifting a branch to create a spy hole. For minutes he stood watching the figure. It wasn't until he released the branch to swat a mosquito that she turned to face the tree.

He couldn't run. She'd see him if he moved. He looked over his shoulder towards Bessy's house, then pushed deeper into the fig tree.

'Ellie, love. Where are you? We're going to have to get a move on.'

'I thought I heard something. Shush, Bob.'

It was her, but she'd done something to her hair. Bob? And who was bloody Bob? The back verandah light came on and bloody Bob was standing in the doorway, and he looked bloody familiar. Jack stopped breathing, let the mosquitoes feast.

'Are you ready, love? Everyone will be waiting for you.'

Ellie wiped her earthy hands against each other, wiped her earthy knees. 'I'm all ready. I've just got to get my good shoes on, that's all.'

'What are you up to out there in the dark?'

'It wasn't dark until you put the light on,' she said. 'There's snails all over my strawberries. Benjie watered before he left and they're out in their thousands.'

'Have you got any snail bait?'

'Yes. It's in the laundry cupboard. And bring out a torch, Bob.' Head to one side then, she peered at the fig tree. A step forward, and a second step, faster steps to the fence.

Only a wire fence and the fig tree between them. Nothing between them. Jack waited while the mosquito drank its fill from his ear, waited motionless until Ellie stepped back to friend Bob, taking the torch, lighting the earth while he sprinkled snail bait.

Then the bastard stood up and put his bloody hand on her shoulder and Jack mashed the mosquito and ground it into his ear.

'Listen.' Ellie's torch light swung towards the peach tree; it searched there, slowly roving backwards, back, back to the fig tree. 'Do you think there's someone out there pinching my peaches?'

'Probably possums. They won't take more than they can eat, love.'

Mosquito buzzing in his ear, Jack cowered from the light. Bloody stupid bastard. He shouldn't have come here. Bloody stupid bastard of a man he was.

The torch turned off, Ellie walked back to the verandah. 'It's such a funny old night, Bob. It's so still and sort of . . . sort of eerie.'

'I don't know about eerie, but it's bloody hot.'

'It's … it's like it's waiting for something. Like it knows something that we don't know.' Then the verandah light was off, and the night was dark.

'You'll feel better about it all in the morning, love. Come on. Get your shoes on and let's go. I'm as dry as a wooden god.'

'Did you see where Johnny went?'

Jack didn't hear the reply. The door closed on it, and he ran, ran for the river, heart thumping, legs pumping, over the fence, and down the slope to the water's edge, where he leaned against the roots of a tree, sucking air, his hand on his heart.

Poetic justice if he dropped dead, had a heart attack on her property while she was having her party to celebrate his death. What the hell was he doing here? Nothing here for him and never had been. Always wanting what he didn't have.

Always.

He'd sat with her in this place when she was sixteen, and her old man had caught him kissing her. Ordered him off the land.

Stay away from her, boy. She's not for you. Go home to your people and make something of your life.

But he'd wanted Ellie, and he'd got what he wanted, and when he found out it wasn't what he'd wanted after all, he'd punished her for his mistake – bruised her, abused her, burned the footbridge that had given her too easy access to her father.

Mummy's boy Benjie had rebuilt it. No black Burton in him. Pure bloody Vevers and Hamstead, that one. He hadn't wanted more. Hadn't gone off looking for more.

Jack stood and walked along the riverbank, not wanting to face that footbridge again. He tripped over logs and stepped in cow shit, slipped in it, and bloody near slipped into the river. Not enough water in it to drown him. Maybe he might choke on mud.

Time heals, they all said to him. Time heals. But old man time had to know what he was supposed to be healing before he could heal it, didn't he?

'Time, that knits the ravelled sleeve of care – or was it sleep that did the knitting?' Jack stood and brushed leaves and soil from the seat of his jeans. 'I used to know it. Used to know a lot of things.' He walked off, quietly quoting and misquoting the words he'd made his own at nineteen. 'Balm of hurt minds, great nature's second course, chief nourisher in life's feast.'

'Bloody boyfriend Bob. Bob who?'

Ellie was the only woman who hadn't wanted him. May had wanted him. Half the women in Mallawindy had wanted him, and he'd taken his pick, just to nark the one who didn't want him.

Amy O'Rouke had wanted him, or hadn't wanted to be alone. Thought she'd paid for him too, with a bloody beautiful feed of fish and chips. He should have taken her up on her offer, or her coffee. But he hadn't.

'Later,' he'd said.

'Do you think we have a later, Samuel Burton?'

'Of all the bars in Melbourne, you had to walk into mine. It's got to mean something.' They'd had a few laughs, but he'd wanted to get away. May's death was still too close. His own death imminent.

'Come out for Christmas dinner, Sam.'

'Can't,' he'd said. 'A prior appointment.'

'Boxing Day then. I'll meet you at the bar. We'll play it again, Sam.'

'Samuel, and why not? Why not?'

Samuel.

That's who he was now. Who he had to be now. No May to coerce into calling him Jack, and no more Jack after midnight.

He was Samuel Burton of Narrawee, and maybe the grey-bearded old bugger still had some time left. Time for a laugh or two. Time to work out the difference between a good bull and one not so good – or learn how to fake it.

He walked around to the main bridge, crossed over, and as the last glimmer of light became lost behind the trees, he reached into his pocket for Sam's glasses – not to hide behind, either. He needed them these days to see where he was going, needed them to drive. Old age was a bastard.

The road a lighter dark than the trees, he walked on, counting the white posts, his sneakers whispering in the dust, his mind wandering as a hand reached for his pocket and cigarettes. Matches. Gratefully he lit up, drawing the smoke deep, coughing it out.

Bob? Bobby Willis? Robbie West. Bob Collins? Bob? That voice, that shape had been familiar. 'Bob?' he said, then he saw his car and stepped eagerly towards it.

And into instant blindness.

'Get that bloody thing out of my eyes, you stupid bastard.'

The tone, the words spoken, were Jack's. There was no taking any of them back. But with the flash of light came an inner illumination.

The friend. It was Ellie's tame copper. Bob bloody Johnson!

retribution

~

Malcolm had seen the big car drive by, seen it turn, watched it stop. Through his binoculars he had spied on the driver, seen him close the car door, watched him walk away from the car.

Jack was back.

Binoculars to his eyes, Malcolm had tracked him to the gate, and as he'd opened it, he'd turned, and for an instant the binoculars had looked Jack Burton in the eye. That was when Malcolm had exchanged them, first for his brandy bottle, then for his gun.

The bottle empty, he had poured the bullets from the worn matchbox into his palm. Two bullets. He'd fingered them, inserted them lovingly into the small handgun – as they had been inserted many times before. Something sensuous about this action.

And the words, elusive words, had begun to play with him.

Edward Edwards felt the weight of the gun in his hand. He knew what he must do. That bastard did not deserve to live.

Malcolm's slipper-clad feet had attempted to walk him to his study where Number 10, *Untitled*, still waited. Unfinished.

'No.'

But Mack was back and Malcolm's word-well, dry too long, was filling.

Edward had never been a violent man. He looked down at his
hands to the gun he had inherited from his father. Why had he kept
it, if not to use on the eradication of vermin? Tonight Mack Curtin
would die.

He had stood there, between his empty brandy bottle and his
study door, and like Edward Edwards, had stared at the gun dangling from his hand, pointing at his flattened slipper.

'Tomorrow,' he'd said, forgetting for a moment that he would
have no tomorrow.

Two bullets he had purchased with this gun. His plan, dredged
from the last drops of his brandy bottle, was to use both bullets. One
for that obnoxious bastard, then one into his own temple. He'd go
out in a blaze of glory.

'A blaze of glory. No more the impotent old fool. We will show
this town what we are made of.'

But the word 'impotent' had led him back to Mack Curtin, led
him to chapter eleven – also unfinished.

In his youth, Mack had been hung like a stallion. So the years had
taken their toll, but the old war horse was not yet ready to be put
out to pasture. He sniffed at the scent of battle as he closed his
eyes. Old mares became young again in the dark.

'Oh yes. Yes, Coll. You are so good. This one could well be your
best yet.'

His slippers had tried to lead him to his study door, but he'd
fought them, forced them to flip-flop to the laundry where he'd
taken up his flashlight. A cumbersome yellow thing, its battery was
new, its light bright. He'd tested it, shining it around the walls, and
through the window.

With a sigh for dreams unrealised, he'd dropped the loaded gun
deep in his trouser pocket then, torch in one hand, walking stick in
the other, he'd flip-flapped across the road to the big car, each flip,

each flap making him aware that he should not have emptied his brandy bottle, but should have changed his footwear. However, had he not emptied the brandy bottle he would have been sitting at his window looking out, instead of outside, looking in.

Slippers were not the optimum footwear for traversing gravelled roads. He prodded and stepped more slowly, knowing he must not fall and pump the precious bullets into his own well-padded buttock.

His heart, playing a wild tattoo amid the fat, was surely loud enough to be heard across the river, strong enough to crush his throat, but not enough to kill those inner words. They had kept coming at him, eating away at his conscious mind. Were his last minutes on this earth to be spent mentally completing Number 10?

But he had found his end. The bastard of a thing had eluded him until tonight.

Mack could smell his future in the heated mulch beneath his feet. Heavy soil. Dust to dust. They were coming to get him and he knew it. For years he had evaded them, hiding out in Sydney, changing his name, but for the last six months the hounds had been baying at his heels.

Breath short, his well of words spilling over, Malcolm found a tree. His back pressed to its trunk, he'd let the words play, fill a minute or an hour.

He hadn't planned to be here tonight. Just passing through, but the bloody old car had let him down. It had rolled over and died three miles out of town.

A too-deep sigh had shaken him. 'It's over, Coll. It's over. Vacate the space. I have more important work to do.' Tonight he would fight his own war against tyranny. And he would win.

Number 10 was roughed out. Only fifty thousand words and no

end in sight, but his death would assure its sales. Let his publishers write their own end, edit it as they wished.

Who would miss him, mourn his passing? Ann, perhaps. And he would miss her. Miss watching her tiny Bethany grow.

'Time's great plan, Malcolm. Time for the old to make way for the new.'

John Burton may miss the Sunday evenings spent in discussion. John, named as Malcolm's own son had been named, and tonight he would be with his son and poor Jillian.

Or would they disown him?

'You're good for me, Mack,' she panted. 'You make me young again. Only you. Only ever you. We've got years of life to live.'

'Speak for yourself, Bell. And you haven't got the legs for life on the run.' His hand slid down to her knee, bone and sinew, and not much else.

'A pity you can't write your own end, Coll. You make me young again. But the world will know who you were tomorrow.'

On his death, Ann was to give up his secret. Let them laugh at him then. Let them call him impotent old fool then. He'd have the last laugh. Pleasure in that thought. Something to look forward to.

'A pity I won't be around to see it.'

His eyes had long given up the fight to see by night. Not knowing from which direction Jack Burton would approach, Malcolm didn't bother looking. He rested his eyes and allowed his ears to work for him. His hearing was good. He'd hear him, and from his position against the tree he could see the outline of the car.

But it was his eyes that had seen the bright spark of a match being struck before his ears had picked up the sound of footsteps. His walking stick placed against the tree, he'd tugged his gun free.

Armpits dripping with perspiration, hands dripping, shaking, he'd pointed both gun and flashlight, and heard the walking stick fall, hit the mulch-covered earth. Still, he would not need it to prod its slow way home tonight. He would not be going home. Let the laconic lawman worry about getting him out, bring in a bulldozer, a fork-lift.

One fat index finger ready on the trigger, his second index finger poised over the on/off flashlight switch, Malcolm had spread his feet and begun counting down his seconds of life.

He'd have to be close. Two metres. He'd need to be that close. With only two bullets he couldn't afford to miss.

Soft the mumble of feet through dust and gravel. Soft the sigh, slow the footsteps. Small orange glow-worm of cigarette.

A breath. Deep drawn. The air had tasted sweet, heavy with eucalypt and honey. The arm holding the gun lifted, Malcolm braced himself to fight his last war, his weapon saved fifty years for this night. For this moment. He would do it. He could do it.

And no thinking, Malcolm. No change of heart. Him first, then a fast shot into the temple and no backward glance.

The glow of cigarette close enough, Malcolm had stepped forward, his left index finger bearing down on the flashlight switch.

Instant light, finding, blinding his quarry.

'Get that bloody thing out of my eyes, you stupid bastard.'

Jack threw a hand up to cover his eyes as Malcolm swayed there, looking at the trees, so green by torchlight as his finger moved against the trigger.

And drew a blank.

So it was not meant to be a murder/suicide, so change the script Malcolm, but quickly. One bullet would be enough. But his torch slipped, fell to the earth. Day birds above complained at the spot-light in their eyes and Jack Burton laughed and kicked the light, sending it flying, a fluorescent football aimed accurately between the goalposts of river gums as Malcolm clumsily ejected the bullet and stepped back. His weight applied to one end of his fallen walking stick, it leaped up from the mulch, hit him in his knee, and his knee went. He swayed back. The trunk of the tree stopped his fall, leant its support.

Laughter. Light now behind the laughter. Bright light from the old Burton verandah. He could see Jack Burton in silhouette.

Both hands on the gun, Malcolm pushed off from the tree, two, three steps forwards, the gun aimed up at the silhouette, up at the laughter.

And his finger squeezed the trigger as the bars of a padded cell squeezed his heart.

The gun exploded in his hands, echoing and re-echoing through the forest.

Faulty German workmanship! the fat man thought as he fell.

seeing stars

~

His mind away on the planet Dune, Johnny had been seated in the kitchen, his novel two-thirds read, when he'd seen a light sweep by his window. He'd placed the book face down and stood, walked to the passage, turning on the outside lights before making his way around the house, seeking a torch bearer – someone looking for a cheap chicken dinner. Most of the town families had received invitations to Ellie's party at the beer garden, but there were a few who had not. A good night for prowling, and Ellie's free-range chickens were tempting.

He'd been on the front verandah when he'd seen the glow, and he'd frowned, his head to one side, staring at what appeared to be a spotlight sending its bright alien beam high into the heavens.

Old Robbie West out star-gazing, or a UFO homing in on the west paddock? The light had not moved, so he'd walked off to investigate.

A strange sweating night. Though the sun had long left for Perth, it hadn't taken its heat with it. Not the breath of breeze about.

He had left Ben's house after a late dinner. No excuses given. None asked. A few months back Ellie would have pleaded with him to go, but she had her friend now.

Johnny had known Bob Johnson as the local cop back in the late sixties. He'd aged some, lost most of his hair, but he still had that same quiet good sense about him. Let him celebrate Jack Burton's life – or his death – with Ellie. Johnny would take no part in the farce.

Annie? She hadn't said that she would drive down with Bronwyn – or that she wouldn't.

'Ann,' he said. 'Annie.'

David called her Ann. Malcolm and Kerrie called her Ann. Only to the family she remained Annie.

'Annie Lizabeth.'

Bethany had brought memories of that other dark-eyed baby flooding back this afternoon, and for a moment they'd threatened to submerge him. Silly little gaping smile, perfect little grasping hands. And the chuckle.

He could remember the day his father had brought Annie home from the hospital. They'd propped her in the old pram in the kitchen. No tears, just that little head turning, and those big eyes staring at all the faces.

Maybe he'd go to Warran tomorrow.

The spotlight in the paddock wasn't moving. It was in the far corner, close to the road, and the shortest route there was through the fowl yard. That was the route he'd taken.

Space debris, he'd thought. A Martian landing? Or careless chicken thief who had taken a fall?

He was squeezing between the fence wires when he heard the explosion. It halted his progress, and his head lifted, his ears seeking direction, his eyes seeking the stationary light, expecting it to flare or die.

It didn't.

When he moved forward once more, he was sucking a wire cut on his palm – until he heard the car, saw the headlights on the road.

Then he ran.

one. two. three.

~

Jack's motor was running and so was he when his headlights picked up the hulk of flesh in his pathway. He couldn't run over it, so he backed up. And his lights saw red, saw the colour of blood.

'You stupid old bastard,' he moaned and he turned off the motor and stepped back to the road. The headlights died. Left him in the dark. 'Bloody modern, bloody inventions!' he snarled, and again turned the key in the ignition. The motor running, lights blazing, he walked to the hump of flesh sprawled like a beached whale on the verge of the road.

'Get up. You're not dead.' He prodded a flat slipper with his own shoe. Malcolm Fletcher didn't move. Jack looked down at the blood and at the mutilated hand that had pumped the blood. 'You're bleeding. You can't be dead. Get off the bloody road.'

No movement. No sound.

'I didn't do anything to you, you rattlesnake-brained old slug,' he said, stooping, prodding at whale blubber. 'Are you dead, or dead bloody drunk?'

Then he was down, slow to his knees, an ear placed close to where a heart might be. No heart – or too much blubber between it and the ear placed to hear it. He picked up the right hand first, let it drop back. He picked up the left.

'I've seen worse on bonfire night. Get up,' he yelled. 'Where's Number 10, you eavesdropping old bastard?' He felt the wrist for a pulse and couldn't find one. Got blood on his hands for his trouble. The hand dropped fast, it flopped like a dead fish onto the gravel, and Jack pulled back. 'Number 10 placed on hold. Permanently too, by the look of bloody things.'

His face turned then to his car, motor still purring, calling him away. He had to get out of here. The lights were on at the old place now and he had a fair idea of who had turned them on and it wasn't Ellie or her boyfriend. The old slug's heart might have stopped, but his own was beating in his brain. Go. Go. Go.

He placed his palm close to the mouth. No air. 'Shit,' he snarled as two uneasy fingers felt for the carotid artery. Not a flutter, not a mutter. Malcolm Fletcher was a goner, and he stunk of sweated brandy.

Jack looked over his shoulder. 'Run, you crazy bastard. Find a phone and ring someone.' He tried to gain his feet, but his knee pressed hard on a baked clay ridge, and the pain drove his heart rate higher. He repositioned the knee and decided to stay down.

'Shit,' he said, feeling for his cigarettes; his hand came out holding a box of matches. He squinted at it, considered it, then tossed the tray and matches onto the earth and manoeuvred the sturdy outer casing between the teeth of the dead man before applying his mouth to the other end of the box. And he blew.

It didn't do any good. The dead stayed dead. Always, they'd stayed dead. His mother, Liza, Linda, May.

The box left in the mouth like a rectangular cigar, Jack placed the heels of his hands at the base of the breastbone, or where the breastbone might have been – if he'd had one. He pushed down hard, trying to remember what the blonde doctor had done on the television show last week. Not that it had done much good. She'd ended up hitting the corpse with electricity. A hairy old bugger, it'd set the hairs of his chest on fire.

But he bore down anyway.

One. Two. Three. And a One. Two. Three. Again he blew into the matchbox. That's what they did. Pumped half a dozen times or so, then blew.

The air wasn't going anywhere.

You had to move the head back or something, so they weren't blocking off their own windpipes. He grabbed a handful of hair and dragged the head down. It flopped to the side then rolled back to its original place. 'Bloody shit, to it.' He snatched at a slipper, then the other, small, but big enough to scrape up a neck-rest of gravel, big enough to prop the bloody head back, open up the windpipe, then he blew again through his matchbox and this time the chest rose! He leaned on fat, pushed the air out.

'Shit!' he said, getting into the rhythm. External heart massage was supposed to compress the heart between spine and ribs. It might be possible to compress it between fat.

One. Two. Three. Blow. And the matchbox almost disappeared down the gaping maw. He fished it out, wiped his fingers on his jeans.

'Breathe, you bastard,' he said. One. Two. Three. 'Breathe. I don't need any more bloody guilt.'

Involved in his rhythm, Jack was unaware of the second presence until the shadow fell across him. He knew who it was before he heard the voice, which sounded like him doing a Sam – without the sibilant Ss.

'Added another notch to your gun?'

Jack's head turned slowly, and his hands became still. So the old war wasn't over. He tried to rise then, to ready himself for war, to push off from the hump of dead fat, but he was too bloody old and his knees were too stiff. Getting down had been bad enough; getting up again was worse. He stayed down, turned back to what he'd started. Blew.

'What did you do to him?'

One. Two. Three.

'Don't blame me for this one. And get out of my bloody light or I'll lose my box down his throat.'

The shadow moved. Johnny Burton was squatting over the old man, looking at the matchbox in the mouth, feeling for a pulse at the throat.

'Who else do I blame?'

'I don't give a shit who you blame, do I? Take your blame and go to buggery with it.' One. Two. Three. 'I've had enough of your bloody blame.'

One. Two. Three. Blow.

'Have you called an ambulance?'

'Yeah. Telephone dangling from every bloody tree. Doctors hiding in the bushes.' One. Two. Three. 'The crazy old bastard tried to shoot me.' One. Two. Three. 'Blew his bloody hands up.' One. Two. Three. 'Might slow his typing down.'

Nothing Johnny could say to that. But he could make the phone call. He ran to Malcolm's house and was back in moments, just standing to the side, looking down at an old man on his knees, blowing air through a disintegrating matchbox.

So close to the scene but distanced, he didn't know what he was supposed to do. Lock his hands around that throat and squeeze? Lash out with a boot, kick that head in?

What was he supposed to say?

Why?

Too late for whys.

'Breathe, you crazy old bastard. Suck on bloody life.' The voice was the same, and the jolt of that head as it turned to him. 'Get on your knees and perform a bloody miracle or something. I'm not wearing any more guilt and I can't keep this up all night.'

But he kept it up.

One. Two. Three. Blow.

'You came back.'

One. Two. Three. Blow. Jack sucked air for himself and his lungs howled. He coughed, coughed, lost his rhythm.

'I came back. That's my guilt. I'll wear it.' One. Two. Three. Blow. And the matchbox cover split at the seam. Jack pitched it, pitched it to buggery, and he sucked air deep. 'I came back . . . came back to mourn for poor bloody old Jack Burton. That's why I came back.' One. Two. Three. 'Nobody else will.' One. Two. Three. 'She's up there celebrating her $250,000 . . . with her bloody new boyfriend, Bob.'

One. Two. Three.

'You're worth more dead than you ever were alive.'

'Yeah.' One. Two. Three. 'You're probably right.' One. Two. Three. 'And I'm too bloody old to argue, so climb down off your pulpit and do something useful.' One. Two. Three. 'He's that author, Chef-bloody-Marlet, the old bastard. We've got to keep getting air into him – and by the living Jesus, I draw the line at kissing that bloody mouth.'

Two old men beside a dark road. Old adversaries. One not breathing and the other tiring fast. His matchbox gone, Jack made a funnel of his hand and he held the hand to the gaping mouth, blew his air through it. Too much escaped his fingers.

Johnny Burton knelt then at the old teacher's head, one hand cupping the many chins, he closed off the nostrils with his cheek and forced his air in. Close to his father. Head to head with his father. Eye to eye with his father. He glanced at the eyes, and for an instant they met, then Jack's head was down as he pumped. One. Two. Three. One. Two. Three. He rested, sat back and shook his bad wrist as he watched his son inflate the tired old lungs.

Eyeball to eyeball these two, and not a word spoken.

Motor purring, lights glaring. John looked at his father's hair, almost white under the car's headlights. At his beard. Almost white. Glasses glinting. Nothing left of that black-headed bastard who had given him life.

Nothing.

And not so big.

Only those hands, familiar, and close. Crossed now, pumping, pumping, pumping life. Old face sweating, mouth grimacing as he sucked air enough for his own lungs.

Father and son. Enemies. Sworn enemies, but fighting side by side tonight for a worthwhile cause.

celebration of life

~

Soft sigh of the river as it started its long slow curve, lonely cry of a night bird, and on the sand dunes, rabbits, up to their old habits, courted and cavorted beneath a black blanket sky. A well-worn blanket this one – enough to hold in the heat of the day, but here, there, and everywhere, ragged holes allowed old heaven's light straight through.

Star light, star bright, first star I see tonight. A choir of mosquitoes hummed in the reed beds and in the hot mulch of the forest floor. They had fed and bred and their eggs were spread.

'*Might*,' a lone frog croaked. '*Might*.' And he swallowed a few contraltos before giving them his slow, clap, clap, clap.

In the trees an owl hooted, and possums coughed their agreement like a meeting of consumptive old men.

'*Wish tonight*,' a feral cat hissed and crouched, ready to pounce. Small possum was sweet, and a cat had to eat. '*Wish tonight*.'

Old familiar song of the Mallawindy bush. But into it came the discordant scream of an ambulance siren, and the flashing light, and movement of shadow.

And the owl flew, and the cat looked up, its eyes glinted gold as the frog stopped his slow clap, clap to dive deep beneath a rotting log, and on the sand dunes, the rabbits ceased their play.

A hot, sweating night in Mallawindy, courtship and death all around.

There was a diamond sparkling on Kerrie Fogarty's finger, and two in Ben Burton's eyes. Try as he might, he couldn't stop smiling.

Jeff Rowan couldn't stop scowling. 'Not the time or the place for it.' If he'd said it once, he'd said it forty times, and he'd only spoken to a third of Ellie's guests. 'Bloody poor taste, I call it.'

Or sour grapes.

Ann, Bron and Ben had always been a close-knit threesome, now Kerrie had joined them. They sat at a corner table for four. Nick and David were in Warran, babysitting and watching a video.

Father Fogarty had been droning on for half an hour. Few were listening – which was to the good. The priest was old, his memory wasn't what it ought to be, and the man he spoke of was unknown in Mallawindy.

Ellie sighed. Still no sign of Sam. She'd been expecting him all day, and it wouldn't have hurt him to put off his overseas trip for his only brother. She glanced at the priest, and for once wished he'd stop praying. Jack would have hated this. After weeks of planning and three days of baking, the night wasn't turning out the way she'd imagined it would. She looked towards the corner table, flinched.

It wasn't as if the engagement had been announced tonight. Benjie wouldn't do a thing like that! Still, a stranger walking in on this party wouldn't know it. Everyone seemed to be crowded around their table, shaking Benjie's hand and kissing Kerrie. Everyone was laughing. Annie and Bron too. And Father Fogarty still droning on.

'How am I supposed to get all that way to Bega for their wedding, Bob?'

'It will be a nice drive in autumn, Ellie.' And maybe just what the doctor ordered, Bob thought. Two days in the car, no Bessy in the back seat. He'd make sure of that.

Then Father Fogarty closed his mouth and Joe Willis was up there, edging him away.

'Jack always did my tax returns in the early years. Always got me a bloody good refund too, until the bloody tax man decided to audit me one year – '

Ellie knew all about audits. She turned her back, offered the cream puffs around. 'Jack used to love these,' she said, taking up a cake, biting into it.

But was it Jack or her father who had loved her cream puffs? Jack had loved her pumpkin cake. Johnny loved her Christmas cake. Annie loved her pastry.

'It's . . . it's like people say, isn't it, Bob? When people go, we start to forget the little things, don't we?'

Bronwyn was pointing to the drip of cream on Ellie's chin. Bob wiped it away with his handkerchief, then he touched her short wash-and-wear waves.

'We go on, love. That's what we do – and you look like a new woman tonight with all that hair cut off.'

'It still feels a bit funny. Sort of . . . sort of like I'm light-headed. I'm glad I did it, though. You know, the hardest part of doing anything is letting yourself do it. Like with getting over Jack. I tried to hold on to him by remembering all the good parts.'

'Where there any bloody good parts?' Bessy said.

'Bessy! Remember where you are and why you're here. And you know there were. Jack mightn't have always been an easy man to live with, but we've all got our faults.' Ellie's head and voice lifted.

Loyal Ellie. Not an intentional mean bone in her body, Bob thought, but he'd had about enough of Jack for one night. 'Young Annie turned up, I see.'

Ellie looked across to the far corner, to the girl who was Jack in woman's clothing. 'I had a feeling that she'd come. She used to love Jack, you know. Used to sit with him for hours when she was little,

383

and talk to him with her little hands. He could understand her too. I couldn't . . . or not more than a few words. I should have tried harder with her.'

'It's never too late to start, Ellie.' Bob poured another beer. 'Why don't you go over and give her a kiss? Tell her how pleased you are that she came down.'

Ellie took two steps forward, but Granny Bourke was making her way towards the corner table, so Ellie stepped back.

A walking frame used as a battering ram before her, Gran cleared a pathway through. Not that she needed a bleeding walking frame. They'd stuck her ankle together with a metal plate and screws when they realised she had no intention of dying.

'I say. I say, weddings and wakes. That's the way it ought to be. As long as it's not my wake, eh?'

'You just plan to be the last one standing, Gran,' Bronwyn said.

'Too right I do. They're running a book in the bar, you know. Two to one odds that your mother won't hold out more than three months.'

'Jesus! That's a bit rough!'

'Her and Bob Johnson,' Gran said, aiming a slap at Bronwyn's arm. 'You knew what I meant.'

'We did not. We thought you were offering us odds on our own mother's funeral, didn't we, Annie?'

Ann nodded, but her attention was on Bill Dooley, now having his say about the deceased. She was tempted to toss her wineglass at him, or its contents at the old dame. Shouldn't have come. It was a farce. Shouldn't have come.

'Bob will make a good catch for your mother; he's not after her for her money or her land; he's got his cop pension.' She eyed Jim Watson, who was eyeing Bessy, who also had good river frontage. 'Still, there's more ways of killing a cat than choking him with cream. They'd make a fine pair, they would. Ugly as a bag full of rats.'

'You're evil, Gran.'

'Yeah, I am, aren't I?' The old dame prodded Bronwyn's stomach with a gnarled finger. 'You look as if you're going to pop out of your britches any minute. How long have you been married?'

'It's quads. They're not due for another five months.'

'Pull the other one, it's made out of rubber – or on second thoughts, you'd better not. It's got more metal in it than rubber these days. I say, did I ever tell you about old Jimmy Willis, Joe's father? Well he come back from the war with a bleedin' metal plate in his head. It fried his brain every time he went out in the sun. Took fits, he did, and one day . . . '

Bill Dooley was out of words, or beer. He wandered off and Father Fogarty started in again.

'It's a fiasco,' Ann said, and she stood.

'If you're going to the loo, I'll come with you, Annie.'

'Give me two minutes, Bron.'

She walked to Father Fogarty, interrupting his discourse on the hereafter, then from her pocket took a page of printed text. She'd planned to read it, but decided against it. Maybe it was right for him. Maybe it was wrong for Ellie. She didn't know, but somehow it suddenly felt right for her.

She drew a deep breath and found her mother's eyes, held them as she drew a second deeper breath. Then her chin lifted.

Her voice was low, but strong. It silenced the drinkers. They'd known her as a mute, seen her on television, but rarely saw her in Mallawindy.

Old knight, the lonely wanderer, is restless with unrest.
A shadow amid shadows, hiding secrets, guarding fears,
And cold, the dank mist clinging to his ageless breast,
Like frozen tears.

On feet of clay he stands outside the circle of pure light,
Never asked to come within, unwanted by new day,
Yet ever hoping for reward and what should be his right,

To watch her play.

She bathes the grass with dewdrops and paints the sky at dawn,
She makes the birds awaken; he's listened to their call.
He's seen her golden beauty, and felt her chill of scorn.
And that is all.

Lost to him the children of his cold and barren earth,
The cloak he wears is held too close, his dark hand offered not.
None will greet him from their beds. None can see his worth.
He's best forgot.

Old knight, old weary warrior, go shed your cloak of black,
That covers, yet can not disguise, the lost one hid beneath.
Step now into morning, and walk ahead, not back.
Forget your grief.

Ellie was weeping and she didn't know why, but Bob's arm was around her, and he was guiding her forward, towards that tall daughter. Such a crowd here tonight, and all of them wanting to talk. Maybe with Bob beside her she'd make it to the other side.

Ambulance siren in the distance. Outside the Grand Central Hotel, King Billy's dogs lifted their heads. No circular hole in the black blanket sky for a full moon tonight, no reason to howl, but they howled anyway. Didn't like that siren. Bad day when the siren came to town.

They killed its noise then, their work done, great heads dropped back to paws and they dreamed on.

But Granny Bourke's reptilian eyes had turned to the road. 'I say. I say, they only turn the siren off if they're already dead.' Her walking frame left standing, she hobbled off towards the bar for a stout and the latest news.

So the river crept onward, twisting, turning, fighting the will of the Dreamtime gods, who had charted its course west towards the arid centre. It crept into billabongs, seeped underground, until the gods washed their hands of this matter and let it flow where it would, while it still could.

And in the gum trees beside the river a night bird swooped, and a small possum tumbled from its mother's back to the mulch below. The feral cat pounced, licked warm blood, while the lone frog swallowed a few sopranos, just to keep the mosquito chorus in balance, then with a clap-clap, he frog-kicked downstream in search of a mate.

And on the sand dunes out Dead Man's Lane, the rabbits played.

Hero Sam Saves Author on Dark Road

Malcolm Fletcher, the 76-year-old author of nine best sellers, was clinically dead when Samuel Burton, in town for the celebration of his twin brother, Jack's, life, came upon the old man, collapsed on the side of a dark road, two kilometres west of Mallawindy on Christmas Eve. The quick actions of Samuel saved the life of the elderly man.

Having ascertained there was no heartbeat and that breathing had ceased, Samuel Burton commenced mouth-to-mouth resuscitation, and heart massage.

John Burton, son of the deceased Jack, and Mallawindy primary school teacher, saw the stationary headlights of his uncle's car. 'I walked up to the road to investigate,' he said.

Believing Malcolm Fletcher to be beyond the help of man, John called the local police station, and when Jeff Rowan could not be raised, he called for an ambulance, before returning to the scene where he found his uncle still on his knees, working over the old author.

'There was definitely no heartbeat, John told reporters. 'He was clinically dead.'

But Samuel, who had recently lost his wife of over forty years, refused to give up. He and John then continued the resuscitation.

By the time the Daree ambulance arrived, half an hour later, Malcolm Fletcher was propped against the car, breathing without assistance. Samuel Burton, his work done, helped lift the 200 kilogram Malcolm Fletcher into the ambulance, then quietly returned to his car and drove away from the scene.

It was Constable Jeff Rowan who discovered the secret identity of Malcolm Fletcher, a retired school-teacher, who has lived in Mallawindy since the 1960s.

Having gone to his house after learning that the old author had been in possession of an illegal handgun he had owned since the war of 1945, Constable Rowan found bookshelves filled with copies of the author's novels and also several letters addressed to Coll M Chef-Marlet.

'I'm his Number 1 fan. It didn't take long for me to deduce that the name was an anagram,' Constable Rowan said. 'We had a celebrity living in town and nobody knew it!'

Mr Fletcher, from his hospital bed, said yesterday that he had come upon the old gun in a drawer, and that he hadn't sighted it in over thirty years. He said he had no idea that there had been a bullet in it, or why he had taken it with him when he'd walked outside.

'I was not thinking logically at the time. Having previously suffered three heart attacks, I recognised the pain and thought to walk across the road to my neighbour's house. I recall little else.'

It is assumed that when he fell, the handgun, a piece of German memorabilia Mr Fletcher had brought with him from England, exploded in his hands.

Doctors operated on the damaged hands yesterday. A portion of the right index finger was removed, but when asked this morning if this would affect his writing, the old author said, 'I'm a two finger typist.'

'How much longer are you going to make your readers wait for Number 10?' a reporter asked.

'Coming soon,' Chef-Marlet replied. 'Coming soon.'

MORE BESTSELLING FICTION AVAILABLE FROM PAN MACMILLAN

Joy Dettman
Mallawindy

Ann Burton was born on a river bank the night her father tried to burn their house down.

Six years later her sister Liza disappears while they are staying at their uncle's property. What Ann sees that day robs her of her memory and her speech.

A stroke of unexpected humanity releases Ann from her world of silence, and she escapes her anguished childhood, finding love and a new life away from Mallawindy.

But there is no escape from the Burton family and its dark secrets. Ann must return to Mallawindy and confront the past if she is ever to be set free.

'We ride the crests and troughs of the Burtons' 30-year history with open mouths and saucer eyes . . . Dettman is an adept storyteller'
THE AGE

'A highly competent and confident debut novel'
SUNDAY TELEGRAPH

'A compelling story, well told . . . it holds promise of further enthralling fiction from its author'
CANBERRA TIMES

'A stunning debut; a rich and engrossing read; a tale of page-turning suspense and mystery; a postmortem of family ties; all this and more, *Mallawindy* will grab you hook, line and sinker'
QUEENSLAND TIMES